Acclaim for **Philip Roth**'s
*American Pastoral*

"Never before has Roth written with such clear conviction. Never before has he assembled so many fully formed characters." —*Time*

"An incandescent fiction. . . . *American Pastoral* scintillates with more Rothian wit, paradox, eloquent tantrums and absurd pratfalls placed at the exit of each irresistible argument than can be counted. . . . He strikes a vivid blaze."
—*Los Angeles Times Book Review*

"Roth has beaten pain and rage into a beautiful shape. *American Pastoral* is elaborately patterned and layered, ingeniously crafted to contain, even as it amplifies, a cathartic, barbaric yawp." —*New York Observer*

"Wrenching, skillfully told . . . a novel not to be missed."
—*St. Louis Post-Dispatch*

"Deeply moving. . . . Roth achieves a masterpiece . . . a literary triumph." —*Playboy*

"A gripping, emotionally charged novel." —*People*

BOOKS BY Philip Roth

ZUCKERMAN BOOKS

*The Ghost Writer*
*Zuckerman Unbound*
*The Anatomy Lesson*
*The Prague Orgy*

*The Counterlife*

*American Pastoral*
*I Married a Communist*
*The Human Stain*

ROTH BOOKS

*The Facts*
*Deception*
*Patrimony*
*Operation Shylock*

KEPESH BOOKS

*The Breast*
*The Professor of Desire*
*The Dying Animal*

OTHER BOOKS

*Goodbye, Columbus* • *Letting Go*
*When She Was Good* • *Portnoy's Complaint*
*Our Gang* • *The Great American Novel*
*My Life as a Man* • *Reading Myself and Others*
*Sabbath's Theater*

# Philip Roth
## *American Pastoral*

In the 1990s Philip Roth won America's four major literary awards in succession: the National Book Critics Circle Award for *Patrimony* (1991), the PEN/Faulkner Award for *Operation Shylock* (1993), the National Book Award for *Sabbath's Theater* (1995), and the Pulitzer Prize in fiction for *American Pastoral* (1997). He won the Ambassador Book Award of the English-Speaking Union for *I Married a Communist* (1998); in the same year he received the National Medal of Arts at the White House. Previously he won the National Book Critics Circle Award for *The Counterlife* (1986) and the National Book Award for his first book, *Goodbye, Columbus* (1959). In 2000 he published *The Human Stain*, concluding a trilogy that depicts the ideological ethos of postwar America. For *The Human Stain* Roth received his second PEN/Faulkner Award as well as Britain's W.H. Smith Award for the Best Book of the Year. In 2001 he received the highest award of the American Academy of Arts and Letters, the Gold Medal in Fiction, given every six years "for the entire work of the recipient."

VINTAGE INTERNATIONAL

# American Pastoral

◆

# Philip Roth

VINTAGE INTERNATIONAL

Vintage Books

A Division of Random House, Inc.

New York

To J. G.

FIRST VINTAGE INTERNATIONAL EDITION, FEBRUARY 1998

Library of Congress Cataloging-in-Publication Data
Roth, Philip.
American pastoral / Philip Roth.—1st Vintage International ed.
p.   cm.
ISBN 0-375-70142-7
1. United States—History—1961–1969—Fiction. I. Title.
PS3568.O855A77   1998   97-35623
813'.54—dc21   CIP

Random House Web address: http://www.randomhouse.com/

Printed in the United States of America
9B8

Dream when the day is thru,
Dream and they might come true,
Things never are as bad as they seem,
So dream, dream, dream.

— JOHNNY MERCER,
*from "Dream," popular song of the 1940s*

the rare occurrence of the expected . . .

— WILLIAM CARLOS WILLIAMS,
*from "At Kenneth Burke's Place," 1946*

# I

# Paradise
# Remembered

———— ◆ ————

# 1

THE SWEDE. During the war years, when I was still a grade
school boy, this was a magical name in our Newark neighborhood,
even to adults just a generation removed from the city's old Prince
Street ghetto and not yet so flawlessly Americanized as to be bowled
over by the prowess of a high school athlete. The name was magical; so was the anomalous face. Of the few fair-complexioned Jewish students in our preponderantly Jewish public high school, none
possessed anything remotely like the steep-jawed, insentient Viking
mask of this blue-eyed blond born into our tribe as Seymour Irving
Levov.

The Swede starred as end in football, center in basketball, and
first baseman in baseball. Only the basketball team was ever any
good—twice winning the city championship while he was its leading scorer—but as long as the Swede excelled, the fate of our sports
teams didn't matter much to a student body whose elders, largely
undereducated and overburdened, venerated academic achievement above all else. Physical aggression, even camouflaged by athletic uniforms and official rules and intended to do no harm to
Jews, was not a traditional source of pleasure in our community—
advanced degrees were. Nonetheless, through the Swede, the neighborhood entered into a fantasy about itself and about the world,
the fantasy of sports fans everywhere: almost like Gentiles (as they

imagined Gentiles), our families could forget the way things actually work and make an athletic performance the repository of all their hopes. Primarily, they could forget the war.

The elevation of Swede Levov into the household Apollo of the Weequahic Jews can best be explained, I think, by the war against the Germans and the Japanese and the fears that it fostered. With the Swede indomitable on the playing field, the meaningless surface of life provided a bizarre, delusionary kind of sustenance, the happy release into a Swedian innocence, for those who lived in dread of never seeing their sons or their brothers or their husbands again.

And how did this affect him—the glorification, the sanctification, of every hook shot he sank, every pass he leaped up and caught, every line drive he rifled for a double down the left-field line? Is this what made him that staid and stone-faced boy? Or was the mature-seeming sobriety the outward manifestation of an arduous inward struggle to keep in check the narcissism that an entire community was ladling with love? The high school cheerleaders had a cheer for the Swede. Unlike the other cheers, meant to inspire the whole team or to galvanize the spectators, this was a rhythmic, foot-stomping tribute to the Swede alone, enthusiasm for his perfection undiluted and unabashed. The cheer rocked the gym at basketball games every time he took a rebound or scored a point, swept through our side of City Stadium at football games any time he gained a yard or intercepted a pass. Even at the sparsely attended home baseball games up at Irvington Park, where there was no cheerleading squad eagerly kneeling at the sidelines, you could hear it thinly chanted by the handful of Weequahic stalwarts in the wooden stands not only when the Swede came up to bat but when he made no more than a routine putout at first base. It was a cheer that consisted of eight syllables, three of them his name, and it went, Bah bah-*bah!* Bah bah bah . . . bah-*bah!* and the tempo, at football games particularly, accelerated with each repetition until, at the peak of frenzied adoration, an explosion of skirt-billowing cartwheels was ecstatically discharged and the orange gym bloomers of ten sturdy little cheerleaders flickered like fireworks before our marveling eyes . . . and not for love of you or me but of the wonderful Swede. "Swede Levov! It rhymes with . . . 'The Love'! . . . Swede Levov! It rhymes with . . . 'The Love'! . . . Swede Levov! It rhymes with . . . 'The Love'!"

Yes, everywhere he looked, people were in love with him. The candy store owners we boys pestered called the rest of us "Hey-you-no!" or "Kid-cut-it-out!"; him they called, respectfully, "Swede." Parents smiled and benignly addressed him as "Seymour." The chattering girls he passed on the street would ostentatiously swoon, and the bravest would holler after him, "Come back, come back, Levov of my life!" And he let it happen, walked about the neighborhood in possession of all that love, looking as though he didn't feel a thing. Contrary to whatever daydreams the rest of us may have had about the enhancing effect on ourselves of total, uncritical, idolatrous adulation, the love thrust upon the Swede seemed actually to *deprive* him of feeling. In this boy embraced as a symbol of hope by so many—as the embodiment of the strength, the resolve, the emboldened valor that would prevail to return our high school's servicemen home unscathed from Midway, Salerno, Cherbourg, the Solomons, the Aleutians, Tarawa—there appeared to be not a drop of wit or irony to interfere with his golden gift for responsibility.

But wit or irony is like a hitch in his swing for a kid like the Swede, irony being a human consolation and beside the point if you're getting your way as a god. Either there was a whole side to his personality that he was suppressing or that was as yet asleep or, more likely, there wasn't. His aloofness, his seeming passivity as the desired object of all this asexual lovemaking, made him appear, if not divine, a distinguished cut above the more primordial humanity of just about everybody else at the school. He was fettered to history, an *instrument* of history, esteemed with a passion that might never have been if he'd broken the Weequahic basketball record—by scoring twenty-seven points against Barringer—on a day other than the sad, sad day in 1943 when fifty-eight Flying

Fortresses were shot down by Luftwaffe fighter planes, two fell victim to flak, and five more crashed after crossing the English coast on their way back from bombing Germany.

The Swede's younger brother was my classmate, Jerry Levov, a scrawny, small-headed, oddly overflexible boy built along the lines of a licorice stick, something of a mathematical wizard, and the January 1950 valedictorian. Though Jerry never really had a friendship with anyone, in his imperious, irascible way, he took an interest in me over the years, and that was how I wound up, from the age of ten, regularly getting beaten by him at Ping-Pong in the finished basement of the Levovs' one-family house, on the corner of Wyndmoor and Keer—the word "finished" indicating that it was paneled in knotty pine, domesticated, and not, as Jerry seemed to think, that the basement was the perfect place for finishing off another kid.

The explosiveness of Jerry's aggression at a Ping-Pong table exceeded his brother's in any sport. A Ping-Pong ball is, brilliantly, sized and shaped so that it cannot take out your eye. I would not otherwise have played in Jerry Levov's basement. If it weren't for the opportunity to tell people that I knew my way around Swede Levov's house, nobody could have got me down into that basement, defenseless but for a small wooden paddle. Nothing that weighs as little as a Ping-Pong ball can be lethal, yet when Jerry whacked that thing murder couldn't have been far from his mind. It never occurred to me that this violent display might have something to do with what it was like for him to be the kid brother of Swede Levov. Since I couldn't imagine anything better than being the Swede's brother—short of being the Swede himself—I failed to understand that for Jerry it might be difficult to imagine anything worse.

The Swede's bedroom—which I never dared enter but would pause to gaze into when I used the toilet outside Jerry's room—was tucked under the eaves at the back of the house. With its slanted ceiling and dormer windows and Weequahic pennants on the walls, it looked like what I thought of as a real boy's room. From the two windows that opened out over the back lawn you could see the roof of the Levovs' garage, where the Swede as a grade school kid practiced hitting in the wintertime by swinging at a baseball taped to a cord hung from a rafter—an idea he might have got from a baseball novel by John R. Tunis called *The Kid from Tomkinsville*. I came to that book and to other of Tunis's baseball books—*Iron Duke, The Duke Decides, Champion's Choice, Keystone Kids, Rookie of the Year*—by spotting them on the built-in shelf beside the Swede's bed, all lined up alphabetically between two solid bronze bookends that had been a bar mitzvah gift, miniaturized replicas of Rodin's "The Thinker." Immediately I went to the library to borrow all the Tunis books I could find and started with *The Kid from Tomkinsville*, a grim, gripping book to a boy, simply written, stiff in places but direct and dignified, about the Kid, Roy Tucker, a clean-cut young pitcher from the rural Connecticut hills whose father dies when he is four and whose mother dies when he is sixteen and who helps his grandmother make ends meet by working the family farm during the day and working at night in town at "MacKenzie's drugstore on the corner of South Main."

The book, published in 1940, had black-and-white drawings that, with just a little expressionistic distortion and just enough anatomical skill, cannily pictorialize the hardness of the Kid's life, back before the game of baseball was illuminated with a million statistics, back when it was about the mysteries of earthly fate, when major leaguers looked less like big healthy kids and more like lean and hungry workingmen. The drawings seemed conceived out of the dark austerities of Depression America. Every ten pages or so, to succinctly depict a dramatic physical moment in the story—"He was able to put a little steam in it," "It was over the fence," "Razzle limped to the dugout"—there is a blackish, ink-heavy rendering of a scrawny, shadow-faced ballplayer starkly silhouetted on a blank page, isolated, like the world's most lonesome soul, from both nature and man, or set in a stippled simulation of ballpark grass, dragging beneath him the skinny statuette of a wormlike shadow. He is unglamorous even in a baseball uniform; if he is the pitcher, his gloved hand looks like a paw; and what image after image makes graphically clear is that playing up in the majors, heroic though it may seem, is yet another form of backbreaking, unremunerative labor.

*The Kid from Tomkinsville* could as well have been called *The Lamb from Tomkinsville*, even *The Lamb from Tomkinsville Led to the Slaughter*. In the Kid's career as the spark-plug newcomer to a last-place Brooklyn Dodger club, each triumph is rewarded with a punishing disappointment or a crushing accident. The staunch attachment that develops between the lonely, homesick Kid and the Dodgers' veteran catcher, Dave Leonard, who successfully teaches him the ways of the big leagues and who, "with his steady brown eyes behind the plate," shepherds him through a no-hitter, comes brutally undone six weeks into the season, when the old-timer is dropped overnight from the club's roster. "Here was a speed they didn't often mention in baseball: the speed with which a player rises—and goes down." Then, after the Kid wins his fifteenth consecutive game—a rookie record that no pitcher in either league has ever exceeded—he's accidentally knocked off his feet in the shower by boisterous teammates who are horsing around after the great victory, and the elbow injury sustained in the fall leaves him unable ever to pitch again. He rides the bench for the rest of the year, pinch-hitting because of his strength at the plate, and then, over the snowy winter—back home in Connecticut spending days on the farm and evenings at the drugstore, well known now but really Grandma's boy all over again—he works diligently by himself on Dave Leonard's directive to keep his swing level ("A tendency to keep his right shoulder down, to swing up, was his worst fault"), suspending a ball from a string out in the barn and whacking at it on cold winter mornings with "his beloved bat" until he has worked himself into a sweat. "'Crack . . .' The clean sweet sound of a bat squarely meeting a ball." By the next season he is ready to return to the Dodgers as a speedy right fielder, bats .325 in the second spot, and leads his team down to the wire as a contender. On the last day of the season, in a game against the Giants, who are in first place by only half a game, the Kid kindles the Dodgers' hitting attack, and in the bottom of the fourteenth—with two down, two men on, and the Dodgers ahead on a run scored by the Kid with his audacious, characteristically muscular baserunning— he makes the final game-saving play, a running catch smack up against the right center-field wall. That tremendous daredevil feat sends the Dodgers into the World Series and leaves him "writhing in agony on the green turf of deep right center." Tunis concludes like this: "Dusk descended upon a mass of players, on a huge crowd pouring onto the field, on a couple of men carrying an inert form through the mob on a stretcher. . . . There was a clap of thunder. Rain descended upon the Polo Grounds." Descended, descended, a clap of thunder, and thus ends the boys' Book of Job.

I was ten and I had never read anything like it. The cruelty of life. The injustice of it. I could not believe it. The reprehensible member of the Dodgers is Razzle Nugent, a great pitcher but a drunk and a hothead, a violent bully fiercely jealous of the Kid. And yet it is not Razzle carried off "inert" on a stretcher but the best of them all, the farm orphan called the Kid, modest, serious, chaste, loyal, naive, undiscourageable, hard-working, soft-spoken, courageous, a brilliant athlete, a beautiful, austere boy. Needless to say, I thought of the Swede and the Kid as one and wondered how the Swede could bear to read this book that had left me near tears and unable to sleep. Had I had the courage to address him, I would have asked if he thought the ending meant the Kid was finished or whether it meant the possibility of yet another comeback. The word "inert" terrified me. Was the Kid *killed* by the last catch of the year? Did the Swede know? Did he care? Did it occur to him that if disaster could strike down the Kid from Tomkinsville, it could come and strike the great Swede down too? Or was a book about a sweet star savagely and unjustly punished—a book about a greatly gifted innocent whose worst fault is a tendency to keep his right shoulder down and swing up but whom the thundering heavens destroy nonetheless—simply a book between those "Thinker" bookends up on his shelf?

*

Keer Avenue was where the rich Jews lived—or rich they seemed to most of the families who rented apartments in the two-, three-, and four-family dwellings with the brick stoops integral to our after-school sporting life: the crap games, the blackjack, and the stoop-ball, endless until the cheap rubber ball hurled mercilessly against the steps went pop and split at the seam. Here, on this grid of locust-tree-lined streets into which the Lyons farm had been partitioned during the boom years of the early twenties, the first postimmigrant generation of Newark's Jews had regrouped into a community that took its inspiration more from the mainstream of American life than from the Polish shtetl their Yiddish-speaking parents had re-created around Prince Street in the impoverished Third Ward. The Keer Avenue Jews, with their finished basements, their screened-in porches, their flagstone front steps, seemed to be at the forefront, laying claim like audacious pioneers to the normalizing American amenities. And at the vanguard of the vanguard were the Levovs, who had bestowed upon us our very own Swede, a boy as close to a goy as we were going to get.

The Levovs themselves, Lou and Sylvia, were parents neither more nor less recognizably American than my own Jersey-born Jewish mother and father, no more or less refined, well spoken, or cultivated. And that to me was a big surprise. Other than the one-family Keer Avenue house, there was no division between us like the one between the peasants and the aristocracy I was learning about at school. Mrs. Levov was, like my own mother, a tidy house-keeper, impeccably well mannered, a nice-looking woman tremendously considerate of everyone's feelings, with a way of making her sons feel important—one of the many women of that era who never dreamed of being free of the great domestic enterprise centered on the children. From their mother both Levov boys had inherited the long bones and fair hair, though since her hair was redder, frizzier, and her skin still youthfully freckled, she looked less startlingly Aryan than they did, less vivid a genetic oddity among the faces in our streets.

The father was no more than five seven or eight—a spidery man even more agitated than the father whose anxieties were shaping my own. Mr. Levov was one of those slum-reared Jewish fathers whose rough-hewn, undereducated perspective goaded a whole generation of striving, college-educated Jewish sons: a father for whom everything is an unshakable duty, for whom there is a right way and a wrong way and nothing in between, a father whose compound of ambitions, biases, and beliefs is so unruffled by careful thinking that he isn't as easy to escape from as he seems. Limited men with limitless energy; men quick to be friendly and quick to be fed up; men for whom the most serious thing in life is *to keep going despite everything.* And we were their sons. It was our job to love them.

The way it fell out, my father was a chiropodist whose office was for years our living room and who made enough money for our family to get by on but no more, while Mr. Levov got rich manufacturing ladies' gloves. His own father—Swede Levov's grandfather—had come to Newark from the old country in the 1890s and found work fleshing sheepskins fresh from the lime vat, the lone Jew alongside the roughest of Newark's Slav, Irish, and Italian immigrants in the Nuttman Street tannery of the patent-leather tycoon T. P. Howell, then *the* name in the city's oldest and biggest industry, the tanning and manufacture of leather goods. The most important thing in making leather is water—skins spinning in big drums of water, drums spewing out befouled water, pipes gushing with cool and hot water, hundreds of thousands of gallons of water. If there's soft water, good water, you can make beer and you can make leather, and Newark made both—big breweries, big tanneries, and, for the immigrant, lots of wet, smelly, crushing work.

The son Lou—Swede Levov's father—went to work in the tannery after leaving school at fourteen to help support the family of nine and became adept not only at dyeing buckskin by laying on the clay dye with a flat, stiff brush but also at sorting and grading skins. The tannery that stank of both the slaughterhouse and the chemical plant from the soaking of flesh and the cooking of flesh and the dehairing and pickling and degreasing of hides, where round the clock in the summertime the blowers drying the thousands and thousands of hanging skins raised the temperature in the low-ceilinged dry room to a hundred and twenty degrees, where the vast vat rooms were dark as caves and flooded with swill, where brutish workingmen, heavily aproned, armed with hooks and staves, dragging and pushing overloaded wagons, wringing and hanging waterlogged skins, were driven like animals through the laborious storm that was a twelve-hour shift—a filthy, stinking place awash with water dyed red and black and blue and green, with hunks of skin all over the floor, everywhere pits of grease, hills of salt, barrels of solvent—this was Lou Levov's high school and college. What was amazing was not how tough he turned out. What was amazing was how civil he could sometimes still manage to be.

From Howell & Co. he graduated in his early twenties to found, with two of his brothers, a small handbag outfit specializing in alligator skins contracted from R. G. Salomon, Newark's king of cordovan leather and leader in the tanning of alligator; for a time the business looked as if it might flourish, but after the crash the company went under, bankrupting the three hustling, audacious Levovs. Newark Maid Leatherware started up a few years later, with Lou Levov, now on his own, buying seconds in leather goods—imperfect handbags, gloves, and belts—and selling them out of a pushcart on weekends and door-to-door at night. Down Neck—the semi-peninsular protuberance that is easternmost Newark, where each fresh wave of immigrants first settled, the lowlands bounded to the north and east by the Passaic River and to the south by the salt marshes—there were Italians who'd been glovers in the old country and they began doing piecework for him in their homes. Out of the skins he supplied they cut and sewed ladies' gloves that he peddled around the state. By the time the war broke out, he had a collective of Italian families cutting and stitching kid gloves in a small loft on West Market Street. It was a marginal business, no real money, until, in 1942, the bonanza: a black, lined sheepskin dress glove, ordered by the Women's Army Corps. He leased the old umbrella factory, a smoke-darkened brick pile fifty years old and four stories high on Central Avenue and 2nd Street, and very shortly purchased it outright, leasing the top floor to a zipper company. Newark Maid began pumping out gloves, and every two or three days the truck backed up and took them away.

A cause for jubilation even greater than the government contract was the Bamberger account. Newark Maid cracked Bamberger's, and then became the major manufacturer of their fine ladies' gloves, because of an unlikely encounter between Lou Levov and Louis Bamberger. At a ceremonial dinner for Meyer Ellenstein, a city commissioner since 1933 and the only Jew ever to be mayor of Newark, some higher-up from Bam's, hearing that Swede Levov's father was present, came over to congratulate him on his boy's selection by the *Newark News* as an all-county center in basketball. Alert to the opportunity of a lifetime—the opportunity to cut through all obstructions and go right to the top—Lou Levov brazenly talked his way into an introduction, right there at the Ellenstein dinner, to the legendary L. Bamberger himself, founder of Newark's most prestigious department store and the philanthropist who'd given the city its museum, a powerful personage as meaningful to local Jews as Bernard Baruch was meaningful to Jews around the country for his close association with FDR. According to the gossip that permeated the neighborhood, although Bamberger barely did more than shake Lou Levov's hand and quiz him (about the Swede) for a couple of minutes at most, Lou Levov had dared to say to his face, "Mr. Bamberger, we've got the quality, we've got the price—why can't we sell you people gloves?" And before the month was out, Bam's had placed an order with Newark Maid, its first, for five hundred dozen pairs.

By the end of the war, Newark Maid had established itself—in no small part because of Swede Levov's athletic achievement—as one of the most respected names in ladies' gloves south of Gloversville, New York, the center of the glove trade, where Lou Levov shipped his hides by rail, through Fultonville, to be tanned by the best glove tannery in the business. Little more than a decade later, with the opening of a factory in Puerto Rico in 1958, the Swede would himself become the young president of the company, commuting every morning down to Central Avenue from his home some thirty-odd miles west of Newark, out past the suburbs—a short-range pioneer living on a hundred-acre farm on a back road in the sparsely habitated hills beyond Morristown, in wealthy, rural Old Rimrock, New Jersey, a long way from the tannery floor where Grandfather Levov had begun in America, paring away from the true skin the rubbery flesh that had ghoulishly swelled to twice its thickness in the great lime vats.

The day after graduating Weequahic in June '45, the Swede had joined the Marine Corps, eager to be in on the fighting that ended the war. It was rumored that his parents were beside themselves and did everything to talk him out of the marines and get him into the navy. Even if he surmounted the notorious Marine Corps anti-Semitism, did he imagine himself surviving the invasion of Japan? But the Swede would not be dissuaded from meeting the manly, patriotic challenge—secretly set for himself just after Pearl Harbor—of going off to fight as one of the toughest of the tough should the country still be at war when he graduated high school. He was just finishing up his boot training at Parris Island, South Carolina—where the scuttlebutt was that the marines were to hit the Japanese beaches on March 1, 1946—when the atomic bomb was dropped on Hiroshima. As a result, the Swede got to spend the rest of his hitch as a "recreation specialist" right there on Parris Island. He ran the calisthenic drill for his battalion for half an hour before breakfast every morning, arranged for the boxing smokers to entertain the recruits a couple of nights a week, and the bulk of the time played for the base team against armed forces teams throughout the South, basketball all winter long, baseball all summer long. He was stationed down in South Carolina about a year when he became engaged to an Irish Catholic girl whose father, a marine major and a one-time Purdue football coach, had procured him the cushy job as drill instructor in order to keep him at Parris Island to play ball. Several months before the Swede's discharge, his own father made a trip to Parris Island, stayed for a full week, near the base at the hotel in Beaufort, and departed only when the engagement to Miss Dunleavy had been broken off. The Swede returned home in '47 to enroll at Upsala College, in East Orange, at twenty unencumbered by a Gentile wife and all the more glamorously heroic for having made his mark as a Jewish marine—a drill instructor no less, and at arguably the cruelest military training camp anywhere in the world. Marines are made at boot camp, and Seymour Irving Levov had helped to make them.

We knew all this because the mystique of the Swede lived on in the corridors and classrooms of the high school, where I was by then a student. I remember two or three times one spring trekking out with friends to Viking Field in East Orange to watch the Upsala baseball team play a Saturday home game. Their star cleanup hitter and first baseman was the Swede. Three home runs one day against Muhlenberg. Whenever we saw a man in the stands wearing a suit and a hat we would whisper to one another, "A scout, a scout!" I was away at college when I heard from a schoolyard pal still living in the neighborhood that the Swede had been offered a contract with a Double A Giant farm club but had turned it down to join his father's company instead. Later I learned through my parents about the Swede's marriage to Miss New Jersey. Before competing at Atlantic City for the 1949 Miss America title, she had been Miss Union County, and before that Spring Queen at Upsala. From Elizabeth. A shiksa. Dawn Dwyer. He'd done it.

One night in the summer of 1985, while visiting New York, I went out to see the Mets play the Astros, and while circling the stadium with my friends, looking for the gate to our seats, I saw the Swede, thirty-six years older than when I'd watched him play ball for Upsala. He wore a white shirt, a striped tie, and a charcoal-gray summer suit, and he was still terrifically handsome. The golden hair was a shade or two darker but not any thinner; no longer was it cut short but fell rather fully over his ears and down to his collar.

In this suit that fit him so exquisitely he seemed even taller and leaner than I remembered him in the uniform of one sport or another. The woman with us noticed him first. "*Who* is that? That's— that's . . . Is that John Lindsay?" she asked. "No," I said. "My God. You know who that is? It's Swede Levov." I told my friends, "That's the Swede!"

A skinny, fair-haired boy of about seven or eight was walking alongside the Swede, a kid under a Mets cap pounding away at a first baseman's mitt that dangled, as had the Swede's, from his left hand. The two, clearly a father and his son, were laughing about something together when I approached and introduced myself. "I knew your brother at Weequahic."

"You're Zuckerman?" he replied, vigorously shaking my hand. "The author?"

"I'm Zuckerman the author."

"Sure, you were Jerry's great pal."

"I don't think Jerry had great pals. He was too brilliant for pals. He just used to beat my pants off at Ping-Pong down in your basement. Beating me at Ping-Pong was very important to Jerry."

"So you're the guy. My mother says, 'And he was such a nice, quiet child when he came to the house.' You know who this is?" the Swede said to the boy. "The guy who wrote those books. Nathan Zuckerman."

Mystified, the boy shrugged and muttered, "Hi."

"This is my son Chris."

"These are friends," I said, sweeping an arm out to introduce the three people with me. "And this man," I said to them, "is the greatest athlete in the history of Weequahic High. A real artist in three sports. Played first base like Hernandez—thinking. A line-drive doubles hitter. Do you know that?" I said to his son. "Your dad was our Hernandez."

"Hernandez's a lefty," he replied.

"Well, that's the only difference," I said to the little literalist, and put out my hand again to his father. "Nice to see you, Swede."

"You bet. Take it easy, Skip."

"Remember me to your brother," I said.

He laughed, we parted, and someone was saying to me, "Well, well, the greatest athlete in the history of Weequahic High called you 'Skip.'"

"I know. I can't believe it." And I did feel almost as wonderfully singled out as I had the one time before, at the age of ten, when the Swede had got so personal as to recognize me by the playground nickname I'd acquired because of two grades I skipped in grade school.

Midway through the first inning, the woman with us turned to me and said, "You should have seen your face—you might as well have told us he was Zeus. I saw just what you looked like as a boy."

The following letter reached me by way of my publisher a couple of weeks before Memorial Day, 1995.

> Dear Skip Zuckerman:
>
> I apologize for any inconvenience this letter may cause you. You may not remember our meeting at Shea Stadium. I was with my oldest son (now a first-year college student) and you were out with some friends to see the Mets. That was ten years ago, the era of Carter-Gooden-Hernandez, when you could still watch the Mets. You can't anymore.
>
> I am writing to ask if we might meet sometime to talk. I'd be delighted to take you to dinner in New York if you would permit me.
>
> I'm taking the liberty of proposing a meeting because of something I have been thinking about since my father died last year. He was ninety-six. He was his feisty, combative self right down to the end. That made it all the harder to see him go, despite his advanced age.
>
> I would like to talk about him and his life. I have been trying to write a tribute to him, to be published privately for friends, family, and business associates. Most everybody thought of my father as indestructible, a thick-skinned man on a short fuse. That was far from the truth. Not everyone

knew how much he suffered because of the shocks that befell his loved ones.

Please be assured that I will understand if you haven't time to respond.

Sincerely,
Seymour "Swede" Levov, WHS 1945

Had anyone else asked if he could talk to me about a tribute he was writing to his father, I would have wished him luck and kept my nose out of it. But there were compelling reasons for my getting off a note to the Swede—within the hour—to say that I was at his disposal. The first was *Swede Levov wants to meet me*. Ridiculously, perhaps, at the onset of old age, I had only to see his signature at the foot of the letter to be swamped by memories of him, both on and off the field, that were some fifty years old and yet still captivating. I remembered going up every day to the playing field to watch football practice the year that the Swede first agreed to join the team. He was already a high-scoring hook-shot artist on the basketball court, but no one knew he could be just as magical on the football field until the coach pressed him into duty as an end and our losing team, though still at the bottom of the city league, was putting up one, two, even three touchdowns a game, all scored on passes to the Swede. Fifty or sixty kids gathered along the sidelines at practice to watch the Swede—in a battered leather helmet and the brown jersey numbered, in orange, 11—working out with the varsity against the JVs. The varsity quarterback, Lefty Leventhal, ran pass play after pass play ("Lev-en-*thal* to Le-*vov!* Lev-en-*thal* to Le-*vov!*" was an anapest that could always get us going back in the heyday of the Swede), and the task of the JV squad, playing defense, was to stop Swede Levov from scoring every time. I'm over sixty, not exactly someone with the outlook on life that he'd had as a boy, and yet the boy's beguilement has never wholly evaporated, for to this day I haven't forgotten the Swede, after being smothered by tacklers, climbing slowly to his feet, shaking himself off, casting an upward, remonstrative glance at the darkening fall sky, sighing ruefully, and then trotting undamaged back to the huddle. When he scored, that was one kind of glory, and when he got tackled and piled on hard, and just stood up and shook it off, that was another kind of glory, even in a scrimmage.

And then one day I shared in that glory. I was ten, never before touched by greatness, and would have been as beneath the Swede's attention as anyone else along the sidelines had it not been for Jerry Levov. Jerry had recently taken me on board as a friend; though I was hard put to believe it, the Swede must have noticed me around their house. And so late on a fall afternoon in 1943, when he got slammed to the ground by the whole of the JV team after catching a short Leventhal bullet and the coach abruptly blew the whistle signaling that was it for the day, the Swede, tentatively flexing an elbow while half running and half limping off the field, spotted me among the other kids, and called over, "Basketball was never like this, Skip."

The god (himself all of sixteen) had carried me up into athletes' heaven. The adored had acknowledged the adoring. Of course, with athletes as with movie idols, each worshiper imagines that he or she has a secret, personal link, but this was one forged openly by the most unostentatious of stars and before a hushed congregation of competitive kids—an amazing experience, and I was thrilled. I blushed, I was thrilled, I probably thought of nothing else for the rest of the week. The mock jock self-pity, the manly generosity, the princely graciousness, the athlete's self-pleasure so abundant that a portion can be freely given to the crowd—this munificence not only overwhelmed me and wafted through me because it had come wrapped in my nickname but became fixed in my mind as an embodiment of something grander even than his talent for sports: the talent for "being himself," the capacity to be this strange engulf-ing force and yet to have a voice and a smile unsullied by even a flicker of superiority—the natural modesty of someone for whom there were no obstacles, who appeared never to have to struggle to clear a space for himself. I don't imagine I'm the only grown man who was a Jewish kid aspiring to be an all-American kid during the patriotic war years—when our entire neighborhood's wartime hope seemed to converge in the marvelous body of the Swede— who's carried with him through life recollections of this gifted boy's unsurpassable style.

The Jewishness that he wore so lightly as one of the tall, blond athletic winners must have spoken to us too—in our idolizing the Swede and his unconscious oneness with America, I suppose there was a tinge of shame and self-rejection. Conflicting Jewish desires awakened by the sight of him were simultaneously becalmed by him; the contradiction in Jews who want to fit in and want to stand out, who insist they are different and insist they are no different, resolved itself in the triumphant spectacle of this Swede who was actually only another of our neighborhood Seymours whose fore-bears had been Solomons and Sauls and who would themselves beget Stephens who would in turn beget Shawns. Where was the Jew in him? You couldn't find it and yet you knew it was there. Where was the irrationality in him? Where was the crybaby in him? Where were the wayward temptations? No guile. No artifice. No mischief. All that he had eliminated to achieve his perfection. No striving, no ambivalence, no doubleness—just the style, the natural physical refinement of a star.

Only . . . what did he do for subjectivity? What *was* the Swede's subjectivity? There had to be a substratum, but its composition was unimaginable.

That was the second reason I answered his letter—the substra-tum. What sort of mental existence had been his? What, if anything, had ever threatened to destabilize the Swede's trajectory? No one gets through unmarked by brooding, grief, confusion, and loss. Even those who had it all as kids sooner or later get the average share of misery, if not sometimes more. There had to have been consciousness and there had to have been blight. Yet I could not picture the form taken by either, could not desimplify him even now: in the residuum of adolescent imagination I was still con-vinced that for the Swede it had to have been pain-free all the way.

But what had he been alluding to in that careful, courteous letter when, speaking of the late father, a man not as thick-skinned as people thought, he wrote, "Not everyone knew how much he suffered because of the shocks that befell his loved ones"? No, the Swede had suffered a shock. And it was suffering the shock that he wanted to talk about. It wasn't the father's life, it was his own that he wanted revealed.

I was wrong.

We met at an Italian restaurant in the West Forties where the Swede had for years been taking his family whenever they came over to New York for a Broadway show or to watch the Knicks at the Garden, and I understood right off that I wasn't going to get anywhere near the substratum. Everybody at Vincent's knew him by name—Vincent himself, Vincent's wife, Louie the maitre d', Carlo the bartender, Billy our waiter, everybody knew Mr. Levov and everybody asked after the missus and the boys. It turned out that when his parents were alive he used to bring them to celebrate an anniversary or a birthday at Vincent's. No, I thought, he's invited me here to reveal only that he is as admired on West 49th Street as he was on Chancellor Avenue.

Vincent's is one of those oldish Italian restaurants tucked into the midtown West Side streets between Madison Square Garden and the Plaza, small restaurants three tables wide and four chandeliers deep, with decor and menus that have changed hardly at all since before arugula was discovered. There was a ballgame on the TV set by the small bar, and a customer every once in a while would get up, go look for a minute, ask the bartender the score, ask how Mattingly was doing, and head back to his meal. The chairs were upholstered in electric-turquoise plastic, the floor was tiled in speckled salmon, one wall was mirrored, the chandeliers were fake brass, and for decoration there was a five-foot-tall bright red pepper grinder standing in one corner like a Giacometti (a gift, said the Swede, to Vincent from his hometown in Italy); counterbalancing it in the opposite corner, on a stand like statuary, stood a stout jeroboam of Barolo. A table piled with jars of Vincent's Marinara

Sauce was just across from the bowl of free after-dinner mints beside Mrs. Vincent's register; on the dessert cart was the napoleon, the tiramisù, the layer cake, the apple tart, and the sugared strawberries; and behind our table, on the wall, were the autographed photographs ("Best regards to Vincent and Anne") of Sammy Davis, Jr., Joe Namath, Liza Minelli, Kaye Ballard, Gene Kelly, Jack Carter, Phil Rizzuto, and Johnny and Joanna Carson. There should have been one of the Swede, of course, and there would have been if we were still fighting the Germans and the Japanese and across the street were Weequahic High.

Our waiter, Billy, a small, heavyset bald man with a boxer's flattened nose, didn't have to ask what the Swede wanted to eat. For over thirty years the Swede had been ordering from Billy the house specialty, ziti à la Vincent, preceded by clams posillipo. "Best baked ziti in New York," the Swede told me, but I ordered my own old-fashioned favorite, the chicken cacciatore, "off the bone" at Billy's suggestion. While writing up our order, Billy told the Swede that Tony Bennett had been in the evening before. For a man with Billy's compact build, a man you might have imagined lugging around a weightier burden all his life than a plate of ziti, Billy's voice—high-pitched and intense, taut from some distress too long endured—was unexpected and a real treat. "See where your friend is sitting? See his chair, Mr. Levov? Tony Bennett sat in that chair." To me he said, "You know what Tony Bennett says when people come up to his table and introduce themselves to him? He says, 'Nice to see you.' And you're in his seat."

That ended the entertainment. It was work from there on out.

He had brought photographs of his three boys to show me, and from the appetizer through to dessert virtually all conversation was about eighteen-year-old Chris, sixteen-year-old Steve, and four-teen-year-old Kent. Which boy was better at lacrosse than at base-ball but was being pressured by a coach . . . which was as good at soccer as at football but couldn't decide . . . which was the diving champion who had also broken school records in butterfly and backstroke. All three were hardworking students, A's and B's; one was "into" the sciences, another was more "community-minded," while the third . . . etc. There was one photograph of the boys with their mother, a good-looking fortyish blonde, advertising manager for a Morris County weekly. But she hadn't begun her career, the Swede was quick to add, until their youngest had entered second grade. The boys were lucky to have a mom who still put staying at home and raising kids ahead of . . .

I was impressed, as the meal wore on, by how assured he seemed of everything commonplace he said, and how everything he said was suffused by his good nature. I kept waiting for him to lay bare something more than this pointed unobjectionableness, but all that rose to the surface was more surface. What he has instead of a being, I thought, is blandness—the guy's radiant with it. He has devised for himself an incognito, and the incognito has become him. Several times during the meal I didn't think I was going to make it, didn't think I'd get to dessert if he was going to keep praising his family and praising his family . . . until I began to wonder if it wasn't that he was incognito but that he was mad.

Something was on top of him that had called a halt to him. Something had turned him into a human platitude. Something had warned him: You must not run counter to anything.

The Swede, some six or seven years my senior, was close to seventy, and yet he was no less splendid-looking for the crevices at the corners of his eyes and, beneath the promontory of cheekbones, a little more hollowing out than classic standards of ruggedness required. I chalked up the gauntness to a regimen of serious jogging or tennis, until near the end of the meal I found out that he'd had prostate surgery during the winter and was only beginning to regain the weight he'd lost. I don't know if it was learning that he'd suffered an affliction or his confessing to one that most surprised me. I even wondered if it might not be his recent experience of the surgery and its aftereffects that was feeding my sense of someone who was not mentally sound.

At one point I interrupted and, trying not to appear in any way desperate, asked about the business, what it was like these days running a factory in Newark. That's how I discovered that Newark Maid hadn't been in Newark since the early seventies. Virtually the whole industry had moved offshore: the unions had made it more and more difficult for a manufacturer to make any money, you could hardly find people to do that kind of piecework anymore, or to do it the way you wanted it done, and elsewhere there was an availability of workers who could be trained nearly to the standards that had obtained in the glove industry forty and fifty years ago. His family had kept their operation going in Newark for quite a long time; out of duty to long-standing employees, most of whom were black, the Swede had hung on for some six years after the '67 riots, held on in the face of industry-wide economic realities and his father's imprecations as long as he possibly could, but when he was unable to stop the erosion of the workmanship, which had deteriorated steadily since the riots, he'd given up, managing to get out more or less unharmed by the city's collapse. All the Newark Maid factory had suffered in the four days of rioting were some broken windows, though fifty yards from the gate to his loading dock, out on West Market, two other buildings had been gutted by fire and abandoned.

"Taxes, corruption, and race. My old man's litany. Anybody at all, people from all over the country who couldn't care less about the fate of Newark, made no difference to him—whether it was down in Miami Beach at the condo, on a cruise ship in the Caribbean, they'd get an earful about his beloved old Newark, butchered to death by taxes, corruption, and race. My father was one of those Prince Street guys who loved that city all his life. What happened to Newark broke his heart.

"It's the worst city in the world, Skip," the Swede was telling me. "Used to be the city where they manufactured everything. Now it's the car-theft capital of the world. Did you know that? Not the most gruesome of the gruesome developments but it's awful enough. The thieves live mostly in our old neighborhood. Black kids. Forty cars stolen in Newark every twenty-four hours. That's the statistic.

Something, isn't it? And they're murder weapons—once they're stolen, they're flying missiles. The target is anybody in the street—old people, toddlers, doesn't matter. Out in front of our factory was the Indianapolis Speedway to them. That's another reason we left. Four, five kids drooping out the windows, eighty miles an hour—right on Central Avenue. When my father bought the factory, there were trolley cars on Central Avenue. Further down were the auto showrooms. Central Cadillac. LaSalle. There was a factory where somebody was making something in every side street. Now there's a liquor store in every street—a liquor store, a pizza stand, and a seedy storefront church. Everything else in ruins or boarded up. But when my father bought the factory, a stone's throw away Kiler made watercoolers, Fortgang made fire alarms, Lasky made corsets, Robbins made pillows, Honig made pen points—Christ, I *sound* like my father. But he was right—'The joint's jumpin',' he used to say. The major industry now is car theft. Sit at a light in Newark, anywhere in Newark, and all you're doing is looking around you. Bergen near Lyons is where I got rammed. Remember Henry's, 'the Sweet Shop,' next to the Park Theater? Well, right there, where Henry's used to be. Took my first high school date to Henry's for a soda. In a booth there. Arlene Danziger. Took her for a black-and-white soda after the movie. But a black-and-white doesn't mean a soda anymore on Bergen Street. It means the worst kind of hatred in the world. A car coming the wrong way on a one-way street and they ram me. Four kids drooping out the windows. Two of them get out, laughing, joking, and point a gun at my head. I hand over the keys and one of them takes off in my car. Right in front of what used to be Henry's. It's something horrible. They ram cop cars in broad daylight. Front-end collisions. To explode the air bags. Doughnuting. Heard of doughnuting? Doing doughnuts? You haven't heard about this? This is what they steal the cars for. Top speed, they slam on the brakes, yank the emergency brake, twist the steering wheel, and the car starts spinning. Wheeling the car in circles at tremendous speeds. Killing pedestrians means nothing to them. Killing motorists means nothing to them. Killing *themselves* means nothing to them. The skid marks are enough to frighten you. They killed a woman right out in front of our place, same week my car was stolen. Doing a doughnut. I witnessed this. I was leaving for the day. Tremendous speed. The car groaning. Ungodly screeching. It was terrifying. It made my blood run cold. Just driving her own car out of 2nd Street, and this woman, young black woman, gets it. Mother of three kids. Two days later it's one of my own employees. A black guy. But they don't care, black, white doesn't matter to them. They'll kill anyone. Fellow named Clark Tyler, my shipping guy—all he's doing is pulling out of our lot to go home. Twelve hours of surgery, four months in a hospital. Permanent disability. Head injuries, internal injuries, broken pelvis, broken shoulder, fractured spine. A high-speed chase, crazy kid in a stolen car and the cops are chasing him, and the kid plows right into him, crushes the driver's-side door, and that's it for Clark. Eighty miles an hour down Central Avenue. The car thief is twelve years old. To see over the wheel he has to roll up the floor mats to sit on. Six months in Jamesburg and he's back behind the wheel of another stolen car. No, that was it for me, too. My car's robbed at gunpoint, they cripple Clark, the woman gets killed—that week did it. That was enough."

Newark Maid manufactured now exclusively in Puerto Rico. For a while, after leaving Newark, he'd contracted with the Communist government in Czechoslovakia and divided the work between his own factory in Ponce, Puerto Rico, and a Czech glove factory in Brno. However, when a plant that suited him went up for sale in Aguadilla, Puerto Rico, over near Mayagüez, he'd bailed out on the Czechs, whose bureaucracy had been irritating from the start, and unified his manufacturing operation by purchasing a second Puerto Rico facility, another good-sized factory, moved in the machinery, started a training program, and hired an additional three hundred people. By the eighties, though, even Puerto Rico began to grow expensive and about everybody but Newark Maid fled to wherever in the Far East the labor force was abundant and cheap, to the Philippines first, then Korea and Taiwan, and now to China.

Even baseball gloves, the most American glove of all, which used to be made by friends of his father's, the Denkerts up in Johnstown, New York, for a long time now had been manufactured in Korea. When the first guy left Gloversville, New York, in '52 or '53 and went to the Philippines to make gloves, they laughed at him, as though he were going to the moon. But when he died, around 1978, he had a factory there with four thousand workers and the whole industry had gone essentially from Gloversville to the Philippines. Up in Gloversville, when the Second World War began, there must have been ninety glove factories, big and small. Today there isn't a one—all of them out of business or importers from abroad, "people who don't know a fourchette from a thumb," the Swede said. "They're business people, they know if they need a hundred thousand pair of this and two hundred thousand pair of that in so many colors and so many sizes, but they don't know the details on how to get it done." "What's a fourchette?" I asked. "The part of the glove between the fingers. Those small oblong pieces between the fingers, they're die-cut along with the thumbs—those are the fourchettes. Today you've got a lot of underqualified people, probably don't know half what I knew when I was five, and they're making some pretty big decisions. A guy buying deerskin, which can run up to maybe three dollars and fifty cents a foot for a garment grade, he's buying this fine garment-grade deerskin to cut a little palm patch to go on a pair of ski gloves. I talked to him just the other day. A novelty part, runs about five inches by one inch, and he pays three fifty a foot where he could have paid a dollar fifty a foot and come out a long, long ways ahead. You multiply this over a large order, you're talking a hundred-thousand-dollar mistake, and he never knew it. He could have put a hundred grand in his pocket."

The Swede found himself hanging on in P.R., he explained, the way he had hung on in Newark, in large part because he had trained a lot of good people to do the intricate work of making a glove carefully and meticulously, people who could give him what Newark Maid had demanded in quality going back to his father's days; but also, he had to admit, staying on because his family so much enjoyed the vacation home he'd built some fifteen years ago on the Caribbean coast, not very far from the Ponce plant. The life the kids lived there they just loved . . . and off he went again, Kent, Chris, Steve, water-skiing, sailing, scuba diving, catamaraning . . . and though it was clear from all he had just been telling me that this guy could be engaging if he wanted to be, he didn't appear to have any judgment at all as to what was and wasn't interesting about his world. Or, for reasons I couldn't understand, he didn't want his world to be interesting. I would have given anything to get him back to Kiler, Fortgang, Lasky, Robbins, and Honig, back to the fourchettes and the details of how to get a good glove done, even back to the guy who'd paid three fifty a foot for the wrong grade of deerskin for a novelty part, but once he was off and running there was no civil way I could find to shift his focus for a second time from the achievements of his boys on land and sea.

While we waited for dessert, the Swede let pass that he was indulging himself in a fattening zabaglione on top of the ziti only because, after having had his prostate removed a couple of months back, he was still some ten pounds underweight.

"The operation went okay?"

"Just fine," he replied.

"A couple friends of mine," I said, "didn't emerge from that surgery as they'd hoped to. That operation can be a real catastrophe for a man, even if they get the cancer out."

"Yes, that happens, I know."

"One wound up impotent," I said. "The other's impotent and incontinent. Fellows my age. It's been rough for them. Desolating. It can leave you in diapers."

The person I had referred to as "the other" was me. I'd had the surgery in Boston, and—except for confiding in a Boston friend who had helped me through the ordeal till I was back on my feet—when I returned to the house where I live alone, two and a half hours west of Boston, in the Berkshires, I had thought it best to keep to myself both the fact that I'd had cancer and the ways it had left me impaired.

"Well," said the Swede, "I got off easy, I guess."

"I'd say you did," I replied amiably enough, thinking that this big jeroboam of self-contentment really was in possession of all he ever had wanted. To respect everything one is supposed to respect; to protest nothing; never to be inconvenienced by self-distrust; never to be enmeshed in obsession, tortured by incapacity, poisoned by resentment, driven by anger . . . life just unraveling for the Swede like a fluffy ball of yarn.

This line of thinking brought me back to his letter, his request for professional advice about the tribute to his father that he was trying to write. I wasn't myself going to bring up the tribute, and yet the puzzle remained not only as to why *he* didn't but as to why, if he didn't, he had written me about it in the first place. I could only conclude—given what I now knew of this life neither overly rich in contrasts nor troubled too much by contradiction—that the letter and its contents had to do with the operation, with something uncharacteristic that arose in him afterward, some surprising new emotion that had come to the fore. Yes, I thought, the letter grew out of Swede Levov's belated discovery of what it means to be not healthy but sick, to be not strong but weak; what it means to not look great—what physical shame is, what humiliation is, what the gruesome is, what extinction is, what it is like to ask "Why?" Betrayed all at once by a wonderful body that had furnished him only with assurance and had constituted the bulk of his advantage over others, he had momentarily lost his equilibrium and had clutched at me, of all people, as a means of grasping his dead father and calling up the father's power to protect him. For a moment his nerve was shattered, and this man who, as far as I could tell, used himself mainly to conceal himself had been transformed into an impulsive, devitalized being in dire need of a blessing. Death had burst into the dream of his life (as, for the second time in ten years, it had burst into mine), and the things that disquiet men our age disquieted even him.

I wondered if he was willing any longer to recall the sickbed vulnerability that had made certain inevitabilities as real for him as the exterior of his family's life, to remember the shadow that had insinuated itself like a virulent icing between the layers and layers of contentment. Yet he'd showed up for our dinner date. Did that mean the unendurable wasn't blotted out, the safeguards weren't back in place, the emergency wasn't yet over? Or was showing up and going blithely on about everything that *was* endurable his way of purging the last of his fears? The more I thought about this simple-seeming soul sitting across from me eating zabaglione and exuding sincerity, the farther from him my thinking carried me. The man within the man was scarcely perceptible to me. I could not make sense of him. I couldn't imagine him at all, having come down with my own strain of the Swede's disorder: the inability to draw conclusions about anything but exteriors. Rooting around trying to figure this guy out is ridiculous, I told myself. This is the jar you cannot open. This guy cannot be cracked by thinking. That's the mystery of his mystery. It's like trying to get something out of Michelangelo's David.

I'd given him my number in my letter—why hadn't he called to break the date if he was no longer deformed by the prospect of death? Once it was all back to how it had always been, once he'd recovered that special luminosity that had never failed to win whatever he wanted, what use did he have for me? No, his letter, I thought, cannot be the whole story—if it were, he wouldn't have come. Something remains of the rash urge to change things. Something that overtook him in the hospital is still there. An unexamined existence no longer serves his needs. He wants something recorded. That's why he's turned to me: to record what might otherwise be forgotten. Omitted and forgotten. What could it be?

Or maybe he was just a happy man. Happy people exist too. Why shouldn't they? All the scattershot speculation about the Swede's motives was only my professional impatience, my trying to imbue Swede Levov with something like the tendentious meaning Tolstoy assigned to Ivan Ilych, so belittled by the author in the uncharitable story in which he sets out to heartlessly expose, in clinical terms, what it is to be ordinary. Ivan Ilych is the well-placed high-court official who leads "a decorous life approved of by society" and who on his deathbed, in the depths of his unceasing agony and terror, thinks, "'Maybe I did not live as I ought to have done.'" Ivan Ilych's life, writes Tolstoy, summarizing, right at the outset, his judgment of the presiding judge with the delightful St. Petersburg house and a handsome salary of three thousand rubles a year and friends all of good social position, *had been most simple and most ordinary and therefore most terrible.* Maybe so. Maybe in Russia in 1886. But in Old Rimrock, New Jersey, in 1995, when the Ivan Ilyches come trooping back to lunch at the clubhouse after their morning round of golf and start to crow, "It doesn't get any better than this," they may be a lot closer to the truth than Leo Tolstoy ever was.

*Swede Levov's life,* for all I knew, *had been most simple and most ordinary and therefore just great, right in the American grain.*

"Is Jerry gay?" I suddenly asked.

"My brother?" The Swede laughed. "You're kidding."

Maybe I was and had asked the question out of mischief, to alleviate the boredom. Yet I did happen to be remembering that line the Swede had written me about how much his father "suffered because of the shocks that befell his loved ones," which led me to wondering again what he'd been alluding to, which spontaneously reminded me of the humiliation Jerry had brought upon himself in our junior year of high school when he attempted to win the heart of a strikingly unexceptional girl in our class who you wouldn't have thought required a production to get her to kiss you.

As a Valentine present, Jerry made a coat for her out of hamster skins, a hundred and seventy-five hamster skins that he cured in the sun and then sewed together with a curved sewing needle pilfered from his father's factory, where the idea dawned on him. The high school biology department had been given a gift of some three hundred hamsters for the purpose of dissection, and Jerry diligently finagled to collect the skins from the biology students; his oddness and his genius made credible the story he told about "a scientific experiment" he was conducting at home. He finagled next to find out the girl's height, he designed a pattern, and then, after he got most of the stink out of the hides—or thought he had—by drying them in the sun on the roof of his garage, he meticulously sewed the skins together, finishing the coat off with a silk lining made out of a section of a white parachute, an imperfect parachute his brother had sent home to him as a memento from the marine air base in Cherry Point, North Carolina, where the Parris Island team won the last game of the season for the Marine Corps baseball championship. The only person Jerry told about the coat was me, the Ping-Pong stooge. He was going to send it to the girl in a Bamberger's coat box of his mother's, wrapped in lavender tissue paper and tied with velvet ribbon. But when the coat was finished, it was so stiff—because of the idiotic way he'd dried the skins, his father would later explain—that he couldn't get it to fold up in the box.

Across from the Swede in Vincent's restaurant, I suddenly recalled seeing it in the basement: this big thing sitting on the floor with sleeves. Today, I was thinking, it would win all kinds of prizes at the Whitney Museum, but back in Newark in 1949 nobody knew dick about what great art was and Jerry and I racked our brains trying to figure out what he could do to get the coat into the box. He was set on that box because she would think, when she began to open it, that it contained an expensive coat from Bam's. I was thinking of what she would think when she saw that *wasn't* what it contained; I was thinking that surely it didn't take such hard work to gain the attention of a chubby girl with bad skin and no boyfriend. But I cooperated with Jerry because he had a cyclonic personality you either fled or yielded to and because he was Swede Levov's brother and I was in Swede Levov's house and everywhere you looked were Swede Levov's trophies. Eventually Jerry tore the entire coat apart and resewed it so that the stitching lay straight across the chest, creating a hinge of sorts where the coat could be bent and placed in the box. I helped him—it was like sewing a suit of armor. Atop the coat he placed a heart that he cut out of cardboard and painted his name on in Gothic letters, and the package was sent parcel post. It had taken him three months to transform an improbable idea into nutty reality. Brief by human standards.

She screamed when she opened the box. "She had a fit," her girlfriends said. Jerry's father also had a fit. "This is what you do with the parachute your brother sent you? You cut it up? You cut up a parachute?" Jerry was too humiliated to tell him that it was to get the girl to fall into his arms and kiss him the way Lana Turner kissed Clark Gable. I happened to be there when his father went after him for curing the skins in the midday sun. "A skin must be preserved *properly*. Properly! And properly is not in the sun—you must dry a skin in the shade. You don't want them sunburned, damn it! Can I teach you once and for all, Jerome, how to preserve a skin?" And that he proceeded to do, in a boil at first, barely able to contain his frustration with his own son's ineptitude as a leather worker, explaining to both of us what they had taught the traders to do to the sheepskins in Ethiopia before they shipped them to Newark Maid to be contracted out to the tanner. "You can salt it, but salt's expensive. Especially in Africa, very, very expensive. And they steal the salt there. These people don't have salt. You have to put poison into the salt over there so they won't steal it. Other way is to pack the skin up, various ways, either on a board or on a frame, you tie it, and make little cuts, tie it up and dry it in the shade. *In the shade,* boys. That's what we call flint-dried skin. Sprinkle a little flint on it, keeps it from deteriorating, prevents the bugs from entering—" Much to my own relief, the outrage had given way surprisingly fast to a patient, if tedious, pedagogical assault, which seemed to gall Jerry even more than being blown down by his father's huffing and puffing. It could well have been that very day when Jerry swore to himself never to go near his father's business.

To deal with malodorous skins, Jerry had doused the coat with his mother's perfume, but by the time the coat was delivered by the postman it had begun to stink as it had intermittently all along, and the girl was so revolted when she opened the box, so insulted and horrified, that she never spoke to Jerry again. According to the other girls, she thought he had gone out and hunted and killed all those tiny beasts and then sent them to her because of her blemished skin. Jerry was in a rage when he got the news and, in the midst of our next Ping-Pong game, cursed her and called all girls fucking idiots. If he hadn't before had the courage to ask anyone out on a date, he never tried after that and was one of only three boys who didn't show up at the senior prom. The other two were what we identified as "sissies." And that was why I now asked the Swede a question about Jerry that I would never have dreamed of asking in 1949, when I had no clear idea what a homosexual was and couldn't imagine that anybody I knew could be one. At the time I thought Jerry was Jerry, a genius, with obsessive naiveté and colossal innocence about girls. In those days, that explained it all. Maybe it still does. But I was really looking to see what, if anything, could roil the innocence of this regal Swede—and to prevent myself from being so rude as to fall asleep on him—so I asked him, "Is Jerry gay?"

"As a kid there was always something secretive about Jerry," I said. "There were never any girls, never close friends, always something about him, even *besides* his brains, that set him apart. . . ."

The Swede nodded, looking at me as though he understood my deeper meaning as no human being ever had before, and because of this probing stare that I would swear saw nothing, all this giving that gave nothing and gave away nothing, I had no idea where his thoughts might be or if he even had "thoughts." When, momentarily, I stopped speaking, I sensed that my words, rather than falling into the net of the other person's awareness, got linked up with nothing in his brain, went in there and vanished. Something about the harmless eyes—the promise they made that he could never do anything other than what was right—was becoming annoying to me, which has to be why I next brought up his letter instead of keeping my mouth shut until the bill came and I could get away from him for another fifty years so that when 2045 rolled around I might actually look forward to seeing him again.

You fight your superficiality, your shallowness, so as to try to come at people without unreal expectations, without an overload of bias or hope or arrogance, as untanklike as you can be, sans cannon and machine guns and steel plating half a foot thick; you come at them unmenacingly on your own ten toes instead of tearing up the turf with your caterpillar treads, take them on with an open mind, as equals, man to man, as we used to say, and yet you never fail to get them wrong. You might as well have the *brain* of a tank. You get them wrong before you meet them, while you're anticipating meeting them; you get them wrong while you're with them; and then you go home to tell somebody else about the meeting and you get them all wrong again. Since the same generally goes for them with you, the whole thing is really a dazzling illusion empty of all perception, an astonishing farce of misperception. And yet what are we to do about this terribly significant business of *other people*, which gets bled of the significance we think it has and takes on instead a significance that is ludicrous, so ill-equipped are we all to envision one another's interior workings and invisible aims? Is everyone to go off and lock the door and sit secluded like the lonely writers do, in a soundproof cell, summoning people out of words and then proposing that these word people are closer to the real thing than the real people that we mangle with our ignorance every day? The fact remains that getting people right is not what living is all about anyway. It's getting them wrong that is living, getting them wrong and wrong and wrong and then, on careful reconsideration, getting them wrong again. That's how we know we're alive: we're wrong. Maybe the best thing would be to forget being right or wrong about people and just go along for the ride. But if you can do that—well, lucky you.

"When you wrote me about your father, and the shocks he'd suffered, it occurred to me that maybe Jerry had been the shock. Your old man wouldn't have been any better than mine at coming to grips with a queer son."

The Swede smiled the smile that refused to be superior, that was meant to reassure me that nothing in him ever could or would want to resist me, that signaled to me that, adored as he was, he was no better than me, even perhaps a bit of a nobody beside me. "Well, fortunately for my father, he didn't have to. Jerry was the-son-the-doctor. He couldn't have been prouder of anyone than he was of Jerry."

"Jerry's a physician?"

"In Miami. Cardiac surgeon. Million bucks a year."

"Married? Jerry married?"

The smile again. The vulnerability in that smile was the surprising element—the vulnerability of our record-breaking muscleman faced with all the crudeness it takes to stay alive. The smile's refusal to recognize, let alone to sanction in himself, the savage obstinacy that seven decades of surviving requires of a man. As though anyone over ten believes you can subjugate with a smile, even one that kind and warm, all the things that are out to get you, with a smile hold it all together when the strong arm of the unforeseen comes crashing down on your head. Once again I began to think that he might be mentally unsound, that this smile could perhaps be an indication of derangement. There was no sham in it—and that was the worst of it. The smile wasn't insincere. He wasn't imitating anything. This caricature was *it*, arrived at spontaneously after a lifetime of working himself deeper and deeper into . . . what? The idea of himself neighborhood stardom had wreathed him in— had that mummified the Swede as a boy forever? It was as though he had abolished from his world everything that didn't suit him— not only deceit, violence, mockery, and ruthlessness but anything remotely coarse-grained, any threat of contingency, that dreadful harbinger of helplessness. Not for a second did he stop trying to make his relation to me appear as simple and sincere as his seeming relationship to himself.

Unless, unless, he was just a mature man, as devious as the next mature man. Unless what was awakened by the cancer surgery—

and what had momentarily managed to penetrate a lifelong comfy take on things—the hundred percent recovery had all but extinguished. Unless he was not a character with no character to reveal but a character with none that he wished to reveal—just a sensible man who understands that if you regard highly your privacy and the well-being of your loved ones, the last person to take into your confidence is a working novelist. Give the novelist, instead of your life story, the brazen refusal of the gorgeous smile, blast him with the stun gun of your prince-of-blandness smile, then polish off the zabaglione and get the hell back to Old Rimrock, New Jersey, where your life is your business and not his.

"Jerry's been married four times," said the Swede, smiling. "Family record."

"And you?" I had already figured, from the ages of his three boys, that the fortyish blonde with the golf clubs was more than likely a second wife and perhaps a third. Yet divorce didn't fit my picture of someone who so refused to register life's irrational element. If there had been a divorce, it had to have been initiated by Miss New Jersey. Or she had died. Or being married to someone who had to keep the achievement looking perfect, someone devoted heart and soul to the illusion of stability, had led her to suicide. Maybe *that* was the shock that had befallen . . . Perversely, my attempts to come up with the missing piece that would make the Swede whole and coherent kept identifying him with disorders of which there was no trace on his beautifully aging paragon's face. I could not decide if that blankness of his was like snow covering something or snow covering nothing.

"Me? Two wives, that's my limit. I'm a piker next to my brother. His new one's in her thirties. Half his age. Jerry's the doctor who marries the nurse. All four, nurses. They revere the ground Dr. Levov walks on. Four wives, six kids. *That* drove my dad a little nuts. But Jerry's a big guy, a gruff guy, the high-and-mighty prima donna surgeon—got a whole *hospital* by the short hairs—and so even my dad fell in line. Had to. Would have lost him otherwise.

My kid brother doesn't screw around. Dad kicked and screamed through each divorce, wanted to shoot Jerry a hundred times over, but as soon as Jerry remarried, the new wife, in my father's eyes, was more of a princess than the wife before. 'She's a doll, she's a sweetheart, she's my girl. . . .' Anybody said anything about any of Jerry's wives, my father would have murdered him. Jerry's kids he outright adored. Five girls, one boy. My dad loved the boy, but the girls, they were the apple of his eye. There's nothing he wouldn't do for those kids. For any of our kids. When he had everybody around him, all of us, all the kids, my old man was in heaven. Ninety-six and never sick a day in his life. After the stroke, for the six months before he died, that was the worst. But he had a good run. Had a good life. A real fighter. A force of nature. Unstoppable guy." A light, floating tone to the words when he goes off on the subject of his father, the voice resonant with amorous reverence, disclosing unashamedly that nothing had permeated more of his life than his father's expectations.

"The suffering?"

"Could have been a lot worse," the Swede said. "Just the six months, and even then he didn't know half the time what was going on. He just slipped away one night . . . and we lost him."

By "suffering" I had meant that suffering he had referred to in his letter, provoked in his father by the shocks "that befell his loved ones." But even if I had thought to bring his letter with me and had rattled it in his face, the Swede would have eluded his own writing as effortlessly as he'd shaken off his tacklers on that Saturday fifty years before, at City Stadium, against South Side, our weakest rival, and set a state record by scoring four times on consecutive pass plays. Of course, I thought, of course—my urge to discover a substratum, my continuing suspicion that more was there than what I was looking at, aroused in him the fear that I might go ahead and tell him that he wasn't what he wanted us to believe he was. . . . But then I thought, Why bestow on him all this thinking? Why the appetite to know this guy? Ravenous because once upon a time he said to you and to you alone, "Basketball was never like this, Skip"? Why clutch at him? What's the matter with you? There's nothing here but what you're looking at. He's all about being looked at. He always was. He is not faking all this virginity. You're craving depths that don't exist. This guy is the embodiment of nothing.

I was wrong. Never more mistaken about anyone in my life.

# 2

Let's remember the energy. Americans were governing not only themselves but some two hundred million people in Italy, Austria, Germany, and Japan. The war-crimes trials were cleansing the earth of its devils once and for all. Atomic power was ours alone. Rationing was ending, price controls were being lifted; in an explosion of self-assertion, auto workers, coal workers, transit workers, maritime workers, steel workers—laborers by the millions demanded more and went on strike for it. And playing Sunday morning softball on the Chancellor Avenue field and pickup basketball on the asphalt courts behind the school were all the boys who had come back alive, neighbors, cousins, older brothers, their pockets full of separation pay, the GI Bill inviting them to break out in ways they could not have imagined possible before the war. Our class started high school six months after the unconditional surrender of the Japanese, during the greatest moment of collective inebriation in American history. And the upsurge of energy was contagious. Around us nothing was lifeless. Sacrifice and constraint were over. The Depression had disappeared. Everything was in motion. The lid was off. Americans were to start over again, en masse, everyone in it together.

If that wasn't sufficiently inspiring—the miraculous conclusion of this towering event, the clock of history reset and a whole people's aims limited no longer by the past—there was the neighborhood, the communal determination that we, the children, should escape poverty, ignorance, disease, social injury and intimidation—escape, above all, insignificance. You must not come to nothing! *Make something of yourselves!*

Despite the undercurrent of anxiety—a sense communicated daily that hardship was a persistent menace that only persistent diligence could hope to keep at bay; despite a generalized mistrust of the Gentile world; despite the fear of being battered that clung to many families because of the Depression—ours was not a neighborhood steeped in darkness. The place was bright with industriousness. There was a big belief in life and we were steered relentlessly in the direction of success: a better existence was going to be ours. The goal was to *have* goals, the aim to *have* aims. This edict came entangled often in hysteria, the embattled hysteria of those whom experience had taught how little antagonism it takes to wreck a life beyond repair. Yet it was this edict— emotionally overloaded as it was by the uncertainty in our elders, by their awareness of all that was in league against them—that made the neighborhood a cohesive place. A whole community perpetually imploring us not to be immoderate and screw up, imploring us to grasp opportunity, exploit our advantages, remember *what matters.*

The shift was not slight between the generations and there was plenty to argue about: the ideas of the world they wouldn't give up; the rules they worshiped, for us rendered all but toothless by the passage of just a couple of decades of American time; those uncertainties that were theirs and not ours. The question of how free of them we might dare to be was ongoing, an internal debate, ambivalent and exasperated. What was most cramping in their point of view a few of us did find the audacity to strain against, but the intergenerational conflict never looked like it would twenty years later. The neighborhood was never a field of battle strewn with the bodies of the misunderstood. There was plenty of haranguing to ensure obedience; the adolescent capacity for upheaval was held in check by a thousand requirements, stipulations, prohibitions—restraints that proved insuperable. One was our own highly realistic appraisal of what was most in our interest, another the pervasive rectitude of the era, whose taboos we'd taken between our teeth at birth; not least was the enacted ideology of parental self-sacrifice that bled us of wanton rebelliousness and sent underground almost every indecent urge.

It would have taken a lot more courage—or foolishness—than most of us could muster to disappoint their passionate, unflagging illusions about our perfectibility and roam very far from the permissible. Their reasons for asking us to be both law-abiding and superior were not reasons we could find the conscience to discount, and so control that was close to absolute was ceded to adults who were striving and improving themselves through us. Mild forms of scarring may have resulted from this arrangement but few cases of psychosis were reported, at least at the time. The weight of all that expectation was not necessarily killing, thank God. Of course there were families where it might have helped if the parents had eased up a little on the brake, but mostly the friction between generations was just sufficient to give us purchase to move forward.

Am I wrong to think that we delighted in living there? No delusions are more familiar than those inspired in the elderly by nostalgia, but am I completely mistaken to think that living as well-born children in Renaissance Florence could not have held a candle to growing up within aromatic range of Tabachnik's pickle barrels? Am I mistaken to think that even back then, in the vivid present, the fullness of life stirred our emotions to an extraordinary extent? Has anywhere since so engrossed you in its ocean of details? The *detail*, the immensity of the detail, the force of the detail, the weight of the detail—the rich endlessness of detail surrounding you in your young life like the six feet of dirt that'll be packed on your grave when you're dead.

Perhaps by definition a neighborhood is the place to which a child spontaneously gives undivided attention; that's the unfiltered way meaning comes to children, just flowing off the surface of things. Nonetheless, fifty years later, I ask you: has the immersion ever again been so complete as it was in those streets, where every block, every backyard, every house, every *floor* of every house—the walls, ceilings, doors, and windows of every last friend's family apartment—came to be so absolutely individualized? Were we ever again to be such keen recording instruments of the microscopic surface of things close at hand, of the minutest gradations of social position conveyed by linoleum and oilcloth, by yahrzeit candles and cooking smells, by Ronson table lighters and venetian blinds? About one another, we knew who had what kind of lunch in the bag in his locker and who ordered what on his hot dog at Syd's; we knew one another's every physical attribute— who walked pigeon-toed and who had breasts, who smelled of hair oil and who oversalivated when he spoke; we knew who among us was belligerent and who was friendly, who was smart and who was dumb; we knew whose mother had the accent and whose father had the mustache, whose mother worked and whose father was dead; somehow we even dimly grasped how every family's different set of circumstances set each family a distinctive difficult human problem.

And, of course, there was the mandatory turbulence born of need, appetite, fantasy, longing, and the fear of disgrace. With only adolescent introspection to light the way, each of us, hopelessly pubescent, alone and in secret, attempted to regulate it—and in an era when chastity was still ascendant, a national cause to be embraced by the young like freedom and democracy.

It's astonishing that everything so immediately visible in our lives as classmates we still remember so precisely. The intensity of feeling that we have seeing one another today is also astonishing. But most astonishing is that we are nearing the age that our grandparents were when we first went off to be freshmen at the annex on February 1, 1946. What is astonishing is that we, who had no idea how anything was going to turn out, now know exactly what happened. That the results are in for the class of January 1950—the unanswerable questions answered, the future revealed—is that not astonishing? To have lived—and in this country, and in our time, and as who we were. Astonishing.

This is the speech I didn't give at my forty-fifth high school reunion, a speech to myself masked as a speech to them. I began to compose it only *after* the reunion, in the dark, in bed, groping to understand what had hit me. The tone—too ruminative for a country club ballroom and the sort of good time people were looking for there—didn't seem at all ill-conceived between three and six A.M., as I tried, in my overstimulated state, to comprehend the union underlying the reunion, the common experience that had joined us as kids. Despite gradations of privation and privilege, despite the array of anxieties fostered by an impressively nuanced miscellany of family quarrels—quarrels that, fortunately, promised more unhappiness than they always delivered—something powerful united us. And united us not merely in where we came from but in where we were going and how we would get there. We had new means and new ends, new allegiances and new aims, new innards— a new *ease,* somewhat less agitation in facing down the exclusions the goyim still wished to preserve. And out of what context did these transformations arise—out of what historical drama, acted unsuspectingly by its little protagonists, played out in classrooms and kitchens looking nothing at all like the great theater of life? Just what collided with what to produce the spark in us?

I was still awake and all stirred up, formulating these questions and their answers in my bed—blurry, insomniac shadows of these questions and their answers—some eight hours after I'd driven back from New Jersey, where, on a sunny Sunday late in October, at a country club in a Jewish suburb far from the futility prevailing in the streets of our crime-ridden, drug-infested childhood home, the reunion that began at eleven in the morning went ebulliently on all afternoon long. It was held in a ballroom just at the edge of the country club's golf course for a group of elderly adults who, as Weequahic kids of the thirties and forties, would have thought a niblick (which was what in those days they called the nine iron) was a hunk of schmaltz herring. Now I couldn't sleep—the last thing I could remember was the parking valet bringing my car around to the steps of the portico, and the reunion's commander in chief, Selma Bresloff, kindly asking if I'd had a good time, and my telling her, "It's like going out to your old outfit after Iwo Jima."

Around three A.M., I left my bed and went to my desk, my head vibrant with the static of unelaborated thought. I wound up working there until six, by which time I had got the reunion speech to read as it appears above. Only after I had built to the emotional peroration culminating in the word "astonishing" was I at last sufficiently unastonished by the force of my feelings to be able to put together a couple of hours of sleep—or something resembling sleep, for, even half out of it, I was a biography in perpetual motion, memory to the marrow of my bones.

Yes, even from as benign a celebration as a high school reunion it's not so simple to instantaneously resume existence back behind the blindfold of continuity and routine. Perhaps if I were thirty or forty, the reunion would have faded sweetly away in the three hours it took me to drive home. But there is no easy mastery of such events at sixty-two, and only a year beyond cancer surgery. Instead of recapturing time past, I'd been captured by it in the present, so that passing seemingly out of the world of time I was, in fact, rocketing through to its secret core.

For the hours we were all together, doing nothing more than hugging, kissing, kibitzing, laughing, hovering over one another recollecting the dilemmas and disasters that hadn't in the long run made a damn bit of difference, crying out, "Look who's here!" and "Oh, it's been a long time" and "You remember me? I remember you," asking each other, "Didn't we once . . . ," "Were you the kid who . . . ," commanding one another—with those three poignant words I heard people repeat all afternoon as they were drawn and tugged into numerous conversations at once—"Don't go away!" . . . and, of course, dancing, cheek-to-cheek dancing our outdated dance steps to a "one-man band," a bearded boy in a tuxedo, his brow encircled with a red bandanna (a boy born at least two full decades after we'd marched together out of the school auditorium to the rousing recessional tempo of *Iolanthe*), accompanying himself on a synthesizer as he imitated Nat "King" Cole, Frankie Laine, and Sinatra—for those few hours time, the chain of time, the whole damn drift of everything called time, had seemed as easy to understand as the dimensions of the doughnut you effortlessly down with your morning coffee. The one-man band in the bandanna played "Mule Train" while I thought, The Angel of Time is passing over us and breathing with each breath all that we've lived through—the Angel of Time unmistakably as present in the ballroom of the Cedar Hill Country Club as that kid doing "Mule Train" like Frankie Laine. Sometimes I found myself looking at everyone as though it were still 1950, as though "1995" were merely the futuristic theme of a senior prom that we'd all come to in humorous papier-mâché masks of ourselves as we might look at the close of the twentieth century. That afternoon time had been invented for the mystification of no one but us.

Inside the commemorative mug presented by Selma to each of us as we were departing were half a dozen little *rugelach* in an orange tissue-paper sack, neatly enclosed in orange cellophane and tied shut with striped curling ribbon of orange and brown, the school colors. The *rugelach*, as fresh as any I'd ever snacked on at home after school—back then baked by the recipe broker of her mahjongg club, my mother—were a gift from one of our class members, a Teaneck baker. Within five minutes of leaving the reun-

ion, I'd undone the double wrapping and eaten all six *rugelach,*
each a snail of sugar-dusted pastry dough, the cinammon-lined
chambers microscopically studded with midget raisins and
chopped walnuts. By rapidly devouring mouthful after mouthful of
these crumbs whose floury richness—blended of butter and sour
cream and vanilla and cream cheese and egg yolk and sugar—I'd
loved since childhood, perhaps I'd find vanishing from Nathan
what, according to Proust, vanished from Marcel the instant he
recognized "the savour of the little *madeleine*": the apprehensive-
ness of death. "A mere taste," Proust writes, and "the word 'death'
. . . [has] . . . no meaning for him." So, greedily I ate, gluttonously,
refusing to curtail for a moment this wolfish intake of saturated fat
but, in the end, having nothing like Marcel's luck.

Let's speak further of death and of the desire—understandably in
the aging a desperate desire—to forestall death, to resist it, to resort
to whatever means are necessary to see death with anything, anything, *anything* but clarity:
   One of the boys up from Florida—according to the reunion
booklet we each received at the door, twenty-six out of a graduating
class of a hundred and seventy-six were now living in Florida . . . a
good sign, meant we still had more people in Florida (six more)
than we had who were dead; and all afternoon, by the way, it was
not in my mind alone that the men were tagged the boys and the
women the girls—told me that on the way to Livingston from
Newark Airport, where his plane had landed and he'd rented a car,
he'd twice had to pull up at service stations and get the key to the
restroom, so wracked was he by trepidation. This was Mendy Gurlik, in 1950 voted the handsomest boy in the class, in 1950 a broad-
shouldered, long-lashed beauty, our most important jitterbugger,
who loved to go around saying to people, "Solid, Jackson!" Having
once been invited by his older brother to a colored whorehouse on
Augusta Street, where the pimps hung out, virtually around the
corner from his father's Branford Place liquor store—a whorehouse where, he eventually confessed, he'd sat fully clothed, waiting

in an outer hallway, flipping through a *Mechanix Illustrated* that he'd found on a table there, while his brother was the one who "did it"—Mendy was the closest the class had to a delinquent. It was Mendy Gurlik (now Garr) who'd taken me with him to the Adams Theater to hear Illinois Jacquet, Buddy Johnson, and "Newark's own" Sarah Vaughan; who'd got the tickets and taken me with him to hear Mr. B., Billy Eckstine, in concert at the Mosque; who, in '49, had got tickets for us to the Miss Sepia America Beauty Contest at Laurel Garden. It was Mendy who, some three or four times, took me to watch, broadcasting in the flesh, Bill Cook, the smooth late-night Negro disc jockey of the Jersey station WAAT. *Musical Caravan,* Bill Cook's show, I ordinarily listened to in my darkened bedroom on Saturday nights. The opening theme was Ellington's "Caravan," very exotic, very sophisticated, Afro-Oriental rhythms, a belly-dancing beat—just by itself it was worth tuning in for; "Caravan," in the Duke's very own rendition, made me feel nicely illicit even while tucked up between my mother's freshly laundered sheets. First the tom-tom opening, then winding curvaceously up out of the casbah that great smoky trombone, and then the insinuating, snake-charming flute. Mendy called it "boner music."

To get to WAAT, and Bill Cook's studio, we took the 14 bus downtown, and only minutes after we'd settled quietly like churchgoers in the row of chairs outside his glass-enclosed booth, Bill Cook would come out from behind the microphone to greet us. With a "race record" spinning on the turntable—for listeners still unadventurously at home—Cookie would cordially shake the hands of the two tall, skinny white sharpies, all done up in their one-button-roll suits from the American Shop and their shirts from the Custom Shoppe, with the spread collars. (The clothes on my back were on loan from Mendy for the night.) "And what might I play for you gentlemen?" Cookie graciously inquired of us in a voice whose mellow resonance Mendy would imitate whenever we talked on the phone. I asked for the melodious stuff, "Miss" Dinah Washington, "Miss" Savannah Churchill—and how arresting that was back then, the salacious chivalry of the dj's "Miss"—while

Mendy's taste, spicier, racially far more authoritative, was for musicians like the lowdown saloon piano player Roosevelt Sykes, for Ivory Joe Hunter ("*When* . . . I lost my *bay-bee* . . . I *aahll* . . . *most* lost my *mind*"), and for a quartet that Mendy seemed to me to take excessive pride in calling "the *Ray*-O-Vacs," emphasizing the first syllable exactly as did the black kid from South Side, Melvyn Smith, who delivered for Mendy's father's store after school. (Mendy and his brother did the Saturday deliveries.) Mendy boldly accompanied Melvyn Smith one night to hear live bebop at the lounge over the bowling alley on Beacon Street, Lloyd's Manor, a place to which few whites other than a musician's reckless Desdemona would venture. It was Mendy Gurlik who first took me down to the Radio Record Shack on Market Street, where we picked out bargains from the 19-cent bin and could listen to the record in a booth before we bought it. During the war, when, to keep up morale on the home front, there'd be dances one night a week during July and August at the Chancellor Avenue playground, Mendy used to scramble through the high-spirited crowd—neighborhood parents and schoolkids and little kids up late who ran gleefully round and round the painted white bases where we played our perpetual summer softball game—dispensing for whoever cared to listen a less conventional brand of musical pleasure than the Glenn Miller–Tommy Dorsey–inspired arrangements that most everybody else liked dancing to beneath the dim floodlights back of the school. Regardless of the dance tune the band up on the flag-festooned bandstand happened to be playing, Mendy would race around most of the evening singing, "Cal*don*ia, Cal*don*ia, what makes your big head so *hard?* Rocks!" He sang it, as he blissfully proclaimed, "free of charge," just as nuttily as Louis Jordan and his Tympany Five did on the record he obliged all the Daredevils to listen to whenever, for whatever refractory purpose (to play dollar-limit seven-card stud, to examine for the millionth time the drawings in his Tillie the Toiler "hot book," on rare occasions to hold a circle jerk), we entered his nefarious bedroom when nobody else was home.

And here now was Mendy in 1995, the Weequahic boy with the biggest talent for being less than a dignified model child, a personality halfway between mildly repellent shallowness and audacious, enviable deviance, flirting back then with indignity in a way that hovered continuously between the alluring and the offensive. Here was Dapper, Dirty, Daffy Mendy Gurlik, not in prison (where I was certain he'd wind up when he'd urge us to sit in a circle on the floor of his bedroom, some four or five Daredevils with our pants pulled down, competing to win the couple of bucks in the pot by being the one to "shoot" first), not in hell (where I was sure he'd be consigned after being stabbed to death at Lloyd's Manor by a colored guy "high on reefer"—whatever that meant), but simply a retired restaurateur—owner of three steakhouses called Garr's Grill in suburban Long Island—at no place more disreputable than his high school class's forty-fifth reunion.

"You shouldn't worry, Mend—you still got your build, your looks. You're amazing. You look great."

He did, too: well tanned, slender, a tall narrow-faced jogger wearing black alligator boots and a black silk shirt beneath a green cashmere jacket. Only the head of brimming silver-white hair looked suspiciously not quite his own but as though it had had an earlier life as the end of a skunk.

"I take care of myself—that isn't my point. I called Mutty"—Marty "Mutty" Sheffer, star sidearm pitcher of the Daredevils, the team we three played on in the playground softball league, and, according to the biographical listing in the reunion booklet, a "Financial Consultant" and, too (unlikely as it seemed when I remembered that, paralyzingly shy of girls, babyfaced Mutty had made pitching pennies his major adolescent diversion), progenitor of "Children 36, 34, 31. Grandchildren 2, 1"—"I told Mutty," Mendy said, "that if he didn't sit next to me I wasn't coming. I had to deal with the real goons in my business. Dealt with the fucking Mob. But this I could not deal with from day one. Not twice, Skip, *three* times I had to stop the car to take a crap."

"Well," I said, "after years and years of painting ourselves opaque, this carries us straight back to when we were sure we were transparent."

"Is that it?"

"Maybe. Who knows."

"Twenty kids dead in our class." He showed me at the back of the booklet the page headed "In Memoriam." "Eleven of the guys dead," Mendy said. "*Two* from the Daredevils. Bert Bergman. Utty Orenstein." Utty was Mutty's battery mate, Bert played second base. "Prostate cancer. The both of them. And both in the last three years. I get the blood test. I get it every six months since I heard about Utty. You get the test?"

"I get it." Of course, I didn't any longer because I no longer had a prostate.

"How often?"

"Every year."

"Not enough," he told me. "Every six months."

"Okay. I'll do that."

"You been all right though?" he asked, taking hold of me by the shoulders.

"I'm in good shape," I said.

"Hey, I taught you to jerk off, you know that?"

"That you did, Mendel. Anywhere from ninety to a hundred twenty days before I would have happened upon it myself. You're the one who got me going."

"I'm the guy," he said, laughing loudly, "who taught Skip Zuckerman to jerk off. My claim to fame," and we embraced, the bald first baseman and white-haired left fielder of the dwindling Daredevil Athletic Club. The torso I could feel through his clothes attested to just how well he did take care of himself.

"I'm still at it," Mendy said happily. "Fifty years later. A Daredevil record."

"Don't be so sure," I said. "Check with Mutty."

"I heard you had a heart attack," he said.

"No, just a bypass. Years ago."

"The fucking bypass. They stick that tube down your throat, don't they?"

"They do."

"I saw my brother-in-law with the tube down his throat. That's all I need," Mendy said. "I didn't want to be here in the worst fucking way, but Mutty keeps calling and saying, 'You're not going to live forever,' and I keep telling him, 'I *am*, Mutt. I have to!' Then I'm schmuck enough to come, and the first thing I see when I open up this booklet is obituaries."

When Mendy went off to get a drink and find Mutty, I looked for his name in the booklet: "Retired Restaurateur. Children 36, 33, 28. Grandchildren 14, 12, 9, 5, 5, 3." I wondered if the six grand-children, including what appeared to be a set of twins, were what made Mendy so fearful of death or if there were other reasons, like reveling still in whores and sharp clothes. I should have asked him.

I should have asked people a lot of things that afternoon. But later, though regretting that I hadn't, I understood that to have gotten answers to any of my questions beginning "Whatever happened to . . ." would not have told me why I had the uncanny sense that what goes on *behind* what we see is what I was seeing. It didn't take more than one of the girls' saying to the photographer, the instant before he snapped the class photo, "Be sure and leave the wrinkles out," didn't take more than laughing along with everyone else at the nicely timed wisecrack, to feel that Destiny, the most ancient enigma of the civilized world—and our first composition topic in freshman Greek and Roman Mythology, where I wrote "the Fates are three goddesses, called the Moerae, Clotho who spins, Lachesis who determines its length, and Atropos who cuts the thread of life"—Destiny had become perfectly understandable while every-thing unenigmatic, such as standing for the photograph in the third row back, with my one arm on the shoulder of Marshall Goldstein ("Children 39, 37. Grandchildren 8, 6") and my other on the shoulder of Stanley Wernikoff ("Children 39, 38. Grandchildren 5, 2, 8 mo."), had become inexplicable.

A young NYU film student named Jordan Wasser, the grandson of fullback Milton Wasserberger, had come along with Milt to make a documentary of our reunion for one of his classes; from time to time, as I floated around the room documenting the event in my own outdated way, I overheard Jordan interviewing somebody on camera. "It was like no other school," sixty-three-year-old Marilyn Koplik was telling him. "The kids were great, we had good teachers, the worst crime we could commit was chewing gum. . . ." "Best school around," said sixty-three-year-old George Kirschenbaum, "best teachers, best kids. . . ." "Mind for mind," said sixty-three-year-old Leon Gutman, "this is the smartest group of people I've ever worked with. . . ." "School was just different in those days," said sixty-three-year-old Rona Siegler, and to the next question Rona replied with a laugh—a laugh without much delight in it— "Nineteen fifty? It was just a couple of years ago, Jordan."

"I always tell people," somebody was saying to me, "when they ask if I went to school with you, how you wrote that paper for me in Wallach's class. On *Red Badge of Courage*." "But I didn't." "You did." "What could I know about *Red Badge of Courage*? I didn't even read it till college." "No. You wrote a paper for me on *Red Badge of Courage*. I got an A plus. I handed it in a week late and Wallach said to me, 'It was worth waiting for.'"

The person telling me this, a small, dour man with a close-clipped white beard, a brutal scar beneath one eye, and two hearing aids, was one of the few I saw that afternoon on whom time had done a job and then some; on him time had worked overtime. He walked with a limp and spoke to me leaning on a cane. His breathing was heavy. I did not recognize him, not when I looked squarely at him from six inches away and not even after I read on his name tag that he was Ira Posner. Who was Ira Posner? And why would I have done him that favor, especially when I couldn't have? Did I write the paper for Ira without bothering to read the book? "Your father meant a lot to me," Ira said. "Did he?" I asked. "In the few moments I spent with him in my life I felt better about myself than the entire life I spent with my own father." "I didn't know that." "My own father was a very marginal person in my life." "What did he do? Remind me." "He scraped floors for a living. Spent his whole life scraping floors. Your father was always pushing you to get the best grades. My father's idea of setting me up in business was buying me a shoeshine kit so I could give quarter shines at a newsstand. That's what he got me for graduation. Dumb fuck. I really suffered in that family. A really benighted family. I lived in a dark place with those people. You get shunted aside by your father, Nathan, you wind up a touchy fellow. I had a brother we had to put in an institution. You didn't know that. Nobody did. We weren't allowed even to mention his name. Eddie. Four years older than me. He would go into wild rages and bite his hands until they would bleed. He would scream like a coyote until my parents quieted him down. At school they asked if I had brothers or sisters and I wrote 'None.' While I was at college, my parents signed some permission form for the nuthouse and they gave Eddie a lobotomy and he went into a coma and died. Can you imagine? Tells me to shine shoes on Market Street outside the courthouse—that is a father's advice to a son." "So what'd you do instead?" "I'm a psychiatrist. It's your father I got my inspiration from. He was a physician." "Not exactly. He wore a white coat but he was a chiropodist." "Whenever I came with the guys to your house, your mother always put out a bowl of fruit and your father always said to me, 'What is your idea on this subject, Ira? What is your idea on that subject, Ira?' Peaches. Plums. Nectarines. Grapes. I never saw an apple in my house. My mother is ninety-seven. I got her in a home now. She sits there crying in a chair all day long but I honestly don't believe she's any more depressed than she was when I was a kid. I assume your father is dead." "Yes. Yours?" "Mine couldn't wait to die. Failure went to his head in a really big way." And still I had no idea who Ira was or what he was talking about, because, as much as I was remembering that day of all that had once happened, far more was so beyond recall that it might never have happened, regardless of how many Ira Posners stood face to face with me attesting otherwise. As best I could tell, when Ira was in my house being inspired by my father I could as well not have been born. I had run out of the power to remember even faintly my father's asking Ira what he thought while Ira was eating a piece of our fruit. It was one of those things that get torn out of you and thrust into oblivion just because they didn't matter enough. And yet what I had missed completely took root in Ira and changed his life.

So you don't have to look much further than Ira and me to see why we go through life with a generalized sense that everybody is wrong except us. And since we don't just forget things because they don't matter but also forget things because they matter too much—because each of us remembers and forgets in a pattern whose labyrinthine windings are an identification mark no less distinctive than a fingerprint—it's no wonder that the shards of reality one person will cherish as a biography can seem to someone else who, say, happened to have eaten some ten thousand dinners at the very same kitchen table, to be a willful excursion into mythomania. But then nobody really bothers to send in their fifty bucks for a forty-fifth high school reunion so as to turn up and stage a protest against the other guy's sense of the-way-it-was; the truly important thing, the supreme delight of the afternoon, is simply finding that you haven't yet made it onto the "In Memoriam" page.

"How long is your father dead?" Ira asked me. "Nineteen sixty-nine. Twenty-six years. A long time," I replied. "To whom? To him? I don't think so. To the dead," said Ira, "it's a drop in the bucket." Just then, from directly behind me, I heard Mendy Gurlik saying to someone, "Whoja jerk off over?" "Lorraine," a second man replied. "Sure. Everyone did. Me too. Who else?" said Mendy. "Diane." "Right. Diane. Absolutely. Who else?" "Selma." "Selma? I didn't realize that," Mendy said. "I'm surprised to hear that. No, I never wanted to fuck Selma. Too short. For me it was always twirlers. Watch 'em practicing up on the field after school and then go home and beat off. The pancake makeup. Cocoa-colored pancake makeup. On their legs. Drove me nuts. You notice something? The guys on the whole don't look too bad, a lot of them work out, but the girls, you know . . . no, a forty-fifth reunion is not the best place to come looking for ass." "True, true," said the other man, who spoke softly and seemed not to have found in the occasion quite the nostalgic license that Mendy had, "time has not been kind to the women." "You know who's dead? Bert and Utty," Mendy said. "Prostate cancer. Went to the spine. Spread. Ate 'em up. Both of them. Thank God I get the test. You get the test?" "What test?" the other fellow asked. "Shit, you don't get the test?" "Skip," said Mendy, pulling me away from Ira, "Meisner doesn't get the test."

Now Meisner was Mr. Meisner, Abe Meisner, a short, swarthy, heavyset man with stooped shoulders and a jutting head, proprietor of Meisner's Cleaners—"5 Hour Cleaning Service"—situated on Chancellor between the shoe repair shop, where the Italian radio station was always playing while you waited on the seat behind the swinging half-door for Ralph to fix your heels, and the beauty salon, Roline's, from which my mother once brought home the copy of *Silver Screen* where I read an article that stunned me called "George Raft Is a Lonely Man." Mrs. Meisner, a short, indestructible earthling like her husband, worked with him in the store and one year also sold war bonds and stamps with my mother in a booth right out on Chancellor Avenue. Alan, their son, had gone through school with me, beginning with kindergarten, skipping the same grades I did all through grade school. Alan Meisner and I used to be thrown into a room together by our teacher and, as though we were George S. Kaufman and Moss Hart, told to turn something out whenever a play was needed at assembly for a national holiday. For a couple of seasons right after the war Mr. Meisner—through some miracle—got to be the dry cleaner for the Newark Bears, the Yankees' Triple A farm team, and one summer day, and a great day it was, I was enlisted by Alan to help him carry the Bears' freshly dry-cleaned away uniforms, via three buses, to the Ruppert Stadium clubhouse all the way down on Wilson Avenue.

"Alan. Jesus," I said, "you are your old man." "Who else's old man should I be?" he replied, and, taking my face between his hands, gave me a kiss. "Al," Mendy said, "tell Skippy what you heard Schrimmer telling his wife. Schrimmer's got a new wife, Skip. Six feet tall. Three years ago he went to a psychiatrist. He was depressed. The psychiatrist said to him, 'What do you think when I ask you to imagine your wife's body.' 'I think I should slit my throat,' Schrim said. So he divorces her and marries the shiksa secretary. Six feet tall. Thirty-five. Legs to the ceiling. Al, tell Skip what she said, the *langer loksh*." "She said to Schrim," said Alan, the two of us grinning as we clutched each other's diminished biceps, "she said, 'Why are they all Mutty and Utty and Dutty and Tutty? If his name is Charles, why is he called Tutty?' 'I shouldn't have brought you,' Schrim said to her. 'I knew I shouldn't. I can't explain it,' Schrim said to her, '*nobody* can. It's *beyond* explanation. *It just is.*'"

And what was Alan now? Raised by a dry cleaner, worked after school for a dry cleaner, himself a dead ringer for a dry cleaner, he was a superior court judge in Pasadena. In his father's pocket-sized dry-cleaning shop there had been a rotogravure picture of FDR framed on the wall above the pressing machine, beside an autographed photo of Mayor Meyer Ellenstein. I remembered these photographs when Alan told me that he had twice been a member of Republican delegations to the presidential convention. When Mendy asked if Alan could get him tickets to the Rose Bowl, Alan Meisner, with whom I used to travel to Brooklyn to see Dodger Sunday doubleheaders the year that Robinson broke in, with whom I'd start out at eight A.M. on a bus from our corner, take it downtown to Penn Station, switch to the tubes to New York, in New York switch to the subway to Brooklyn, all to get to Ebbets Field and eat our sandwiches from our lunch bags before batting practice began—Alan Meisner, who, once the ballgame got under way, drove everybody around us crazy with his vocally unmodulated play-by-play of both ends of the doubleheader—this same Alan Meisner took a pocket diary out of his jacket and carefully inscribed a note to himself. I saw what he'd written from over his shoulder: "R.B. tix for Mendy G."

Meaningless? Unspectacular? Nothing very enormous going on there? Well, what you make of it would depend on where you grew up and how life got opened up to you. Alan Meisner could not be said to have risen out of nothing; however, remembering him as a little hick obliviously yapping away nonstop in his seat at Ebbets Field, remembering him delivering the dry cleaning through our streets late on a winter afternoon, hatless and in a snow-laden pea jacket, one could easily imagine him destined for something less than the Tournament of Roses.

Only after strudel and coffee had capped off a chicken dinner that, what with barely anyone able to stay seated very long in one place to eat it, had required nearly all afternoon to get through; after the kids from Maple got up on the bandstand and sang the Maple Avenue School song; after classmate upon classmate had taken the microphone to say "It's been a great life" or "I'm proud of all of you"; after people had just about finished tapping one another on the shoulder and falling into one another's arms; after the ten-member reunion committee stood on the dance floor and held hands while the one-man band played Bob Hope's theme song, "Thanks for the Memory," and we applauded in appreciation of all their hard work; after Marvin Lieb, whose father sold my father our Pontiac and offered each of us kids a big cigar to smoke whenever we came to get Marvin from the house, told me about his alimony miseries—"A guy takes a leak with more forethought than I gave to my two marriages"—and Julius Pincus, who'd always been the kindest kid and who now, because of tremors resulting from taking the cyclosporin essential to the long-term survival of his transplant, had had to give up his optometry practice, told me ruefully how he'd come by his new kidney—"If a little fourteen-year-old girl didn't die of a brain hemorrhage last October, I would be dead today"—and after Schrimmer's tall young wife had said to me,

"You're the class writer, maybe you can explain it. Why are they all called Utty, Dutty, Mutty, and Tutty?"; only after I had shocked Shelly Minskoff, another Daredevil, with a nod of the head when he asked, "Is it true what you said at the mike, you don't have kids or anything like that?," only after Shelly had taken my hand in his and said, "Poor Skip," only then did I discover that Jerry Levov, having arrived late, was among us.

# 3

I HADN'T EVEN thought to look for him. I knew from the Swede that Jerry lived in Florida, but even more to the point, he'd always been such an isolated kid, so little engaged by anything other than his own abstruse interests, that it didn't seem likely he'd have any more desire now than he'd had then to endure the wisdom of his classmates. But only minutes after Shelly Minskoff had bid me good-bye, Jerry came bounding over, a big man in a double-breasted blue blazer like my own, but with a chest like a large birdcage, and bald except for a ropelike strand of white hair draped across the crown of his skull. His body had really achieved a strange form: despite the majestic upper torso that had replaced the rolling-pin chest of the gawky boy, he locomoted himself on the same ladderlike legs that had made his the silliest gait in the school, legs no heavier or any shapelier than Olive Oyl's in the *Popeye* comic strip. The face I recognized immediately, from those afternoons when my own face was target for its focused animosity, when I used to see it weaving wildly above the Ping-Pong table, crimson with belligerence and lethal intention—yes, the core of that face I could never forget, long-limbed Jerry's knotted little face, the determined mask of the prowling beast that won't let you be until you're driven from your lair, the ferret face that declares, "Don't talk to me about compromise! I know nothing of compromise!" Now in that face was the obstinacy of a *lifetime* of smashing the ball back at the other guy's gullet. I could imagine that Jerry had made himself important to people by means different from his brother's.

"I didn't expect to see you here," Jerry said.

"I didn't expect to see you."

"I wouldn't have thought this was a big enough stage for you," he said, laughing. "I was sure you'd find the sentimentality repellent."

"Exactly what I was thinking about you."

"You're somebody who has banished all superfluous sentiments from his life. No asinine longings to be home again. No patience for the nonessential. Only time for what's indispensable. After all, what they sit around calling the 'past' at these things isn't a fragment of a fragment of the past. It's the past undetonated—nothing is really brought back, nothing. It's nostalgia. It's bullshit."

These few sentences telling me what I was, what *everything* was, would have accounted not merely for four wives but for eight, ten, sixteen of them. Everyone's narcissism is strong at a reunion, but this was an outpouring of another magnitude. Jerry's body may have been divided between the skinny kid and the large man but not the character—he had the character of one big unified thing, coldly accustomed to being listened to. What an evolution this was, the eccentric boy elaborated into a savagely sure-of-himself man. The original unwieldy impulses appeared to have been brought into a crude harmony with the enormous intelligence and willfulness; the effect was not only of somebody who called the shots and would never dream of doing what he was told but of somebody you could count on to churn things up. It seemed truer even than it had been when we were boys that if Jerry got an idea in his head, however improbable, something big would come of it. I could see why I had been infatuated with him as a kid, understood for the first time that my fascination had been not solely with his being the Swede's brother but with the Swede's brother's being so decisively odd, his masculinity so imperfectly socialized compared with the masculinity of the three-letterman.

"Why *did* you come?" Jerry asked.

About the cancer scare of the year before, and the impact on urogenital function of the ensuing prostate surgery, I said nothing directly. Or rather, said everything that was necessary—and perhaps not merely for myself—when I replied, "Because I'm sixty-two. I figured that of all the forms of bullshit-nostalgia available, this was the one least likely to be without unsettling surprises."

He enjoyed that. "You like unsettling surprises."

"Might as well. Why did you come?"

"I happened to be up here. At the end of the week I had to be up here, so I came." Smiling at me, he said, "I don't think they were expecting their writer to be so laconic. I don't think they were expecting quite so *much* modesty." Keeping in mind what I took to be the spirit of the occasion, when I'd been called up to the microphone near the end of the meal by the MC (Erwin Levine, Children 43, 41, 38, 31. Grandchildren 9, 8, 3, 1, 6 weeks), I'd said only, "I'm Nathan Zuckerman. I was vice president of our class in 4B and a member of the prom committee. I have neither child nor grandchild but I did, ten years ago, have a quintuple bypass operation of which I am proud. Thank you." That was the history I gave them, as much as was called for, medical or otherwise—enough to be a little amusing and sit down.

"What were you expecting?" I asked Jerry.

"That. Exactly that. Unassuming. The Weequahic Everyman. What else? Always behave contrary to their expectations. You even as a kid. Always found a practical method to guarantee your freedom."

"I'd say that was a better description of you, Jer."

"No, no. I found the *impractical* method. Rashness personified, Little Sir Hothead—just went nuts and started screaming when I couldn't have it my way. You were the one with the big outlook on things. You were more theoretical than the rest of us. Even back then you had to hook up everything with your thoughts. Sizing up the situation, drawing conclusions. You kept a sharp watch over yourself. All the crazy stuff contained inside. A sensible boy. No, not like me at all."

"Well, we both had a big investment in being right," I said.

"Yeah, being wrong," Jerry said, "was unendurable to me. Absolutely unendurable."

"And it's easier now?"

"Don't have to worry about it. The operating room turns you into somebody who's never wrong. Much like writing."

"Writing turns you into somebody who's always wrong. The illusion that you may get it right someday is the perversity that draws you on. What else could? As pathological phenomena go, it doesn't *completely* wreck your life."

"How is your life? Where are you? I read somewhere, on the back of some book, you were living in England with an aristocrat."

"I live in New England now, without an aristocrat."

"So who instead?"

"No one instead."

"Can't be. What do you do for somebody to eat dinner with?"

"I go without dinner."

"For now. The Wisdom of the Bypass. But my experience is that personal philosophies have a shelf life of about two weeks. Things'll change."

"Look, this is where life has left me. Rarely see anyone. Where I live in western Massachusetts, a tiny place in the hills there, I talk to the guy who runs the general store and to the lady at the post office. The postmistress. That's it."

"What's the name of the town?"

"You wouldn't know it. Up in the woods. About ten miles from a college town called Athena. I met a famous writer there when I was just starting out. Nobody mentions him much anymore, his sense of virtue is too narrow for readers now, but he was revered back then. Lived like a hermit. Reclusion looked awfully austere to a kid. He maintained it solved his problems. Now it solves mine."

"What's the problem?"

"Certain problems having been taken out of my life—that's the problem. At the store the Red Sox, at the post office the weather—that's it, my social discourse. Whether we deserve the weather.

When I come to pick up my mail and the sun is shining outside, the postmistress tells me, 'We don't deserve this weather.' Can't argue with that."

"And pussy?"

"Over. Live without dinner, live without pussy."

"Who are you, Socrates? I don't buy it. Purely the writer. The single-minded writer. Nothing more."

"Nothing more all along and I could have saved myself a lot of wear and tear. That's all I've had anyway to keep the shit at bay."

"What's 'the shit'?"

"The picture we have of one another. Layers and layers of misunderstanding. The picture we have of *ourselves*. Useless. Presumptuous. Completely cocked-up. Only we go ahead and we *live* by these pictures. 'That's what she is, that's what he is, this is what I am. This is what happened, this is *why* it happened—' Enough. You know who I saw a couple of months ago? Your brother. Did he tell you?"

"No, he didn't."

"He wrote me a letter and invited me to dinner in New York. A nice letter. Out of the blue. I drove down to meet him. He was composing a tribute to your old man. In the letter he asked for my help. I was curious about what he had in mind. I was curious about him writing me to announce that he wanted to write something. To you he's just a brother—to me he's still 'the Swede.' You carry those guys around with you forever. I *had* to drive down. But at dinner he never mentioned the tribute. We just uttered the pleasantries. At some place called Vincent's. That was it. As always, he looked terrific."

"He's dead."

"Your brother's dead?"

"Died Wednesday. Funeral two days ago. Friday. That's why I was in Jersey. Watched my big brother die."

"Of what? *How?*"

"Cancer."

"But he'd had prostate surgery. He told me they got it out."

Impatiently Jerry said, "What else was he going to tell you?"

"He was thin, that was all."

"That wasn't all."

So, the Swede too. What, astoundingly to Mendy Gurlik, was decimating the Daredevils right up the middle; what, astoundingly to me, had, a year earlier, made of me "purely a writer"; what, in the wake of all the other isolating losses, in the wake of everything gone and everyone gone, had stripped me down into someone whose aging powers had now but a single and unswerving aim, a man who would be seeking his solace, like it or not, nowhere but in sentences, had managed the most astounding thing of all by carrying off the indestructible hero of the wartime Weequahic section, our neighborhood talisman, the legendary Swede.

"Did he know," I asked, "when I saw him, that he was in trouble?"

"He had his hopes, but sure he knew. Metastasized. All through him."

"I'm sorry to hear it."

"His *fiftieth* was coming up next month. You know what he said at the hospital on Tuesday? To me and his kids the day before he died? Most of the time he was incoherent, but twice he said, so we could understand him, 'Going to get to my fiftieth.' He'd heard everyone from his class was asking, 'Will the Swede be there?' and he didn't want to let them down. He was very stoical. He was a very nice, simple, stoical guy. Not a humorous guy. Not a passionate guy. Just a sweetheart whose fate it was to get himself fucked over by some real crazies. In one way he could be conceived as completely banal and conventional. An absence of negative values and nothing more. Bred to be dumb, built for convention, and so on. That ordinary decent life that they all want to live, and that's it. The social norms, and that's it. Benign, and that's it. But what he was trying to do was to survive, keeping his group intact. He was trying to get through with his platoon intact. It was a war for him, finally. There was a noble side to this guy. Some excruciating renunciations went on in that life. He got caught in a war he didn't start, and he fought to keep it all together, and he went down. Banal, conventional—maybe, maybe not. People could think that. I don't want to get into judging. My brother was the best you're going to get in this country, by a long shot."

I was wondering while he spoke if this had been Jerry's estimate of the Swede while he was alive, if there wasn't perhaps a touch of mourner's rethinking here, remorse for a harsher Jerry-like view he might once have held of the handsome older brother, sound, well adjusted, quiet, normal, somebody everybody looked up to, the neighborhood hero to whom the smaller Levov had been endlessly compared while himself evolving into something slightly ersatz. This kindly unjudging judgment of the Swede could well have been a new development in Jerry, compassion just a few hours old. That can happen when people die—the argument with them drops away and people so flawed while they were drawing breath that at times they were all but unbearable now assert themselves in the most appealing way, and what was least to your liking the day before yesterday becomes in the limousine behind the hearse a cause not only for sympathetic amusement but for admiration. In which estimate lies the greater reality—the uncharitable one permitted us before the funeral, forged, without any claptrap, in the skirmish of daily life, or the one that suffuses us with sadness at the family gathering afterward—even an outsider can't judge. The sight of a coffin going into the ground can effect a great change of heart—all at once you find you are not so disappointed in this person who is dead—but what the sight of a coffin does for the mind in its search for the truth, this I don't profess to know.

"My father," Jerry said, "was one impossible bastard. Overbearing. Omnipresent. I don't know how people worked for him. When they moved to Central Avenue, the first thing he had the movers move was his desk, and the first place he put it was not in the glass-enclosed office but dead center in the middle of the factory floor, so he could keep his eye on everybody. You can't imagine the noise out there, the sewing machines whining, the clicking machines pounding, hundreds of machines going all at once, and right in the middle his desk and his telephone and the great man himself.

The owner of the glove factory, but he would always sweep his own floors, especially around the cutters, where they cut the leather, because he wanted to see from the size of the scraps who was losing money for him. I told him early on to fuck off, but Seymour wasn't built like me. He had a big, generous nature and with that they really raked him over the coals, all the impossible ones. Unsatisfiable father, unsatisfiable wives, and the little murderer herself, the monster daughter. The monster *Merry*. The solid thing he once was. At Newark Maid he was an absolute, unequivocal success. Charmed a lot of people into giving their all for Newark Maid. Very adroit businessman. Knew how to cut a glove, knew how to cut a deal. Had an in on Seventh Avenue with the fashion people. The designers there would tell the guy anything. That's how he stayed abreast of the pack. In New York, he was always stopping into the department stores, shopping the competition, looking for something unique about the other guy's product, always in the stores taking a look at the leather, stretching the glove, doing everything just the way my old man taught him. Did most of the selling himself. Handled all the big house accounts. The lady buyers went nuts for Seymour. You can imagine. He'd come over to New York, take these tough Jewish broads out to dinner—buyers who could make or break you—wine and dine them, and they'd fall head over heels for the guy. Instead of him buttering them up, by the end of the evening they'd be buttering him up. Come Christmastime they'd be sending my brother the theater tickets and the case of Scotch rather than the other way around. He knew how to get the confidence of these people just by being himself. He'd find out a buyer's favorite charity, get a ticket to the annual dinner at the Waldorf-Astoria, show up like a movie star in his tuxedo, on the spot make a fat donation to cancer, muscular dystrophy, whatever it was, United Jewish Appeal—next thing Newark Maid had the account. Knew all the stuff: what colors are going to be next season's colors, whether the length is going to be up or down. Attractive, responsible, hardworking guy. A couple of unpleasant strikes in the sixties, a lot of tension. But his employees are out on the picket line and they see him pull up in the car and the women who sew the gloves start falling all over themselves apologizing for not being at the machines. They were more loyal to my brother than they were to their union. Everybody loved him, a perfectly decent person who could have escaped stupid guilt forever. No reason for him to know anything about anything except gloves. Instead he is plagued with shame and uncertainty and pain for the rest of his life. The incessant questioning of a conscious adulthood was never something that obstructed my brother. He got the meaning for his life some other way. I don't mean he was simple. Some people thought he was simple because all his life he was so kind. But Seymour was never that simple. Simple is *never* that simple. Still, the self-questioning did take some time to reach him. And if there's anything worse than self-questioning coming too early in life, it's self-questioning coming too late. His life was blown up by that bomb. The real victim of that bombing was him."

"What bomb?"

"Little Merry's darling bomb."

"I don't know what 'Merry's darling bomb' is."

"Meredith Levov. Seymour's daughter. The 'Rimrock Bomber' was Seymour's daughter. The high school kid who blew up the post office and killed the doctor. The kid who stopped the war in Vietnam by blowing up somebody out mailing a letter at five A.M. A doctor on his way to the hospital. Charming child," he said in a voice that was all contempt and still didn't seem to contain the load of contempt and hatred that he felt. "Brought the war home to Lyndon Johnson by blowing up the post office in the general store. Place is so small the post office is in the general store—just a window at the back of the general store and a couple rows of those boxes with the locks, and that's the whole post office. Get your stamps right in there with the Rinso and the Lifebuoy and the Lux. Quaint Americana. Seymour was into quaint Americana. But the kid wasn't. He took the kid out of real time and she put him right back in. My brother thought he could take his family out of human confusion and into Old Rimrock, and she put them right back in.

Somehow she plants a bomb back behind the post office window, and when it goes off it takes out the general store too. And takes out the guy, this doctor, who's just stopping by the collection box to drop off his mail. Good-bye, Americana; hello, real time."

"This passed me by. I had no idea."

"That was '68, back when the wild behavior was still new. People suddenly forced to make sense of madness. All that public display. The dropping of inhibitions. Authority powerless. The kids going crazy. Intimidating everybody. The adults don't know what to make of it, they don't know what to do. Is this an act? Is the 'revolution' real? Is it a game? Is it cops and robbers? What's going on here? Kids turning the country upside down and so the adults start going crazy too. But Seymour wasn't one of them. He was one of the people who knew his way. He understood that something was going wrong, but he was no Ho-Chi-Minhite like his darling fat girl. Just a liberal sweetheart of a father. The philosopher-king of ordinary life. Brought her up with all the modern ideas of being rational with your children. Everything permissible, everything forgivable, and she hated it. People don't like to admit how much they resent other people's children, but this kid made it easy for you. She was miserable, self-righteous—little shit was no good from the time she was born. Look, I've got kids, kids galore—I know what kids are like growing up. The black hole of self-absorption is bottomless. But it's one thing to get fat, it's one thing to let your hair grow long, it's one thing to listen to rock-and-roll music too loud, but it's another to jump the line and throw a bomb. That crime could never be made right. There was no way back for my brother from that bomb. That bomb detonated his life. His perfect life was over. Just what she had in mind. That's why they had it in for him, the daughter and her friends. He was so in love with his own good luck, and they hated him for it. Once we were all up at his place for Thanksgiving, the Dwyer mother, Dawn's kid brother Danny, Danny's wife, all the Levovs, our kids, everybody, and Seymour got up to make a toast and he said, 'I'm not a religious man, but when I look around this table, I know that something is shining down on me.' It was him they were really out to get. And they did it. They got him. The bomb might as well have gone off in their living room. The violence done to his life was awful. Horrible. Never in his life had occasion to ask himself, 'Why are things the way they are?' Why should he bother, when the way they were was always perfect? Why are things the way they are? The question to which there is no answer, and up till then he was so blessed he didn't even know the question existed."

Had Jerry ever before been so full of his brother's life and his brother's story? It did not strike me that all the despotic determination concentrated in that strange head could ever have allowed him to divide his attention into very many parts. Not that death ordinarily impinges upon the majesty of self-obsession; generally it intensifies it: "What about me? What if this happens to me?"

"He told you it was horrible?"

"Once. Only once," Jerry replied. "No, Seymour just took it and took it. You could stay on this guy and stay on this guy and he'd just keep making the effort," Jerry said bitterly. "Poor son of a bitch, that was his fate—built for bearing burdens and taking shit," and with his saying this, I remembered those scrimmage pileups from which the Swede would extricate himself, always still clutching the ball, and how seriously I'd fallen in love with him on that late-autumn afternoon long ago when he'd transformed my ten-year-old existence by selecting me to enter the fantasy of Swede Levov's life—when for a moment it had seemed that I, too, had been called to great things and that nothing in the world could ever obstruct my way now that our god's benign countenance had shed its light on me alone. "Basketball was never like this, Skip." How captivatingly that innocence spoke to my own. The significance he had given me. It was everything a boy could have wanted in 1943.

"Never caved in. He could be tough. Remember, when we were kids, he joined the marines to fight the Japs? Well, he *was* a goddamn marine. Caved in only once, down in Florida," Jerry said. "It just got to be too much for him. He'd brought the whole family down to visit us, the boys and the second superbly selfish Mrs.

Levov. That was two years ago. We all went to this stone-crab place. Twelve of us for dinner. Lots of noise, the kids all showing off and laughing. Seymour loved it. The whole handsome family there, life just the way it's supposed to be. But when the pie and coffee came he got up from the table, and when he didn't come back right away I went out and found him. In the car. In tears. Shaking with sobs. I'd never seen him like that. My brother the rock. He said, 'I miss my daughter.' I said, 'Where is she?' I knew he always knew where she was. He'd been going to see her in hiding for years. I believe he saw her frequently. He said, 'She's dead, Jerry.' I didn't believe him at first. It was to throw me off the track, I thought. I thought he must have just seen her somewhere. I thought, He's still going to wherever she is and treating this killer like his own child—this killer who is now in her forties while everybody she killed is still killed. But then he threw his arms around me and he just let go, and I thought, Is it true, the family's fucking monster's really dead? But why is he crying if she's dead? If he had half a brain, he would have realized that it was just too extraordinary to have a child like that—if he had half a brain, he would have been enraged by this kid and estranged from this kid long ago. Long ago he would have torn her out of his guts and let her go. The angry kid who gets nuttier and nuttier— and the sanctified cause to hang her craziness on. Crying like that—for her? No, I couldn't buy it. I said to him, 'I don't know whether you're lying to me or you're telling me the truth. But if you're telling me the truth, that she's dead, it's the best news I ever heard. Nobody else is going to say this to you. Everybody else is going to commiserate. But I grew up with you. I talk straight to you. The best thing for you is for her to be dead. She did not belong to you. She did not belong to anything that you were. She did not belong to anything anyone is. *You* played ball—there was a field of play. She was not on the field of play. She was nowhere near it. Simple as that. She was out of bounds, a freak of nature, *way* out of bounds. You are to stop your mourning for her. You've kept this wound open for twenty-five years. And twenty-five years is enough. It's driven you mad. Keep it open any longer and it's going to kill you. She's dead? Good! Let her go. Otherwise it will rot in your gut and take your life too.' That's what I told him. I thought I could let the rage out of him. But he just cried. He couldn't let it go. I said this guy was going to get killed from this thing, and he did."

Jerry said it and it happened. It is Jerry's theory that the Swede is nice, that is to say passive, that is to say trying always to do the right thing, a socially controlled character who doesn't burst out, doesn't yield to rage ever. Will not have the angry quality as his liability, so doesn't get it as an asset either. According to this theory, it's the no-rage that kills him in the end. Whereas aggression is cleansing or curing.

It would seem that what kept Jerry going, without uncertainty or remorse and unflaggingly devoted to his own take on things, was that he had a special talent for rage and another special talent for not looking back. Doesn't look back at all, I thought. He's unseared by memory. To him, all looking back is bullshit-nostalgia, including even the Swede's looking back, twenty-five years later, at his daughter before that bomb went off, looking back and helplessly weeping for all that went up in that explosion. Righteous anger at the daughter? No doubt that would have helped. Incontestable that nothing is more uplifting in all of life than righteous anger. But given the circumstances, wasn't it asking a lot, asking the Swede to overstep the limits that made him identifiably the Swede? People must have been doing that to him all his life, assuming that because he was once upon a time this mythic character the Swede he had no limits. I'd done something like that in Vincent's restaurant, childishly expecting to be wowed by his godliness, only to be confronted by an utterly ordinary humanness. One price you pay for being taken for a god is the unabated dreaminess of your acolytes.

"You know Seymour's 'fatal attraction'? Fatally attracted to his duty," Jerry said. "Fatally attracted to responsibility. He could have played ball anywhere he wanted, but he went to Upsala because my father wanted him near home. Giants offered him a Double A contract, might have played one day with Willie Mays—instead he went down to Central Avenue to work for Newark Maid. My father started him off at a tannery. Puts him for six months working in a tannery on Frelinghuysen Avenue. Up six mornings a week at five A.M. You know what a tannery is? A tannery is a shithole. Remember those days in the summer? A strong wind from the east and the tanning stench wafts over Weequahic Park and covers the whole neighborhood. Well, he gets out of the tannery, Seymour does, strong as an ox, and my father sits him down at a sewing machine for another six months and Seymour doesn't let out a peep. Just masters the fucking machine. Give him the pieces of a glove and he can close it up better than the sewers and in half the time. He could have married any beauty he wanted. Instead he marries the bee-yoo-ti-full Miss Dwyer. You should have seen them. Knockout couple. The two of them all smiles on their outward trip into the USA. She's post-Catholic, he's post-Jewish, together they're going to go out there to Old Rimrock to raise little post-toasties. Instead they get that fucking kid."

"What was wrong with Miss Dwyer?"

"No house they lived in was right. No amount of money in the bank was enough. He set her up in the cattle business. That didn't work. He set her up in the nursery tree business. That didn't work. He took her to Switzerland for the world's best face-lift. Not even into her fifties, still in her forties, but that's what the woman wants, so they schlep to Geneva for a face-lift from the guy who did Princess Grace. He would have been better off spending his life in Double A ball. He would have been better off knocking up some waitress down there in Phoenix and playing first base for the Mudhens. That fucking kid! She stuttered, you know. So to pay everybody back for her stuttering, she set off the bomb. He took her to speech therapists. He took her to clinics, to psychiatrists. There wasn't enough he could do for her. And the reward? Boom! Why does this girl hate her father? This great father, this truly great father. Good-looking, kind, providing, thinks about nothing really but them, his family—why does she take off after him? That our own ridiculous father should have produced such a *brilliant* father—and that he should then produce *her*? Somebody tell me what caused it. The genetic need to separate? For that she has to run from Seymour Levov to Che Guevara? No, no. What is the poison that caused it, that caused this poor guy to be placed outside his life for the rest of his life? He kept peering in from outside at his own life. The struggle of his life was to bury this thing. But could he? How? How could a big, sweet, agreeable putz like my brother be expected to deal with this bomb? One day life started laughing at him and it never let up."

That was as far as we got, as much of an earful as I was to hear from Jerry—anything more I wanted to know, I'd have to make up—because just then a small, gray-haired woman in a brown pantsuit came up to introduce herself, and Jerry, not a man equipped by nature to stand around more than five seconds while someone else was getting a third party's attention, shot me a mock salute and disappeared, and when I went looking for him later, I heard that he'd had to leave, to catch a Newark plane back to Miami.

After I'd already written about his brother—which is what I would do in the months to come: think about the Swede for six, eight, sometimes ten hours at a stretch, exchange my solitude for his, inhabit this person least like myself, disappear into him, day and night try to take the measure of a person of apparent blankness and innocence and simplicity, chart his collapse, make of him, as time wore on, the most important figure of my life—just before I set about to alter names and disguise the most glaring marks of identification, I had the amateur's impulse to send Jerry a copy of the manuscript to ask what he thought. It was an impulse I quashed: I hadn't been writing and publishing for nearly forty years not to know by now to quash it. "That's not my brother," he'd tell me, "not in any way. You've misrepresented him. My brother couldn't think like that, didn't talk like that," etc.

Yes, by this time Jerry might well have recovered the objectivity that had deserted him directly after the funeral, and with it the old resentment that helped make him the doctor at the hospital everybody was afraid to talk to because he was never wrong. Also, unlike most people whose dear one winds up as a model for the life-drawing class, Jerry Levov would probably be amused rather than outraged by my failure to grasp the Swede's tragedy the way he did. A strong possibility: Jerry's flipping derisively through my pages and giving me, item by item, the bad news. "The wife was nothing like this, the kid was nothing like this—got even my father wrong. I won't talk about what you do with me. But missing my father, man, that's missing the side of a barn. Lou Levov was a brute, man. This guy is a pushover. He's *charming*. He's *conciliatory*. No, we had something over us light-years away from that. We had a sword. Dad on the rampage—laid down the law and that was it. No, nothing bears the slightest resemblance to . . . here, for instance, giving my brother a mind, awareness. This guy responds with consciousness to his loss. But my brother is a guy who had cognitive *problems*— this is nowhere *like* the mind he had. This is the mind he *didn't* have. Christ, you even give him a mistress. Perfectly misjudged, Zuck. Absolutely off. How could a big man like you fuck up like this?"

Well, Jerry wouldn't have gotten much of an argument from me had that turned out to be his reaction. I had gone out to Newark and located the abandoned Newark Maid factory on a barren stretch of lower Central Avenue. I went out to the Weequahic section to look at their house, now in disrepair, and to look at Keer Avenue, a street where it didn't seem like a good idea to get out of the car and walk up the driveway to the garage where the Swede used to practice his swing in the wintertime. Three black kids were sitting on the front steps eyeing me in the car. I explained to them, "A friend of mine used to live here." When I got no answer, I added, "Back in the forties." And then I drove away. I drove to Morristown to look at Merry's high school and then on west to Old Rimrock, where I found the big stone house up on Arcady Hill Road where the Seymour Levovs once had lived as a happy young family; later, down in the village, I drank a cup of coffee at the counter of the new general store (McPherson's) that had replaced the old general store (Hamlin's) whose post office the teenage Levov daughter had blown up "to bring the war home to America." I went to Elizabeth, where the Swede's beautiful Dawn was born and raised, and walked around her pleasant neighborhood, the residential Elmora section; I drove by her family's church, St. Genevieve's, and then headed due east to her father's neighborhood, the old port on the Elizabeth River, where the Cuban immigrants and their offspring replaced, back in the sixties, the last of the Irish immigrants and their offspring. I was able to get the New Jersey Miss America Pageant office to dig up a glossy photo of Mary Dawn Dwyer, age twenty-two, being crowned Miss New Jersey in May of 1949. I found another picture of her—in a 1961 number of a Morris County weekly—standing primly before her fireplace mantel in a blazer, a skirt, and a turtleneck sweater, a picture captioned, "Mrs. Levov, the former Miss New Jersey of 1949, loves living in a 170-year-old home, an environment which she says reflects the values of her family." At the Newark Public Library I scanned microfilmed sports pages of the *Newark News* (expired 1972), looking for accounts and box scores of games in which the Swede had shined for Weequahic High (in extremis 1995) and Upsala College (expired 1995). For the first time in fifty years I reread the baseball books of John R. Tunis and at one point even began to think of my book about the Swede as *The Kid from Keer Avenue*, calling it after Tunis's 1940 story for boys about the Tomkinsville, Connecticut, orphan whose only fault, as a major leaguer, is a tendency to keep his right shoulder down and his swing up, but a fault, alas, that is provocation enough for the gods to destroy him.

Yet despite these efforts and more to uncover what I could about the Swede and his world, I would have been willing to admit that my Swede was not the primary Swede. Of course I was working with traces; of course essentials of what he was to Jerry were gone, expunged from my portrait, things I was ignorant of or I didn't want; of course the Swede was concentrated differently in my pages from how he'd been concentrated in the flesh. But whether that meant I'd imagined an outright fantastical creature, lacking entirely the unique substantiality of the real thing; whether that meant my conception of the Swede was any more fallacious than the conception held by Jerry (which he wasn't likely to see as in any way fallacious); whether the Swede and his family came to life in me any less truthfully than in his brother—well, who knows? Who *can* know? When it comes to illuminating someone with the Swede's opacity, to understanding those regular guys everybody likes and who go about more or less incognito, it's up for grabs, it seems to me, as to whose guess is more rigorous than whose.

"You don't remember me, do you?" asked the woman who had sent Jerry scurrying. Smiling warmly, she had taken my two hands in hers. Beneath the short-cropped hair, her head looked imposingly well made, large and durable, its angular mass like the antique stone head of a Roman sovereign. Though the broad planes of her face were deeply scored as if with an engraving stylus, the skin beneath the rosy makeup looked to be seriously wrinkled only around the mouth, which, after nearly six hours of exchanging kisses, had lost most of its lipstick; otherwise there was an almost girlish softness to her flesh, indicating that perhaps she hadn't partaken of every last one of the varied forms of suffering available to a woman over a lifetime.

"Don't look at my name tag. Who was I?"

"You tell me," I said.

"Joyce. Joy Helpern. I had a pink angora sweater. Originally my cousin's. Estelle's. She was three years ahead of us. She's dead, Nathan—in the ground. My beautiful cousin, Estelle, who smoked and dated older guys. In high school she was dating a guy who shaved twice a day. Her parents had the dress and corset shop on Chancellor. Grossman's. My mother worked there. You took me on a class hayride. Believe it or not, I used to be Joy Helpern."

Joy: a bright little girl with curly reddish hair, freckles, a round face, a girl with a provocative chubbiness that did not go unobserved by Mr. Roscoe, our stout, red-nosed Spanish teacher who on the mornings when Joy came to school in a sweater was always asking her to stand at her desk to recite her homework. Mr. Roscoe called her Dimples. Amazing what you could get away with back in those days when it didn't seem to me anybody got away with anything.

Because of an association of words not entirely implausible, Joy's figure had continued to tantalize me, no less than it had Mr. Roscoe, long after I last saw her springing up Chancellor Avenue to school in that odd but stirring pair of unclasped galoshes obviously outgrown by her older brother and handed down to Joy like her beautiful cousin's angora sweater. Whenever a couple of famous lines from John Keats happened, for whatever reason, to fall into my head, I'd invariably remember the full, plump feel of her beneath me, the wonderful buoyancy of her that my adolescent boy's exquisite radar sensed even through my mackinaw on that hayride. The lines are from "Ode on Melancholy": ". . . him whose strenuous tongue / Can burst Joy's grape against his palate fine."

"I remember that hayride, Joy Helpern. You weren't as kind on that hayride as you might have been."

"And now I look like Spencer Tracy," she said, breaking into laughter. "Now that I'm no longer frightened it's much too late. I used to be shy—I'm not shy anymore. Oh, Nathan, aging," she cried, as we embraced each other, "aging, aging—it is so very strange. You wanted to touch my bare breasts."

"I would have settled for that."

"Yes," she said. "They were new then."

"You were fourteen and they were about one."

"There's *always* been a thirteen-year difference. Back then I was thirteen years older than they were and now they're about thirteen years older than I am. But we certainly did kiss, didn't we, darling?"

"Kissed and kissed and kissed."

"I had practiced. All that afternoon I practiced kissing."

"On whom?"

"My fingers. I *should* have let you undo my bra. Undo it now if you'd like to."

"I'm afraid I haven't the daring anymore to undo a brassiere in front of the class."

"What a surprise. Just when I'm ready, Nathan's grown up."

We bantered back and forth, our arms tight around each other, and leaning backwards from the waist so each could see clearly what had happened to the other's face and figure, the external shape that half a century of living had bestowed.

Yes, the overwhelming spell that we continue to cast on one another, right down to the end, with the body's surface, which turns out to be, as I suspected on that hayride, about as serious a thing as there is in life. The body, from which one cannot strip oneself however one tries, from which one is not to be freed this side of death. Earlier, looking at Alan Meisner I was looking at his father, and looking now at Joy I was looking at her mother, the stout seamstress with her stockings rolled down to her knees in the back room of Grossman's Dress Shop on Chancellor Avenue. . . . But who I was thinking of was the Swede, the Swede and the tyranny that his body held over him, the powerful, the gorgeous, the lonely Swede, whom life had never made shrewd, who did not want to pass through life as a beautiful boy and a stellar first baseman, who wanted instead to be a serious person for whom others came before himself and not a baby for whose needs alone the wide, wide world of satisfactions had been organized. He wanted to have been born something more than a physical wonder. As if for one person that gift isn't enough. The Swede wanted what he took to be a higher calling, and his bad luck was to have found one. The responsibility of the school hero follows him through life. Noblesse oblige. You're the hero, so then you have to behave in a certain way—there is a prescription for it. You have to be modest, you have to be forbearing, you have to be deferential, you have to be understanding. And it all began—this heroically idealistic maneuver, this strategic, strange spiritual desire to be a bulwark of duty and ethical obligation—because of the war, because of all the terrible uncertainties bred by the war, because of how strongly an emotional community whose beloved sons were far away facing death had been drawn to a lean and muscular, austere boy whose talent it was to be able to catch anything anybody threw anywhere near him. It all began for the Swede—as what doesn't?—in a circumstantial absurdity.

And ended in another one. A bomb.

When we'd met at Vincent's, perhaps he insisted on how well his three boys had turned out because he assumed I knew about the bomb, about the daughter, the Rimrock Bomber, and had judged him harshly, as some people must have. Such a sensational thing, in his life certainly—even twenty-seven years later, how could anybody not know or have forgotten? Maybe that explains why he couldn't stop himself, even had he wanted to, from going interminably on and on to me about the myriad nonviolent accomplishments of Chris, Steve, and Kent. Maybe that explains what he had wanted to talk about in the first place. "The shocks" that had befallen his father's loved ones was the daughter—*she* was "the shocks" that had befallen them all. *This* was what he had summoned me to talk about—had wanted me to help him *write* about. And I missed it—I, whose vanity is that he is never naive, was more naive by far than the guy I was talking to. Sitting there at Vincent's getting the shallowest bead I could on the Swede when the story he had to tell me was this one, the revelation of the interior life that was unknown and unknowable, the story that is tragic and awful and impossible to ignore, the ultimate reunion story, and I missed it entirely.

The father was the cover. The burning subject was the daughter. How much of that was he aware of? All of it. He was aware of everything—I had that wrong too. The unconscious one was me. He knew he was dying, and this terrible thing that had happened to him—that over the years he'd been partially able to bury, that somewhere along the way he had somewhat overcome—came back at him worse than ever. He'd put it aside as best he could, new wife, new kids—the three terrific boys; he sure seemed to me to have put it aside the night in 1985 I saw him at Shea Stadium with young

Chris. The Swede had got up off the ground and he'd done it—a second marriage, a second shot at a unified life controlled by good sense and the classic restraints, once again convention shaping everything, large and small, and serving as barrier against the improbabilities—a second shot at being the traditional devoted husband and father, pledging allegiance all over again to the standard rules and regulations that are the heart of family order. He had the talent for it, had what it took to avoid anything disjointed, anything special, anything improper, anything difficult to assess or understand. And yet not even the Swede, blessed with all the attributes of a monumental ordinariness, could shed that girl the way Jerry the Ripper had told him to, could go all the way and shed completely the frantic possessiveness, the paternal assertiveness, the obsessive love for the lost daughter, shed every trace of that girl and that past and shake off forever the hysteria of "my child." If only he could have just let her fade away. But not even the Swede was that great.

He had learned the worst lesson that life can teach—that it makes no sense. And when that happens the happiness is never spontaneous again. It is artificial and, even then, bought at the price of an obstinate estrangement from oneself and one's history. The nice gentle man with his mild way of dealing with conflict and contradiction, the confident ex-athlete sensible and resourceful in any struggle with an adversary who is fair, comes up against the adversary who is not fair—the evil ineradicable from human dealings—and he is finished. He whose natural nobility was to be exactly what he seemed to be has taken in far too much suffering to be naively whole again. Never again will the Swede be content in the trusting old Swedian way that, for the sake of his second wife and their three boys—for the sake of *their* naive wholeness—he ruthlessly goes on pretending to be. Stoically he suppresses his horror. He learns to live behind a mask. A lifetime experiment in endurance. A performance over a ruin. Swede Levov lives a double life.

And now he is dying and what sustained him in a double life can sustain him no longer, and that horror mercifully half submerged, two-thirds submerged, even at times nine-tenths sub-merged, comes back distilled despite the heroic creation of that second marriage and the fathering of the wonderful boys; in the final months of the cancer, it's back worse than ever; *she's* back worse than ever, the first child who was the cancellation of every-thing, and one night in bed when he cannot sleep, when every effort fails to control his runaway thoughts, he is so depleted by his anguish he thinks, "There's this guy who was in my brother's class, and he's a writer, and maybe if I told him. . . ." But what would happen if he told the writer? He doesn't even know. "I'll write him a letter. I know he writes about fathers, about sons, so I'll write him about my father—can he turn that down? Maybe he'll respond to that." The hook to which I am to be the eye. But I come because he is the Swede. No other hook is necessary. He is the hook.

Yes, the story was back worse than ever, and he thought, "If I can give it to a pro . . . ," but when he got me there he couldn't deliver. Once he got my attention he didn't want it. He thought better of it. And he was right. It was none of my business. What good would it have done him? None at all. You go to someone and you think, "I'll tell him this." But why? The impulse is that the telling is going to relieve you. And that's why you feel awful later—you've relieved yourself, and if it truly is tragic and awful, it's not better, it's worse—the exhibitionism inherent to a confession has only made the misery worse. The Swede realized this. He was nothing like the chump I was imagining, and he had figured this out simply enough. He realized that there was nothing to be had through me. He certainly didn't want to cry in front of me the way he had with his brother. I wasn't his brother. I wasn't anyone—that's what he saw when he saw me. So he just blabbered deliberately on about the boys and went home and, the story untold, he died. And I missed it. He turned to me, of all people, and he was conscious of everything and I missed everything.

And now Chris, Steve, Kent, and their mother would be at the Rimrock house, perhaps along with the Swede's old mother, with Mrs. Levov. The mother must be ninety. Sitting shiva at ninety for her beloved Seymour. And the daughter, Meredith, Merry . . . obviously hadn't attended the funeral, not with that outsized uncle around who hated her guts, that vindictive uncle who might even take it upon himself to turn her in. But with Jerry now gone, she dares to leave her hideout to join in the mourning, makes her way to Old Rimrock, perhaps in disguise, and there, alongside her half-brothers and her stepmother and Grandma Levov, weeps her heart out over her father's death. . . . But no, she was dead too. If the Swede had been telling Jerry the truth, the daughter in hiding had died—perhaps in hiding she had been murdered or had even taken her own life. Anything might have occurred—and "anything" wasn't supposed to occur, not to him.

The brutality of the destruction of this indestructible man. Whatever Happened to Swede Levov. Surely not what befell the Kid from Tomkinsville. Even as boys we must have known that it couldn't have been as easy for him as it looked, that a part of it was a mystique, but who could have imagined that his life would come apart in this horrible way? A sliver off the comet of the American chaos had come loose and spun all the way out to Old Rimrock and him. His great looks, his larger-than-lifeness, his glory, our sense of his having been exempted from all self-doubt by his heroic role— that all these manly properties had precipitated a political murder made me think of the compelling story not of John R. Tunis's sacrificial Tomkinsville Kid but of Kennedy, John F. Kennedy, only a decade the Swede's senior and another privileged son of fortune, another man of glamour exuding American meaning, assassinated while still in his mid-forties just five years before the Swede's daughter violently protested the Kennedy-Johnson war and blew up her father's life. I thought, But of course. He is our Kennedy.

Meanwhile Joy was telling me things about her life that I'd never known as a single-minded kid searching the neighborhood for a grape to burst—Joy was tossing into this agitated pot of memory called "the reunion" yet more stuff no one knew at the time, that no one *had* to know back when all our storytelling about ourselves was still eloquently naive. Joy was telling me about how her father had died of a heart attack when she was nine and the family was living in Brooklyn; about how she and her mother and Harold, her older brother, had moved from Brooklyn to the Newark haven of Grossman's Dress Shop; about how, in the attic space above the shop, she and her mother slept in the double bed in their one big room while Harold slept in the kitchen, on a sofa he made up each night and unmade each morning so they could eat breakfast there before going to school. She asked if I remembered Harold, now a retired pharmacist in Scotch Plains, and told me how just the week before she'd gone out to the cemetery in Brooklyn to visit her father's grave—as frequently as once a month she went out there, all the way to Brooklyn, she said, surprised herself by how much this graveyard now mattered to her. "What do you do at the cemetery?" "I unabashedly talk to him," Joy said. "When I was ten it wasn't nearly as bad as it is now. I thought then it was odd that people had two parents. Our threesome seemed right." "Well, all this," I told her, as we stood there just swaying together to the one-man band closing the day down singing, "Dream . . . when you're feelin' blue, . . . dream . . . that's the thing to do"—"all this I did not know," I told her, "on the harvest moon hayride in October 1948."

"I didn't want you to know. I didn't want anybody to know. I didn't want anybody to find out Harold slept in the kitchen. That's why I wouldn't let you undo my bra. I didn't want you to be my boyfriend and come to pick me up and see where my brother had to sleep. It had nothing to do with you, sweetheart."

"Well, I feel better for being told that. I wish you'd told me sooner."

"I wish I had," she said, and first we were laughing and then, unexpectedly, Joy began to cry and, perhaps because of that damn song, "Dream," which we used to dance to with the lights turned down in somebody or other's basement back when the Pied Pipers still had Jo Stafford and used to sing it the way it's supposed to be sung—in locked harmony, to that catatonic forties beat, with the ethereal tinkle of the xylophone hollowly sounding behind them—

or perhaps because Alan Meisner had become a Republican and second baseman Bert Bergman had become a corpse and Ira Posner, instead of shining shoes at the newsstand outside the Essex County courthouse, had escaped his Dostoyevskian family and become a psychiatrist, because Julius Pincus had disabling tremors from the drug that prevented the rejection from his body of the fourteen-year-old girl's kidney keeping him alive and because Mendy Gurlik was still a horny seventeen-year-old kid and because Joy's brother, Harold, had slept for ten years in a kitchen and because Schrimmer had married a woman nearly half his age who had a body that didn't make him want to slit his throat but to whom he now had to explain every single thing about the past, or perhaps because I seemed alone in having wound up with no children, grandchildren, or, in Minskoff's words, "anything like that," or perhaps because after all these years of separation this reuniting of perfect strangers had all gone on a little too long, a load of unruly emotion began sliding around in me, too, and there I was thinking again of the Swede, of the notorious significance that an outlaw daughter had thrust on him and his family during the Vietnam War. A man whose discontents were barely known to himself, awakening in middle age to the horror of self-reflection. All that normalcy interrupted by murder. All the small problems any family expects to encounter exaggerated by something so impossible ever to reconcile. The disruption of the anticipated American future that was simply to have unrolled out of the solid American past, out of each generation's getting smarter—smarter for knowing the inadequacies and limitations of the generations before—out of each new generation's breaking away from the parochialism a little further, out of the desire to go the limit in America with your rights, forming yourself as an ideal person who gets rid of the traditional Jewish habits and attitudes, who frees himself of the pre-America insecurities and the old, constraining obsessions so as to live unapologetically as an equal among equals.

And then the loss of the daughter, the fourth American generation, a daughter on the run who was to have been the perfected image of himself as he had been the perfected image of his father, and his father the perfected image of his father's father . . . the angry, rebarbative spitting-out daughter with no interest whatever in being the next successful Levov, flushing him out of hiding as if he were a fugitive—initiating the Swede into the displacement of another America entirely, the daughter and the decade blasting to smithereens his particular form of utopian thinking, the plague America infiltrating the Swede's castle and there infecting everyone. The daughter who transports him out of the longed-for American pastoral and into everything that is its antithesis and its enemy, into the fury, the violence, and the desperation of the counterpastoral— into the indigenous American berserk.

The old intergenerational give-and-take of the country-that-used-to-be, when everyone knew his role and took the rules dead seriously, the acculturating back-and-forth that all of us here grew up with, the ritual postimmigrant struggle for success turning pathological in, of all places, the gentleman farmer's castle of our superordinary Swede. A guy stacked like a deck of cards for things to unfold entirely differently. In no way prepared for what is going to hit him. How could he, with all his carefully calibrated goodness, have known that the stakes of living obediently were so high? Obedience is embraced to *lower* the stakes. A beautiful wife. A beautiful house. Runs his business like a charm. Handles his hand-ful of an old man well enough. He was really living it out, his version of paradise. This is how successful people live. They're good citizens. They feel lucky. They feel grateful. God is smiling down on them. There are problems, they adjust. And then everything changes and it becomes impossible. Nothing is smiling down on anybody. And who can adjust then? Here is someone not set up for life's working out poorly, let alone for the impossible. But who is set up for the impossible that is going to happen? Who is set up for tragedy and the incomprehensibility of suffering? Nobody. The tragedy of the man not set up for tragedy—that is every man's tragedy.

*He kept peering in from outside at his own life. The struggle of his life was to bury this thing. But how could he?*

*Never in his life had occasion to ask himself, "Why are things the way they are?" Why should he bother, when the way they were was always perfect? Why are things the way they are? The question to which there is no answer, and up till then he was so blessed he didn't even know the question existed.*

After all the effervescent strain of resuscitating our class's mid-century innocence—together a hundred aging people recklessly turning back the clock to a time when time's passing was a matter of indifference—with the afternoon's exhilarations finally coming to an end, I began to contemplate the very thing that must have baffled the Swede till the moment he died: how had he become history's plaything? History, American history, the stuff you read about in books and study in school, had made its way out to tranquil, untrafficked Old Rimrock, New Jersey, to countryside where it had not put in an appearance that was notable since Washington's army twice wintered in the highlands adjacent to Morristown. History, which had made no drastic impingement on the daily life of the local populace since the Revolutionary War, wended its way back out to these cloistered hills and, improbably, with all its predictable unforeseenness, broke helter-skelter into the orderly household of the Seymour Levovs and left the place in a shambles. People think of history in the long term, but history, in fact, is a very sudden thing.

In earnest, right then and there, while swaying with Joy to that out-of-date music, I began to try to work out for myself what exactly had shaped a destiny unlike any imagined for the famous Weequahic three-letterman back when this music and its sentimental exhortation was right to the point, when the Swede, his neighborhood, his city, and his country were in their exuberant heyday, at the peak of confidence, inflated with every illusion born of hope. With Joy Helpern once again close in my arms and quietly sobbing to hear the old pop tune enjoining all of us sixty-odd-year-olds,

"Dream . . . and they might come true," I lifted the Swede up onto the stage. That evening at Vincent's, for a thousand different excellent reasons, he could not bring himself to ask me to do this. For all I know he had no intention of asking me to do this. To get me to write his story may not have been why he was there at all. Maybe it was only why I was there.

Basketball was never like this.

He'd invoked in me, when I was a boy—as he did in hundreds of other boys—the strongest fantasy I had of being someone else. But to wish oneself into another's glory, as boy or as man, is an impossibility, untenable on psychological grounds if you are not a writer, and on aesthetic grounds if you are. To embrace your hero in his destruction, however—to let your hero's life occur within you when everything is trying to diminish him, to imagine yourself into his bad luck, to implicate yourself not in his mindless ascendancy, when he is the fixed point of your adulation, but in the bewilderment of his tragic fall—well, that's worth thinking about.

So then . . . I am out there on the floor with Joy, and I am thinking of the Swede and of what happened to his country in a mere twenty-five years, between the triumphant days at wartime Weequahic High and the explosion of his daughter's bomb in 1968, of that mysterious, troubling, extraordinary historical transition. I am thinking of the sixties and of the disorder occasioned by the Vietnam War, of how certain families lost their kids and certain families didn't and how the Seymour Levovs were one of those that did—families full of tolerance and kindly, well-intentioned liberal goodwill, and theirs were the kids who went on a rampage, or went to jail, or disappeared underground, or fled to Sweden or Canada. I am thinking of the Swede's great fall and of how he must have imagined that it was founded on some failure of his own responsibility. There is where it must begin. It doesn't matter if he was the cause of anything. He makes himself responsible anyway. He has been doing that all his life, making himself unnaturally responsible, keeping under control not just himself but whatever else threatens to be uncontrollable, giving his all to keep his world together. Yes, the cause of the disaster has for him to be a transgression. How else would the Swede explain it to himself? It has to be a transgression, a single transgression, even if it is only he who identifies it as a transgression. The disaster that befalls him begins in a failure of his responsibility, *as he imagines it.*

But what could that have been?

Dispelling the aura of the dinner at Vincent's, when I'd rushed to conclude the most thoughtless conclusion—that simple *was* that simple—I lifted onto my stage the boy we were all going to follow into America, our point man into the next immersion, at home here the way the Wasps were at home here, an American not by sheer striving, not by being a Jew who invents a famous vaccine or a Jew on the Supreme Court, not by being the most brilliant or the most eminent or the best. Instead—by virtue of his isomorphism to the Wasp world—he does it the ordinary way, the natural way, the regular American-guy way. To the honeysweet strains of "Dream," I pulled away from myself, pulled away from the reunion, and I dreamed . . . I dreamed a realistic chronicle. I began gazing into his life—not his life as a god or a demigod in whose triumphs one could exult as a boy but his life as another assailable man—and inexplicably, which is to say lo and behold, I found him in Deal, New Jersey, at the seaside cottage, the summer his daughter was eleven, back when she couldn't stay out of his lap or stop calling him by cute pet names, couldn't "resist," as she put it, examining with the tip of her finger the close way his ears were fitted to his skull. Wrapped in a towel, she would run through the house and out to the clothesline to fetch a dry bathing suit, shouting as she went, "Nobody look!" and several evenings she had barged into the bathroom where he was bathing and, when she saw him, cried out, "Oh, pardonnez-moi—j'ai pensé que—" "Scram," he told her, "get-outahere-moi." Driving alone with him back from the beach one day that summer, dopily sun-drunk, lolling against his bare shoulder, she had turned up her face and, half innocently, half audaciously, precociously playing the grown-up girl, said, "Daddy, kiss me the way you k-k-kiss umumumother." Sun-drunk himself, voluptuously fatigued from rolling all morning with her in the heavy surf, he had looked down to see that one of the shoulder straps of her swimsuit had dropped over her arm, and there was her nipple, the hard red bee bite that was her nipple. "N-n-no," he said—and stunned them both. "And fix your suit," he added feebly. Soundlessly she obeyed. "I'm sorry, cookie—" "Oh, I deserve it," she said, trying with all her might to hold back her tears and be his chirpingly charming pal again. "It's the same at school. It's the same with my friends. I get started with something and I can't stop. I just get c-c-carried awuh-awuh-awuh-awuh—"

It was a while since he'd seen her turn white like that or seen her face contorted like that. She fought for the word longer than, on that particular day, he could possibly bear. "Awuh-awuh—" And yet he knew better than anyone what not to do when, as Merry put it, she "started phumphing to beat the band." He was the parent she could always rely on not to jump all over her every time she opened her mouth. "Cool it," he would tell Dawn, "relax, lay off her," but Dawn could not help herself. Merry began to stutter badly and Dawn's hands were clasped at her waist and her eyes fixed on the child's lips, eyes that said, "I know you can do it!" while saying, "I know that you can't!" Merry's stuttering just killed her mother, and that killed Merry. "I'm not the problem—Mother is!" And so was the teacher the problem when she tried to spare Merry by not calling on her. So was everybody the problem when they started feeling sorry for her. And when she was fluent suddenly and free of stuttering, the problem was the compliments. She resented terribly being praised for fluency, and as soon as she was praised she lost it completely—sometimes, Merry would say, to the point that she was afraid "I'm going to short out my whole *system.*" Amazing how this child could summon up the strength to joke about it—his precious lighthearted jokester! If only it were within Dawn's power to become a little lighthearted about it herself. But it was the Swede alone who could always manage to be close to perfect with her, though even he had all he could do not to cry out in exasperation, "If you dare the gods and are fluent, what terrible thing do you think will happen?" The exasperation never surfaced: he did not wring his hands like her mother, when she was in trouble he did not watch her lips or mouth her words with her like her mother, he did not turn her, every time she spoke, into the most important person not merely in the room but in the entire world—he did everything he could not to make her stigma into Merry's way of being Einstein. Instead his eyes assured her that he would do all he could to help but that when she was with him she must stutter freely if she needed to. And yet he had said to her, "N-n-no." He had done what Dawn would rather die than do—he had made fun of her.

"Awuh-awuh-awuh—"

"Oh, cookie," he said, and at just the moment when he had understood that the summer's mutual, seemingly harmless playacting—the two of them nibbling at an intimacy too enjoyable to swear off and yet not in any way to be taken seriously, to be much concerned with, to be given an excessive significance, something utterly uncarnal that would fade away once the vacation was over and she was in school all day and he had returned to work, nothing that they couldn't easily find their way back from—just when he had come to understand that the summer romance required some readjusting all around, he lost his vaunted sense of proportion, drew her to him with one arm, and kissed her stammering mouth with the passion that she had been asking him for all month long while knowing only obscurely what she was asking for.

Was he supposed to feel that way? It happened before he could think. She was only eleven. Momentarily it was frightening. This was not anything he had ever worried about for a second, this was a taboo that you didn't even think of as a taboo, something you are prohibited from doing that felt absolutely natural not to do, you just proceeded effortlessly—and then, however momentary, *this*. Never in his entire life, not as a son, a husband, a father, even as an employer, had he given way to anything so alien to the emotional rules by which he was governed, and later he wondered if this strange parental misstep was not the lapse from responsibility for which he paid for the rest of his life. The kiss bore no resemblance to anything serious, was not an imitation of anything, had never been repeated, had itself lasted five seconds . . . ten at most . . . but after the disaster, when he went obsessively searching for the origins of their suffering, it was that anomalous moment—when she was eleven and he was thirty-six and the two of them, all stirred up by the strong sea and the hot sun, were heading happily home alone from the beach—that he remembered.

But then he also wondered if after that day he had perhaps withdrawn from her too radically, become physically distant more than was necessary. He had only meant to let her know she needn't be concerned that he would lose his equilibrium again, needn't worry about her *own* natural-enough infatuation, and the result may well have been that having exaggerated the implications of that kiss, having overestimated what constituted provocation, he went on to alter a perfectly harmless spontaneous bond, only to exacerbate a stuttering child's burden of self-doubt. And all he had ever meant was to help her, to help her heal!

What then was the wound? What could have wounded Merry? The indelible imperfection itself or those who had fostered in her the imperfection? But by doing what? What had they done other than to love her and look after her and encourage her, give her the support and guidance and independence that seemed reasonable to them—and still the undisclosed Merry had become tainted! Twisted! Crazed! By what? Thousands upon thousands of young people stuttered—they didn't all grow up to set off bombs! What went wrong with Merry? What did he do to her that was so wrong? The kiss? That kiss? So beastly? How could a kiss make someone into a criminal? The aftermath of the kiss? The withdrawal? Was that the beastliness? But it wasn't as though he'd never held her or touched her or kissed her again—he *loved* her. She *knew* that.

Once the inexplicable had begun, the torment of self-examination never ended. However lame the answers, he never ran out of the questions, he who before had nothing of consequence really to ask himself. After the bomb, he could never again take life as it came or trust that his life wasn't something very different from what he perceived. He found himself recalling his own happy childhood, the success that had been his boyhood, as though that were the cause of their blight. All the triumphs, when he probed them, seemed superficial; even more astonishing, his very virtues came to seem vices. There was no longer any innocence in what he remembered of his past. He saw that everything you say says either more than you wanted it to say or less than you wanted it to say; and everything you do does either more than you wanted it to do or less than you wanted it to do. What you said and did made a difference, all right, but not the difference you intended.

The Swede as he had always known himself—well-meaning, well-behaved, well-ordered Seymour Levov—evaporated, leaving only self-examination in his place. He couldn't disentangle himself from the idea that he was responsible any more than he could resort to the devilishly tempting idea that everything was accidental. He had been admitted into a mystery more bewildering even than Merry's stuttering: there was no fluency anywhere. It was *all* stuttering. In bed at night, he pictured the whole of his life as a stuttering mouth and a grimacing face—the whole of his life without cause or sense and completely bungled. He no longer had any conception of order. There was no order. None. He envisioned his life as a stutterer's thought, wildly out of his control.

Merry's other great love that year, aside from her father, was Audrey Hepburn. Before Audrey Hepburn there had been astronomy and before astronomy, the 4-H Club, and along the way, a bit distressingly to her father, there was even a Catholic phase. Her grandmother Dwyer took her to pray at St. Genevieve's whenever Merry was visiting down in Elizabeth. Little by little, Catholic trinkets made their way into her room—and as long as he could think of them as trinkets, as long as she wasn't going overboard, everything was okay. First there was the palm frond bent into the shape of the cross that Grandma had given her after Palm Sunday. That was all right. Any kid might want that up on the wall. Then came the candle, in thick glass, about a foot tall, the Eternal Candle;

on its label was a picture of the Sacred Heart of Jesus and a prayer that began, "O Sacred Heart of Jesus who said, 'Ask and you shall receive.'" That wasn't so great, but as she didn't seem to be lighting and burning it, as it just seemed to sit there on her dresser for decoration, there was no sense making a fuss. Then, to hang over the bed, came the picture of Jesus, in profile, praying, which really wasn't all right, though still he said nothing to her, nothing to Dawn, nothing to Grandma Dwyer, told himself, "It's harmless, it's a picture, to her a pretty picture of a nice man. What difference does it make?"

What did it was the statue, the plaster statue of the Blessed Mother, a smaller version of the big ones on the breakfront in Grandma Dwyer's dining room and on the dressing table in Grandma Dwyer's bedroom. The statue was what led him to sit her down and ask if she would be willing to take the pictures and the palm frond off the wall and put them away in her closet, along with the statue and the Eternal Candle, when Grandma and Grandpa Levov came to visit. Quietly he explained that though her room was her room and she had the right to hang anything there she wanted, Grandma and Grandpa Levov were Jews, and so, of course, was he, and, rightly or wrongly, Jews don't, etc., etc. And because she was a sweet girl who wanted to please people, and to please her daddy most of all, she was careful to be sure that nothing Grandma Dwyer had given her was anywhere to be seen when next the Swede's parents visited Old Rimrock. And then one day everything Catholic came down off the wall and off her dresser for good. She was a perfectionist who did things passionately, lived intensely in the new interest, and then the passion was suddenly spent and everything, including the passion, got thrown into a box and she moved on.

Now it was Audrey Hepburn. Every newspaper and magazine she could get hold of she combed for the film star's photograph or name. Even movie timetables—"Breakfast at Tiffany's, 2, 4, 6, 8, 10"—were clipped from the newspaper after dinner and pasted in her Audrey Hepburn scrapbook. For months she went in and out of pretending to be gaminish instead of herself, daintily walking to her room like a wood sprite, smiling with meaningfully coy eyes into every reflecting surface, laughing what they call an "infectious" laugh whenever her father said a word. She bought the soundtrack from *Breakfast at Tiffany's* and played it in her bedroom for hours. He could hear her in there singing "Moon River" in the charming way that Audrey Hepburn did, and absolutely fluently—and so, however ostentatious and singularly self-conscious was the shameless playacting, nobody in the house ever indicated that it was tiresome, let alone ludicrous, an improbable dream of purification that had taken possession of her. If Audrey Hepburn could help her shut down just a little of the stuttering, then let her go on ludicrously pretending, a girl blessed with golden hair and a logical mind and a high IQ and an adultlike sense of humor even about herself, blessed with long, slender limbs and a wealthy family and her own brand of dogged persistence—with everything except fluency. Security, health, love, every advantage imaginable—missing only was the ability to order a hamburger without humiliating herself.

How hard she tried! Two afternoons she went to ballet class after school and two afternoons Dawn drove her to Morristown to see a speech therapist. On Saturday she got up early, made her own breakfast, and then bicycled the five hilly miles into Old Rimrock village to the tiny office of the local circuit-riding psychiatrist, who had a slant that made the Swede furious when he began to see Merry's struggle getting worse rather than better. The psychiatrist got Merry thinking that the stutter was a choice she made, a way of being special that she had chosen and then locked into when she realized how well it worked. The psychiatrist asked her, "How do you think your father would feel about you if you didn't stutter? How do you think your mother would feel?" He asked her, "Is there anything good that stuttering brings you?" The Swede did not understand how it was going to help the child to make her feel responsible for something she simply could not do, and so he went to see the man. And by the time he left he wanted to kill him.

It seemed that the etiology of Merry's problem had largely to do with her having such good-looking and successful parents. As best the Swede could follow what he was hearing, her parental good fortune was just too much for Merry, and so, to withdraw from the competition with her mother, to get her mother to hover over and focus on her and eventually climb the walls—and, in addition, to win the father away from the beautiful mother—she chose to stigmatize herself with a severe stutter, thereby manipulating everyone from a point of seeming weakness. "But Merry is made miserable by her stutter," the Swede reminded him. "That's why we brought her to see you." "The benefits may far outweigh the penalties." For the moment, the Swede couldn't understand what the doctor was explaining and replied, "But, no, no—watching her stutter is *killing* my wife." "Maybe, for Merry, that's one of the benefits. She is an extremely bright and manipulative child. If she weren't, you wouldn't be so angry with me because I'm telling you that stuttering can be an extremely manipulative, an extremely useful, if not even a vindictive type of behavior." He hates me, thought the Swede. It's all because of the way I look. Hates me because of the way Dawn looks. He's obsessed with our looks. That's why he hates us—we're not short and ugly like him! "It's difficult," the psychiatrist said, "for a daughter to grow up the daughter of somebody who had so much attention for what sometimes seems to the daughter to be such a silly thing. It's tough, on top of the natural competition between mother and daughter, to have people asking a little girl, 'Do you want to grow up to be Miss New Jersey just like your mommy?'" "But nobody asks her that. Who asks her that? We never have. We never talk about it, it never comes up. Why would it? My wife isn't Miss New Jersey—my wife is her *mother*." "But people ask her that, Mr. Levov." "Well, for God's sake, people ask children all sorts of things that don't mean anything—that is not the *problem* here." "But you do see how a child who has reason to feel she doesn't quite measure up to Mother, that she couldn't come close, might choose to adopt—" "She hasn't *adopted* anything. Look, I think that perhaps you put an unfair burden on my daughter by making her see this as a 'choice.' She *has* no choice. It's perfect hell for her when she stutters." "That isn't always what she tells me. Last Saturday, I asked her point-blank, 'Merry, why do you stutter?' and she told me, 'It's just easier to stutter.'" "But you know what she meant by that. It's obvious what she meant by that. She means she doesn't have to go through all that she has to go through when she tries *not* to stutter." "I happen to think she was telling me something more than that. I think that Merry may even feel that if she doesn't stutter, then, oh boy, people are really going to find the real problem with her, particularly in a highly pressured perfectionist family where they tend to place an unrealistically high value on her every utterance. 'If I don't stutter, then my mother is really going to read me the riot act, then she's going to find out my *real* secrets.'" "Who said we're a highly pressured perfectionist family? Jesus. We're an ordinary family. Are you quoting Merry? That's what she told you, about her mother? That she was going to read her *the riot act?*" "Not in so many words." "Because it's not *true*," the Swede said. "That's not the cause. Sometimes I just think it's because her brain is so quick, it's so much quicker than her tongue—" Oh, the pitying way he is looking at me and my pathetic explanation. Superior bastard. Cold, heartless bastard. *Stupid* bastard. That's the worst of it—the stupidity. And all of it is because he looks the way he looks and I look the way I look and Dawn looks the way she looks and . . . "We frequently see fathers who can't accept, who refuse to believe—" Oh, these people are completely useless! They only make things worse! Whose idea was this fucking psychiatrist! "I'm not *not* accepting anything, damn it. I brought her here," the Swede said, "in the first place. I do everything any professional has told me to do to help support her efforts to stop. I just want to know from you what good it is doing my daughter, with her grimacing and her tics and her leg twitches and her banging on the table and turning white in the face, with all of that difficulty, to be told that, on top of everything else, she's doing all this to *manipulate* her mother and father." "Well, who is in charge when she is banging on the table and turning white? Who is in control there?" "*She* certainly isn't!" said the Swede angrily. "You find me taking a very uncharitable view toward her," replied the doctor. "Well . . . in a way, as her father, yes. It never seems to occur to you that there might be some *physiological* basis for this." "No, I didn't say that. Mr. Levov, I can give you organic theories if you want them. But that isn't the way I have found I can be most effective."

Her stuttering diary. When she sat at the kitchen table after dinner writing the day's entry in her stuttering diary, that's when he most wanted to murder the psychiatrist who had finally to inform him—one of the fathers "who can't accept, who refuse to believe"—that she would stop stuttering only when stuttering was no longer necessary for her, when she wanted to "relate" to the world in a different way—in short, when she found a more valuable replacement for the manipulativeness. The stuttering diary was a red three-ring notebook in which, at the suggestion of her speech therapist, Merry kept a record of when she stuttered. Could she have been any more the dedicated enemy of her stuttering than when she sat there scrupulously recalling and recording how the stuttering fluctuated throughout the day, in what context it was least likely to occur, when it was most likely to occur and with whom? And could anything have been more heartbreaking for him than reading that notebook on the Friday evening she rushed off to the movies with her friends and happened to leave it open on the table? "When do I stutter? When somebody asks me something that requires an unexpected, unrehearsed response, that's when I'm likely to stutter. When people are looking at me. People who know I stutter, particularly when *they're* looking at me. Though sometimes it's worse with people who don't know me. . . ." On she went, page after page in her strikingly neat handwriting—and all she seemed to be saying was that she stuttered in all situations. She had written, "Even when I'm doing fine, I can't stop thinking, 'How soon is it going to be before he knows I'm a stutterer? How soon is it going to be before I start stuttering and screw this up?'" Yet, despite every disappointment, she sat where her parents could see her and worked on her stuttering diary every night, weekends included. She worked with her therapist on the different "strategies" to be used with strangers, store clerks, people with whom she had relatively safe conversations; they worked on strategies to be used with the people who were closer to her—teachers, girlfriends, boys, finally her grandparents, her father, her mother. She recorded the strategies in the diary. She listed in the diary what topics she could expect to talk about with different people, wrote down the points she would try to make, anticipating when she was most likely to stutter and getting herself thoroughly prepared. How could she bear the hardship of all that self-consciousness? The planning required of her to make the spontaneous unspontaneous, the persistence with which she refused to shrink from these tedious tasks—was that what the arrogant son of a bitch had meant by "a vindictive exercise"? It was unflagging commitment the likes of which the Swede had never known, not even in himself that fall they turned him into a football player and, reluctant as he was to go banging heads in a sport whose violence he never really liked, he did it, excelled at it, "for the good of the school."

But none of what she diligently worked at did Merry an ounce of good. In the quiet, safe cocoon of her speech therapist's office, taken out of her world, she was said to be terrifically at home with herself, to speak flawlessly, make jokes, imitate people, sing. But outside again, she saw it coming, started to go around it, would do anything, *anything,* to avoid the next word beginning with a *b*— and soon she was sputtering all over the place, and what a field day that psychiatrist had the next Saturday with the letter *b* and "what it unconsciously signified to her." Or what *m* or *c* or *g* "unconsciously signified." And yet nothing of what he surmised meant a goddamn thing. None of his great ideas disposed of a single one of her difficulties. Nothing anybody said meant anything or, in the end, made any sense. The psychiatrist didn't help, the speech therapist's strategies didn't help, the stuttering diary didn't help, he didn't help, Dawn didn't help, not even the light, crisp enunciation of Audrey Hepburn made the slightest dent. She was simply in the hands of something she could not get out of.

And then it was too late: like some innocent in a fairy story who has been tricked into drinking the noxious potion, the grasshopper child who used to scramble delightedly up and down the furniture and across every available lap in her black leotard all at once shot up, broke out, grew stout—she thickened across the back and the neck, stopped brushing her teeth and combing her hair; she ate almost nothing she was served at home but at school and out alone ate virtually all the time, cheeseburgers with French fries, pizza, BLTs, fried onion rings, vanilla milk shakes, root beer floats, ice cream with fudge sauce, and cake of any kind, so that almost overnight she became large, a large, loping, slovenly sixteen-year-old, nearly six feet tall, nicknamed by her schoolmates Ho Chi Levov.

And the impediment became the machete with which to mow all the bastard liars down. "You f-f-fucking madman! You heartless mi-mi-mi-miserable m-monster!" she snarled at Lyndon Johnson whenever his face appeared on the seven o'clock news. Into the televised face of Humphrey, the vice president, she cried, "You prick, sh-sh-shut your lying m-m-mouth, you c-c-coward, you f-f-f-f-filthy fucking collaborator!" When her father, as a member of the ad hoc group calling itself New Jersey Businessmen Against the War, went down to Washington with the steering committee to visit their senator, Merry refused his invitation to come along. "But," said the Swede, who had never belonged to a political group before and would not have joined this one and volunteered for the steering committee and paid a thousand dollars toward their protest ad in the *Newark News* had he not hoped his conspicuous involvement might deflect a little of her anger away from him, "this is your chance to say what's on your mind to Senator Case. You can confront him directly. Isn't that what you want?" "Merry," said her petite mother to the large glowering girl, "you might be able to influence Senator Case—" "C-c-c-c-c-c-case!" erupted Merry and, to the astonishment of her parents, proceeded to spit on the tiled kitchen floor.

She was on the phone now all the time, the child who formerly had to run through her telephone "strategy" just to be sure that when she picked up the phone she could get out the word "Hello" in under thirty seconds. She had conquered the anguishing stutter all right, but not as her parents and her therapist had hoped. No, Merry concluded that what was deforming her life wasn't the stuttering but the futile effort to overturn it. The crazy effort. The ridiculous significance she had given to that stutter to meet the Rimrock expectations of the very parents and teachers and friends who had caused her to so overestimate something as secondary as the way she talked. Not what she said but how she said it was all that bothered them. And all she really had to do to be free of it was to not give a shit about how it made them so miserable when she had to pronounce the letter *b*. Yes, she cut herself away from caring about the abyss that opened up under everybody's feet when she started stuttering; her stuttering was no longer going to be the center of her existence—and she'd make damn sure that it wasn't going to be the center of theirs. Vehemently she renounced the appearance and the allegiances of the good little girl who had tried so hard to be adorable and lovable like all the other good little Rimrock girls—renounced her meaningless manners, her petty social concerns, her family's "bourgeois" values. She had wasted enough time on the cause of herself. "I'm not going to spend my whole life wrestling day and night with a fucking stutter when kids are b-b-b-being b-b-b-b-bu-bu-bu roasted alive by Lyndon B-b-b-baines b-b-b-bu-bu-burn-'em-up Johnson!"

All her energy came right to the surface now, unimpeded, the force of resistance that had previously been employed otherwise; and by no longer bothering with the ancient obstruction, she experienced not only her full freedom for the first time in her life but the exhilarating power of total self-certainty. A brand-new Merry had begun, one who'd found, in opposing the "v-v-v-vile" war, a difficulty to fight that was worthy, at last, of her truly stupendous strength. North Vietnam she called the Democratic Republic of Vietnam, a country she spoke of with such patriotic feeling that, according to Dawn, one would have thought she'd been born not at the Newark Beth Israel but at the Beth Israel in Hanoi. "'The

Democratic Republic of Vietnam'—if I hear that from her one more time, Seymour, I swear, I'll go out of my mind!" He tried to convince her that perhaps it wasn't as bad as it sounded. "Merry has a credo, Dawn, Merry has a political position. There may not be much subtlety in it, she may not yet be its best spokesman, but there is some thought behind it, there's certainly a lot of emotion behind it, there's a lot of *compassion* behind it. . . ."

But there was now no conversation she had with her daughter that did not drive Dawn, if not out of her mind, out of the house and into the barn. The Swede would overhear Merry fighting with her every time the two of them were alone together for two minutes. "Some people," Dawn says, "would be perfectly *happy* to have parents who are contented middle-class people." "I'm sorry I'm not brainwashed enough to be one of them," Merry replies. "You're a sixteen-year-old girl," Dawn says, "and I can tell you what to do and I *will* tell you what to do." "Just because I'm sixteen doesn't make me a g-g-girl! I do what I w-w-want!" "You're not antiwar," Dawn says, "you're anti *everything*." "And what are you, Mom? You're pro c-c-c-cow!"

Night after night now Dawn went to bed in tears. "What is she? What is this?" she asked the Swede. "If someone simply defies your authority, what can you do? Seymour, I'm totally puzzled. How did this happen?" "It happens," he told her. "She's a kid with a strong will. With an idea. With a cause." "Where did this *come* from? It's inexplicable. Am I a bad mother? Is that it?" "You are a good mother. You are a wonderful mother. That is not it." "I don't know why she's turned against me like this. I don't have any sense of what I did to her or even what she perceives I did to her. I don't know what's happened. Who *is* she? Where did *she* come from? I cannot control her. I cannot *recognize* her. I thought she was smart. She's not smart at all. She's become *stupid*, Seymour; she gets more and more stupid each time we talk." "No, it's just a very crude kind of aggression. It's not very well worked out. But she is still smart. She's very smart. This is what teenagers are like. There are these very turbulent sorts of changes. It has nothing to do with you or me.

They just amorphously object to everything." "It's all from the stuttering, isn't it?" "We're doing everything we can for her stutter. We always have." "She's angry because she stutters. She doesn't make friends," Dawn said, "because she stutters." "She's always had friends. She has many friends. Besides, she was on top of her stuttering. Stuttering is not the explanation." "Yes, it is. You never get on top of your stutter," Dawn said, "you're in constant fear." "That's not an explanation, Dawnie, for what is going on." "She's sixteen—is *that* the explanation?" asked Dawn. "Well, if it is," he said, "and maybe an awful lot of it is, we'll do the best we can until she stops being sixteen." "And? When she's not sixteen anymore, she'll be seventeen." "At seventeen she won't be the same. At eighteen she won't be the same. Things change. She'll discover new interests. She'll have college—academic pursuits. We can work this out. The important thing is to keep talking with her." "I can't. I can't talk to her. Now she's even jealous of the cows. It's too maddening." "Then I'll keep talking to her. The important thing is not to abandon her and not to capitulate to her, and to keep talking even if you have to say the same thing over and over and over. It doesn't matter if it all seems hopeless. You can't expect what you say to have an immediate impact." "It's what she says *back* that has the *impact!*" "It doesn't matter what she says back. We have to keep saying to her what we have to say to her, even if saying it seems interminable. We must draw the line. If we don't draw the line, then surely she's not going to obey. If we do draw the line, there's at least a fifty percent chance that she will." "And if she still doesn't?" "All we can do, Dawn, is to continue to be reasonable and continue to be firm and not lose hope or patience, and the day will come when she will outgrow all this objecting to everything." "She doesn't *want* to outgrow it." "Now. Today. But there is tomorrow. There's a bond between us all and it's tremendous. As long as we don't let her go, as long as we keep talking, tomorrow will come. Of course she's maddening. She's unrecognizable to me, too. But if you don't allow her to exhaust your patience and if you keep talking to her and you don't give up on her, she will eventually become herself again."

And so, hopeless as it seemed, he talked, he listened, he was reasonable; endless as the struggle seemed, he remained patient, and whenever he saw her going too far he drew the line. No matter how much it might openly enrage her to answer him, no matter how sarcastic and caustic and elusive and dishonest her answers might be, he continued to question her about her political activities, about her after-school whereabouts, about her new friends; with a gentle persistence that infuriated her, he asked about her Saturday trips into New York. She could shout all she wanted at home—she was still just a kid from Old Rimrock, and the thought of whom she might meet in New York alarmed him.

Conversation #1 about New York. "What do you do when you go to New York? Who do you see in New York?" "What do I do? I go see New York. That's what I do." "What do you do, Merry?" "I do what everyone else does. I window-shop. What else would a girl do?" "You're involved with political people in New York." "I don't know what you're talking about. Everything is political. Brushing your *teeth* is political." "You're involved with people who are against the war in Vietnam. Isn't that who you go to see? Yes or no?" "They're people, yes. They're people with ideas, and some of them don't b-b-b-believe in the war. Most of them don't b-b-b-believe in the war." "Well, I don't happen to believe in the war myself." "So what's your problem?" "Who are these people? How old are they? What do they do for a living? Are they students?" "Why do you want to know?" "Because I'd like to know what you're doing. You're alone in New York on Saturdays. Not everyone's parents would allow a sixteen-year-old girl to go that far." "I go in . . . I, you know, there are people and dogs and streets . . ." "You come home with all this Communist material. You come home with all these books and pamphlets and magazines." "I'm trying to *learn*. You taught me to *learn*, didn't you? Not just to study, but to *learn*. C-c-c-communist . . ." "It *is* Communist. It says on the page that it's Communist." "C-c-c-communists have ideas that aren't always about C-communism." "For instance." "About poverty. About war. About injustice. They have all kinds of ideas. Just b-b-because you're Jewish doesn't mean you just have ideas about Judaism. Well, the same holds for C-c-communism."

Conversation #12 about New York. "Where do you eat your meals in New York?" "Not at Vincent's, thank God." "Where then?" "Where everybody else eats their meals. Restaurants. Cafeterias. People's apartments." "Who are the people who live in these apartments?" "Friends of mine." "Where did you meet them?" "I met some here, I met some in the city—" "Here? Where?" "At the high school. Sh-sh-sh-sherry, for instance." "I never met Sherry." "Sh-sh-sh-sherry is the one, do you remember, who played the violin in all the class plays? And she goes into New York b-because she takes music lessons." "Is she involved with politics too?" "Daddy, everything is political. How can she not be involved if she has a b-b-b-brain?" "Merry, I don't want you to get into trouble. You're angry about the war. A lot of people are angry about the war. But there are some people who are angry about the war who don't have any limits. Do you know what the limits are?" "Limits. That's all you think about. Not going to the extreme. Well, sometimes you have to fucking go to the extreme. What do you think war is? War is an extreme. It isn't life out here in little Rimrock. Nothing is too extreme out here." "You don't like it out here anymore. Would you want to live in New York? Would you like that?" "Of c-c-c-course." "Suppose when you graduate from high school you were to go to college in New York. Would you like that?" "I don't know if I'm going to go to college. Look at the administration of those colleges. Look what they do to their students who are against the war. How can I want to be going to college? Higher education. It's what I call lower education. Maybe I'll go to college, maybe I won't. I wouldn't start p-planning now."

Conversation #18 about New York, after she fails to return home on a Saturday night. "You're never to do that again. You're never to stay over with people who we don't know. Who are these people?" "Never say never." "Who are the people you stayed with?" "They're friends of Sh-sherry's. From the music school." "I don't believe you." "Why? You can't b-b-b-believe that I might have friends? That people might like me—you don't b-b-b-believe that? That people might put me up for the night—you don't b-b-b-believe that? What *do* you b-b-b-b-b-b-b-believe in?" "You're sixteen years old. You're to come home. You cannot stay over in New York City." "Stop reminding me of how old I am. We all have an age." "When you went off yesterday we expected you back at six o'clock. At seven o'clock at night you phoned to say you're staying over. We said you weren't. You insisted. You said you had a place to stay. So I let you do it." "You let me. Sure." "But you can't do it again. If you do it again, you will never be allowed to go into New York by yourself." "Says who?" "Your father." "We'll see." "I'll make a deal with you." "What's the deal, *Father?*" "If you ever go into New York again and you find it's getting late and you have to stay somewhere, you stay with the Umanoffs." "The *Umanoffs?*" "They like you, you like them, they've known you all your life. They have a very nice apartment." "Well, the people I stayed with have a very nice apartment too." "Who are they?" "I told you, they're Sh-sherry's friends." "Who are they?" "Bill and Melissa." "And who are Bill and Melissa?" "They're p-p-p-people. Like everyone else." "What do they do for a living? How old are they?" "Melissa's twenty-two. And Bill is nineteen." "Are they students?" "They were students. Now they organize people for the betterment of the Vietnamese." "Where do they live?" "What are you going to do, come and get me?" "I'd like to know where they live. There are all sorts of neighborhoods in New York. Some are good, some aren't." "They live in a perfectly fine neighborhood and a perfectly fine b-b-b-b-building." "Where?" "They live up in Morningside Heights." "Are they Columbia students?" "They were." "How many people stay in this apartment?" "I don't see why I have to answer all these questions." "Because you're my daughter and you are sixteen years old." "So for the rest of my life, because I'm your daughter—" "No, when you are eighteen and graduate high school, you can do whatever you want." "So the difference we're talking about here is two years." "That's right." "And what's the b-big thing that's going to happen in two years?" "You will be an independent person who can support herself." "I can support myself now if I w-w-w-w-wanted to." "I don't want you to stay with Bill and Melissa." "W-w-w-why?" "It's my responsibility to look after you. I want you to stay with the Umanoffs. If you can agree to do that, then you can go to New York and stay over. Otherwise you won't be permitted to go there at all. The choice is yours." "I'm in there to stay with the people I want to stay with." "Then you're not going to New York." "We'll see." "There is no 'we'll see.' You're not going and that's the end of it." "I'd like to see you stop me." "Think about it. If you can't agree to stay with the Umanoffs, then you can't go to New York." "What about the war—" "My responsibility is to you and not to the war." "Oh, I know your responsibility is not to the war—that's why I have to go to New York. B-b-b-because people there do feel responsible. They feel responsible when America b-blows up Vietnamese villages. They feel responsible when America is b-blowing little b-babies to b-b-b-b-bits. B-but you don't, and neither does Mother. You don't care enough to let it upset a single day of yours. You don't care enough to make *you* spend another night somewhere. You don't stay up at night worrying about it. You don't really care, Daddy, one way or the other."

Conversations #24, 25, and 26 about New York. "I can't have these conversations, Daddy. I won't! I refuse to! Who talks to their parents like this!" "If you are underage and you go away for the day and don't come home at night, then you damn well talk to your parents like this." "B-b-but you drive me c-c-c-crazy, this kind of sensible parent, trying to be understanding! I don't want to be understood—I want to be f-f-f-free!" "Would you like it better if I were a senseless parent trying not to understand you?" "I would! I think I would! Why don't you fucking t-t-try it for a change and let me fucking see!"

Conversation #29 about New York. "No, you can't disrupt our family life until you are of age. Then do whatever you want. So long as you're under eighteen—" "All you can think about, all you can talk about, all you c-c-care about is the well-being of this f-fucking l-l-little f-f-family!" "Isn't that all you think about? Isn't that what you are angry about?" "N-n-no! N-n-never!" "Yes, Merry. You are angry about the families in Vietnam. You are angry about their being destroyed. Those are families too. Those are families just like ours that would like to have the right to have lives like our family has. Isn't that what you yourself want for them? What Bill and Melissa want for them? That they might be able to have secure and peaceful lives like ours?" "To have to live out here in the privileged middle of nowhere? No, I don't think that's what B-b-bill and Melissa want for them. It's not what I want for them." "Don't you? Then think again. I think that to have this privileged middle-of-nowhere kind of life would make them quite content, frankly." "They just want to go to b-bed at night, in their own country, leading their own lives, and without thinking they're going to get b-b-blown to b-b-b-b-b-bits in their sleep. B-b-blown to b-b-b-b-bits all for the sake of the privileged people of New Jersey leading their p-p-peaceful, s-s-secure, acquisitive, meaningless l-l-l-little bloodsucking lives!"

Conversation #30 about New York, after Merry returns from staying overnight with the Umanoffs. "Oh, they're oh-so-liberal, B-b-b-b-Barry and Marcia. With their little comfortable b-b-bourgeois life." "They are professors, they are serious academics who are against the war. Did they have any people there?" "Oh, some English professor against the war, some sociology professor against the war. At least he involves his family against the war. They all march tugu-tugu-tugu-together. That's what I call a family. Not these fucking c-c-c-cows." "So it went all right there." "No. I want to go with my friends. I don't want to go to the Umanoffs at eight o'clock. Whatever is happening is happening *after* eight o'clock! If I wanted to be with your friends after eight o'clock at night, I could stay here in Rimrock. I want to be with my friends after eight o'clock!" "Nonetheless it worked out. We compromised. You didn't get to be with your friends after eight o'clock but you got to spend the day with your friends, which is a lot better than nothing at all. I feel much better about what you have agreed to do. You should too. Are you going to go in next Saturday?" "I don't plan these things y-years in advance." "If you're going in next Saturday, then you're to phone the Umanoffs beforehand and let them know you're coming."

Conversation #34 about New York, after Merry fails to show up at the Umanoffs for the night. "Okay, that's it. You made an agreement and you broke it. You're not leaving this house on a Saturday again." "I'm under house arrest." "Indefinitely." "What is it that you're so afraid of? What is it that you think I'm going to do? I'm hanging out with f-friends. We discuss the war and other important things. I don't know why you want to know so much. You don't ask me a z-z-z-z-zillion fucking questions every time I go down to Hamlin's s-s-store. What are you so afraid of? You're just a b-b-b-b-bundle of fear. You just can't keep hiding out here in the woods. Don't go spewing your fear all over me and making me as fearful as you and Mom are. All you can deal with is c-cows. C-cows and trees. Well, there's something besides c-c-c-c-cows and trees. There are people. People with real pain. Why don't you say it? Are you afraid I'm going to get laid? Is that what you're afraid of? I'm not that moronic to get knocked up. What have I ever done in my life that's irresponsible?" "You broke the agreement. That's the end of it." "This is not a corporation. This isn't b-b-b-b-b-b-business, Daddy. House arrest. Every day in this house is like being under house arrest." "I don't like you very much when you act like this." "Daddy, shut up. I don't like you either. I never d-d-did."

Conversation #44 about New York. The next Saturday. "I'm not driving you to the train. You're not leaving the house." "What are you going to do? B-barricade me in? How you going to stop me? You going to tie me to my high chair? Is that how you treat your daughter? I can't b-b-believe my own father would threaten me with physical force." "I'm not threatening you with physical force." "Then how are you going to keep me in the house? I'm not just one of Mom's dumb c-c-c-c-cows! I'm not going to live here forever and ever and ever. Mr. C-cool, Calm, and Collected. What is it that you're so afraid of? What is it you're so afraid of people for? Haven't you ever heard that New York is one of the world's great cultural centers? People come from the whole world to experience New

York. You always wanted me to experience everything else. Why can't I experience New York? Better than this d-dump here. What are you so angry about? That I might have a real idea of my own? Something that you didn't come up with first? Something that isn't one of your well-thought-out plans for the family and how things should go? All I'm doing is taking a fucking train into the city. Millions of men and women do it every day to go to work. Fall in with the wrong people. God forbid I should ever get another point of view. You married an Irish Catholic. What did your family think about your falling in with the wrong people? She married a J-j-j-j-jew. What did her family think about her falling in with the wrong people? How much worse can I do? Maybe hang out with a guy with an Afro—is that what you're afraid of? I don't think so, *Daddy*. Why don't you worry about something that matters, like the war, instead of whether or not your overprivileged little girl takes a train into the b-big city b-by herself?"

Conversation #53 about New York. "You still won't tell me what kind of horrible fucking fate is going to b-b-befall me if I take a fucking train to the city. They have apartments and roofs in New York too. They have locks and doors too. A lock isn't something that is unique to Old Rimrock, New Jersey. Ever think of that, Seymour-Levov-it-rhymes-with-the-love? You think everything that is f-foreign to you is b-bad. Did you ever think that there are some things that are f-foreign to you that are good? And that as your daughter I would have some instinct to go with the right people at the right time? You're always so sure I'm going to fuck up in some way. If you had any confidence in me, you'd think that I might hang out with the right people. You don't give me any credit." "Merry, you know what I'm talking about. You're involving yourself with political radicals." "Radicals. B-b-because they don't agree with y-y-y-you they're radical." "These are people who have very extreme political ideas—" "That's the only thing that gets anything done is to have strong ideas, Daddy." "But you are only sixteen years old, and they are much older and more sophisticated than you." "Good. So maybe I'll learn something. Extreme is b-b-b-blowing up a little country for some misunderstood notions about freedom. That is extreme. B-b-b-blowing off b-b-boys' legs and b-balls, that is extreme, Daddy. Taking a b-bus or a train into New York and spending a night in a locked, secure apartment—I don't see what's so extreme about that. I think people sleep somewhere every night if they can. T-t-tell me what's so extreme about that. Do you think war is b-bad? Eww—extreme idea, Daddy. It's not the idea that's extreme—it's the fact that someone might care enough about something to try to make it different. You think that's extreme? That's *your* problem. It might mean more to someone to try to save other people's lives than to finish a d-d-d-d-d-degree at Columbia—that's extreme? No, the other is extreme." "You talking about Bill and Melissa?" "Yeah. She dropped out because there are things that are more important to her than a d-d-d-degree. To stop the killing is more important to her than the letters B-b-b.A. on a piece of paper. You call that extreme? No, I think extreme is to continue on with life as usual when this kind of craziness is going on, when people are b-being exploited left, right, and center, and you can just go on and get into your suit and tie every day and go to work. As if nothing is happening. That is extreme. That is extreme s-s-s-stupidity, that is what that is."

Conversation #59 about New York. "Who are they?" "They went to Columbia. They dropped out. I *told* you all this. They live on Morningside Heights." "That doesn't tell me enough, Merry. There are drugs, there are violent people, it is a dangerous city. Merry, you can wind up in a lot of trouble. You can wind up getting raped." "B-because I didn't listen to my daddy?" "That's not impossible." "Girls wind up getting raped whether they listen to their daddies or not. Sometimes the daddies do the raping. Rapists have ch-ch-children too. That's what makes them daddies." "Tell Bill and Melissa to come here and spend the weekend with us." "Oh, they'd really like to stay out here." "Look, how would you like to go away to school in September? To prep school for your last two years. Maybe you've had enough of living at home and living with us here." "Always planning. Always trying to figure out the most reasonable course." "What else should I do? Not plan? I'm a man. I'm a husband. I'm a father. I run a business." "I run a b-b-b-business, therefore I am." "There are all kinds of schools. There are schools with all kinds of interesting people, with all kinds of freedom. . . . You talk to your faculty adviser, I'll make inquiries too—and if you're sick and tired of living with us, you can go away to school. I understand that there isn't much for you to do out here anymore. Let's all of us think seriously about your going away to school."

Conversation #67 about New York. "You can be as active in the antiwar movement as you like here in Morristown and here in Old Rimrock. You can organize people here against the war, in your school—" "Daddy, I want to do it my w-way." "Listen to me. Please listen to me. The people here in Old Rimrock are not antiwar. To the contrary. You want to be in opposition? Be in opposition here." "You can't do anything about it here. What am I going to do, march around the general store?" "You can organize here." "Rimrockians Against the War? That's going to make a b-big difference. Morristown High Against the War." "That's right. Bring the war home. Isn't that the slogan? So do it—bring the war home to your town. You like to be unpopular? You'll be plenty unpopular, I can assure you." "I'm not looking to be unpopular." "Well, you will be. Because it's an unpopular position here. If you oppose the war here with all your strength, believe me, you will make an impact. Why don't you educate people here about the war? This is part of America too, you know." "A minute part." "These people are Americans, Merry. You can be actively against the war right here in the village. You don't have to go to New York." "Yeah, I can be against the war in our living room." "You can be against the war at the Community Club." "All twenty people." "Morristown is the county seat. Go into Morristown on Saturdays. There are people there who are against the war. Judge Fontane is against the war, you know that. Mr. Avery is against the war. They signed the ad with me. The old judge went to Washington with me. People around here weren't very happy to see my name there, you know. But that's my position. You can organize a march in Morristown. You can work on the march."

"And the Morristown High School paper is going to cover it. That'll get the troops out of Vietnam." "I understand you're quite vocal about the war at Morristown High already. Why do you even bother if you don't think it matters? You do think it matters. Everyone's point of view in America matters in terms of this war. Start in your hometown, Merry. That's the way to end the war." "Revolutions don't b-b-begin in the countryside." "We're not talking about revolution." "*You're* not talking about revolution."

And that was the last conversation they ever had to have about New York. It worked. Interminable, but he was patient and reasonable and firm and it worked. As far as he knew, she did not go to New York again. She took his advice and stayed at home, and, after turning their living room into a battlefield, after turning Morristown High into a battlefield, she went out one day and blew up the post office, destroying right along with it Dr. Fred Conlon and the village's general store, a small wooden building with a community bulletin board out front and a single old Sunoco pump and the metal pole on which Russ Hamlin—who, with his wife, owned the store and ran the post office—had raised the American flag every morning since Warren Gamaliel Harding was president of the United States.

# II

# The Fall

# 4

A TINY, bone-white girl who looked half Merry's age but claimed to be some six years older, a Miss Rita Cohen, came to the Swede four months after Merry's disappearance. She was dressed like Dr. King's successor, Ralph Abernathy, in freedom-rider overalls and ugly big shoes, and a bush of wiry hair emphatically framed her bland baby face. He should have recognized immediately who she was—for the four months he had been waiting for just such a person—but she was so tiny, so young, so ineffectual-looking that he could barely believe she was at the University of Pennsylvania's Wharton School of Business and Finance (doing a thesis on the leather industry in Newark, New Jersey), let alone the provocateur who was Merry's mentor in world revolution.

On the day she showed up at the factory, the Swede had not known that Rita Cohen had undertaken some fancy footwork—in and out through the basement door beneath the loading dock—so as to elude the surveillance team the FBI had assigned to observe from Central Avenue the arrival and departure of everyone visiting his office.

Three, four times a year someone either called or wrote to ask permission to see the plant. In the old days, Lou Levov, busy as he might be, always made time for the Newark school classes, or Boy Scout troops, or visiting notables chaperoned by a functionary from City Hall or the Chamber of Commerce. Though the Swede didn't get nearly the pleasure his father did from being an authority on the glove trade, though he wouldn't claim his father's authority on anything pertaining to the leather industry—pertaining to anything else, either—occasionally he did assist a student by answering questions over the phone or, if the student struck him as especially serious, by offering a brief tour.

Of course, had he known beforehand that this student was no student but his fugitive daughter's emissary, he would never have arranged their meeting to take place at the factory. Why Rita hadn't explained to the Swede whose emissary she was, said nothing about Merry until the tour had been concluded, was undoubtedly so she could size up the Swede first; or maybe she said nothing for so long the better to enjoy toying with him. Maybe she just enjoyed the power. Maybe she was just another politician and the enjoyment of power lay behind much of what she did.

Because the Swede's desk was separated from the making department by glass partitions, he and the women at the machines could command a clear view of one another. He had instituted this arrangement so as to wrest relief from the mechanical racket while maintaining access between himself and the floor. His father had refused to be confined to any office, glass-enclosed or otherwise: just planted his desk in the middle of the making room's two hundred sewing machines—royalty right at the heart of the overcrowded hive, the swarm around him whining its buzz-saw bee buzz while he talked to his customers and his contractors on the phone and simultaneously plowed through his paperwork. Only from out on the floor, he claimed, could he distinguish within the contrapuntal din the sound of a Singer on the fritz and with his screwdriver be over the machine before the girl had even alerted her forelady to the trouble. Vicky, Newark Maid's elderly black forelady, so testified (with her brand of wry admiration) at his retirement banquet. While everything was running without a hitch, Lou was impatient, fidgety—in a word, said Vicky, the insufferable boss—but when a cutter came around to complain about the foreman, when the foreman came around to complain about a cutter, when skins arrived months late or in damaged condition or were of poor quality, when he discovered a lining contractor cheating him on the yield or a shipping clerk robbing him blind, when he determined that the glove slitter with the red Corvette and the sunglasses was, on the side, a bookie running a numbers game among the employees, then he was in his element and in his inimitable way set out to make things right—so that when they *were* right, said the next-to-last speaker, the proud son, introducing his father in the longest, most laudatory of the evening's jocular encomiums, "he could begin driving himself—and the rest of us—nuts with worrying again. But then, always expecting the worst, he was never disappointed for long. Never caught off guard either. All of which goes to show that, like everything else at Newark Maid, worrying *works*. Ladies and gentlemen, the man who has been my lifelong teacher— and not just in the art of worrying—the man who has made of my life a lifelong education, a difficult education sometimes but always a profitable one, who explained to me when I was a boy of five the secret of making a product perfect—'You work at it,' he told me— ladies and gentlemen, a man who has worked at it and succeeded at it since the day he went off to begin tanning hides at the age of fourteen, the glover's glover, who knows more about the glove business than anybody else alive, Mr. Newark Maid, my father, Lou Levov." "Look," began Mr. Newark Maid, "don't let anybody kid you tonight. I enjoy working, I enjoy the glove business, I enjoy the challenge, I don't like the idea of retiring, I think it's the first step to the grave. But none of that bothers me for one big reason—because I am the luckiest man in the world. And lucky because of one word. The biggest little word there is: family. If I was being pushed out by a competitor, I wouldn't be standing here smiling—you know me, I would be standing here shouting. But who I am being pushed out by is my own beloved son. I have been blessed with the most wonderful family a man could want: a wonderful wife, two wonderful boys, wonderful grandchildren. . . ."

\*

The Swede had Vicky bring a sheepskin into the office and he gave it to the Wharton girl to feel.

"This has been pickled but it hasn't been tanned," he told her. "It's a hair sheepskin. Doesn't have wool like a domestic sheep but hair."

"What happens to the hair?" she asked him. "Does it get used?"

"Good question. The hair is used to make carpet. Up in Amsterdam, New York. Bigelow. Mohawk. But the primary value is the skins. The hair is a by-product, and how you get the hair off the skin and all the rest of it is another story entirely. Before synthetics came along, the hair mostly went into cheap carpets. There's a company that brokered all the hair from the tanneries to the carpetmakers, but you don't want to go into that," he said, observing how before they'd really even begun she'd filled with notes the top sheet of a fresh yellow legal pad. "Though if you do," he added, touched by—and attracted by—her thoroughness, "because I suppose it does all sort of tie together, I could send you to talk to those people. I think the family is still around. It's a niche that not many people know about. It's interesting. It's *all* interesting. You've settled on an interesting subject, young lady."

"I think I have," she said, warmly smiling over at him.

"Anyway, this skin"—he'd taken it back from her and was stroking it with the side of a thumb as you might stroke the cat to get the purr going—"is called a cabretta in the industry's terminology. Small sheep. Little sheep. They only live twenty or thirty degrees north and south of the equator. They're sort of on a semiwild grazing basis—families in an African village will each own four or five sheep, and they'll all be flocked together and put out in the bush. What you were holding in your hand isn't raw anymore. We buy them in what's called the pickled stage. The hair's been removed and the preprocessing has been done to preserve them to get here. We used to bring them in raw—huge bales tied with rope and so on, skins just dried in the air. I actually have a ship's manifest—it's somewhere here, I can find it for you if you want to see it—a copy of a ship's manifest from 1790, in which skins were landed in Boston similar to what we were bringing in up to last year. And from the same ports in Africa."

It could have been his father talking to her. For all he knew, every word of every sentence uttered by him he had heard from his father's mouth before he'd finished grade school, and then two or three thousand times again during the decades they'd run the business together. Trade talk was a tradition in glove families going back hundreds of years—in the best of them, the father passed the secrets on to the son along with all the history and all the lore. It was true in the tanneries, where the tanning process is like cooking and the recipes are handed down from the father to the son, and it was true in the glove shops and it was true on the cutting-room floor. The old Italian cutters would train their sons and no one else, and those sons accepted the tutorial from their fathers as he had accepted the tutorial from his. Beginning when he was a kid of five and extending into his maturity, the father as the authority was unopposed: accepting his authority was one and the same with extracting from him the wisdom that had made Newark Maid manufacturer of the country's best ladies' glove. The Swede quickly came to love in the same wholehearted way the very things his father did and, at the factory, to think more or less as he did. And to sound as he did—if not on every last subject, then whenever a conversation came around to leather or Newark or gloves.

Not since Merry had disappeared had he felt anything like this loquacious. Right up to that morning, all he'd been wanting was to weep or to hide; but because there was Dawn to nurse and a business to tend to and his parents to prop up, because everybody else was paralyzed by disbelief and shattered to the core, neither inclination had as yet eroded the protective front he provided the family and presented to the world. But now words were sweeping him on, buoying him up, his *father's* words released by the sight of this tiny girl studiously taking them down. She was nearly as small, he thought, as the kids from Merry's third-grade class, who'd been bused the thirty-eight miles from their rural schoolhouse one day back in the late fifties so that Merry's daddy could show them how he made gloves, show them especially Merry's magical spot, the laying-off table, where, at the end of the making process, the men shaped and pressed each and every glove by pulling it carefully down over steam-heated brass hands veneered in chrome. The hands were dangerously hot and they were shiny and they stuck straight up from the table in a row, thin-looking as hands that had been flattened in a mangle and then amputated, beautifully amputated hands afloat in space like the souls of the dead. As a little girl, Merry was captivated by their enigma, called them "the pancake hands." Merry as a little girl saying to her classmates, "You want to make five dollars a dozen," which was what glovemakers were always saying and what she'd been hearing since she was born— five dollars a dozen, that was what you shot for, regardless. Merry whispering to the teacher, "People cheating on piece rates is always a problem. My daddy had to fire one man. He was stealing time," and the Swede telling her, "Honey, let Daddy conduct the tour, okay?" Merry as a little girl reveling in the dazzling idea of stealing *time*. Merry flitting from floor to floor, so proud and proprietary, flaunting her familiarity with all the employees, unaware as yet of the desecration of dignity inherent to the ruthless exploitation of the worker by the profit-hungry boss who unjustly owns the means of production.

No wonder he felt so untamed, craving to spill over with talk. Momentarily it was *then* again—nothing blown up, nothing ruined. As a family they still flew the flight of the immigrant rocket, the upward, unbroken immigrant trajectory from slave-driven great-grandfather to self-driven grandfather to self-confident, accomplished, independent father to the highest high flier of them all, the fourth-generation child for whom America was to be heaven itself. No wonder he couldn't shut up. It was impossible to shut up. The Swede was giving in to the ordinary human wish to live once again in the past—to spend a self-deluding, harmless few moments back in the wholesome striving of the past, when the family endured by a truth in no way grounded in abetting destruction but rather in eluding and outlasting destruction, overcom-

ing its mysterious inroads by creating the utopia of a rational existence.

He heard her asking, "How many come in a shipment?"

"How many skins? A couple of thousand dozen skins."

"A bale is how many?"

He liked finding that she was interested in every last detail. Yes,
talking to this attentive student up from Wharton, he was suddenly
able to like something as he had not been able to like anything, to
bear anything, even to understand anything he'd come up against
for four lifeless months. He'd felt himself instead to be perishing of
everything. "Oh, a hundred and twenty skins," he replied.

She continued taking notes as she asked, "They come right to
your shipping department?"

"They come to the tannery. The tannery is a contractor. We buy
the material and then we give it to them, and we give them the
process to use and then they convert it into leather for us. My
grandfather and my father worked in the tannery right here in
Newark. So did I, for six months, when I started in the business.
Ever been inside a tannery?"

"Not yet."

"Well, you've got to go to a tannery if you're going to write about
leather. I'll set that up for you if you'd like that. They're primitive
places. The technology has improved things, but what you'll see
isn't that different from what you would have seen hundreds of
years ago. Awful work. Said to be the oldest industry of which relics
have been found anywhere. Six-thousand-year-old relics of tanning
found somewhere—Turkey, I believe. First clothing was just skins
that were tanned by smoking them. I told you it was an interesting
subject once you get into it. My father is the leather scholar. He's
who you should be talking to, but he's living in Florida now. Start
my father off about gloves and he'll talk for two days running.
That's typical, by the way. Glovemen love the trade and everything
about it. Tell me, have you ever seen anything manufactured, Miss
Cohen?"

"I can't say I have."

"Never seen anything made?"

"Saw my mother make a cake when I was a kid."

He laughed. She had made him laugh. A feisty innocent, eager to learn. His daughter was easily a foot taller than Rita Cohen, fair where she was dark, but otherwise Rita Cohen, homely little thing though she was, had begun to remind him of Merry before her repugnance set in and she began to become their enemy. The good-natured intelligence that would just waft out of her and into the house when she came home from school overbrimming with what she'd learned in class. How she remembered everything. Everything neatly taken down in her notebook and memorized overnight.

"I'll tell you what we're going to do. We're going to bring you right through the whole process. Come on. We're going to make you a pair of gloves and you're going to watch them being made from start to finish. What size do you wear?"

"I don't know. Small."

He'd gotten up from the desk and come around and taken hold of her hand. "Very small. I'm guessing you're a four." He'd already got from the top drawer of his desk a measuring tape with a D ring at one end, and now he put it around her hand, threaded the other end through the D ring, and pulled the tape around her palm. "We'll see what kind of guesser I am. Close your hand." She made a fist, causing the hand to slightly expand, and he read the size in French inches. "Four it is. In a ladies' size that's as small as they come. Anything smaller is a child's. Come on. I'll show you how it's done."

He felt as though he'd stepped right back into the mouth of the past as they started, side by side, up the wooden steps of the old stairwell. He heard himself telling her (while simultaneously hearing his father telling her), "You always sort your skins at the northern side of the factory, where there's no direct sunlight. That way you can really study the skins for quality. Where the sunlight comes in you can't see. The cutting room and the sorting, always on the northern side. Sorting at the top. The second floor the cutting. And the first floor, where you came, the making. Bottom floor finishing and shipping. We're going to work our way from the top down."

That they did. And he was happy. He could not help himself. It was not right. It was not real. Something must be done to stop this. But she was busy taking notes, and he could not stop—a girl who knew the value of hard work and paying attention, and interested in the right things, interested in the preparation of leather and the manufacture of gloves, and to stop himself was impossible.

When someone is suffering as the Swede was suffering, asking him to be undeluded by a momentary uplifting, however dubious its rationale, is asking an awful lot.

In the cutting room, there were twenty-five men at work, about six to a table, and the Swede led her over to the oldest of them, whom he introduced as "the Master," a small, bald fellow with a hearing aid who continued working at a rectangular piece of leather—"That's the piece the glove is made from," said the Swede, "called a trank"—working at it with a ruler and shears all the time that the Swede was telling her just who this Master was. With a light heart. Still floating free. Doing nothing to stop it. Letting his father's patter flow.

The cutting room was where the Swede had got inspired to follow his father into gloves, the place where he believed he'd grown from a boy into a man. The cutting room, up high and full of light, had been his favorite spot in the factory since he was just a kid and the old European cutters came to work identically dressed in three-piece suits, starched white shirts, ties, suspenders, and cuff links. Each cutter would carefully remove the suit coat and hang it in the closet, but no one in the Swede's memory had ever removed the tie, and only a very few descended to the informality of removing the vest, let alone turning up shirtsleeves, before donning a fresh white apron and getting down to the first skin, unrolling it from the dampened muslin cloth and beginning the work of stretching. The wall of big windows to the north illuminated the hardwood cutting tables with the cool, even light you needed for grading and matching and cutting skins. The polished smoothness of the table's rounded edge, worked smooth over the years from all the animal skins stretched across it and pulled to length, was so provocative to the boy that he always had to restrain himself from rushing to press the concavity of his cheek against the convexity of the wood—restrained himself until he was alone. There was a blurry line of footprints worn into the wood floor where the men stood all day at the cutting tables, and when no one else was up there he liked to go and stand with his shoes where the floor was worn away. Watching the cutters work, he knew that they were the elite and that they knew it and the boss knew it. Though they considered themselves to be men more aristocratic than anyone around, including the boss, a cutter's working hand was proudly calloused from cutting with his big, heavy shears. Beneath those white shirts were arms and chests and shoulders full of a workingman's strength—powerful they had to be, to pull and pull on leather all their lives, to squeeze out of every skin every inch of leather there was.

A lot of licking went on, a lot of saliva went into every glove, but, as his father joked, "The customer never knows it." The cutter would spit into the dry inking material in which he rubbed the brush for the stencil that numbered the pieces he cut from each trank. Having cut a pair of gloves, he would touch his finger to his tongue so as to wet the numbered pieces, to stick them together before they were rubber-banded for the sewing forelady and the sewers. What the boy never got over were those first German cutters employed by Newark Maid, who used to keep a schooner of beer beside them and sip from it, they said, "to keep the whistle wet" and their saliva flowing. Quickly enough Lou Levov had done away with the beer, but the saliva? No. Nobody could want to do away with the saliva. That was part and parcel of all that they loved, the son and heir no less than the founding father.

"Harry can cut a glove as good as any of them." Harry, the Master, stood directly beside the Swede, indifferent to his boss's words and doing his work. "He's only been forty-one years with Newark Maid but he works at it. The cutter has to visualize how the skin is going to realize itself into the maximum number of gloves.

Then he has to cut it. Takes great skill to cut a glove right. Table cutting is an art. No two skins are alike. The skins all come in different according to each animal's diet and age, every one different as far as stretchability goes, and the skill involved in making every glove come out like every other is amazing. Same thing with the sewing. Kind of work people don't want to do anymore. You can't just take a sewer who knows how to run a traditional sewing machine, or knows how to sew dresses, and start her here on gloves. She has to go through a three- or four-month training process, has to have finger dexterity, has to have patience, and it's six months before she's proficient and reaches even eighty percent efficiency. Glove sewing is a tremendously complicated procedure. If you want to make a better glove, you have to spend money and train workers. Takes a lot of hard work and attention, all the twists and turns where the finger crotches are sewn—it's very hard. In the days when my father first opened a glove shop, the people were in it for life—Harry's the last of them. This cutting room is one of the last in this hemisphere. Our production is still always full. We still have people here who know what they're doing. Nobody cuts gloves this way anymore, not in this country, where hardly anybody's left to cut them, and not anywhere else either, except maybe in a little family-run shop in Naples or Grenoble. These were people, the people who worked here, who were in it for life. They were born into the glove industry and they died in the glove industry. Today we're constantly retraining people. Today our economy is such that people take a job here and if something comes along for another fifty cents an hour, they're gone."

She wrote all this down.

"When I first came into the business and my father sent me up here to learn how to cut, all I did was stand right here at the cutting table and watch this guy. I learned this business in the old-fashioned way. From the ground up. My father started me literally sweeping the floors. Went through every single department, getting a feel for each operation and why it was being done. From Harry I learned how to cut a glove. I wouldn't say I was a proficient glove cutter. If I cut two, three pairs a day it was a lot, but I learned the rudimentary principles—right, Harry? A demanding teacher, this fellow. When he shows you how to do something, he goes all the way. Learning from Harry almost made me yearn for my old man. First day I came up here Harry set me straight—he told me that down where he lived boys would come to his door and say, 'Could you teach me to be a glove cutter?' and he would tell them, 'You've got to pay me fifteen thousand first, because that's how much time and leather you're going to destroy till you get to the point where you can make the minimum wage.' I watched him for a full two months before he let me anywhere near a hide. An average table cutter will cut three, three and a half dozen a day. A good, fast table cutter will cut five dozen a day. Harry was cutting five and a half dozen a day. 'You think I'm good?' he told me. 'You should have seen my dad.' Then he told me about his father and the tall man from Barnum and Bailey. Remember, Harry?" Harry nodded. "When the Barnum and Bailey circus came to Newark . . . this is 1917, 1918?" Harry nodded again without stopping his work. "Well, they came to town and they had a tall man, approaching nine feet or so, and Harry's father saw him one day in the street, walking along the street, at Broad and Market, and he got so excited he ran over to the tall man and he took his shoelace off his own shoe, measured the guy's hand right out there on the street, and he went home and made up a perfect size-seventeen pair of gloves. Harry's father cut it and his mom sewed it, and they went over to the circus and gave the gloves to the tall man, and the whole family got free seats, and a big story about Harry's dad ran in the *Newark News* the next day."

Harry corrected him. "The *Star-Eagle*."

"Right, before it merged with the *Ledger*."

"Wonderful," the girl said, laughing. "Your father must have been very skilled."

"Couldn't speak a word of English," Harry told her.

"He couldn't? Well, that just goes to show, you don't have to know English," she said, "to cut a perfect pair of gloves for a man nine feet tall."

Harry didn't laugh but the Swede did, laughed and put his arm around her. "This is Rita. We're going to make her a dress glove, size four. Black or brown, honey?"

"Brown?"

From a wrapped-up bundle of hides dampening beside Harry, he picked one out in a pale shade of brown. "This is a tough color to get," the Swede told her. "British tan. You can see, there's all sorts of variation in the color—see how light it is there, how dark it is down there? Okay. This is sheepskin. What you saw in my office was pickled. This has been tanned. This is leather. But you can still see the animal. If you were to look at the animal," he said, "here it is—the head, the butt, the front legs, the hind legs, and here's the back, where the leather is harder and thicker, as it is over our own backbones. . . ."

Honey. He began calling her honey up in the cutting room and he could not stop, and this even before he understood that by standing beside her he was as close to Merry as he had been since the general store blew up and his honey disappeared. This is a French ruler, it's about an inch longer than an American ruler. . . . This is called a spud knife, dull, beveled to an edge but not sharp. . . . Now he's pulling the trank down like that, to the length again—Harry likes to bet you that he'll pull it right down to the pattern without even touching the pattern, but I don't bet him because I don't like losing. . . . This is called a fourchette. . . . See, all meticulously done. . . . He's going to cut yours and give it to me so we can take it down to the making department. . . . This is called the slitter, honey. Only mechanical process in the whole thing. A press and a die, and the slitter will take about four tranks at a time. . . .

"Wow. This is an elaborate process," said Rita.

"That it is. Hard really to make money in the glove business because it's so labor-intensive—a time-consuming process, many operations to be coordinated. Most of the glove businesses have been family businesses. From father to son. Very traditional business. A product is a product to most manufacturers. The guy who makes them doesn't know anything about them. The glove business isn't like that. This business has a long, long history."

"Do other people feel the romance of the glove business the way you do, Mr. Levov? You really are mad for this place and all the processes. I guess that's what makes you a happy man."

"Am I?" he asked, and felt as though he were going to be dissected, cut into by a knife, opened up and all his misery revealed. "I guess I am."

"Are you the last of the Mohicans?"

"No, most of them, I believe, in this business have that same feeling for the tradition, that same love. Because it does require a love and a legacy to motivate somebody to stay in a business like this. You have to have strong ties to it to be able to stick it out. Come on," he said, having managed momentarily to quash everything that was shadowing him and menacing him, succeeded still to be able to speak with great precision despite her telling him he was a happy man. "Let's go back to the making room."

This is the silking, that's a story in itself, but this is what she's going to do first. . . . This is called a piqué machine, it sews the finest stitch, called piqué, requires far more skill than the other stitches. . . . This is called a polishing machine and that is called a stretcher and you are called honey and I am called Daddy and this is called living and the other is called dying and this is called madness and this is called mourning and this is called hell, pure hell, and you have to have strong ties to be able to stick it out, this is called trying-to-go-on-as-though-nothing-has-happened and this is called paying-the-full-price-but-in-God's-name-for-what, this is called wanting-to-be-dead-and-wanting-to-find-her-and-to-kill-her-and-to-save-her-from-whatever-she-is-going-through-wherever-on-earth-she-may-be-at-this-moment, this unbridled outpouring is called blotting-out-everything *and it does not work, I am half insane, the shattering force of that bomb is too great.* . . . And then they were back at his office again, waiting for Rita's gloves to come from the finishing department, and he was repeating to her a favorite observation of his father's, one that his father had read somewhere and always used to impress visitors, and he heard himself repeating it, word for word, as his own. If only he could get her to stay and not go, if he could keep on talking about gloves to her, about gloves, about skins, about his horrible riddle, implore her, beg her, *Don't leave me alone with this horrible riddle. . . .* "Monkeys, gorillas, they have brains and we have a brain, but they don't have this thing, the thumb. They can't move it opposite the way we do. The inner digit on the hand of man, that might be the distinguishing physical feature between ourselves and the rest of the animals. And the glove protects that inner digit. The ladies' glove, the welder's glove, the rubber glove, the baseball glove, et cetera. This is the root of humanity, this opposable thumb. It enables us to make tools and build cities and everything else. More than the brain. Maybe some other animals have bigger brains in proportion to their bodies than we have. I don't know. But the hand itself is an intricate thing. It moves. There is no other part of a human being that is clothed that is such a complex moving structure. . . ." And that was when Vicky popped in the door with the size-four finished gloves. "Here's your pair of gloves," Vicky said, and gave them to the boss, who looked them over and then leaned across the desk to show them to the girl. "See the seams? The width of the sewing at the edge of the leather—that's where the quality workmanship is. This margin is probably about a thirty-second of an inch between the stitching and the edge. And that requires a high skill level, far higher than normal. If a glove is not well sewn, this edge might come to an eighth of an inch. It also will not be straight. Look at how straight these seams are. This is why a Newark Maid glove is a good glove, Rita. Because of the straight seams. Because of the fine leather. It's well tanned. It's soft. It's pliable. Smells like the inside of a new car. I love good leather, I love fine gloves, and I was brought up on the idea of making the best glove possible. It's in my blood, and nothing gives me greater pleasure"—he clutched at his own effusiveness the way a sick person clutches at any sign of health, no matter how minute—"than giving you these lovely gloves. Here," he said, "with our compliments," and, smiling, he presented the gloves to the girl, who excitedly pulled them onto her little hands—"Slowly, slowly . . . always draw on a pair of gloves by the fingers," he told her, "afterward the thumb, then draw the wrist down in place . . . always the first time draw them on slowly"—and she looked up and, smiling back at him with the pleasure that any child takes in receiving a gift, showed him with her hands in the air how beautiful the gloves looked, how beautifully they fit. "Close your hand, make a fist," the Swede said. "Feel how the glove expands where your hand expands and nicely adjusts to your size? That's what the cutter does when he does his job right—no stretch left in the length, he's pulled that all out at the table because you don't want the fingers to stretch, but an exactly measured amount of hidden stretch left in the width. That stretch in the width is a precise calculation."

"Yes, yes, it's wonderful, absolutely perfect," she told him, opening and closing her hands in turn. "God bless the precise calculators of this world," she said, laughing, "who leave stretch hidden in the width," and only after Vicky had shut the door to his glass-enclosed office and headed back into the racket of the making department did Rita add, very softly, "She wants her Audrey Hepburn scrapbook."

The next morning the Swede met Rita at the Newark airport parking lot to give her the scrapbook. From his office he had first driven to Branch Brook Park, miles in the opposite direction from the airport, where he'd got out of the car to take a solitary walk. He strolled along where the Japanese cherry trees were blooming. For a while he sat on a bench, watching the old people with their dogs. Then, back in the car, he just began to drive—through Italian north Newark and on up to Belleville, making right turns for half an hour until he determined that he was not being followed. Rita had warned him not to make his way to their rendezvous otherwise.

The second week, at the airport parking lot, he handed over the ballet slippers and the leotard Merry had last worn at age fourteen. Three days after that it was her stuttering diary.

"Surely," he said, having decided that now, with the diary in his hands, the time had come to repeat the words his wife had spoken to him before each of his meetings with Rita, meetings in which he had scrupulously done nothing other than what Rita asked and deliberately asked nothing of her in return—"surely you can now tell me something about Merry. If not where she is, how she is."

"I surely cannot," Rita said sourly.

"I'd like to speak with her."

"Well, she wouldn't like to speak with you."

"But if she wants these things . . . why else would she want these things?"

"Because they're hers."

"So are we hers, Miss."

"Not to hear her tell it."

"I can't believe that."

"She hates you."

"Does she?" he asked lightly.

"She thinks you ought to be shot."

"Yes, that too?"

"What do you pay the workers in your factory in Ponce, Puerto Rico? What do you pay the workers who stitch gloves for you in Hong Kong and Taiwan? What do you pay the women going blind in the Philippines hand-stitching designs to satisfy the ladies shopping at Bonwit's? You're nothing but a shitty little capitalist who exploits the brown and yellow people of the world and lives in luxury behind the nigger-proof security gates of his mansion."

Till now the Swede had been civil and soft-spoken with Rita no matter how menacing she was determined to be. Rita was all they had, she was indispensable, and though he did not expect to change her any by keeping his emotions to himself, each time he steeled himself to show no desperation. Taunting him was the project she had set herself; imposing her will on this conservatively dressed success story six feet three inches tall and worth millions clearly provided her with one of life's great moments. But then it was all great moments these days. They had Merry, sixteen-year-old stuttering Merry. They had a live human being and her family to play with. Rita was no longer an ordinary wavering mortal, let alone a novice in life, but a creature in clandestine harmony with the brutal way of the world, entitled, in the name of historical justice, to be just as sinister as the capitalist oppressor Swede Levov.

The *unreality* of being in the hands of this child! This loathsome kid with a head full of fantasies about "the working class"! This tiny being who took up not even as much space in the car as the Levov sheepdog, pretending that she was striding on the world stage! This utterly insignificant *pebble!* What was the whole sick enterprise other than angry, infantile egoism thinly disguised as identification with the oppressed? Her weighty responsibility to the workers of the world! Egoistic pathology bristled out of her like the hair that nuttily proclaimed, "I go wherever I want, as far as I want—all that matters is what I want!" Yes, the nonsensical hair constituted half of their revolutionary ideology, about as sound a justification for her actions as the other half—the exaggerated jargon about changing the world. She was twenty-two years old, no more than five feet tall, and off on a reckless adventure with a very potent thing way beyond her comprehension called power. Not the least need of thought. Thought just paled away beside their ignorance. They were omniscient without even thinking. No wonder his tremendous effort to hide his agitation was thwarted momentarily by uncontrollable rage, and sharply he said to her—as though he were not joined to her maniacally uncompromising mission in the most unimaginable way, as though it could matter to him that she enjoyed thinking the worst of him—"You have no idea what you're talking about! American firms make gloves in the Philippines and Hong Kong and Taiwan and India and Pakistan and all over the place—but not mine! I own two factories. *Two.* One of my factories you visited in Newark. You saw how unhappy my employees were. That's why they've worked for us for forty years, because they're exploited so miserably. The factory in Puerto Rico employs two hundred and sixty people, Miss Cohen—people we have trained, trained from scratch, people we trust, people who before we came to Ponce had barely enough work to go around. We furnish employment where there was a shortage of employment, we have taught needle skills to Caribbean people who had few if any of these skills. You know nothing. You know nothing about anything—you didn't even know what a factory *was* till I showed you one!"

"I know what a plantation is, Mr. Legree—I mean, Mr. Levov. I know what it means to run a plantation. You take good care of your niggers. Of course you do. It's called paternal capitalism. You own 'em, you sleep with 'em, and when you're finished with 'em you toss 'em out. Lynch 'em only when necessary. Use them for your sport and use them for your profit—"

"Please, I haven't two minutes' interest in childish clichés. You don't know what a factory is, you don't know what manufacturing is, you don't know what capital is, you don't know what labor is, you haven't the faintest idea what it is to be employed or what it is to be unemployed. You have no idea what *work* is. You've never held a job in your life, and if you even cared to find one, you wouldn't last a single day, not as a worker, not as a manager, not as an owner. Enough nonsense. I want you to tell me where my daughter is. That is all I want to hear from you. She needs help, she needs serious help, not ridiculous clichés. I want you to tell me where I can find her!"

"Merry never wants to see you again. *Or* that mother."

"You don't know anything about Merry's mother."

"Lady Dawn? Lady Dawn of the Manor? I know all there is to know about Lady Dawn. So ashamed of her class origins she has to make her daughter into a debutante."

"Merry shoveled cowshit from the time she was six. You don't know what you're talking about. Merry was in the 4-H Club. Merry rode tractors. Merry—"

"Fake. All fake. The daughter of the beauty queen and the captain of the football team—what kind of nightmare is that for a girl with a soul? The little shirtwaist dresses, the little shoes, the little this and the little that. Always playing with her hair. You think she wanted to fix Merry's hair because she loved her and the way she looked or because she was disgusted with her, disgusted she couldn't have a baby beauty queen that could grow up in her own image to become Miss Rimrock? Merry has to have dancing lessons. Merry has to have tennis lessons. I'm surprised she didn't get a nose job."

"You don't know what you are talking about."

"Why do you think Merry had the hots for Audrey Hepburn? Because she thought that was the best chance she had with that vain little mother of hers. Miss Vanity of 1949. Hard to believe you could fit so much vanity into that cutesy figure. Oh, but it does, it fits, all right. Just doesn't leave much room for Merry, does it?"

"You don't know what you're saying."

"No imagination for somebody who isn't beautiful and lovable and desirable. None. The frivolous, trivial beauty-queen mentality and no imagination for her own daughter. 'I don't want to see anything messy, I don't want to see anything dark.' But the world isn't like that, Dawnie dear—it *is* messy, it *is* dark. It's *hideous!*"

"Merry's mother works a farm all day. She works with animals all day, she works with farm machinery all day, she works from six A.M. to—"

"Fake. Fake. Fake. She works a farm like a fucking upper-class—"

"You don't know anything about any of this. Where is my daughter? Where is she? The conversation is pointless. Where is Merry?"

"You don't remember the 'Now You Are a Woman Party'? To celebrate her first menstruation."

"We're not talking about any party. What party?"

"We're talking about the humiliation of a daughter by her beauty-queen mother. We're talking about a mother who completely colonized her daughter's self-image. We're talking about a mother who didn't have an inch of feeling for her daughter—who has about as much depth as those gloves you make. A whole family and all you really fucking care about is skin. Ectoderm. Surface. But what's underneath, you don't have a clue. You think that was real affection she had for that stuttering girl? She tolerated that stuttering girl, but you can't tell the difference between affection and tolerance because you're too stupid yourself. Another one of your fucking fairy tales. A menstruation party. A party for it! Jesus!"

"You mean—*no*, that wasn't that. The party? You mean when she took all her friends to Whitehouse for dinner? That was her twelfth birthday. What is this 'Now You Are a Woman' crap? It was a *birthday* party. Nothing to do with menstruating. *Nothing*. Who told you this? Merry didn't tell you this. I remember that party. *She* remembers that party. It was a simple birthday party. We took all those girls down to that restaurant in Whitehouse. They had a wonderful time. We had ten twelve-year-old girls. This is all cracked. Somebody is dead. My daughter is being accused of murder."

Rita was laughing. "Mr. Law-abiding New Jersey Fucking Citizen, a little bit of fake affection looks just like love to him."

"But what you are describing never *happened*. What you are saying never *happened*. It wouldn't have mattered if it did, but *it did not*."

"Don't you know what's made Merry Merry? Sixteen years of living in a household where she was hated by that mother."

"For what? Tell me. Hated her for *what*?"

"Because she was everything Lady Dawn wasn't. Her mother hated her, Swede. It's a shame you're so late in finding out. Hated her for not being petite, for not being able to have her hair pulled back in that oh-so-spiffy country way. Merry was hated with that hatred that seeps into you like toxin. Lady Dawn couldn't have done a better job if she'd slipped poison into her a meal at a time. Lady Dawn would look at her with that look of hatred and Merry was turned into a piece of shit."

"There was no look of hatred. Something may have gone wrong . . . but that wasn't it. That wasn't hatred. I know what she's talking about. What you're calling hatred was her mother's anxiety. I know the look. But it was about the stuttering. My God, it wasn't *hatred*. It was the *opposite*. It was concern. It was distress. It was *helplessness*."

"Still protecting that wife of yours," said Rita, laughing at him again. "Incredible incomprehension. Simply incredible. You know why else she hated her? She hated her because she's your daughter. It's all fine and well for Miss New Jersey to marry a Jew. But to raise a Jew? That's a whole other bag of tricks. You have a shiksa wife, Swede, but you didn't get a shiksa daughter. Miss New Jersey is a bitch, Swede. Merry would have been better off sucking the cows if she wanted a little milk and nurturance. At least the cows have maternal feelings."

He had allowed her to talk, he had allowed himself to listen, only because he wanted to know; if something had gone wrong, of course he wanted to know. What *is* the grudge? What *is* the grievance? That was the central mystery: how did Merry get to be who she is? But none of this explained anything. This could not be what it was all about. This could not be what lay behind the blowing up of the building. No. A desperate man was giving himself over to a treacherous girl not because she could possibly begin to know what went wrong but because there was no one else to give himself over to. He felt less like someone looking for an answer than like someone mimicking someone who was looking for an answer. This whole exchange had been a ridiculous mistake. To expect this kid to talk to him truthfully. She couldn't insult him enough. Everything about their lives transformed absolutely by *her* hatred. *Here* was the hater—this insurrectionist child!

"Where is she?"

"Why do you want to know where she is?"

"I want to see her," he said.

"Why?"

"She's my daughter. Somebody is dead. My daughter is being accused of murder."

"You're really stuck on that, aren't you? Do you know how many Vietnamese have been killed in the few minutes we've had the luxury to talk about whether or not Dawnie loves her daughter? It's all relative, Swede. Death is all relative."

"Where is she?"

"Your daughter is safe. Your daughter is loved. Your daughter is fighting for what she believes in. Your daughter is finally having an experience of the world."

"Where is she, damn you!"

"She's not a possession, you know—she's not property. She's not powerless anymore. You don't own Merry the way you own your Old Rimrock house and your Deal house and your Florida condo and your Newark factory and your Puerto Rico factory and your Puerto Rican workers and all your Mercedes and all your Jeeps and all your beautiful handmade suits. You know what I've come to realize about you kindly rich liberals who own the world? Nothing is further from your understanding than the nature of reality."

No one begins like this, the Swede thought. This can't be what she is. This bullying infant, this obnoxious, stubborn, angry bullying infant cannot be my daughter's protector. She is her jailer. Merry with all her intelligence under the spell of this childlike cruelty and meanness. There's more human sense in one page of the stuttering diary than in all the sadistic idealism in this reckless child's head. Oh, to crush that hairy, tough little skull of hers—right now, between his two strong hands, to squeeze it and squeeze it until all the vicious ideas came streaming from her nose!

How does a child get to be like this? Can anyone be utterly without thoughtfulness? The answer is yes. His only contact with his daughter was this child who did not know anything and would say anything and more than likely do anything—resort to anything to excite herself. Her opinions were all stimuli: the goal was excitement.

"The paragon," Rita said, speaking to him out of the side of her mouth, as though that would make it all the easier to wreck his life. "The cherished and triumphant paragon who is in actuality the criminal. The great Swede Levov, all-American capitalist criminal."

She was some clever child crackpot gorging herself on an escapade entirely her own, a reprehensible child lunatic who'd never laid eyes on Merry except in the paper; some "politicized" crazy was what she was—the streets of New York were full of them—a criminally insane Jewish kid who'd picked up her facts about their lives from the newspapers and the TV and from the school friends of Merry's who were all out peddling the same quotation: "Quaint Old Rimrock is in for a big surprise." From the sound of it, Merry had gone around school the day before the bombing telling that to four hundred kids. That was the evidence against her, all these kids on TV claiming they heard her say it—that hearsay and her disappearance were the whole of the evidence. The post office had been blown up, and the general store along with it, but nobody had seen her anywhere near it, nobody had seen her do the thing, nobody would have even thought of her as the bomber if she hadn't disappeared. "She's been tricked!" For days Dawn went around the house crying, "She's been abducted! She's been tricked! She's somewhere right now being brainwashed! Why does everybody say she did it? Nobody's had any *contact* with her. She is not connected with it in any way *at all*. How can they believe this of a *child*? Dynamite? What does Merry have to do with dynamite? No! It isn't true! Nobody knows a *thing!*"

He should have informed the FBI of Rita Cohen's visit the day she'd come to ask for the scrapbook—at the very least should have demanded proof from her of Merry's existence. And he should have taken into his confidence someone other than Dawn, formulated strategy with a person less likely to kill herself if he proceeded other than as her desperation demanded. Answering the needs of a wife incoherent with grief, in no condition to think or act except out of hysteria, was an inexcusable error. He should have heeded his mistrust and contacted immediately the agents who had interviewed him and Dawn at the house the day after the bombing. He should have picked up the phone the moment he understood who Rita Cohen was, even while she was seated in his office. But instead he had driven directly home from the office and, because he could never calculate a decision free of its emotional impact on those who claimed his love; because seeing them suffer was his greatest hardship; because ignoring their importuning and defying their expectations, even when they would not argue reasonably or to the point, seemed to him an illegitimate use of his superior strength; because he could not disillusion anyone about the kind of selfless son, husband, and father he was; because he had come so highly *recommended* to everyone, he sat across from Dawn at the kitchen table, watching her deliver a long, sob-wracked, half-demented speech, a plea to tell the FBI nothing.

Dawn begged him to do whatever the girl wanted: it remained possible for Merry to go unapprehended if only they kept her out of sight until the destruction of the store—and the death of Dr. Conlon—had been forgotten. If only they hid her somewhere, provided for her, maybe even in another country, until this war-mad witch-hunt was over and a new time had begun; then she could be treated fairly for something she never, never could have done. "She's been *tricked!*" and he believed this himself—what else *could* a father believe?—until he heard it, day after day, a hundred times a day, from Dawn.

So he'd turned over the Audrey Hepburn scrapbook, the leotard, the ballet slippers, the stuttering book; and now he was to meet Rita Cohen at a room in the New York Hilton, this time bearing five thousand dollars in unmarked twenties and tens. And just as he'd known to call the FBI when she asked for the scrapbook, he now understood that if he acceded any further to her malicious daring there'd be no bottom to it, there would only be misery on a scale incomprehensible to all of them. With the scrapbook, the leotard, the ballet slippers, and the stuttering book he had been craftily set up; now for the disastrous payoff.

But Dawn was convinced that if he traveled over to Manhattan, got himself lost in the crowds, then, at the appointed afternoon hour, certain he wasn't being tailed, made his way to the hotel, Merry herself would be there waiting for him—an absurd fairy-tale hope for which there wasn't a shred of justification, but which he didn't have the heart to oppose, not when he saw his wife shedding another layer of sanity whenever the telephone rang.

For the first time she was got up in a skirt and blouse, gaudily floral bargain-basement stuff, and wearing high-heeled pumps; when she unsteadily crossed the carpet in them, she looked tinier even than she had in her work boots. The hairdo was as aboriginal as before but her face, ordinarily a little pot, soulless and unadorned, had been emblazoned with lipstick and painted with eye shadow, her cheekbones highlighted with pink grease. She looked like a third grader who had ransacked her mother's room, except that the cosmetics caused her expressionlessness to seem even more frighteningly psychopathic than when her face was just unhumanly empty of color.

"I have the money," he said, standing in the hotel room doorway towering above her and knowing that what he was doing was as wrong as it could be. "I have the money," he repeated, and prepared himself for the retort about the sweat and blood of the workers from whom he had stolen it.

"Oh, hi. Do come in," the girl said. *I'd like you to meet my parents. Mom and Dad, this is Seymour.* An act for the factory, an act for the hotel. "Please, do come in. Do make yourself at home."

He had the money packed into his briefcase, not just the five thousand in the tens and twenties she'd asked for but five thousand more in fifties. A total of ten thousand dollars—and with no idea why. What good would any of it do Merry? Merry wouldn't see a penny of it. Still, he said yet again—summoning all his strength so as not to lose hold—"I've brought the money you requested." He was trying hard to continue to exist as himself despite the unlikeliness of everything.

She had moved onto the bedspread and, with her legs crossed at the ankle and two pillows propped up behind her head, began lightly to sing: "Oh Lydia, oh Lydia, my encyclo-pid-e-a, oh Lydia, the tattooed lady . . ."

It was one of the old, silly songs he'd taught his little daughter once they saw that singing, she could always be fluent.

"Come to fuck Rita Cohen, have you?"

"I've come," he said, "to deliver the money."

"Let's f-f-f-fuck, D-d-d-dad."

"If you have any feeling for what everyone is going through—"

"Come off it, Swede. What do you know about 'feeling'?"

"Why are you treating us like this?"

"Boo-hoo. Tell me another. You came here to fuck me. Ask anybody. Why does a middle-aged capitalist dog come to a hotel room to meet a young piece of ass? To fuck her. Say it, just say, 'I came to fuck you. To fuck you good.' Say it, Swede."

"I don't want to say any such thing. Stop all this, please."

"I'm twenty-two years old. I do everything. I do it all. Say it, Swede."

Could this lead to Merry, this onslaught of sneering and mockery? She could not insult him enough. Was she impersonating someone, acting from a script prepared beforehand? Or was he dealing with a person who could not be dealt with because she was mad? She was like a gang member. Was she the gang *leader*, this tiny white-faced thug? In a gang the authority is given to the one who is most ruthless. Is she the most ruthless or are there others who are worse, those others who are holding Merry captive right now? Maybe she is the most intelligent. Their actress. Maybe she is the most corrupt. Their budding whore. Maybe this is all a *game* to them, middle-class kids out on a spree.

"Don't I suit you?" she asked. "No crude desires in a big guy like you? Come on, I'm not such a frightening person. You can't have met your match in little me. Look at you. Like a naughty boy. A child in terror of being disgraced. Isn't there anything else in there except your famous purity? I bet there is. I bet you've got yourself quite a pillar in there," she said. "The pillar of society."

"What is the aim of all this talk? Will you tell me?"

"The aim? Sure. To introduce you to reality. That's the aim."

"And how much ruthlessness is necessary?"

"To introduce you to reality? To get you to admire reality? To get you to partake of reality? To get you out there on the frontiers of reality? It ain't gonna be no picnic, jocko."

He had braced himself not to become entangled in her loathing for him, not to be affronted by anything she said. He was prepared for the verbal violence and prepared, this time, not to react. She was not unintelligent and she was not afraid to say anything—he knew that much. But what he had not counted on was lust, an urge—he had not counted on being assailed by something *other* than the verbal violence. Despite the repugnance inspired by the sickly whiteness of her flesh, by the comically childish makeup and the cheap cotton clothes, half reclining on the bed was a young woman half reclining on a bed, and the Swede himself, the superman of certainties, was one of the people whom he could not deal with.

"Poor thing," she said scornfully. "Little Rimrock rich boy. All locked up like that. Let's fuck, D-d-d-daddy. I'll take you to see your daughter. We'll wash your prick and zip up your fly and I'll take you to where she is."

"Do I know you will? How do I know you will?"

"Wait. See how things turn out. The worst is you get yourself some twenty-two-year-old gash. Come on, Dad. Come on over to the bed, D-d-d—"

"Stop this! My daughter has nothing to do with *any* of this! My daughter has nothing to do with *you!* You little shit—you're not fit to wipe my daughter's *shoes!* My daughter had nothing to do with that bombing. You know that!"

"Calm down, Swede. Calm down, lover boy. If you want to see your daughter as much as you say, you'll just calm down and come on over here and give Rita Cohen a nice big fuck. First the fuck, then the dough."

She had raised her knees toward her chest and now, with either foot planted on the bed, she let her legs fall open. The floral skirt was gathered up by her hips and she wore no underwear.

"There," she said softly. "Put it right there. Attack there. It's all permissible, baby."

"Miss Cohen . . ." He did not know what to reach for in his estimable strongbox of reactions—this boiling up of something so visceral in with the rhetorical was not the attack he had prepared himself for. She'd brought to the hotel a stick of dynamite to throw. This was it. To blow *him* up.

"What is it, dear?" she replied. "You must speak up like a big boy if you wish to be heard."

"What does this display have to do with what has happened?"

"Everything," she said. "You'll be surprised by what a very clear picture of things you're going to get from this display." She edged her two hands down onto her pubic hair. "Look at it," she told him and, by rolling the labia lips outward with her fingers, exposed to him the membranous tissue veined and mottled and waxy with the moist tulip sheen of flayed flesh. He looked away.

"It's a jungle down there," she said. "Nothing in its place. Nothing on the left side like anything on the right side. How many extras are there? Nobody knows. Too many to count. There are glands down there. There's another hole. There are flaps. Don't you see what this has to do with what happened? Take a look. Take a good long look."

"Miss Cohen," he said, fixing on her eyes, the one mark of beauty she was blessed with—a child's eyes, he discovered, a *good* child's eyes that had nothing in common with what she was up to, "my daughter is missing. Someone is dead."

"You don't get the point. You don't get the point about anything. Look at it. Describe it to me. Have I got it wrong? What do you see? Do you see anything? No, you don't see anything. You don't see anything because you don't look at anything."

"This makes no sense," he said. "You are subjugating no one by this. Only yourself."

"You know what size it is? Let's see what kind of guesser you are. It's small. I'm guessing that it's a size four. In a ladies' size that's as small as cunts come. Anything smaller is a child's. Let's see how you'll fit into a teeny size four. Let's see if a size four doesn't provide just the nicest, warmest, snuggest fuck you've ever dreamed of fucking. You love good leather, you love fine gloves—stick it in. But slowly, slowly. Always the first time stick it in slowly."

"Why don't you stop right now?"

"Okay, if that's your decision, that you're such a brave man you won't even *look* at it, shut your eyes and step right up and smell it. Step right up and take a whiff. The swamp. It *sucks* you in. Smell it, Swede. You know what a glove smells like. It smells like the inside of a new car. Well, this is what life smells like. Smell this. Smell the inside of a brand-new pussy."

Her dark child's eyes. Full of excitement and fun. Full of audacity. Full of unreasonableness. Full of oddness. Full of *Rita*. And only half of it was performance. To agitate. To infuriate. To arouse. She was in an altered state. The imp of upheaval. The genie of disaster. As though in being his tormentor and wrecking his family she had found the malicious meaning for her own existence. Kid Mayhem.

"Your physical restraint is amazing," she said. "Isn't there *anything* that can get you off dead center? I didn't believe there were any left like you. Any other man would have been overcome by his hard-on hours ago. You *are* a throwback. *Taste it.*"

"You're not a woman. This does not make you a woman in any way. This makes you a *travesty* of a woman. This is loathsome." Rapidly firing back at her like a soldier under attack.

"And a man who won't look, what's he a travesty of?" she asked him. "Isn't it just human *nature* to look? What about a man always averting his eyes because it's all too steeped in reality for him? Because nothing is in harmony with the world as he knows it? *Thinks* he knows it. *Taste* it! Of *course* it's loathsome, you great big Boy Scout—I'm *depraved!*" and merrily laughing off his refusal to lower his gaze by so much as an inch, she cried, "*Here!*"

She must have reached inside herself with her hand, her hand must have disappeared inside her, because a moment later it was the whole of her hand that she was extending upward to him. The tips of her fingers bore the smell of her right up to him. That he could not shut out, the fecund smell released from within.

"This'll unlock the mystery. You want to know what this has to do with what happened?" she said. "This'll tell you."

There was so much emotion in him, so much uncertainty, so much inclination and counterinclination, he was bursting so with impulse and counterimpulse that he could no longer tell which of them had drawn the line that he would not pass over. All his thinking seemed to be taking place in a foreign language, but still he knew enough not to pass over the line. He would not pick her up and hurl her against the window. He would not pick her up and throw her onto the floor. He would not pick her up for any reason. All the strength left in him would be marshaled to keep him paralyzed at the foot of the bed. He would not go near her.

The hand she'd offered him she now carried slowly up to her face, making loony, comical little circles in the air as she approached her mouth. Then, one by one, she slipped each finger between her lips to cleanse it. "You know what it tastes like? Want me to tell you? It tastes like your d-d-d-daughter."

Here he bolted the room. With all his strength.

That was it. Ten, twelve minutes and it was over. By the time the FBI responded to his phone call and got to the hotel, she was gone, as was the briefcase he had abandoned. He'd bolted not from the childlike cruelty and meanness, not even from the vicious provocation, but from something that he could no longer name.

Faced with something he could not name, he had done everything wrong.

Five years pass. In vain, the Rimrock Bomber's father waits for Rita to reappear at his office. He did not take her photograph, did not save her fingerprints—no, whenever they met, for those few minutes, she, a child, was boss. And now she's disappeared. With an agent and a sketch artist to assist him, he is asked to construct a picture of Rita for the FBI, while alone he studies the daily paper and the weekly newsmagazines, searching for the real thing. He waits for Rita's picture to turn up. She is bound to be there. Bombs are going off everywhere. In Boulder, Colorado, bombs destroy a

Selective Service office and the ROTC headquarters at the University of Colorado. In Michigan there are explosions at the university and dynamite attacks on a police headquarters and the draft board. In Wisconsin a bomb destroys a National Guard armory; a small plane flies over and drops two jars filled with gunpowder on an ammunition plant. College buildings are attacked with bombs at the University of Wisconsin. In Chicago a bomb destroys the memorial statue to the policemen killed in the Haymarket riots. In New Haven someone firebombs the home of the judge in the trial of nineteen Black Panthers accused of planning to destroy department stores, the police station, and the New Haven Railroad. Buildings are bombed at universities in Oregon, Missouri, and Texas. A Pittsburgh shopping mall, a Washington nightclub, a Maryland courtroom—all bombed. In New York there are a series of explosions—at the United Fruit Line pier, at the Marine Midland Bank, at Manufacturers Trust, at General Motors, at the Manhattan headquarters of Mobil Oil, IBM, and General Telephone and Electronics. A downtown Manhattan Selective Service center is bombed. The criminal courts building is bombed. Three Molotov cocktails go off in a Manhattan high school. Bombs explode in safe-deposit boxes in banks in eight cities. She has to have set off one of them. They'll find Rita, catch her red-handed—catch the whole bunch of them—and she will lead them to Merry.

In his pajamas, in their kitchen, he sits watching every night for her soot-covered face at the window. He sits alone in the kitchen, waiting for his enemy, Rita Cohen, to return.

A TWA jet is bombed in Las Vegas. A bomb goes off on the *Queen Elizabeth*. A bomb goes off in the Pentagon—in a women's restroom on the fourth floor of an air force area of the Pentagon! The bomber leaves a note: "Today we attacked the Pentagon, the center of the American military command. We are reacting at a time when growing U.S. air and naval shelling are being carried out against the Vietnamese; while U.S. mines and warships are used to block the harbors of the Democratic Republic of Vietnam; while plans for even more escalation are being made in Washington." *The*

*Democratic Republic of Vietnam—if I hear that from her once again,
Seymour, I swear, I'll go out of my mind.* It's their daughter! Merry
has bombed the Pentagon.

"D-d-dad!" Above the noise of the sewing machines he hears her
crying for him in his office. "D-d-d-daddy!"

Two years after her disappearance, there is a bomb blast in the
most elegant Greek Revival house on the most peaceful residential
street in Greenwich Village—three explosions and a fire destroy the
old four-story brick townhouse. The house is owned by a prosperous New York couple who are on vacation in the Caribbean. After
the explosion, two dazed young women stumble, bruised and lacer-
ated, out of the building. One of them, who is naked, is described as
being between sixteen and eighteen. The two are sheltered by a
neighbor. She gives them clothes to wear, but while the neighbor
rushes off to the bombed-out building to see what more she can do,
the two young women disappear. One is the twenty-five-year-old
daughter of the owners of the townhouse, a member of a violent
revolutionary faction of the Students for a Democratic Society
called the Weathermen. The other is unidentified. The other is Rita.
The other is *Merry.* They've roped her into this too!

He waits all night in the kitchen for his daughter and the girl
Weatherman. It is safe now—the surveillance of the house, of the
factory, the monitoring of the phones, were dropped more than a
year before. It's okay now to show up. He defrosts some soup to
feed them. He thinks back to when she had begun to lean toward
the sciences. Because of Dawn's cattle, she thought she'd be a vet. It
was the stuttering, too, that sent her into the sciences, because when
she was focused and concentrated on one of her science projects,
doing close work, the stuttering always abated a little. No parent in
the world could have seen the connection to a bomb. Everyone
would have missed it, not just him. Her interest in science was
totally innocent. *Everything* was.

The body of a young man found in the rubble of the burned-out
house is identified the next day as that of a one-time Columbia
student, a veteran of violent antiwar demonstrations, the founder

of a radical SDS splinter group, the Mad Dogs. The following day the second young woman who fled the bomb scene is identified: another radical activist but not Merry—the twenty-six-year-old daughter of a left-wing New York lawyer. Even worse is news of another corpse discovered in the rubble at the Village townhouse: the torso of a young woman. "The body of the second victim of the blast was not immediately identified and Dr. Elliott Gross, associate medical examiner, said, 'It will take some time before we have any idea who she is.'"

Alone at the kitchen table, her father knows who she is. Sixty sticks of dynamite, thirty blasting caps, a cache of homemade bombs—twelve-inch pipes packed with dynamite—are found only twenty feet from the body. It was a pipe packed with dynamite that blew up Hamlin's. She was putting the components of a new bomb together, did something wrong, and blew up the townhouse. First Hamlin's, now herself. She did do it, gave the quaint town its big surprise—and this is the result. "Dr. Gross confirmed that the torso had a number of puncture wounds, caused by nails, giving credence to the report from the police source that the bombs were apparently being wrapped to act more as antipersonnel weapons than just as explosive devices."

The next day more explosions are reported in Manhattan: three midtown buildings bombed simultaneously at about one-forty A.M. The torso's not hers! Merry is alive! Hers is not the body skewered by nails and blown apart! "As a result of the telephoned warning police arrived at the building at 1:20 and evacuated 24 janitors and other workers before the explosion occurred." The midtown bomber and the Rimrock Bomber *must* be one and the same. Had she known enough to telephone before her first bomb was set to go off, no one would have been killed and she would not be wanted for murder. So at least she has learned something, at least she is alive and there is reason to be sitting every night in the kitchen waiting to see her at the window with Rita.

He reads about the parents of the two young women who are missing and wanted for questioning in the townhouse explosion.

The mother and father of one of them appeal to their daughter on television to disclose how many people were in the building when it exploded. "If there were no others," the mother says, "the search could be called off until the surrounding walls are removed. I believe in you," the mother tells the missing daughter, who, with SDS comrades, used the house as a bomb factory, "and know that you would not wish to add more sorrow to this tragedy. Please, please telephone or wire or have someone call for you with this information. There is nothing else that we need to know except that you are safe, and nothing we need to say except that we love you and want desperately to help."

The very words spoken to the press and television by the father of the Rimrock Bomber when *she* disappeared. *We love you and want to help.* "Asked if he had been 'communicating well' with his daughter, the father of the townhouse bomber replied," and no less truthfully or miserably than the father of the Rimrock Bomber answering a similar question, "'As parents, we'd have to say no, not in recent years.'" His daughter is quoted by him as fighting for what Merry too—in her dinner-table outbursts decrying her selfish mother and father and their bourgeois life—proclaimed as the motive for her own struggle: "To change the system and give power to the 90 percent of the people who have no economic or political control now."

The father of the other missing girl is said by the police investigator to be "very uncommunicative." He says only, "I have no knowledge concerning her whereabouts." And the father of the Rimrock Bomber believes him, understands his uncommunicativeness all too well, knows better than any other father in America the burden of anguish concealed by the emotionless formulation "I have no knowledge concerning her whereabouts." If it hadn't happened to him, he would probably have marveled at the tight-lipped façade. But he knows the truth is that the missing girl's parents are drowning exactly as he is, drowning day and night in inadequate explanations.

A third body is found in the townhouse rubble, the body of an adult male. Then, a week later, a statement appears in the paper, attributed to the mother of the second missing girl, that dissipates his compassion for both sets of parents. Asked about her daughter, the mother says, "We know she is safe."

Their daughter has killed three people and they know she is safe, while about his daughter, who has not been proved by anyone to have killed anybody—about his daughter, who is being used by radical little thugs just like these privileged townhouse bombers, who has been framed, who is *innocent*—he knows nothing. What has he got to do with them? *His* daughter *didn't* do it. She no more set off the bomb at Hamlin's than she set off the bomb in the Pentagon. Since '68 thousands of bombs have been exploded in America, and his daughter has had nothing to do with a single one of them. How does he know? Because Dawn knows. Because Dawn knows for sure. Because if their daughter had been going to do it, she would never have gone around school telling kids that the town of Old Rimrock was in for a big surprise. Their daughter was too smart for that. If she had been going to do it, she would have said nothing.

Five years pass, five years searching for an explanation, going back over everything, over the circumstances that shaped her, the people and the events that influenced her, and none of it adequate to begin to explain the bombing until he remembers the Buddhist monks, the self-immolation of the Buddhist monks. . . . Of course she was just ten then, maybe eleven years old, and in the years between then and now a million things had happened to her, to them, to the world. Though she had been terrified for weeks afterward, crying about what had appeared on television that night, talking about it, awakened from her sleep by dreaming about it, it hardly stopped her in her tracks. And yet when he remembers her sitting there and seeing that monk going up in flames—as unprepared as the rest of the country for what she was seeing, a kid half watching the news with her mother and father one night after dinner—he is sure he has unearthed the reason for what happened.

It was back in '62 or '63, around the time of Kennedy's assassination, before the war in Vietnam had begun in earnest, when, as far as everybody knew, America was merely at the periphery of whatever was going haywire over there. The monk who did it was in his seventies, thin, with a shaved head and wearing a saffron robe. Cross-legged and straight-backed on an empty city street somewhere in South Vietnam, gracefully seated like that in front of a crowd of monks who had gathered to witness the event as though to observe a religious ritual, the monk had upended a large plastic canister, poured the gasoline or the kerosene, whatever it was, out of the canister and over himself and drenched the asphalt around him. Then he struck the match, and a nimbus of ragged flames came roiling out of him.

There is sometimes a performer in a circus, advertised as the fire eater, who makes flames seemingly shoot out of his mouth, and there on the street of some city in South Vietnam, this shaven-headed monk somehow made it look as though flames, instead of assaulting him from without, were shooting forward into the air from within him, not just from his mouth, however, but in an instantaneous eruption from his scalp and his face and his chest and his lap and his legs and his feet. Because he remained perfectly upright, indicating in no way that he could feel himself to be on fire, because he did not so much as move a muscle, let alone cry out, it at first looked very much like a circus stunt, as though what was being consumed were not the monk but the air, the monk setting the air on fire while no harm at all befell him. His posture remained exemplary, the posture of someone altogether elsewhere leading another life entirely, a servant of selfless contemplation, meditative, serene, a mere link in the chain of being untouched by what happened to be happening to him within view of the entire world. No screaming, no writhing, just his calmness at the heart of the flames—no pain registering on anyone on camera, only on Merry and the Swede and Dawn, horrified together in their living room. Out of nowhere and into their home, the nimbus of flames, the upright monk, and the sudden liquefaction before he keels over;

into their home all those other monks, seated along the curbstone impassively looking on, a few with their hands pressed together before them in the Asian gesture of peace and unity; into their home on Arcady Hill Road the charred and blackened corpse on its back in that empty street.

That was what had done it. Into their home the monk came to stay, the Buddhist monk calmly sitting out his burning up as though he were a man both fully alert and anesthetized. The television transmitting the immolation *must* have done it. If their set had happened to be tuned to another channel or turned off or broken, if they had all been out together as a family for the evening, Merry would never have seen what she shouldn't have seen and would never have done what she shouldn't have done. What other explanation was there? "These gentle p-p-people," she said, while the Swede gathered her into his lap, a lanky eleven-year-old girl, held her to him, rocking and rocking her in his arms, "these gentle p-p-p-people. . . ." At first she was so frightened she couldn't even cry—she could get out of her just those three words. Only later, a moment after going to bed, when she got up and with a yelp ran from her room down the corridor and into their room and asked, as she hadn't since she was five, to get into bed with them, was she able to let everything out of her, everything awful that she was thinking. All the lights remained on in their bedroom and they let her go on and on, sitting up between them in their bed and talking until there were no words left inside her to panic or terrorize her. When she fell asleep, sometime after three, it was with their lights all still burning—she would not let him turn them off—but she had at least by then talked herself out enough and cried herself out enough to succumb to her exhaustion. "Do you have to m-m-melt yourself down in fire to bring p-p-people to their s-senses? Does anybody care? Does anybody have a conscience? Doesn't anybody in this w-world have a conscience left?" Every time "conscience" crossed her lips she began to cry.

What could they tell her? How could they answer her? Yes, some people have a conscience, many people have a conscience, but unfortunately there are people who don't have a conscience, that is true. You are lucky, Merry, you have a very well-developed conscience. It's admirable for someone your age to have such a conscience. We're proud of having a daughter who has so much conscience and who cares so much about the well-being of others and who is able to sympathize with the sufferings of others. . . .

She couldn't sleep alone in her room for a week. The Swede carefully read the papers in order to be able to explain to her why the monk had done what he did. It had to do with the South Vietnamese president, General Diem, it had to do with corruption, with elections, with complex regional and political conflicts, it had to do with something about Buddhism itself. . . . But for her it had only to do with the extremes to which gentle people have to resort in a world where the great majority are without an ounce of conscience.

Just when she seemed to have gotten over the self-immolation of that elderly Buddhist monk on that street in South Vietnam and began to be able to sleep in her own room and without a light on and without awakening screaming two and three times a night, it happened again, another monk in Vietnam set himself on fire, then a third, then a fourth . . . and once that started up he found that he couldn't keep her away from the television set. If she missed a self-immolation on the evening news, she got up early to see it on the morning news before she left for school. They did not know how to stop her. What was she doing by watching and watching as though she intended never to stop watching? He wanted her to be not upset, but not to be not upset like this. Was she simply trying to make sense of it? To master her fear of it? Was she trying to figure out what it was like to be able to do something like that to yourself? Was she imagining herself as one of those monks? Was she watching because she was still appalled or was she watching now because she was excited? What was starting to unsettle him, to frighten him, was the idea that Merry was less horrified now than curious, and soon he himself became obsessed, though not, like her, by the self-immolators in Vietnam but by the change of demeanor in his eleven-year-old. That she'd always wanted to know things had made him tremendously proud of her from the time she was small, but did he really want her to want to know so much about something like this?

Is it a sin to take your own life? How can the others stand by and just watch? Why don't they stop him? Why don't they put out the flames? They stand by and let it be televised. They *want* it televised. Where has *their* morality gone? What about the morality of the television crews who are doing the filming? . . . Were these the questions she was asking herself? Were they a necessary part of her intellectual development? He didn't know. She watched in total silence, as still as the monk at the center of the flames, and afterward she would say nothing; even if he spoke to her, questioned her, she just sat transfixed before that set for minutes on end, her gaze focused somewhere else than on the flickering screen, focused inward—inward where the coherence and the certainty were supposed to be, where everything she did not know was initiating a gigantic upheaval, where nothing that registered would ever fade away. . . .

Though he didn't know how to stop her, he did try to find ways to divert her attention, to make her forget this madness that was going on halfway around the world for reasons having nothing to do with her or her family—he took her at night to drive golf balls with him, he took her to a couple of Yankee games, he took her and Dawn for a quick trip down to the factory in Puerto Rico and a week of vacation in Ponce by the beach, and then, one day, she did forget, but not because of anything he had done. It had to do with the immolations—they stopped. There were five, six, seven immolations and then there were no more, and shortly thereafter Merry did become herself again, thinking again about things immediate to her daily life and more appropriate to her years.

When this South Vietnamese president, Diem, the man against whom the martyred Buddhist monks had been directing their protest—when some months later he was assassinated (according to a CBS Sunday morning show, assassinated by the USA, by the CIA, who had propped him up in power in the first place), the news seemed to pass Merry by, and the Swede didn't convey it to her. By then this place called Vietnam no longer even existed for Merry, if it ever had except as an alien, unimaginable backdrop for a ghastly TV spectacle that had embedded itself in her impressionable mind when she was eleven years old.

She never spoke again of the martyrdom of the Buddhist monks, even after she became so committed to her own political protest. The fate of those monks back in 1963 appeared to have nothing whatsoever to do with what galvanized into expression, in 1968, a newly hatched vehemence against capitalist America's imperialist involvement in a peasant war of national liberation . . . and yet her father spent days and nights trying to convince himself that no other explanation existed, that nothing else sufficiently awful had ever happened to her, nothing causal even remotely large enough or shocking enough to explain how his daughter could be the bomber.

Five years pass. Angela Davis, a black philosophy professor of about Rita Cohen's age—born in Alabama in 1944, eight years before the birth in New Jersey of the Rimrock Bomber—a Communist professor at UCLA who is against the war, is tried in San Francisco for kidnapping, murder, and conspiracy. She is charged with supplying guns used in an armed attempt to free three black San Quentin convicts during their trial. A shotgun that killed the trial judge is said to have been purchased by her only days before the courthouse battle. For two months she lived underground, dodging the FBI, until she was apprehended in New York and extradited to California. All around the world, as far away as France and Algeria and the Soviet Union, her supporters claim that she is the victim of a political frame-up. Everywhere she is transported by the police as a prisoner, blacks and whites are waiting in the nearby streets, holding up placards for the TV cameras and shouting, "Free Angela! End political repression! End racism! End the war!"

Her hair reminds the Swede of Rita Cohen. Every time he sees that bush encircling her head he is reminded of what he should have done that afternoon in the hotel. He should not have let her get away from him, no matter what.

Now he watches the news to see Angela Davis. He reads everything he can about her. He knows that Angela Davis can get him to his daughter. He remembers how, when Merry was still at home, he went into her room one Saturday when she was off in New York, opened the bottom drawer of the dresser and, seated at her desk, read through everything in there, all that political stuff, the pamphlets, the paperbacks, the mimeographed booklets with the satiric cartoons. There was a copy of *The Communist Manifesto*. Where did she get that? Not in Old Rimrock. Who was supplying her with all this literature? Bill and Melissa. These weren't just diatribes against the war—they were written by people wanting to overthrow capitalism and the U.S. government, people screaming for violence and revolution. It was awful for him to come upon passages that, being the good student she was, she had neatly underlined, but he could not stop reading . . . and now he believes he can remember something in that drawer written by Angela Davis. There was no way of his knowing for sure because the FBI had confiscated it all, put all those publications into evidence bags, sealed them, and removed them from the house. They had dusted her room, looking for a solid set of fingerprints that they could use to match up with anything incriminating. They collected the household phone bills to trace Merry's calls. They searched her room for hiding places: pried up floorboards from beneath her rug, removed wainscoting from the walls, took the globe off the ceiling light—they went through the clothes in her closet, looking for things hidden in the sleeves. After the bombing, the state police stopped all traffic on Arcady Hill Road, closed off the area, and twelve FBI agents spent sixteen hours combing the house from the attic to the basement; when finally, in the kitchen, they searched the dustbag of the vacuum cleaner for "papers," Dawn had let out a scream. And all because of Merry's reading Karl Marx and Angela Davis! Yes, now he remembers clearly sitting at Merry's desk trying to read Angela

Davis himself, working at it, wondering how his child did it, think-ing, Reading this stuff is like deep-sea diving. It's like being in an Aqua-Lung with the window right up against your face and the air in your mouth and no place to go, no place to move, no place to put a crowbar and escape. It's like reading those tiny pamphlets and illustrated holy cards about the saints that the old lady Dwyer used to give her in Elizabeth. Luckily the child outgrew them, but for a while, whenever she misplaced her fountain pen, she'd pray to St. Anthony, and whenever she thought she hadn't studied enough for a test, she prayed to St. Jude, and whenever her mother made her spend a Saturday morning cleaning up her messy room, she prayed to St. Joseph, the patron saint of laborers. Once when she was nine and some diehards down at Cape May reported that the Virgin Mary appeared to their children in their barbecue and people flocked in from miles around and kept vigil in their yard, Merry was fascinated, perhaps less by the mystery of the Virgin's appear-ance in New Jersey than by a child's having been singled out to see her. "I wish I could see that," she told her father, and she told him about how apparitions of the Virgin Mary had appeared to three shepherd children in Fátima, in Portugal, and he nodded and held his tongue, though when her grandfather got wind of the Cape May vision from his granddaughter, he said to her, "I guess next they'll see her at the Dairy Queen," a remark Merry repeated down in Elizabeth. Grandma Dwyer then prayed to St. Anne to help Merry stay Catholic despite her upbringing, but in a couple of years saints and prayer had disappeared from Merry's life; she stopped wearing the Miraculous Medal, with the impression on it of the Blessed Virgin, which she had sworn to Grandma Dwyer to wear "perpetually" without even taking it off to bathe. She outgrew the saints just as she would have outgrown the Communism. And she *would* have outgrown it—Merry outgrew everything. It was merely a matter of months. Maybe weeks and the stuff in that drawer would have been completely forgotten. All she had to do was wait. If only she could have waited. That was Merry's story in a nutshell. She was impatient. She was always impatient. Maybe it was the stuttering that made her impatient, I don't know. But whatever it was she was passionate about, she was passionate for a year, she did it in a year, and then she got rid of it overnight. Another year and she would have been ready for college. And by then she would have found something new to hate and new to love, something new to be intense about, and that would have been that.

At the kitchen table one night Angela Davis appears to the Swede, as Our Lady of Fátima did to those children in Portugal, as the Blessed Virgin did down in Cape May. He thinks, Angela Davis can get me to her—and there she is. Alone in the kitchen at night the Swede begins to have heart-to-heart talks with Angela Davis, at first about the war, then about everything important to both of them. As he envisions her, she has long lashes and wears large hoop earrings and is more beautiful even than she looks on television. Her legs are long and she wears colorful minidresses to expose them. The hair is extraordinary. She peers defiantly out of it like a porcupine. The hair says, "Do not approach if you don't like pain."

He tells her whatever she wants to hear, and whatever she tells him he believes. He has to. She praises his daughter, whom she calls "a soldier of freedom, a pioneer in the great struggle against repression." He should take pride in her political boldness, she says. The antiwar movement is an anti-imperialist movement, and by lodging a protest in the only way America understands, Merry, at sixteen, is in the forefront of the movement, a Joan of Arc of the movement. His daughter is the spearhead of the popular resistance to a fascist government and its terrorist suppression of dissent. What she did was criminal only inasmuch as it is defined as criminal by a state that is itself criminal and will commit ruthless aggression anywhere in the world to preserve the unequal distribution of wealth and the oppressive institutions of class domination. The disobedience of oppressive laws, she explains to him, including violent disobedience, goes back to abolitionism—his daughter is one with John Brown!

Merry's was not a criminal act but a political act in the power struggle between the counterrevolutionary fascists and the forces of

resistance—blacks, Chicanos, Puerto Ricans, Indians, draft resist-
ers, antiwar activists, heroic white kids like Merry herself, working,
either by legal means or by what Angela calls extralegal means, to
overthrow the capitalist-inspired police state. And he should not
fear for her fugitive life—Merry is not alone, she is part of an army
of eighty thousand radical young people who have gone underground the better to fight the social wrongs fostered by an oppressive politico-economic order. Angela tells him that everything he
has heard about Communism is a lie. He must go to Cuba if he
wants to see a social order that has abolished racial injustice and the
exploitation of labor and is in harmony with the needs and aspira-
tions of its people.

Obediently he listens. She tells him that imperialism is a weapon
used by wealthy whites to pay black workers less for their work, and
that's when he seizes the opportunity to tell her about the black
forelady, Vicky, thirty years with Newark Maid, a tiny woman of
impressive wit, stamina, and honesty, with twin sons, Newark Rut-
gers graduates, Donny and Blaine, both of them now in medical
school. He tells her how Vicky alone stayed with him in the building, round the clock, during the '67 riots. On the radio, the mayor's
office was advising everyone to get out of the city immediately, but
he had stayed, because he thought that by being there he could
perhaps protect the building from the vandals and also for the
reason that people stay when a hurricane hits, because they cannot
leave behind the things they cherish. For something like that reason, Vicky stayed.

In order to appease any rioters who might be heading from
South Orange Avenue with their torches, Vicky had made signs and
stuck them where they would be visible, in Newark Maid's first-
floor windows, big white cardboard signs in black ink: "Most of
this factory's employees are NEGROES." Two nights later every
window with a sign displayed in it was shot out by a band of white
guys, either vigilantes from north Newark or, as Vicky suspected,
Newark cops in an unmarked car. They shot the windows out and
drove away, and that was the total damage done to the Newark

Maid factory during the days and nights when Newark was on fire. And he tells this to St. Angela.

A platoon of the young National Guardsmen who were on Bergen Street to seal off the riot zone had camped out back by the Newark Maid loading dock on the second day of fighting, and when he and Vicky went down with hot coffee, Vicky talked to each of them—uniformed kids, in helmets and boots, conspicuously armed with knives and rifles and bayonets, white country boys up from south Jersey who were scared out of their wits. Vicky told them, "Think before you shoot into somebody's window! These aren't 'snipers'! These are people! These are good people! Think!" The Saturday afternoon the tank sat out in front of the factory—and the Swede, seeing it there, could at last phone Dawn to tell her, "We'll make it"—Vicky had gone up and knocked on the lid with her fists until they opened up. "Don't go nuts!" she shouted at the soldiers inside. "Don't go crazy! People have to live here when you're gone! This place is their *home!*" There'd been a lot of criticism afterward of Governor Hughes for sending in tanks, but not from the Swede—those tanks put a stop to what could have been total disaster. Though this he does not say to Angela.

For the two worst, most terrifying days, Friday and Saturday, July 14 and 15, 1967, while he kept in touch with the state police on a walkie-talkie and with his father on the phone, Vicky would not desert him. She told him, "This is mine too. You just own it." He tells Angela how he knew the way things worked between Vicky and his family, knew it was an old and lasting relationship, knew how close they all were, but he had never properly understood that her devotion to Newark Maid was no less than his. He tells Angela how, after the riots, after living under siege with Vicky at his side, he was determined to stand alone and not leave Newark and abandon his black employees. He does not, of course, tell her that he wouldn't have hesitated—and wouldn't still—to pick up and move were it not for his fear that, if he should join the exodus of businesses not yet burned down, Merry would at last have her airtight case against him. *Victimizing black people and the working class and the poor solely for self-gain, out of filthy greed!*

In the idealistic slogans there was no reality, not a drop of it, and yet what else could he do? He could not provide his daughter with the justification for doing something crazy. So he stayed in Newark, and after the riots Merry did something crazier than crazy. The Newark riots, then the Vietnam War; the city, then the entire country, and that took care of the Seymour Levovs of Arcady Hill Road. First the one colossal blow—seven months later, in February '68, the devastation of the next. The factory under siege, the daughter at large, and that took care of their future.

On top of everything else, after the sniper fire ended and the flames were extinguished and twenty-one Newarkers were counted dead by gunfire and the National Guard was withdrawn and Merry had disappeared, the quality of the Newark Maid line began to fall off because of negligence and indifference on the part of his employees, a marked decline in workmanship that had the effect of sabotage even if he couldn't call it that. He does not tell Angela, for all that he is tempted to, about the struggle his decision to stay on in Newark has precipitated between himself and his own father; might only antagonize her against Lou Levov and deter her from leading them to Merry.

"What we've got now," his father argued each time he flew up from Florida to plead with his son to get the hell out before a second riot destroyed the rest of the city, "is that every step of the way we're no longer making one step, we're making two, three, and four steps. Every step of the way you have got to go back a step to get it cut again, to get it stitched again, and nobody is doing a day's work and nobody is doing it right. A whole business is going down the drain because of that son of a bitch LeRoi Jones, that Peek-A-Boo-Boopy-Do, whatever the hell he calls himself in that goddamn hat. I built this with my *hands*! With my blood! They think somebody gave it to me? Who? Who gave it to me? Who gave me anything, ever? Nobody! What I have I built! With work—w-o-r-k! But they took that city and now they are going to take that business and everything that I built up a day at a time, an *inch* at a time, and they are going to leave it *all* in ruins! And that'll do 'em a world of good! They burn down their own houses—that'll show whitey! Don't fix 'em up—burn 'em down. Oh, that'll do wonders for a man's black pride—a totally ruined city to live in! A great city turned into a total nowhere! They're just going to love living in that! And *I* hired 'em! How's that for a laugh? *I hired 'em!* 'You're nuts, Levov'—this is what my friends in the steam room used to tell me—'What are you hiring schvartzes for? You won't get gloves, Levov, you'll get dreck.' But I hired 'em, treated them like human beings, kissed Vicky's ass for twenty-five years, bought all the girls a Thanksgiving turkey every goddamn Thanksgiving, came in every morning with my tongue hanging out of my mouth so I could lick their asses with it. 'How is everybody,' I said, 'how are we all, my time is yours, I don't want you complaining to anybody but me, here at this desk isn't just a boss, here is your ally, your buddy, your friend.' And the party I gave for Vicky's twins when they graduated? And what a jerk-off I was. *Am.* To this day! I'm by the pool and my wonderful friends look up from the paper and they tell me they ought to take the schvartzes and line 'em up and shoot 'em, and I'm the one who has to remind them that's what Hitler did to the Jews. And you know what they tell me, as an answer? 'How can you compare schvartzes to Jews?' They are telling me to shoot the schvartzes and I am hollering no, and meanwhile I'm the one whose business they are ruining because they cannot make a glove that fits. Bad cutting, the stretch is wrong—the glove won't even go *on.* Careless people, careless, and it is inexcusable. One operation goes wrong, the whole operation is spoiled all the way through, and, still, when I am arguing with these fascist bastards, Seymour, Jewish men, men of my age who have seen what I've seen, who should know better *a million times over,* when I am arguing with them, *I am arguing against what I should be arguing for!*" "Well, sometimes you wind up doing that," the Swede said. "Why? Tell me why!" "I suppose out of conscience." "*Conscience?* Where is *theirs,* the schvartzes' conscience? Where is *their* conscience after working for me for twenty-five years?"

Whatever it cost him to deny his father relief from his suffering, stubbornly to defy the truth of what his father was saying, the Swede could not submit to the old man's arguments, for the simple reason that if Merry were to learn—and she would, through Rita Cohen, if Rita Cohen actually had anything to do with her—that Newark Maid had fled the Central Avenue factory she would be all too delighted to think, "He did it! He's as rotten as the rest! My own father! Everything justified by the profit principle! Everything! Newark's just a black colony for my own father. Exploit it and exploit it and then, when there's trouble, fuck it!"

These thoughts and thoughts even stupider—engendered in her by the likes of *The Communist Manifesto*—would surely foreclose any chance of ever seeing her again. Despite all that he could tell Angela Davis that might favorably influence her about his refusal to desert Newark and his black employees, he knows that the personal complications of that decision could not begin to conform to the utter otherworldliness of the ideal of St. Angela, and so he decides instead to explain to a vision that he is one of two white trustees (this is not true—the father of a friend is the trustee) of an antipoverty organization that meets regularly in Newark to promote the city's comeback, which (also not true—how could it be?) he still believes in. He tells Angela that he attends evening meetings all over Newark despite his wife's fears. He is trying to do everything he can for the liberation of her people. He reminds himself to repeat these words to her every night: the liberation of the people, America's black colonies, the inhumanity of the society, embattled humanity.

He does not tell Angela that his daughter is childishly boasting, lying in order to impress her, that his daughter knows nothing about dynamite or revolution, that these are just words to her and she blurts them out to make herself feel powerful despite her speech impediment. No, Angela is the person who knows Merry's whereabouts, and if Angela has come to him like this, it's no mere friendly visit. Why would Angela Davis drop out of nowhere into the Levovs' Old Rimrock kitchen at midnight every single night if she weren't the revolutionary leader assigned to looking after his daughter's well-being? What's in it for her otherwise—why else would she keep coming back?

So he says to her *yes,* his daughter *is* a soldier of freedom, yes, he *is* proud, yes, everything he has heard about Communism *is* a lie, yes, the United States *is* concerned solely with making the world safe for business and keeping the have-nots from encroaching on the haves—yes, the United States is responsible for oppression *everywhere.* Everything is justified by her cause, Huey Newton's cause, Bobby Seale's cause, George Jackson's cause, Merry Levov's cause. Meanwhile he mentions Angela's name to no one, certainly not to Vicky, who thinks Angela Davis is a troublemaker and who says as much to the girls at work. Alone then and in secret he prays—ardently prays to God, to Jesus, to anyone, to the Blessed Virgin, to St. Anthony, St. Jude, St. Anne, St. Joseph—for Angela's acquittal. And when it happens he is jubilant. She is free! But he does not send her the letter that he sits up writing in the kitchen that night, nor does he some weeks later when Angela, in New York, behind a four-sided shield of bulletproof glass and before fifteen thousand exultant supporters, demands the freedom of political prisoners deprived of due process and unjustly imprisoned. Free the Rimrock Bomber! Free my daughter! Free her, please! cries the Swede. "I think it's about time," Angela says, "for all of us to begin to teach the rulers of this country a few lessons," and yes, cries the Swede, yes, it *is* about time, a socialist revolution in the United States of America! But nonetheless he remains alone at his kitchen table because he still cannot do anything that he should do or believe anything that he should believe or even know any longer what it is he does believe. Did she do it or didn't she do it? He should have fucked Rita Cohen, if only to find out—fucked the conniving little sexual terrorist until she was his slave! Until she took him to the hideout where they made the bombs! *If you want to see your daughter as much as you say, you'll just calm down and come over here and give Rita Cohen a nice big fuck.* He should have looked at her cunt and tasted it and fucked her. Is that what any father would have done? If he would do anything for Merry, why not that? Why did he run?

And this is just a part of what is meant by "Five years pass." A very tiny part. Everything he reads or sees or hears has a single significance. Nothing is impersonally perceived. For one whole year he cannot go into the village without seeing where the general store used to be. To buy a newspaper or a quart of milk or a tank of gas he has to drive almost clear into Morristown, and so does everybody else in Old Rimrock. The same to buy a stamp. Basically the village is one street. Going east there is the new Presbyterian church, a white pseudocolonial building that doesn't look like much of anything and that replaced the old Presbyterian church that burned to the ground in the twenties. Just a little ways from the church are The Oaks, a pair of two-hundred-year-old oak trees that are the town's pride. Some thirty yards beyond The Oaks is the old blacksmith shop that was converted, just before Pearl Harbor, into the Home Shop, where local women go to buy wallpaper and lampshades and decorative knicknacks and to get advice from Mrs. Fowler about interior decorating. Down at the far end of the street is the auto-repair garage run by Perry Hamlin, a hard-drinking cousin of Russ Hamlin's who also canes chairs, and then beyond that, encompassing some five hundred acres, is the rolling terrain of the dairy farm owned and worked by Paul Hamlin, who is Perry's younger brother. Hills like these where Hamlins have farmed now for close to two hundred years run northeast to southwest, in a thirty- or forty-mile-wide swath, crossing north Jersey at around Old Rimrock, a range of small hills that continue up into New York to become the Catskills and from there all the way up to Maine.

Diagonally across from where the store used to be is the yellow-stuccoed six-room schoolhouse. Before they sent her to the Montessori school and then on to Morristown High, Merry had been a pupil there for the first four grades. Every kid who goes there now sees every day where the store used to be, as do their teachers, as do their parents when they drive into the village. The Community Club meets at the school, they hold their chicken suppers there, people vote there, and everybody who drives up there and sees where the store used to be thinks about the explosion and the good man it killed, thinks about the girl who set off the explosion, and, with varying degrees of sympathy or of contempt, thinks about her family. Some people are overly friendly; others, he knows, try their best to avoid running into him. He receives anti-Semitic mail. It is so vile it sickens him for days on end. He overhears things. Dawn overhears things. "Lived here all my life. Never saw anything like this before." "What can you expect? They have no business being out here to begin with." "I thought they were nice people, but you never know." An editorial from the local paper, recording the tragedy and commemorating Dr. Conlon, is thumbtacked to the Community Club bulletin board and hangs there, right out by the street. There is no way that the Swede can take it down, much as he would like to, for Dawn's sake at least. You would think that what with exposure to the rain and the wind and the sun and the snow the thing would rot away in a matter of weeks, but it not only remains intact but is almost completely legible for one whole year. The editorial is called "Dr. Fred." "We live in a society where violence is becoming all too prevalent . . . we do not know why and we may never understand . . . the anger that all of us feel . . . our hearts go out to the victim and his family, to the Hamlins, and to an entire community that is trying to understand and to cope with what has happened . . . a remarkable man and a wonderful physician who touched all our lives . . . a special fund in memory of 'Doctor Fred' . . . to contribute to this memorial, which will help indigent local families in time of medical need . . . in this time of grief, we must rededicate ourselves, in his memory. . . ." Alongside the editorial is an article headlined "Distance Heals All Wounds," which begins, "We'd all just as soon forget . . ." and continues, ". . . that soothing distance will come quicker to some than others. . . . The Rev. Peter

Baliston of the First Congregational Church, in his sermon, sought to find some good in all the tragedy . . . will bring the community closer together in a shared sorrow. . . . The Rev. James Viering of St. Patrick's Church gave an impassioned homily. . . ." Beside that article is a third clipping, one that has no business being there, but he cannot tear that one down any more than he can go ahead and tear down the others, so it, too, hangs there for a year. It is the interview with Edgar Bartley—both the interview and the picture of Edgar from the paper, showing him standing in front of his family's house with a shovel and his dog and behind him the path to the house freshly cleared of snow. Edgar Bartley is the boy from Old Rimrock who'd taken Merry to the movies in Morristown some two years before the bombing. He was a year ahead of her at the high school, a boy as tall as Merry and, as the Swede remembered him, nice enough looking though terrifically shy and a bit of an oddball. The newspaper story describes him as Merry's boyfriend at the time of the bombing, though as far as her parents knew, Merry's date with Edgar Bartley two years earlier was the one and only date she'd ever had with him or with anyone. Whatever, someone has underlined in black all the quotations attributed to Edgar. Maybe a friend of his did it as a joke, a high school joke. Maybe the article with the photograph was hung there as a joke in the first place. Joke or not, there it remains, month after month, and the Swede cannot get rid of it. "It doesn't seem real. . . . I never thought she would do something like this. . . . I knew her as a very nice girl. I never heard her say anything vicious. I'm sure something snapped. . . . I hope they find her so that she can get the help that she needs. . . . I always thought of Old Rimrock as a place where nothing can happen to you. But now I'm like everybody, I'm looking over my shoulder. It's going to take time before things return to normal. . . . I'm just moving on. I have to. I have to forget about it. Like nothing happened. But it's very sad."

The only solace the Swede can take from the Community Club bulletin board is that no one has posted there the clipping whose headline reads "Suspected Bomber Is Described as Bright, Gifted but with 'Stubborn Streak.'" That one he *would* have torn down. He would have had to go there in the middle of the night and just do it. This one article is no worse, probably, than any of the others that were appearing then, not just in their local weekly but in the New York papers—the *Times,* the *Daily News,* the *Daily Mirror,* the *Post;* in the Jersey dailies—the *Newark News,* the *Newark Star-Ledger,* the *Morristown Record,* the *Bergen Record,* the *Trenton Times,* the *Paterson News;* in the nearby Pennsylvania papers—the *Philadelphia Inquirer,* the *Philadelphia Bulletin,* and the *Easton Express;* and in *Time* and *Newsweek.* Most of the papers and the wire services dropped the story after the first week, but the *Newark News* and the *Morristown Record* in particular wouldn't let up—the *News* had three star reporters on the case, and both papers were churning out their stories about the Rimrock Bomber every single day for weeks. The *Record,* with its local orientation, couldn't stop reminding its readers that the Rimrock bombing was the most shattering disaster in Morris County since the September 12, 1940, Hercules Powder Company explosion, some twelve miles away in Kenvil, when fifty-two people were killed and three hundred injured. There had been a murder of a minister and a choirmaster in the late twenties, down in Middlesex County, in a lane just outside New Brunswick, and in the Morris village of Brookside there had been a murder by an inmate who had walked off the grounds of the Greystone mental asylum, visited his uncle in Brookside, and split the man's head open with an ax—and these stories, too, are dug up and rehashed. And, of course, the Lindbergh kidnapping down in Hopewell, New Jersey, the abduction and murder of the infant son of Charles A. Lindbergh, the famous transatlantic aviator—that, too, the papers luridly recall, reprinting details over thirty years old about the ransom, the baby's battered corpse, the Flemington trial, reprinting newspaper excerpts from April 1936 about the electrocution of the convicted kidnapper-murderer, an immigrant carpenter named Bruno Hauptmann. Day after day, Merry Levov is mentioned in the context of the region's slender history of atrocities—her name several times appearing right alongside Hauptmann's—and yet nothing of what's written wounds him as savagely as the story about her "stubborn streak" in the local weekly. There is something concealed there—yet implicit—a degree of provincial smugness, of simplemindedness, of sheer stupidity, that is so enraging to him that he could not have borne to see it hanging up for everybody to read and to shake their heads over at the Community Club bulletin board. Whatever Merry may or may not have done, he could not have allowed her life to be on display like that just outside the school.

## SUSPECTED BOMBER IS DESCRIBED AS BRIGHT, GIFTED BUT WITH "STUBBORN STREAK"

To her teachers at Old Rimrock Community School, Meredith "Merry" Levov, who allegedly bombed Hamlin's General Store and killed Old Rimrock's Dr. Fred Conlon, was known as a multi-talented child, an excellent student and somebody who never challenged authority. People looking to her childhood for some clue about her alleged violent act remained stymied when they remembered her as a cooperative girl full of energy.

"We are in disbelief," ORCS Principal Eileen Morrow said about the suspected bomber. "It is hard to understand why this happened."

As a student at the six-room elementary school, Principal Morrow said, Merry Levov was "very helpful and never in trouble."

"She's not the kind of person who would do that," Mrs. Morrow said. "At least not when we knew her here."

At ORCS, Merry Levov had a straight A average and was involved in school activities, Mrs. Morrow said, and was well liked by both students and faculty.

"She was hard-working and enthusiastic and set very high standards for herself," Mrs. Morrow said. "Her teachers respected her as a quality student and her peers admired her."

At ORCS Merry Levov was a talented art student and a leader in team sports, particularly kickball. "She was just a normal kid growing up," Mrs. Morrow said. "This is something we would never have dreamt could happen," the principal said. "Unfortunately, nobody can see the future."

Mrs. Morrow said that Meredith associated with "model students" at the school, though she did show a "stubborn streak," for example, sometimes refusing to do school assignments which she thought unnecessary.

Others remembered the alleged bomber's stubborn streak, when she went on to become a student at Morristown High School. Sally Curren, a 16-year-old classmate, described Meredith as someone with an attitude she described as "arrogant and superior to everybody else."

But 16-year-old Barbara Turner said Meredith "seemed nice enough, though she had her beliefs."

Though Morristown High students asked about Merry had many different impressions, all the students who knew her agreed that she "talked a lot about the Vietnam war." Some students remembered her "lashing out in anger" if somebody else opposed her way of thinking about the presence of American troops in Vietnam.

According to her homeroom teacher, Mr. William Paxman, Meredith had been "working hard and doing well, A's or B's" and had expressed a strong interest in attending his alma mater, Penn State.

"If you mention her family, people say, 'What a nice family,'" Mr. Paxman said. "We just can't believe this has happened."

The only ominous note about her activities came from one of the alleged bomber's teachers who has been interviewed by agents from the FBI. "They told me, 'We have received a great deal of information about Miss Levov.'"

For a year there is "where the store used to be." Then construction begins on a new store, and month after month he watches it

going up. One day a big red, white, and blue banner appears—
"Greatly Expanded! New! New! New! McPherson's Store!"—an-
nouncing the grand opening on the Fourth of July. He has to sit
Dawn down and tell her they are going to shop at the new store like
everyone else and, though for a while it will not be easy for them,
eventually. . . . But it is never easy. He cannot go into the new store
without remembering the old store, even though the Russ Hamlins
have retired and the new store is owned by a young couple from
Easton who care nothing about the past and who, in addition to an
expanded general store, have put in a bakery that turns out delicious cakes and pies as well as bread and rolls baked fresh every day.
At the back of the store, alongside the post office window, there is
now a little counter where you can buy a cup of coffee and a fresh
bun and sit and chat with your neighbor or read your paper if you
want to. McPherson's is a tremendous improvement over Hamlin's,
and soon everybody around seems to have forgotten their blown-
up old-fashioned country store, except for the local Hamlins and
for the Levovs. Dawn cannot go near the new place, simply refuses
to go in there, while the Swede makes it his business, on Saturday
mornings, to sit at the counter with his paper and a cup of coffee,
despite what anybody who sees him there may be thinking. He buys
his Sunday paper there too. He buys his stamps there. He could
bring stamps home from his office, could do all the family mailing
in Newark, but he prefers to patronize the post office window at
McPherson's and to linger there musing over the weather with
young Beth McPherson the way he used to enjoy the same moment
with Mary Hamlin, Russ's wife.

That is the outer life. To the best of his ability, it is conducted just
as it used to be. But now it is accompanied by an inner life, a
gruesome inner life of tyrannical obsessions, stifled inclinations,
superstitious expectations, horrible imaginings, fantasy conversations, unanswerable questions. Sleeplessness and self-castigation
night after night. Enormous loneliness. Unflagging remorse, even
for that kiss when she was eleven and he was thirty-six and the two
of them, in their wet bathing suits, were driving home together

from the Deal beach. Could *that* have done it? Could *anything* have done it? Could *nothing* have done it?

*Kiss me the way you k-k-kiss umumumother.*

And in the everyday world, nothing to be done but respectably carry on the huge pretense of living as himself, with all the shame of masquerading as the ideal man.

# 5

Dear Mr. Levov,

Merry is working in the old dog and cat hospital on New Jersey Railroad Avenue in the Ironbound Section of Newark, 115 N.J. Railroad Avenue, five minutes from Penn Station. She is there every day. If you wait outside you can catch her leaving work and heading home just after four P.M. She doesn't know I'm writing this letter to you. I am at the breaking point and can't go on. I want to go away but I can leave her to no one. You have to take over. Though I warn you that if you tell her that it was from me that you discovered her whereabouts, you will be doing her serious harm. She is an incredible spirit. She has changed everything for me. I got into this over my head because I couldn't ever resist her power. That is too much to get into here. You must believe me when I tell you that I never said anything or did anything other than what Merry demanded me to say and to do. She is an overwhelming force. You and I were in the same boat. I lied to her only once. That was about what happened at the hotel. If I had told her that you refused to make love with me she would have refused to take the money. She would have been back begging on the streets. I would never have made you suffer so if I hadn't the strength of my love for Merry to help me. To you that will sound crazy. I am telling you it is so. Your daughter is divine. You cannot be in the presence of such suffering without succumbing to its holy power. You don't know what a nobody I was before I met Merry. I was headed for oblivion. But I can't take anymore. YOU MUST NOT MENTION ME TO MERRY EXCEPT AS SOMEONE WHO TORMENTED YOU EXACTLY AS I DID. DO NOT MENTION THIS LETTER IF YOU CARE ABOUT MERRY'S SURVIVAL. You must take every precaution before getting to the hospital. She could not survive the FBI. Her name is Mary Stoltz. She must be allowed to fulfill her destiny. We can only stand as witnesses to the anguish that sanctifies her.

The Disciple Who Calls Herself "Rita Cohen"

He could never root out the unexpected thing. The unexpected thing would be waiting there unseen, for the rest of his life ripening, ready to explode, just a millimeter behind everything else. The unexpected thing was the other *side* of everything else. He had already parted with everything, then remade everything, and now, when everything appeared to be back under his control, he was being incited to part with everything again. And if that should happen, the unexpected thing becoming the only thing . . .

Thing, thing, thing, thing—but what other word was tolerable? They could not be forever in bondage to this fucking thing! For five years he had been waiting for just such a letter—it had to come. Every night in bed he begged God to deliver it the following morning. And then, in this amazing transitional year, 1973, the year of Dawn's miracle, during these months when Dawn was giving herself over to designing the new house, he had begun to dread what he might find in the morning's mail or hear each time he picked up the phone. How could he allow the unexpected thing back into their lives now that Dawn had ruled out of their lives forever the improbability of what had happened? Leading his wife back to herself had been like flying them through a five-year storm. He had fulfilled every demand. To disentangle her from her horror, there

wasn't anything he had omitted to do. Life had returned to something like its recognizable proportions. Now tear the letter up and
throw it away. Pretend it never arrived.

Because Dawn had twice been hospitalized in a clinic near
Princeton for suicidal depression, he had come to accept that the
damage was permanent and that she would be able to function only
under the care of psychiatrists and by taking sedatives and an anti-
depressant medication—that she would be in and out of psychiatric hospitals and that he would be visiting her in those places for
the rest of their lives. He imagined that once or twice a year he
would find himself sitting at the side of her bed in a room where
there were no locks on the door. There would be flowers he'd sent
her in a vase on the writing desk; on a windowsill, the ivy plants
he'd brought from her study, thinking it might help her to care for
something; on the bedside table framed photographs of himself
and Merry and Dawn's parents and brother. At the side of the bed
he himself would be holding her hand while she sat propped up
against the pillows in her Levi's and a big turtleneck sweater and
wept. "I'm frightened, Seymour. I'm frightened all the time." He
would sit patiently there beside her whenever she began to tremble
and he would tell her to just breathe, slowly breathe in and out and
think of the most pleasant place on earth that she knew of, imagine
herself in the most wonderfully calming place in the entire world,
a tropical beach, a beautiful mountain, a holiday landscape from
her childhood . . . and he would do this even when the trembling
was brought on by a tirade aimed at him. Sitting up on the bed,
with her arms crossed in front of her as though to warm herself,
she would hide the whole of her body inside the sweater—turn
the sweater into a tent by extending the turtleneck up over her
chin, stretching the back under her buttocks, and drawing the front
across her bent knees, down over her legs, and beneath her feet.
Often she sat tented like that all the time he was there. "You know
when I was in Princeton last? I do! I was invited by the governor. To
his mansion. Here, to Princeton, to his mansion. I had dinner at the
governor's mansion. I was twenty-two—in an evening gown and

scared to death. His chauffeur drove me from Elizabeth and I danced in my crown with the governor of New Jersey—so how did *this* happen? How have I wound up *here?* You, that's how! You wouldn't leave me alone! *Had* to have me! *Had* to marry me! I just wanted to become a teacher! That's what I *wanted.* I *had* the job. I had it *waiting.* To teach kids music in the Elizabeth system, and to be left alone by boys, and that was it. I never wanted to be Miss America! I never wanted to marry *anyone!* But you wouldn't let me *breathe*—you wouldn't let me out of your *sight.* All I ever wanted was my college education and that job. I should never have left Elizabeth! Never! Do you know what Miss New Jersey did for my life? It ruined it. I only went after the damn scholarship so Danny could go to college and my father wouldn't have to pay. Do you think if my father didn't have the heart attack I would have entered for Miss Union County? No! I just wanted to win the money so Danny could go to college without the burden on my dad! I didn't do it for boys to go traipsing after me everywhere—I was trying to help out at home! But then you arrived. You! Those hands! Those shoulders! Towering over me with your *jaw!* This huge animal I couldn't get rid of! You wouldn't leave me be! Every time I looked up, there was my boyfriend, gaga because I was a ridiculous beauty queen! You were like some *kid!* You had to make me into a *princess.* Well, look where I have wound up! In a madhouse! Your princess is in a *madhouse!*"

For years to come she would be wondering how what happened to her could have happened to her and blaming him for it, and he would be bringing her food she liked, fruit and candy and cookies, in the hope that she might eat something aside from bread and water, and bringing her magazines in the hope that she might be able to concentrate on reading for even just half an hour a day, and bringing clothes that she could wear around the hospital grounds to accommodate to the weather when the seasons changed. At nine o'clock every evening, he would put away in her dresser whatever he'd brought for her, and he would hold her and kiss her good-bye, hold her and tell her he'd be seeing her the next night after work, and then he would drive the hour in the dark back to Old Rimrock remembering the terror in her face when, fifteen minutes before visiting hours were to end, the nurse put her head in the door to kindly tell Mr. Levov that it was almost time for him to go.

The next night she'd be angry all over again. He had swayed her from her real ambitions. He and the Miss America Pageant had put her off her program. On she went and he couldn't stop her. Didn't try. What did any of what she said have to do with why she was suffering? Everybody knew that what had broken her was quite enough in itself and that what she said had no bearing on anything. That first time she was in the hospital, he simply listened and nodded, and strange as it was to hear her going angrily on about an adventure that at the time he was certain she couldn't have enjoyed more, he sometimes wondered if it wasn't better for her to identify what had happened to her in 1949, not what had happened to her in 1968, as the problem at hand. "All through high school people were telling me, 'You should be Miss America.' I thought it was ridiculous. Based on what should I be Miss America? I was a clerk in a dry-goods store after school and in the summer, and people would come up to my cash register and say, 'You should be Miss America.' I couldn't stand it. I couldn't stand when people said I should do things because of the way that I looked. But when I got a call from the Union County pageant to come to that tea, what could I do? I was a baby. I thought this was a way for me to kick in a little money so my father wouldn't have to work so hard. So I filled out the application and I went, and after all the other girls left, that woman put her arm around me and she told all her neighbors, 'I want you to know that you've just spent the afternoon with the next Miss America.' I thought, 'This is all so silly. Why do people keep saying these things to me? I don't want to be doing this.' And when I won Miss Union County, people were already saying to me, 'We'll see you in Atlantic City'—people who know what they're talking about saying I'm going to win this thing, so how could I back out? I couldn't. The whole front page of the *Elizabeth Journal* was about me winning Miss Union County. I was mortified. I *was*. I thought somehow I could keep it all a secret and just win the money. I was a *baby!* I was sure *at least* I wasn't going to win Miss New Jersey, I was *positive*. I looked around and there was this sea of good-looking girls and they all knew what to do, and I didn't know anything. They knew how to use hair rollers and put false eyelashes on, and I couldn't roll my hair right until I was halfway through my Miss New Jersey year. I thought, 'Oh, my God, look at their makeup,' and they had beautiful wardrobes and I had a prom dress and borrowed clothes, and so I was convinced there was no way I could *ever* win. I was so *introverted*. I was so *unpolished*. But I won *again*. And then they were coaching me on how to sit and how to stand, even how to *listen*—they sent me to a model agency to learn how to *walk*. They didn't like the way I walked. I didn't *care* how I walked—I *walked!* I walked well enough to become Miss New Jersey, didn't I? If I don't walk well enough to become Miss America, the hell with it! But you have to *glide*. No! I will walk the way I walk! Don't swing your arms too much, but don't hold them stiffly at your side. All these little tricks of the trade to make me so self-conscious I could barely *move!* To land not on your heels but on the balls of your feet—this is the kind of thing I went through. If I can just drop out of this thing! How can I back out of this thing? Leave me alone! All of you leave me alone! I never wanted this in the first place! Do you see why I married you? *Now* do you understand? One reason only! I wanted something that seemed normal! So desperately after that year, I wanted something *normal!* How I wish it had never happened! *None of it!* They put you up on a pedestal, which I didn't ask for, and then they rip you off it so damn fast it can *blind* you! And I did not ask for *any* of it! I had nothing in common with those other girls. I hated them and they hated me. Those tall girls with their big feet! None of them gifted. All of them so *chummy!* I was a serious music student! All I wanted was to be left alone and not to have that goddamn crown sparkling like crazy up on top of my head! I never wanted *any* of it! *Never!*"

It was a great help to him, driving home after one of those visits, to remember her as the girl she had really been back then, who, as he recalled it, was nothing like the girl she portrayed as herself in those tirades. During the week in September of 1949 leading up to the Miss America Pageant, when she called Newark every night from the Dennis Hotel to tell him about what happened to her that day as a Miss America contestant, what radiated from her voice was sheer *delight* in being herself. He'd never heard her like that before—it was almost frightening, this undisguised exulting in being where she was and who she was and what she was. Suddenly life existed rapturously and for Dawn Dwyer alone. The surprise of this new and uncharacteristic immoderation even made him wonder if, when the week was over, she could ever again be content with Seymour Levov. And suppose she should win. What chance would he have against all the men who set their sights on marrying Miss America? Actors would be after her. Millionaires would be after her. They'd flock to her—the new life opening up to her could attract a host of powerful new suitors and wind up excluding him. Nonetheless, as the current suitor, he was spellbound by the prospect of Dawn's winning; the more real a possibility it was, the more reasons he had to flush and perspire.

They would talk long distance for as long as an hour at a time—she was too excited to sleep, even though she had been on the go since breakfast, which she'd eaten in the dining room with her chaperone, just the two of them at the table, the chaperone a large local woman in a small hat, Dawn wearing her Miss New Jersey sash pinned to her suit and, on her hands, white kid gloves, tremendously expensive gloves, a present to her from Newark Maid, where the Swede was beginning his training to take over the business. All the girls wore the same style of white kid glove, four-button in length, up over the wrist. Dawn alone had got hers for nothing, along with a second pair of gloves—opera length, in black, Newark Maid's formal, sixteen-button kid glove (a small fortune at Saks), the table-cut workmanship as expert as anything from Italy or France—and, in addition, a third pair of gloves, above the elbow, custom made to match her evening gown. The Swede had asked Dawn for a yard of fabric the same as her gown, and a friend of the family's who did fabric gloves made them for Dawn as a courtesy to Newark Maid. Three times a day, seated across from the chaperones in the small hats, the girls, with their beautiful, nicely combed hair and neat, nice dresses and four-button gloves, attempted to have a meal, something of each course, at least, between giving autographs to all the people in the dining room who came over to gawk and to say where they were from. Because Dawn was Miss New Jersey and the hotel guests were *in* New Jersey, she was the most popular girl by far, and so she had to say a kind word to everyone and smile and sign autographs and still try to get something to eat. "This is what you have to do," she told him on the phone, "this is why they give you the free room."

When she arrived at the train station, they'd put her in a little convertible, a Nash Rambler, that had her name and her state on it, and her chaperone was in the convertible too. Dawn's chaperone was the wife of a local real-estate dealer, and everywhere Dawn went the chaperone was sure to go—in the car with her when she got in, and out of the car with her when she got out. "She does not leave my side, Seymour. You don't see a man the whole time except the judges. You can't even *talk* to one. A few boyfriends are here. Some are even fiancés. But what's the sense? The girls aren't allowed to see them. There's a book of rules so long I can hardly read through it. 'Members of the male sex are not permitted to talk to contestants except in the presence of their hostesses. At no time is a contestant permitted to enter a cocktail lounge or partake of an intoxicating beverage. Other rules include no padding—'" The Swede laughed. "Uh-oh." "Let me finish, Seymour—it just goes on and on. 'No one is permitted an interview with a contestant without her hostess present to protect her interests. . . .'"

Not just Dawn but all the girls got the little Nash Rambler convertibles—though not to keep. You got to keep it only if you became Miss America. Then it would be the car from which you waved to the capacity crowd when you were driven around the edge of the field at the most famous of college football games. The pageant was pushing the Rambler because American Motors was one of the sponsors.

There had been a box of Fralinger's Original saltwater taffy in the room when she arrived, and a bouquet of roses; everybody got both, compliments of the hotel, but Dawn's roses never opened, and the rooms the girls got—at least the girls put up at Dawn's hotel—were small, ugly, and at the back. But the hotel itself, as Dawn excitedly described it, at Boardwalk and Michigan Avenue, was one of the swanky ones where every afternoon they had a proper tea with little sandwiches and croquet was played on the lawn by the paying guests, who rightly enough got the big, beautiful rooms and the ocean views. Every night she'd come back exhausted to the ugly back room with the faded wallpaper, check to see if the roses had opened, and then phone to answer his questions about her chances.

She was one of four or five girls whose photographs kept appearing in the papers, and everybody said that one of these girls had to win—the New Jersey pageant people were sure they had a winner, especially when the photographs of her popped up every morning. "I hate to let them down," she told him. "You're not going to. You're going to win," he told her. "No, this girl from Texas is going to win. I know it. She's so pretty. She has a round face. She has a dimple. Not a beauty but very, very cute. And a great figure. I'm scared to death of her. She's from some tacky little town in Texas and she tap-dances and she's the one." "Is she in the papers with you?" "Always. She's one of the four or five *always*. I'm there because it's Atlantic City and I'm Miss New Jersey and the people on the boardwalk see me in my sash and they go nuts, but that happens to Miss New Jersey *every* year. And she *never* wins. But Miss Texas is there in those papers, Seymour, because she's going to win."

Earl Wilson, the famous syndicated newspaper columnist, was one of the ten judges, and when he heard that Dawn was from Elizabeth he was reported to have said to someone at the float parade, in which Dawn had ridden along the boardwalk with two other girls on the float of her hotel, that Elizabeth's longtime mayor, Joe Brophy, was one of his friends. Earl Wilson told someone who told someone who then told Dawn's chaperone. Earl Wilson and Joe Brophy were old friends—that was all Earl Wilson said, or was able to say in public, but Dawn's chaperone was sure he'd said it because after he'd seen Dawn in her evening gown on the float she'd become his candidate. "Okay," said the Swede, "one down, nine to go. You're on your way, Miss America."

All she talked about with her chaperone was who they thought her closest competition was; apparently this was all any of the girls talked about with their chaperones and all they wound up talking about when they called home, even if, among themselves, they pretended to love one another. The southern girls in particular, Dawn told him, could really lay it on: "Oh, you're just so wonderful, your hair's so wonderful. . . ." The veneration of hair took some getting used to for a girl as down-to-earth as Dawn; you might almost think, from listening to the conversation among the other girls, that life's possibilities resided in hair—not in the hands of your destiny but in the hands of your hair.

Together with the chaperones, they visited the Steel Pier and had a fish dinner at Captain Starn's famous seafood restaurant and yacht bar, and a steak dinner at Jack Guischard's Steak House, and the third morning they had their picture taken together in front of Convention Hall, where a pageant official told them the picture was one they would treasure for the rest of their lives, that the friendships they were making would last the rest of their lives, that they would keep up with one another for the rest of their lives, that when the time arrived they would name their children after one another—and meanwhile, when the papers came out in the morning, the girls said to their chaperones, "Oh God, I'm not in this. Oh God, this one looks like she's going to win."

Every day there were rehearsals and every night for a week they gave a show. Year after year people visited Atlantic City just for the Miss America contest and bought tickets for the nightly show and came all dressed up to see the girls on the stage individually exhibiting their talent and performing as an ensemble in costumed musical numbers. The one other girl who played piano played "Clair de Lune" for her solo performance and so Dawn had to herself the much flashier number, the currently popular hit "Till the End of Time," a danceable arrangement of a Chopin polonaise. "I'm in *show* business. I don't stop all day. You don't have a moment. Because New Jersey's host state there's all this focus on me, and I don't want to let everybody down, I really don't, I couldn't bear it—" "You won't, Dawnie. Earl Wilson's in your pocket, and he's the most famous of all the judges. I feel it. I know it. You're going to win."

But he was wrong. Miss Arizona won. Dawn didn't make it even into the top ten. In those days the girls waited backstage while the winners were announced. There was row after row of mirrors and tables lined up alphabetically by state, and Dawn was right in the middle of everyone when the announcement was made, so she had to start smiling to beat the band and clapping like crazy because she had lost and then, to make matters worse, had to rush back onstage and march around with the other losers, singing along with MC Bob Russell the Miss America song of that era: "Every flower, every rose, stands up on her tippy toes . . . when Miss America marches by!" while a girl just as short and slight and dark as she was—little Jacque Mercer from Arizona, who won the swimsuit competition but who Dawn never figured would win it all—took the crowd at Convention Hall by storm. Afterward, at the farewell ball, though it was for Dawn a terrific letdown, she wasn't nearly as depressed as most of the others. The same thing she had been told by the New Jersey pageant people they'd been told by *their* state pageant people: "You're going to make it. You're going to be Miss America." So the ball, she told him, was the saddest sight she'd ever seen. "You have to go and smile and it's awful," she said. "They have these people from the Coast Guard or wherever they're from—Annapolis. They have fancy white uniforms and braid and ribbons. I guess they're considered safe enough for us to dance with. So they dance with you with their chin tucked in, and the evening's over, and you go home."

Still, for months afterward the superstimulating adventure refused to die; even while she was being Miss New Jersey and going around snipping ribbons and waving at people and opening department stores and auto showrooms, she wondered aloud if anything so wonderfully unforeseen as that week in Atlantic City would ever happen to her again. She kept beside her bed the 1949 Official Yearbook of the Miss America Pageant, a booklet prepared by the pageant that was sold all week at Atlantic City: individual photos of the girls, four to a page, each with a tiny outline drawing of her state and a capsule biography. Where Miss New Jersey's photoportrait appeared—smiling demurely, Dawn in her evening gown with the matching twelve-button fabric gloves—the corner of the page had been neatly turned back. "Mary Dawn Dwyer, 22 year old Elizabeth, N.J. brunette, carries New Jersey's hopes in this year's Pageant. A graduate of Upsala College, East Orange, N.J., where she majored in music education, Mary Dawn has the ambition of becoming a high school music teacher. She is 5-2½ and blue-eyed, and her hobbies are swimming, square dancing, and cooking. (*Left above*)" Reluctant to give up excitement such as she'd never known before, she talked on and on about the fairy tale it had been for a kid from Hillside Road, a plumber's daughter from Hillside Road, to have been up in front of all those people, competing for the title of Miss America. She almost couldn't believe the courage she'd shown. "Oh, that ramp, Seymour. That's a long ramp, a long runway, it's a long way to go just smiling. . . ."

In 1969, when the invitation arrived in Old Rimrock for the twentieth reunion of the Miss America contestants of her year, Dawn was back in the hospital for the second time since Merry's disappearance. It was May. The psychiatrists were as nice as they were the first time, and the room was as pleasant, and the rolling landscape as pretty, and the walks were even prettier, with tulips around the bungalows where the patients lived, the huge fields green this time around, beautiful, beautiful views—and because this *was* the second time in two years, and because the place *was* beautiful, and because when he arrived directly from Newark in the early evening, after they had just cut the grass, there was a smell in the air as fresh and sharp as the smell of chives, it was all a thousand times worse. And so he did not show Dawn the invitation for the 1949 reunion. Things were bad enough—the things she was saying to him were bizarre enough; the relentless crying about her shame, her mortification, the futility of her life was all quite sad enough—without any more of the Miss New Jersey business.

And then the change occurred. Something made her decide to want to be free of the unexpected, improbable thing. She was not going to be deprived of her life.

The heroic renewal began with the face-lift at the Geneva clinic she'd read about in *Vogue*. Before going to bed he'd see her at her bathroom mirror drawing the crest of her cheekbones back between her index fingers while simultaneously drawing the skin at her jawline back and upward with her thumbs, firmly tugging the loose flesh until she had eradicated even the natural creases of her face, until she was staring at a face that looked like the polished kernel of a face. And though it was clear to her husband that she had indeed begun to age like a woman in her mid-fifties at only forty-five, the remedy suggested in *Vogue* in no way addressed anything that mattered; so remote was it from the disaster that had befallen them he saw no reason to argue with her, thinking she knew the truth better than anyone, however much she might prefer to imagine herself another prematurely aging reader of *Vogue* rather than the mother of the Rimrock Bomber. But because she had run out of psychiatrists to see and medications to try and because she was terrified at the prospect of electric shock therapy should she have to be hospitalized a third time, the day came when he took her to Geneva. They were met at the airport by the liveried chauffeur and the limousine, and she booked herself into Dr. LaPlante's clinic.

In their suite of rooms the Swede slept in the bed beside hers. The night after the operation, when she could not stop vomiting, he was there to clean her up and to comfort her. During the next several days, when she wept from the pain, he sat at her bedside and, as he had night after night at the psychiatric clinic, held her hand, certain that this grotesque surgery, this meaningless, futile ordeal, was ushering in the final stage of her downfall as a recognizable human being: far from assisting at his wife's recovery, he understood himself to be acting as the unwitting accomplice to her mutilation. He looked at her head buried in bandages and felt he might as well be witnessing the preparation for burial of her corpse.

He was totally wrong. As it was to turn out, only a few days before the letter from Rita Cohen reached his office, he happened to pass Dawn's desk and to see there a brief handwritten letter beside an envelope addressed to the plastic surgeon in Geneva: "Dear Dr. LaPlante: A year has passed since you did my face. I do not feel that when I last saw you I understood what you have given me. That you would spend five hours of your time for my beauty fills me with awe. How can I thank you enough? I feel it's taken me these full twelve months to recover from the surgery. I believe, as you said, that my system was more beaten down than I had realized. Now it is as if I have been given a new life. Both from within and from the outside. When I meet old friends I have not seen for a while, they are puzzled as to what happened to me. I don't tell them. It is quite wonderful, dear doctor, and without you it would never have been possible. Much love and thank you, Dawn Levov."

Almost immediately after the reconstitution of her face to its former pert, heart-shaped pre-explosion perfection, she decided to build a small contemporary house on a ten-acre lot the other side of Rimrock ridge and to sell the big old house, the outbuildings, and their hundred-odd acres. (Dawn's beef cattle and the farm machinery had been sold off in '69, the year after Merry became a fugitive from justice; by then it was clear that the business was too demanding for Dawn to continue to run on her own, and so he took an ad in one of the monthly cattle magazines and within only weeks had got rid of the baler, the kicker, the rake, the livestock—everything, the works.) When he overheard her telling the architect, their neighbor Bill Orcutt, that she had always hated their house, the Swede was as stunned as if she were telling Orcutt she had always hated her husband. He went for a long walk, needed to walk almost the five miles down into the village to keep reminding himself that it was the *house* she said she'd always hated. But even her meaning no more than that left him so miserable it took all his considerable powers of suppression to turn himself around and head home for lunch, where Dawn and Orcutt were to review with him Orcutt's first set of sketches.

Hated their old stone house, the beloved first and only house? How could she? He had been dreaming about that house since he was sixteen years old and, riding with the baseball team to a game against Whippany—sitting there on the school bus in his uniform, idly rubbing his fingers around the deep pocket of his mitt as they drove along the narrow roads curving westward through the rural Jersey hills—he saw a large stone house with black shutters set on a rise back of some trees. A little girl was on a swing suspended from a low branch of one of those big trees, swinging herself high into the air, just as happy, he imagined, as a kid can be. It was the first house built of stone he'd ever seen, and to a city boy it was an architectural marvel. The random design of the stones *said* "House" to him as not even the brick house on Keer Avenue did, despite the finished basement where he'd taught Jerry Ping-Pong and checkers; despite the screened-in back porch where he'd lie in the dark on the old sofa and listen on hot nights to the Giant games; despite the garage where as a boy he would use a roll of black tape to affix a ball to the end of a rope hanging from a cross beam, where, all winter long, assuming his tall, erect, no-nonsense stance, he would duteously spend half an hour swinging at it with his bat after he came home from basketball practice, so as not to lose his timing; despite the bedroom under the eaves, with the two dormer windows, where the year before high school he'd put himself to sleep reading and rereading *The Kid from Tomkinsville*—"A gray-haired man in a dingy shirt and a blue baseball cap well down over his eyes shoved an armful of clothes at the Kid and indicated his locker. 'Fifty-six. In the back row, there.' The lockers were plain wooden stalls about six feet high with a shelf one or two feet from the top. The front of his locker was open and along the edge at the top was pasted: 'TUCKER. NO. 56.' There was his uniform with the word 'DODGERS' in blue across the front and the number 56 on the back of the shirt. . . ."

The stone house was not only engagingly ingenious-looking to his eyes—all that irregularity regularized, a jigsaw puzzle fitted patiently together into this square, solid thing to make a beautiful shelter—but it looked indestructible, an impregnable house that could never burn to the ground and that had probably been standing there since the country began. Primitive stones, rudimentary stones of the sort that you would see scattered about among the trees if you took a walk along the paths in Weequahic Park, and out there they were a house. He couldn't get over it.

At school he'd find himself thinking about which girl in each of his classes to marry and take to live with him in that house. After the ride with the team to Whippany, he had only to hear someone saying "stone"—even saying "west"—and he would imagine himself going home after work to that house back of the trees and seeing his daughter there, his little daughter high up in the air on the swing he'd built for her. Though he was only a high school sophomore, he could imagine a daughter of his own running to kiss him, see her flinging herself at him, see himself carrying her on his shoulders into that house and straight on through to the kitchen, where standing by the stove in her apron, preparing their dinner, would be the child's adoring mother, who would be whichever Weequahic girl had shimmied down in the seat in front of him at the Roosevelt movie theater just the Friday before, her hair hanging over the back of her chair, within stroking distance, had he dared. All of his life he had this ability to imagine himself completely. Everything always added up to something whole. How could it not when he felt *himself* to add up, add up exactly to one?

Then he saw Dawn at Upsala. She'd be crossing the common to Old Main where the day students hung out between classes; she'd be standing under the eucalyptus trees talking with a couple of the girls who lived in Kenbrook Hall. Once he followed her down Prospect Street toward the Brick Church bus station when suddenly she stopped in front of the window at Best & Co. After she went inside the store, he went up to the window to look at the mannequin in a long "New Look" skirt and imagined Dawn Dwyer in a fitting room trying the skirt on over her slip. She was so lovely that it made him extraordinarily shy even to glance her way, as though glancing were itself touching or clinging, as though if she knew (and how could she not?) that he was uncontrollably looking her way, she'd do what any sensible, self-possessed girl would do, disdain him as a beast of prey. He'd been a U.S. Marine, he'd been engaged to a girl in South Carolina, at his family's request had broken off the engagement, and it was years since he'd thought about that stone house with the black shutters and the swing out front. Sensationally handsome as he was, fresh from the service and a glamorous campus athletic star however determinedly he worked at containing conceit and resisting the role, it took him a full semester to approach Dawn for a date, not only because nakedly confronting her beauty gave him a bad conscience and made him feel shamefully voyeuristic but because once he approached her there'd be no way to prevent her from looking right through him and into his mind and seeing for herself how he pictured her: there at the stove of the stone house's kitchen when he came trundling in with their daughter, Merry, on his back—"Merry" because of the joy she took in the swing he'd built her. At night he played continuously on his phonograph a song popular that year called "Peg o' My Heart." A line in the song went, "It's your Irish heart I'm after," and every time he saw Dawn Dwyer on the paths at Upsala, tiny and exquisite, he went around the rest of the day unaware that he was whistling that damn song nonstop. He would find himself whistling it even during a ballgame, while swinging a couple of bats in the on-deck circle, waiting his turn at the plate. He lived under two skies then—the Dawn Dwyer sky and the natural sky overhead.

But still he didn't immediately approach her, for fear that she'd see what he was thinking and laugh at his intoxication with her, this ex-marine's presumptuous innocence about the Upsala Spring Queen. She would think that his imagining, before they were even *introduced*, that she was especially intended to satisfy Seymour Levov's yearnings meant that he was still a child, vain and spoiled, when in fact what it meant to the Swede was that he was fully charged up with purpose long, long before anyone else he knew, with a grown man's aims and ambitions, someone who excitedly foresaw, in perfect detail, the outcome of his story. He had come home from the service at twenty in a rage to be "mature." If he was a child, it was only insofar as he found himself looking ahead into responsible manhood with the longing of a kid gazing into a candy-store window.

Understanding all too well why she wanted to sell the old house, he acceded to her wish without even trying to make her understand that the reason she wanted to go—because Merry was still there, in every room, Merry at age one, five, ten—was the reason he wanted to stay, a reason no less important than hers. But as she might not survive their staying—and he, it still seemed, could endure anything, however brutally it flew in the face of his own inclinations—he agreed to abandon the house he loved, not least for the memories it held of his fugitive child. He agreed to move into a brand-new house, open everywhere to the sun, full of light, just big enough for the two of them, with only a small extra room for guests out over the garage. A modern dream house—"luxuriously austere" was how Orcutt described it back to Dawn after sounding her out on what she had in mind—with electric baseboard heating (instead of the insufferable forced hot air that gave her sinusitis) and built-in Shaker-like furniture (instead of those dreary period pieces) and recessed ceiling lighting (instead of the million stand-

ing lamps beneath the gloomy oak beams) and large, clear case-
ment windows throughout (instead of those mullioned old sashes
that were always sticking), and with a basement as technologically
up-to-date as a nuclear submarine (instead of that dank, cavernous
cellar where her husband took guests to see the wine he had "laid
down" for drinking in his old age, reminding them as they shuffled
between the mildewed stone walls to be on guard against the low-
slung cast-iron drainage pipes: "Your head, be careful, watch it
there . . ."). He understood everything, all of it, understood just
how awful it was for her, and so what could he do but accede?
"Property is a responsibility," she said. "With no machinery and no
cattle, you grow up a lot of grass. You're going to have to keep this
mowed two or three times a year to keep it down. You have to have
it bush-hogged—you can't just let things grow up into woods.
You've got to keep them mowed and it's just ridiculously expensive
and it's crazy for you to keep laying that money out year after year.
There's keeping the barns from falling down—there's a *responsibility* you have with land. You just can't let it go. The best thing to do,
the *only* thing to do," she told him, "is to move."

Okay. They'd move. But why did she have to tell Orcutt she'd
hated that house "from the day we found it"? That she was there
only because her husband had "dragged" her there when she was
too young to have any idea what it would be like trying to run a
huge, antiquated, dark barn of a place in which something was
always leaking or rotting or in need of repair? The reason she first
went into cattle, she told him, was to get out of that terrible house.

And if that was true? To find this out so late in the game! It was
like discovering an infidelity—all these years she had been unfaith-
ful to the house. How could he have gone around dopily believing
he was making her happy when there was no justification for his
feelings, when they were absurd, when, year in, year out, she was
seething with hatred for their house? How he had loved the providing. Had he only been given the opportunity to provide for *more*
than the three of them. If only there had been more children in that
big house, if only Merry had been raised among brothers and

sisters whom she loved and who loved her, this thing might never have happened to them. But Dawn wanted from life something other than to be the slavish mom to half a dozen kids and the nursemaid to a two-hundred-year-old house—she wanted to raise beef cattle. Because of her being introduced, no matter where they went, as "a former Miss New Jersey," she was sure that even though she had a bachelor's degree people were always dismissing her as a bathing beauty, a mindless china doll, capable of doing nothing more productive for society than standing around looking pretty. It did not matter how many times she patiently explained to them, when they brought up her title, that she had entered at the local Union County level only because her father had the heart attack, and money was tight, and her brother Danny was graduating St. Mary's, and she thought that if she won—and she believed she had a chance not because of having been Upsala Spring Queen but because she was a music-education major who played classical piano—she could use the scholarship money that went with the title for Danny's college tuition, thereby unburdening . . .

But it didn't matter what she said or how much she said or how often she mentioned the piano: nobody believed her. Nobody really believed that she never wanted to look better than everybody else. They only thought that there are lots of other ways to get a scholarship than to go walking around Atlantic City in high heels and a bathing suit. She was always telling people her serious reasons for becoming Miss New Jersey and nobody even listened. They smiled. To them she couldn't have serious reasons. They didn't want her to have serious reasons. All she could have for them was that face. Then they could go away saying, "Oh her, she's nothing but a face," and pretend they weren't jealous or intimidated by her looks. "Thank God," Dawn would mutter to him, "I didn't win Miss Congeniality. If they think Miss New Jersey has to be dumb, imagine if I'd won the booby prize. Though," she'd then add wistfully, "it would have been nice to bring home the thousand dollars."

After Merry was born, when they first began going to Deal in the summer, people used to stare at Dawn in her bathing suit. Of course she never wore the white Catalina one-piece suit that she'd worn on the runway in Atlantic City, with the logo, just below the hip, of the traditional swim girl in her bathing cap. He loved that bathing suit, it fit her so marvelously, but after Atlantic City she never put it on again. They stared at her no matter what style or color suit she wore, and sometimes they would come up and snap her picture and ask for an autograph. More disturbing, however, than the staring and the photographs was their *suspiciousness* of her. "For some strange reason," she said, "the women always think that because I'm a former whatever I want their husbands." And probably, the Swede thought, what made it so frightening for them is that they believed Dawn could get their husbands—they'd noticed how men looked at her and how attentive they were to her wherever she went. He'd noticed it himself but never worried, not about a wife as proper as Dawn who'd been brought up as strictly as she was. But all of this so rankled Dawn that first she gave up going to the beach club in a bathing suit, any bathing suit; then, much as she loved the surf, she gave up going to the beach club at all and whenever she wanted to swim drove the four miles down to Avon, where, as a child, she used to vacation with her family for a week in the summertime. On the beach at Avon she was just a simple, petite Irish girl with her hair pulled back about whom nobody cared one way or another.

She went to Avon to get away from her beauty, but Dawn couldn't get away from it any more than she could openly flaunt it. You have to enjoy power, have a certain ruthlessness, to accept the beauty and not mourn the fact that it overshadows everything else. As with any exaggerated trait that sets you apart and makes you exceptional—and enviable, and hateable—to accept your beauty, to accept its effect on others, to play with it, to make the best of it, you're well advised to develop a sense of humor. Dawn was not a stick, she had spirit and she had spunk, and she could be cutting in a very humorous way, but that wasn't quite the inward humor it took to do the job and make her free. Only after she was married and no longer a virgin did she discover the place where it was okay for her to be as beautiful as she was, and that place, to the profit of both husband and wife, was with the Swede, in bed.

They used to call Avon the Irish Riviera. The Jews without much money went to Bradley Beach, and the Irish without much money went next door to Avon, a seaside town all of ten blocks long. The swell Irish—who had the money, the judges, the builders, the fancy surgeons—went to Spring Lake, beyond the imposing manorial gates just south of Belmar (another resort town, which was more or less a mixture of everybody). Dawn used to get taken to stay in Spring Lake by her mother's sister Peg, who'd married Ned Mahoney, a lawyer from Jersey City. If you were an Irish lawyer in that town, her father told her, and you played ball with City Hall, Mayor "I-am-the-law" Hague took care of you. Since Uncle Ned, a smooth talker, a golfer, and good-looking, had been on the Hudson County gravy train from the day he graduated John Marshall and signed on across the street with a powerful firm right there in Journal Square, and since he seemed to love pretty Mary Dawn best of all his nieces and nephews, every summer after the child had spent her week in the Avon rooming house with her mother and father and Danny, she went on by herself to spend the next week with Ned and Peg and all the Mahoney kids at the huge old Essex and Sussex Hotel right on the oceanfront at Spring Lake, where every morning in the airy dining room overlooking the sea she ate French toast with Vermont maple syrup. The starched white napkin that covered her lap was big enough to wrap around her waist like a sarong, and the sparkling silverware weighed a ton. On Sunday, they all went together to St. Catherine's, the most gorgeous church the little girl had ever seen. You got there by crossing a bridge—the loveliest bridge she had ever seen, narrow and humpbacked and made of wood—that spanned the lake back of the hotel. Sometimes when she was unhappy at the swim club she'd drive beyond Avon into Spring Lake and remember how Spring Lake used to materialize out of nowhere every summer, magically full blown, Mary Dawn's Brigadoon. She remembered how she dreamed of getting married in St. Catherine's, of being a bride there in a white dress, marrying a rich lawyer like her Uncle Ned and living in one of those grand summer houses whose big verandas overlooked the lake and the bridges and the dome of the church while only minutes from the booming Atlantic. She could have done it, too, could have had it just by snapping her fingers. But her choice was to fall in love with and marry Seymour Levov of Newark instead of any one of those dozens and dozens of smitten Catholic boys she'd met through her Mahoney cousins, the smart, rowdy boys from Holy Cross and Boston College, and so her life was not in Spring Lake but down in Deal and up in Old Rimrock with Mr. Levov. "Well, that's the way it happened," her mother would say sadly to whoever would listen. "Could have had a wonderful life there just like Peg's. Better than Peg's. St. Catherine's and St. Margaret's are there. St. Catherine's is right by the lake there. Beautiful building. Just beautiful. But Mary Dawn's the rebel in the family—always was. Always did just what she wanted, and from the time she marched off to be in that contest, fitting in like everybody else is apparently not something she wanted."

Dawn went to Avon strictly to swim. She still hated lying on the beach to take the sun, still resented having been made to expose her fair skin to the sun every day by the New Jersey pageant people—on the runway, they told her, her white swimsuit would look striking against a deep tan. As a young mother she tried to get as far as she could from everything that marked her as "a former whatever" and that aroused insane contempt in other women and made her feel unhappy and like a freak. She even gave away to charity all the clothes the pageant director (who had his own idea of what kind of girl should be presented by New Jersey to the Miss America judges) had picked out for her at the designers' showrooms in New York during Dawn's daylong buying trip for Atlantic City. The Swede thought she'd looked great in those gowns and he hated to see them go, but at least, at his urging, she kept the state crown so that someday she could show it to their grandchildren.

And then, after Merry started at nursery school, Dawn set out to prove to the world of women, for neither the first time nor the last, that she was impressive for something more than what she looked like. She decided to raise cattle. That idea, too, went back to her childhood—way back to her grandfather, her mother's father, who as a twenty-year-old from County Kerry came to the port in the 1880s, married, settled in south Elizabeth close to St. Mary's, and proceeded to father eleven children. His living he earned at first as a hand on the docks, but he bought a couple of cows to provide milk for the family, wound up selling the surplus to the big shots on West Jersey Street—the Moores from Moore Paint, Admiral "Bull" Halsey's family, Nicholas Murray Butler the Nobel Prize winner—and soon became one of the first independent milkmen in Elizabeth. He had about thirty cows on Murray Street, and though he didn't own much property, it didn't matter—in those days you could let them graze anywhere. All his sons went into the business and stayed in it until after the war, when the big supermarkets came along and knocked out the little man. Dawn's father, Jim Dwyer, had worked for her mother's family, and that was how Dawn's parents had met. When he was still only a kid, before refrigeration, Jim Dwyer used to go out on the milk truck at twelve o'clock at night and stay out till morning delivering milk off the back of the truck. But he hated it. Too tough a life. The heck with that, he finally said, and took up plumbing. Dawn, as a small child, loved to visit the cows, and when she was about six or seven, she was taught by one of her cousins how to milk them, and that thrill—squirting the milk out of those udders, the animals just standing there eating hay and letting her tug to her heart's content—she never forgot.

With beef cattle, however, she wouldn't need the manpower to milk and she could run the operation almost entirely by herself. The Simmental, which made a lot of milk but was a beef animal as well, still weren't a registered breed in the United States at that time, so she could get in on the ground floor. Crossbreeding—Simmental to polled Hereford—was what interested her, the genetic vigor, the hybrid vigor, the sheer growth that results from crossbreeding. She studied the books, took the magazines, the catalogs started coming in the mail, and at night she would call him over to where she was paging through a catalog and say, "Isn't that a good-looking heifer? Have to go out and take a look at her." Pretty soon they were traveling together to shows and sales. She loved the auctions. "This reminds me just a little too much," she whispered to the Swede, "of Atlantic City. It's the Miss America Pageant for cows." She wore a tag identifying herself—"Dawn Levov, Arcady Breeders," which was the name of her company, taken from their Old Rimrock address, Box 62, Arcady Hill Road—and found it very hard to resist buying a nice cow.

A cow or a bull would be led into the ring and paraded around and the show sponsors would give the background of the animal, the sire and the dam and what they did, what the potential was, and then the people would bid, and though Dawn bought carefully, her pleasure just in raising her hand and topping the previous bid was serious pleasure. Much as he wanted more children, not more cows, he had to admit that she was never so fascinating to him, not even when he first saw her at Upsala, as in those moments at the auctions when her beauty came enticingly cloaked in the excitement of bidding and buying. Before Count arrived—the champion bull she bought at birth for ten thousand dollars, which her husband, who was a hundred percent behind her, still had to tell her was an awful lot of money—his accountant would look at her figures for Arcady Breeders at the end of each year and tell the Swede, "This is ridiculous, you can't go on this way." But they really couldn't take a beating as long as it was mostly her own time she put into it, and so he told the accountant, "Don't worry, she'll make some money." He wouldn't have dreamed of stopping her, even if eventually she didn't make a cent, because, as he said to himself when he watched her and the dog out with the herd, "These are her friends."

She worked like hell, all by herself, keeping track of the calving, getting the calves drinking out of a plastic bottle with a nipple if they didn't get the idea of sucking, tending to the mothers' feeding before she put them back in the herd. For the fencing she had to hire a man, but she was out there with him baling hay, the eighteen hundred, two thousand bales that saw them through the winter, and when Count was on in years and got lost one winter day she was heroic in hunting him down, for three days combed the woods for him before she found him where he had got himself onto a little island out in the swamp. Getting him back to the barn was ghastly. Dawn weighed a hundred and three pounds and was five feet two inches tall, and Count weighed about twenty-five hundred pounds, a very long, very beautiful animal with big brown spots around either eye, sire of the most sought-after calves. Dawn kept all the bull calves, breeding for other cattle owners, who would keep these bulls in their herds; the heifers she didn't sell often, but when she did, people wanted them. Count's progeny won year after year at the national shows and the investment returned itself many times over. But then Count got stranded out in the swamp because he had thrown his stifle out; it was icy and he must have got his foot caught in a hole, between roots, and when he saw that to get off this little island he had to get through wet mud, he just quit, and it was three days before Dawn could find him anywhere. Then, with the dog and Merry, she went out with a halter and tried to get him out but he hurt too much and didn't want to get up. So they came back later with some pills, loaded him up with cortisone and different things and sat there with him for another few hours in the rain, and then they tried again to move him. They had to get him through roots and stones and deep muck, and he'd walk a bit and stop, walk a bit and stop, and the dog got behind him and she'd bark and so he'd walk another couple of steps, and that was the way it went for hours. They had him on a rope and he'd take his head, this great big head, all curly with those beautiful eyes, and he'd pull the rope and just swing the two of them, Dawn and Merry together—boom! So then they'd get themselves up and start all over again. They had some grain and he'd eat a little and then he'd come a little farther, but all together it took four hours to get him out of the woods. Ordinarily he led very well, but he hurt so that they had to get him home almost piece by piece. Seeing his petite wife—a woman who could, if she'd wanted to, have been just a pretty face—and his small daughter drenched and covered with mud when they emerged with the bull on the rain-soaked field back of the barn was something the Swede never forgot. "This is right," he thought. "She is happy. We have Merry and that's enough." He was not a religious man but at that moment he offered up thanks, saying aloud, "Something is shining down on me."

To get the bull to the barn took Dawn and Merry nearly another hour, and there he just lay down in the hay for four days. They got the vet, and the vet said, "You're not going to get him any better. I can make him more comfortable, that's all I can do for you." Dawn brought him water to drink in buckets and food to eat, and one day (as Merry used to tell the story to whoever came to the house) he decided, "Hey, I'm all right," and he got up and he wandered out and he took it easy and that's when he fell in love with the old mare and they became inseparable. The day they had to ship Count— send him to the butcher—Dawn was in tears and kept saying, "I can't do this," and he kept saying, "You've got to do this," and so they did it. Magically (Merry's word) the night before Count left he bred a perfect little heifer, his parting shot. She got the brown spots around the eyes—"He th-th-th-threw brown eyes all around him"—but after that, though the bulls were well bred, never again was there an animal to compare with the Count.

So did it matter finally that she told people she hated the house? He was now far and away the stronger partner, she was now far and away the weaker; he was the fortunate, doubtlessly undeserving recipient of so much—what the hell, to whatever demand she made on him, he acceded. If he could bear something and Dawn couldn't, he didn't understand how he could do anything *but* accede. That was the only way the Swede knew for a man to go about being a man, especially one as lucky as himself. From the very beginning it had been a far greater strain for him to bear her disappointments than to bear his own; her disappointments seemed to dangerously rob him of himself—once he had absorbed her disappointments it became impossible for him to do nothing about them. Half measures wouldn't suffice. His effort to arrive at what she wanted always had to be wholehearted; never was he free of his quiet wholeheartedness. Not even when everything was on top of him, not even when giving everyone what they needed from him at the factory and everyone what they needed from him at home—dealing promptly with the suppliers' screw-ups, with the union's exactions, with the buyers' complaints; contending with an uncertain marketplace and all the overseas headaches; attending, on demand, to the importuning of a stuttering child, an independent-minded wife, a putatively retired, easily riled-up father—did it occur to him that this relentlessly impersonal use of himself might one day wear him down. He did not think like that any more than the ground under his feet thought like that. He seemed never to understand or, even in a moment of fatigue, to admit that his limitations were not entirely loathsome and that he was not himself a one-hundred-and-seventy-year-old stone house, its weight borne imperturbably by beams carved of oak—that he was something more transitory and mysterious.

It wasn't this house she hated anyway; what she hated were memories she couldn't shake loose from, all of them associated with the house, memories that of course he shared. Merry as a grade school kid lying on the floor of the study next to Dawn's desk, drawing pictures of Count while Dawn did the accounts for the farm. Merry emulating her mother's concentration, enjoying working with the same discipline, silently delighting to feel an equal in a common pursuit, and in some preliminary way offering them a glimpse of herself as the adult—yes, of the adult friend to them that she would someday be. Memories particularly of when they weren't being what parents are nine-tenths of the time—the taskmasters, the examples, the moral authorities, the nags of pick-that-up and you're-going-to-be-late, keepers of the diary of her duties and routines—memories, rather, of when they found one another afresh, beyond the tensions between parental mastery and inept childish uncertainty, of those moments of respite in a family's life when they could reach one another in calm.

The early mornings in the bathroom shaving while Dawn went to wake Merry up—he could not imagine a better start to the morning than catching a glimpse of that ritual. There was never an alarm clock in Merry's life—Dawn was her alarm clock. Before six o'clock Dawn was already out in the barn, but at promptly six-thirty she stopped tending the herd, came back in the house, and went up to the child's room, where, as she sat at the edge of the bed, daybreak's comforting observance began. Without a word it be-gan—Dawn simply stroking Merry's sleeping head, a pantomime that could go on for two full minutes. Next, almost singing the whispered words, Dawn lightly inquired, "A sign of life?" Merry responded not by opening her eyes but by moving a little finger. "Another sign, please?" On the game went—Merry playing along by wrinkling her nose, by moistening her lips, by sighing just audi-bly—till eventually she was up out of bed ready to go. It was a game embodying a loss, for Merry the state of being completely pro-tected, for Dawn the project of completely protecting what once had seemed completely protectable. Waking The Baby: it continued until the baby was nearly twelve, the one rite of infancy that Dawn could not resist indulging, that neither one of them ever appeared eager to outgrow.

How he loved to sight them doing together what mothers and daughters do. To a father's eye, one seemed to amplify the other. In bathing suits rushing out of the surf together and racing each other to the towels—the wife now a little past her robust moment and the daughter edging up to the beginning of hers. A delineation of life's cyclical nature that left him feeling afterward as though he had a spacious understanding of the whole female sex. Merry, with her growing curiosity about the trappings of womanhood, putting on Dawn's jewelry while, beside her at the mirror, Dawn helped her preen. Merry confiding in Dawn about her fears of ostracism—of other kids ignoring her, of her girlfriends ganging up on her. In those quiet moments from which he was excluded (daughter relying on mother, Dawn and Merry emotionally one inside the other like those Russian dolls), Merry appeared more poignantly than ever not a small replica of his wife, or of himself, but an independent little being—something similar, a version of them, yet distinctive and new—for which he had the most passionate affinity.

It wasn't the house Dawn hated—what she hated, he knew, was that the motive for having the house (for making the beds, for setting the table, for laundering the curtains, for organizing the holidays, for apportioning her energies and differentiating her duties by the day of the week) had been destroyed right along with Hamlin's store; the tangible daily fullness, the smooth regularity that was once the underpinning of all of their lives survived in her only as an illusion, as a mockingly inaccessible, bigger-than-life-size fantasy, real for every last Old Rimrock family but hers. He knew this not just because of the million memories but also because in the top drawer of his office desk he still kept handy a ten-year-old copy of a local weekly, the *Denville-Randolph Courier,* featuring on the first page the article about Dawn and her cattle business. She had consented to be interviewed only if the journalist promised not to mention her having been Miss New Jersey of 1949. The journalist agreed and the piece was titled "Old Rimrock Woman Feels Lucky to Love What She's Doing," and concluded with a paragraph that, simple as it was, made him proud of her whenever he went back to read it: "'People are lucky if they get to do what they love and are good at it,' Mrs. Levov declared."

The *Courier* story testified just how much she had loved the house, as well as everything else about their lives. Beneath a photograph of her standing before the pewter plates lined up on the fireplace mantel—in her white turtleneck shirt and cream-colored blazer, with her hair styled in a pageboy and her two delicate hands in front of her, the fingers decorously intertwined, looking sweet though a bit plain—the caption read, "Mrs. Levov, the former Miss New Jersey of 1949, loves living in a 170-year-old home, an environment which she says reflects the values of her family." When Dawn called the paper in a fury about mentioning Miss New Jersey, the journalist answered that he had kept to his promise not to mention it in the article; it was the editor who had put it in the caption.

No, she had not hated the house, of course she hadn't—and that didn't matter anyway. All that mattered now was the restoration of her well-being; the foolish remarks she might make to this one or that one were of no consequence beside the recovery taking hold. Maybe what was agitating him was that the self-adjustments on which she was building a recovery were not regenerative for him or entirely admirable to him, were even something of an affront to him. He could not tell people—certainly couldn't convince himself—that he hated the things he'd loved. . . .

He was back to it. But he couldn't help it, not when he remembered how at seven Merry would eat herself sick with the raw batter while baking two dozen tollhouse cookies, and a week later they'd still be finding batter all over the place, even up on top of the refrigerator. So how could he hate the refrigerator? How could he let his emotions be reshaped, imagine himself being rescued, as Dawn did, by their leaving it behind for an all-but-silent new IceTemp, the Rolls-Royce of refrigerators? He for one could not say he hated the kitchen in which Merry used to bake her cookies and melt her cheese sandwiches and make her baked ziti, even if the cupboards weren't stainless steel or the counters Italian marble. He could not say he hated the cellar where she used to go to play hide-and-seek with her screaming friends, even if sometimes it spooked even him a little to be down there in the wintertime with those scuttling mice. He could not say he hated the massive fireplace adorned with the antique iron kettle that was all at once insufferably corny in Dawn's estimation, not when he remembered how, early every January, he would chop up the Christmas tree and set it afire there, the whole thing in one go, so that the explosive blaze of the bone-dry branches, the great whoosh and the loud crackling and the dancing shadows, cavorting devils climbing to the ceiling from the four walls, would transport Merry into a delirium of terrified delight. He could not say he hated the ball-and-claw-foot bathtub where he used to give her baths, just because decades of indelible mineral stains from the well water streaked the enamel and encircled the drain. He could not even hate the toilet whose handle required all that jiggling to get the thing to stop gushing, not when he remembered her kneeling beside it and throwing up while he knelt next to her, holding her sick little forehead.

Nor could he say he hated his daughter for what she had done— if he could! If only, instead of living chaotically in the world where she wasn't and in the world where she once was and in the world where she might now be, he could come to hate her enough not to care anything about her world, then *or* now. If only he could be back thinking like everybody else, once again the totally natural man instead of this riven charlatan of sincerity, an artless outer Swede and a tormented inner Swede, a visible stable Swede and a concealed beleaguered Swede, an easygoing, smiling sham Swede enshrouding the Swede buried alive. If only he could even faintly reconstitute the undivided oneness of existence that had made for his straightforward physical confidence and freedom before he became the father of an alleged murderer. If only he could be as unknowing as some people perceived him to be—if only he could be as perfectly simple as the legend of Swede Levov concocted by the hero-worshiping kids of his day. If only *he* could say, "I hate this house!" and be Weequahic's Swede Levov again. If he could say, "I hate that child! I never want to see her again!" and then go ahead, disown her, forevermore despise and reject her and the vision for which she was willing, if not to kill, then to cruelly abandon her own family, a vision having nothing whatsoever to do with "ideals" but with dishonesty, criminality, megalomania, and insanity. Blind antagonism and an infantile desire to menace—*those* were her ideals. In search always of something to hate. Yes, it went way, way beyond her stuttering. That violent hatred of America was a disease unto itself. And he loved America. Loved being an *American.* But back then he hadn't dared begin to explain to her why he did, for fear of unleashing the demon, insult. They lived in dread of Merry's stuttering tongue. And by then he had no influence anyway. Dawn had no influence. His parents had no influence. In what way was she "his" any longer if she hadn't even been his then, certainly not his if to drive her into her frightening blitzkrieg mentality it required no more than for her own father to begin to explain why his affections happened to be for the country where he'd been born and raised. Stuttering, sputtering little bitch! Who the fuck did she think she was?

Imagine the vileness with which she would have assaulted him for revealing to her that just reciting the names of the forty-eight states used to thrill him back when he was a little kid. The truth of it was that even the road maps used to give him a kick when they gave them away free at the gas station. So did the offhand way he had got his nickname. The first day of high school, down in the gym for their first class, and him just jerking around with the basketball while the other kids were still all over the place getting into their sneakers. From fifteen feet out he dropped in two hook shots—swish! swish!—just to get started. And then that easygoing way that Henry "Doc" Ward, the popular young phys ed teacher and wrestling coach fresh from Montclair State, laughingly called from his office doorway—called out to this lanky blond fourteen-year-old with the brilliant blue gaze and the easy, effortless style whom he'd never seen in his gym before—"Where'd you learn that, Swede?" Because the name differentiated Seymour Levov from Seymour Munzer and Seymour Wishnow, who were also on the class roll, it stuck all through gym his freshman year; then other teachers and coaches took it up, then kids in the school, and afterward, as long as Weequahic remained the old Jewish Weequahic and people there still cared about the past, Doc Ward was known as the guy who'd christened Swede Levov. It just stuck. Simple as that, an old American nickname, proclaimed by a gym teacher, bequeathed in a gym, a name that made him mythic in a way that Seymour would never have done, mythic not only during his school years but to his schoolmates, in memory, for the rest of their days. He carried it with him like an invisible passport, all the while wandering deeper and deeper into an American's life, forthrightly evolving into a large, smooth, optimistic American such as his conspicuously raw forebears—including the obstinate father whose American claim was not inconsiderable—couldn't have dreamed of as one of their own.

The way his father talked to people, that got him too, the American way his father said to the guy at the pump, "Fill 'er up, Mac. Check the front end, will ya, Chief?" The excitement of their trips in the DeSoto. The tiny, musty tourist cabins they stopped at overnight while meandering up through the scenic back roads of New York State to see Niagara Falls. The trip to Washington when Jerry was a brat all the way. His first liberty home from the marines, the pilgrimage to Hyde Park with the folks and Jerry to stand together as a family looking at FDR's grave. Fresh from boot camp and there at Roosevelt's grave, he felt that something meaningful was happening; hardened and richly tanned from training through the hottest months on a parade ground where the temperature rose some days to a hundred twenty degrees, he stood silent, proudly wearing his new summer uniform, the shirt starched, the khaki pants sleekly pocketless over the rear and perfectly pressed, the tie pulled taut, cap centered on his close-shaven head, black leather dress shoes spit-shined, agleam, and the belt—the belt that made him feel most like a marine, that tightly woven khaki fabric belt with the metal buckle—girding a waist that had seen him through some ten thousand sit-ups as a raw Parris Island recruit. Who was she to sneer at all this, to reject all this, to hate all this and set out to destroy it? The war, winning the war—did she hate that too? The neighbors, out in the street, crying and hugging on V-J Day, blowing car horns and marching up and down front lawns loudly banging kitchen pots. He was still at Parris Island then, but his mother had described it to him in a three-page letter. The celebration party at the playground back of the school that night, everyone they knew, family friends, school friends, the neighborhood butcher, the grocer, the pharmacist, the tailor, even the bookie from the candy store, all in ecstasy, long lines of staid middle-aged people madly mimicking Carmen Miranda and dancing the conga, one-two-three *kick*, one-two-three *kick*, until after two A.M. The war.

Winning that war. Victory, victory, victory had come! No more death and war!

His last months of high school, he'd read the paper every night, following the marines across the Pacific. He saw the photographs in *Life*—photographs that haunted his sleep—of the crumpled bodies of dead marines killed on Peleliu, an island in a chain called the Palaus. At a place called Bloody Nose Ridge, Japs ferreted in old phosphate mines, who were themselves to be burned to a crisp by the flamethrowers, had cut down hundreds and hundreds of young marines, eighteen-year-olds, nineteen-year-olds, boys barely older than he was. He had a map up in his room with pins sticking out of it, pins he had inserted to mark where the marines, closing in on Japan, had assaulted from the sea a tiny atoll or an island chain where the Japs, dug into coral fortresses, poured forth ferocious mortar and rifle fire. Okinawa was invaded on April 1, 1945, Easter Sunday of his senior year and just two days after he'd hit a double and a home run in a losing game against West Side. The Sixth Marine Division overran Yontan, one of the two island air bases, within three hours of wading ashore. Took the Motobu Peninsula in thirteen days. Just off the Okinawa beach, two kamikaze pilots attacked the flagship carrier *Bunker Hill* on May 14—the day after the Swede went four for four against Irvington High, a single, a triple, and two doubles—plunging their planes, packed with bombs, into the flight deck jammed with American planes all gassed up to take off and laden with ammunition. The blaze climbed a thousand feet into the sky, and in the explosive firestorm that raged for eight hours, four hundred sailors and aviators died. Marines of the Sixth Division captured Sugar Loaf Hill, May 14, 1945—three more doubles for the Swede in a winning game against East Side—maybe the worst, most savage single day of fighting in marine history. Maybe the worst in human history. The caves and tunnels that honeycombed Sugar Loaf Hill at the southern end of the island, where the Japs had fortified and hidden their army, were blasted with flamethrowers and then sealed with grenades and demolition charges. Hand-to-hand fighting went on day and night.

Jap riflemen and machine gunners, chained to their positions and unable to retreat, fought until they died. The day the Swede graduated from Weequahic High, June 22—having racked up the record number of doubles in a single season by a Newark City League player—the Sixth Marine Division raised the American flag over Okinawa's second air base, Kadena, and the final staging area for the invasion of Japan was secured. From April 1, 1945, to June 21, 1945—coinciding, give or take a few days, with the Swede's last and best season as a high school first baseman—an island some fifty miles long and about ten miles wide had been occupied by American forces at the cost of 15,000 American lives. The Japanese dead, military and civilian, numbered 141,000. To conquer the Japanese homeland to the north and end the war meant the number of dead on each side could run ten, twenty, thirty times as great. And still the Swede went out and, to be a part of the final assault on Japan, joined the U.S. Marines, who on Okinawa, as on Tarawa, Iwo Jima, Guam, and Guadalcanal, had absorbed casualties that were stupefying.

The marines. Being a marine. Boot camp. Knocked us around every which way, called us all kinds of names, physically and mentally murdered us for three months, and it was the best experience I ever had in my life. Took it on as a challenge and I did it. My name became "Ee-oh." That's the way the southern drill instructors pronounced Levov, dropping the *L* and the two *v*'s—all consonants overboard—and lengthening out the two vowels. "Ee-oh!" Like a donkey braying. "Ee-oh!" "Yes, sir!" Major Dunleavy, the athletic director, big guy, Purdue football coach, stops the platoon one day and the hefty sergeant we called Sea Bag shouts for Private Ee-oh and out I run with my helmet on, and my heart was pounding because I thought my mother had died. I was just a week away from being assigned to Camp Lejeune, up in North Carolina, for advanced weaponry training, but Major Dunleavy pulled the plug on that and so I never got to fire a BAR. And that was why I'd joined the marines—wanted more than anything to fire the BAR from flat on my belly with the barrel elevated on a mount. Eighteen years old and that was the Marine Corps to me, the rapid-firing, air-cooled .30 caliber machine gun. What a patriotic kid that innocent kid was. Wanted to fire the tank killer, the hand-held bazooka rocket, wanted to prove to myself I wasn't scared and could do that stuff. Grenades, flamethrowers, crawling under barbed wire, blowing up bunkers, attacking caves. Wanted to hit the beach in a duck. Wanted to help win the war. But Major Dunleavy had got a letter from his friend in Newark, what an athlete this Levov was, glowing letter about how wonderful I was, and so they reassigned me and made me a drill instructor to keep me on the island to play ball—by then they'd dropped the atomic bomb and the war was over anyway. "You're in my unit, Swede. Glad to have you." A great break, really. Once my hair grew in, I was a human being again. Instead of being called "shithead" all the time or "shithead-move-your-ass," suddenly I was a DI the recruits called Sir. What the DI called the recruits was You People! Hit the deck, You People! On your feet, You People! Double time, You People, double time *hup!* Great, great experience for a kid from Keer Avenue. Guys I would never have met in my life. Accents from all over the place. The Midwest. New England. Some farm boys from Texas and the Deep South I couldn't even understand. But got to know them. Got to like them. Hard boys, poor boys, lots of high school athletes. Used to live with the boxers. Lived with the recreation gang. Another Jewish guy, Manny Rabinowitz from Altoona. Toughest Jewish guy I ever met in my life. What a fighter. A great friend. Didn't even finish high school. Never had a friend like that before or since. Never laughed so hard in my life as I did with Manny. Manny was money in the bank for me. Nobody ever gave us any Jewboy shit. A little back in boot camp, but that was it. When Manny fought, the guys would bet their cigarettes on him. Buddy Falcone and Manny Rabinowitz were always the two winners for us whenever we fought another base. After the fight with Manny the other guy would say that nobody had ever hit him as hard in his life. Manny ran the entertainment with me, the boxing smokers. The duo—the Jewish leathernecks. Manny got the wiseguy recruit who made all the trouble and weighed a hundred and forty-five pounds to fight somebody a hundred and sixty pounds who he could be sure would beat the shit out of him. "Always pick a redhead, Ee-oh," Manny said, "he'll give you the best fight in the world. Redhead'll never quit." Manny the scientist. Manny going up to Norfolk to fight a sailor, a middle-weight contender before the war, and whipping him. Exercising the battalion before breakfast. Marching the recruits down to the pool every night to teach them to swim. We practically threw them in—the old-fashioned way of teaching swimming, but you had to swim to be a marine. Always had to be ready to do ten more push-ups than any of the recruits. They'd challenge me, but I was in shape. Getting on the bus going to play ball. The long distances we flew. Bob Collins on the team, the big St. John's guy. My teammate. Terrific athlete. Boozer. With Bob C. got drunk for the first time in my life, talked for two hours nonstop about playing ball for Weequahic and then threw up all over the deck. Irish guys, Italian guys, Slovaks, Poles, tough little bastards from Pennsylvania, kids who'd run away from fathers who worked in the mines and beat them with belt buckles and with their fists—these were the guys I lived with and ate with and slept alongside. Even an Indian guy, a Cherokee, a third baseman. Called him Piss Cutter, the same as the name for our caps. Don't ask me why. Not all of them decent people but on the whole all right. Good guys. Lots of organized grabass. Played against Fort Benning. Cherry Point, North Carolina, the marine air base. Beat them. Beat Charleston Navy Yard. We had a couple of boys who could throw that ball. One pitcher went on to the Tigers. Went down to Rome, Georgia, to play ball, over to Waycross, Georgia, to an army base. Called the army guys doggies. Beat *them*. Beat everybody. Saw the South. Saw things I never saw. Saw the life the Negroes live. Met every kind of Gentile you can think of. Met beautiful southern girls. Met common whores. Used a condom. Skinned 'er back and squeezed 'er down. Saw Savannah. Saw New Orleans. Sat in a rundown slopchute in Mobile, Alabama, where I was damn glad the shore patrol was just outside the door. Playing basketball and baseball with the Twenty-second Regiment.

Got to be a United States Marine. Got to wear the emblem with the anchor and the globe. "No pitcher in there, Ee-oh, poke it outta here, Ee-oh—" Got to be Ee-oh to guys from Maine, New Hampshire, Louisiana, Virginia, Mississippi, Ohio—guys without an education from all over America calling me Ee-oh and nothing more. Just plain Ee-oh to them. Loved that. Discharged June 2, 1947. Got to marry a beautiful girl named Dwyer. Got to run a business my father built, a man whose own father couldn't speak English. Got to live in the prettiest spot in the world. Hate America? Why, he lived in America the way he lived inside his own skin. All the pleasures of his younger years were American pleasures, all that success and happiness had been American, and he need no longer keep his mouth shut about it just to defuse her ignorant hatred. The loneliness he would feel as a man without all his American feelings. The longing he would feel if he had to live in another country. Yes, everything that gave meaning to his accomplishments had been American. Everything he loved was here.

For her, being an American was loathing America, but loving America was something he could not let go of any more than he could have let go of loving his father and his mother, any more than he could have let go of his decency. How could she "hate" this country when she had no *conception* of this country? How could a child of his be so blind as to revile the "rotten system" that had given her own family every opportunity to succeed? To revile her "capitalist" parents as though their wealth were the product of anything other than the unstinting industry of three generations. The men of three generations, including even himself, slogging through the slime and stink of a tannery. The family that started out in a tannery, at one with, side by side with, the lowest of the low—now to her "capitalist dogs." There wasn't much difference, *and she knew it*, between hating America and hating them. He loved the America she hated and blamed for everything that was imperfect in life and wanted violently to overturn, he loved the "bourgeois values" she hated and ridiculed and wanted to subvert, he loved the mother she hated and had all but murdered by doing what she did. Ignorant little fucking bitch! The price they had paid! Why *shouldn't* he tear up this Rita Cohen letter? Rita Cohen! They were back! The sadistic mischief-makers with their bottomless talent for antagonism who had extorted the money from him, who, for the fun of it, had extracted from him the Audrey Hepburn scrapbook, the stuttering diary, and the ballet shoes, these delinquent young brutes calling themselves "revolutionaries" who had so viciously played with his hopes five years back had decided the time had again rolled around to laugh at Swede Levov.

*We can only stand as witnesses to the anguish that sanctifies her. The Disciple Who Calls Herself "Rita Cohen."* They were laughing at him. They *had* to be laughing. Because the only thing worse than its all being a wicked joke was its *not* being a wicked joke. *Your daughter is divine.* My daughter is anything and everything but. She is all too frail and misguided and wounded—she's hopeless! Why did you tell her that you slept with me? And tell me that it was *she* who wanted you to. You say these things because you hate us. And you hate us because we *don't* do such things. You hate us not because we're reckless but because we're prudent and sane and industrious and agree to abide by the law. You hate us because we haven't failed. Because we've worked hard and honestly to become the best in the business and because of that we have prospered, so you envy us and you hate us and want to destroy us. And so you used her. A sixteen-year-old kid with a stutter. No, nothing small about you people. Made her into a "revolutionary" full of great thoughts and high-minded ideals. Sons of bitches. You *enjoy* the spectacle of our devastation. Cowardly bastards. It isn't clichés that enslaved her, it's *you* who enslaved her in the loftiest of the shallow clichés—and that resentful kid, with her stutterer's hatred of injustice, had no protection at all. You got her to believe she was at one with the downtrodden people—and made her into your patsy, your stooge. And Dr. Fred Conlon, as a result, is dead. That was who you killed to stop the war: the chief of staff up at the hospital in Dover, the guy who in a small community hospital established a coronary care unit of eight beds. That was *his* crime.

Instead of exploding in the middle of the night when the village was empty, the bomb, either as planned or by mistake, went off at five A.M., an hour before Hamlin's store opened for the day and the moment that Fred Conlon turned away from having dropped into the mailbox envelopes containing checks for household bills that he'd paid at his desk the evening before. He was on his way to the hospital. A chunk of metal flying out of the store struck him at the back of the skull.

Dawn was under sedation and couldn't see anyone, but the Swede had gone to Russ and Mary Hamlin's house and expressed his sympathy about the store, told the Hamlins how much the store had meant to Dawn and him, how it was no less a part of their lives than it was of everyone else's in the community; then he went to the wake—in the coffin Conlon looked fine, fit, just as affable as ever—and the following week, with their doctor already arranging for Dawn's hospitalization, the Swede went alone to visit Conlon's widow. How he managed to get to that woman's house for tea is another story—another *book*—but he did it, he did it, and heroically she served him tea while he extended his family's condolences in the words that he had revised in his mind five hundred times but that, when spoken, were still no good, even more hollow than those he'd uttered to Russ and Mary Hamlin: "deep and sincere re-grets . . . the agony of your family . . . my wife would like you to know. . . ." After listening to everything he had to say, Mrs. Conlon quietly replied, displaying an outlook so calm and kind and com-passionate that the Swede wanted to disappear, to hide like a child, while at the same time the urge was nearly overpowering to throw himself at her feet and to remain there forever, begging for her forgiveness. "You are good parents and you raised your daughter the way you thought best," she said to him. "It was not your fault and I don't hold anything against you. You didn't go out and buy the dynamite. You didn't make the bomb. You didn't plant the bomb. You had nothing to do with the bomb. If, as it appears, your daughter turns out to be the one who is responsible, I will hold no one responsible but her. I feel badly for you and your family, Mr.

Levov. I have lost a husband, my children have lost a father. But you have lost something even greater. You are parents who have lost a child. There is not a day that goes by that you won't be in my thoughts and in my prayers." The Swede had known Fred Conlon only slightly, from cocktail parties and charity events where they found themselves equally bored. Mainly he knew him by reputation, a man who cared about his family and the hospital with the same devotion—a hard worker, a good guy. Under him, the hospital had begun to plan a building program, the first since its construction, and in addition to the new coronary care unit, during his stewardship there had been a long-overdue modernization of emergency room facilities. But who gives a shit about the emergency room of a community hospital out in the sticks? Who gives a shit about a rural general store whose owner has been running it since 1921? We're talking about *humanity!* When has there ever been progress for humanity without a few small mishaps and mistakes? The people are angry and they have spoken! Violence will be met by violence, regardless of consequences, until the people are liberated! Fascist America down one post office, facility completely destroyed.

Except, as it happened, Hamlin's was not an official U.S. post *office* nor were the Hamlins U.S. postal employees—theirs was merely a postal *station* contracted, for $x$ number of dollars, to handle a little postal business on the side. Hamlin's was no more a government installation than the office where your accountant makes out your tax forms. But that is a mere technicality to world revolutionaries. Facility destroyed! Eleven hundred Old Rimrock residents forced, for a full year and a half, to drive five miles to buy their stamps and to get packages weighed and to send anything registered or special delivery. That'll show Lyndon Johnson who's boss.

They were laughing at him. *Life* was laughing at him.

Mrs. Conlon had said, "You are as much the victims of this tragedy as we are. The difference is that for us, though recovery will take time, we will survive as a family. We will survive as a loving family. We will survive with our memories intact and with our memories to sustain us. It will not be any easier for us than it will be for you to make sense of something so senseless. But we are the same family we were when Fred was here, and we will survive."

The clarity and force with which she implied that the Swede and his family would *not* survive made him wonder, in the weeks that followed, if her kindness and her compassion were so all-encompassing as he had wanted at first to believe.

He never went to see her again.

He told his secretary that he was going over to New York, to the Czech mission, where he'd already had preliminary discussions about a trip to Czechoslovakia later in the fall. In New York he had examined specimen gloves as well as shoes, belts, pocketbooks, and wallets manufactured in Czechoslovakia, and now the Czechs were working up plans for him to visit factories in Brno and Bratislava so he could see the glove setup firsthand and examine a more extensive sample of their work while it was in production and when it came off the floor. There was no longer any question that in Czechoslovakia leather apparel could be more cheaply made than in Newark or Puerto Rico—and probably better made, too. The workmanship that had begun falling off in the Newark plant since the riots had continued to deteriorate, especially once Vicky retired as making room forelady. Even granting that what he'd seen at the Czech mission might not be representative of day-to-day production, it had been impressive enough. Back in the thirties the Czechs had flooded the American market with fine gloves, over the years excellent Czech cutters had been employed by Newark Maid, and the machinist who for thirty years had been employed full-time tending Newark Maid's sewing machines, keeping those work-horses running—replacing worn-out shafts, levers, throat plates, bobbins, endlessly adjusting each machine's timing and tension—was a Czech, a wonderful worker, expert with every glove machine on earth, able to fix anything. Even though the Swede had assured his father he had no intention of signing over any aspect of their operation to a Communist government until he'd returned with a thorough report, he was confident that pulling out of Newark wasn't far down the line.

Dawn by this time had her new face and had begun the startling comeback, and as for Merry . . . well, Merry dear, Merry darling, my precious one-and-only Merry-child, how can I possibly remain on Central Avenue struggling to keep my production up, taking the beating we're taking there from black people who care nothing any longer about the quality of my product—people who are careless, people who've got me over a barrel because they know there's nobody trainable left in Newark to replace them—for fear that if I leave Central Avenue you will call me a racist and never see me again? I have waited so long to see *you* again, your mother has waited, Grandpa and Grandma have waited, we have all been waiting twenty-four hours a day every day of every year for five years to see you or to hear from you or somehow to get some word of you, and we can postpone our lives no longer. It's 1973. Mother is a new woman. If we are ever again going to live, now is when we must begin.

Nonetheless, he was waiting not for the pleasant consul at the Czech mission to welcome him with a glass of slivovitz (as his father or his wife would think if they happened to phone the office) but across from the dog and cat hospital on New Jersey Railroad Avenue, a ten-minute car ride from the Newark Maid factory.

Ten minutes away. And for years? In Newark, for years? Merry was living in the one place in the world he would never have guessed had he been given a thousand guesses. Was he deficient in intelligence, or was she so provocative, so perverse, so insane he still could not imagine *anything* she might do? Was he deficient also in imagination? What father wouldn't be? It was preposterous. His daughter was living in Newark, working across the Pennsylvania Railroad tracks, and not at the end of the Ironbound where the Portuguese were reclaiming the poor Down Neck streets but here at the Ironbound's westernmost edge, in the shadow of the railroad viaduct that closed off Railroad Avenue all along the western side of the street. That grim fortification was the city's Chinese wall, brownstone boulders piled twenty feet high, strung out for more than a mile and intersected only by half a dozen foul underpasses. Along this forsaken street, as ominous now as any street in any ruined city in America, was a reptilian length of unguarded wall barren even of graffiti. But for the wilted weeds that managed to jut forth in wiry clumps where the mortar was cracked and washed away, the viaduct wall was barren of everything except the affirmation of a weary industrial city's prolonged and triumphant struggle to monumentalize its ugliness.

On the east side of the street, the dark old factories—Civil War factories, foundries, brassworks, heavy-industrial plants blackened from the chimneys pumping smoke for a hundred years—were windowless now, the sunlight sealed out with brick and mortar, their exits and entrances plugged with cinderblock. These were the factories where people had lost fingers and arms and got their feet crushed and their faces scalded, where children once labored in the heat and the cold, the nineteenth-century factories that churned up people and churned out goods and now were unpierceable, airtight tombs. It was Newark that was entombed there, a city that was not going to stir again. The pyramids of Newark: as huge and dark and hideously impermeable as a great dynasty's burial edifice has every historical right to be.

The rioters hadn't crossed beneath the elevated railroad tracks—if they had, these factories, the whole block of them, would be burned-out rubble like the West Market Street factories back of Newark Maid.

His father used to tell him, "Brownstone and brick. There was the business. Brownstone quarried right here. Know that? Out by Belleville, north along the river. This city's got everything. What a business that must have been. The guy who sold Newark brownstone and brick—*he* was sittin' pretty."

On Saturday mornings, the Swede would drive Down Neck alongside his father to pick up the week's finished gloves from the Italian families paid to do piecework in their homes. As the car bounced along the streets paved with bricks, past one poor little frame house after another, the massive railroad viaduct remained brokenly within view. It would not go away. This was the Swede's first encounter with the manmade sublime that divides and dwarfs, and in the beginning it was frightening to him, a child susceptible to his environment even then, with a proclivity to be embraced by it and to embrace it in return. Six or seven years old. Maybe five, maybe Jerry hadn't even been born yet. The dwarfing stones causing the city to be even more gigantic for him than it already was. The manmade horizon, the brutal cut in the body of the giant city—it felt as though they were entering the shadow world of hell, when all the boy was seeing was the railroad's answer to the populist crusade to hoist the tracks above the grade crossings so as to end the crashes and the pedestrian carnage. "Brownstone and brick," said his father admiringly. "*There* was a guy whose worries were over."

That had all taken place before they'd moved to Keer Avenue, when they were living across from the synagogue in a three-family house at the poor end of Wainwright Street. His father didn't have even a loft then but got his skins from a fellow who was also Down Neck and who trafficked out of his garage in whatever the workers could carry from the tanneries hidden within their big rubber boots or wrapped around them beneath their overalls. The hide man was himself a tannery worker, a big, gruff Pole with tattoos up and down his massive arms, and the Swede had vague memories of his father's standing at the garage's one window holding the finished hides up to the light and searching them for defects, then stretching them over his knee before making his selection. "Feel this," he'd say to the Swede once they were safely back in the car, and the child would crease a delicate kidskin as he'd seen his father do, finger the fineness appreciatively, the velvet texture of the skin's close, tight grain. "*That's* leather," his father told him. "What makes kidskin so delicate, Seymour?" "I don't know." "Well, what is a kid?" "A baby goat." "Right. And what does he eat?" "Milk?" "Right. And because all the animal has eaten is milk, that's what makes the grain smooth and beautiful. Look at the pores of this skin with a magnifying glass and they're so fine you can't even see 'em. But the kid starts eating grass, that skin's a different story. The goat eats grass and the skin is like sandpaper. The finest glove leather for a formal glove is what, Seymour?" "Kid." "That's my boy. But it's not only the kid, son, it's the tanning. You've got to know your tannery. It's like a good cook and a bad cook. You get a good piece of meat and a bad cook can spoil it for you. How come someone makes a wonderful cake and the other doesn't? One is moist and nice and the other is dry. Same thing in leather. I worked in the tannery. It's the chemicals, it's the time, it's the temperature. That's where the difference comes in. That, and not buying second-rate skins to begin with. Cost as much to tan a bad skin as a good skin. Cost more to tan a bad one—you work harder at it. Beautiful, beautiful," he said, "wonderful stuff," once again lovingly kneading the kidskin between his fingertips. "You know how you get it like this, Seymour?" "How, Daddy?" "You work at it."

There were eight, ten, twelve immigrant families scattered throughout Down Neck to whom Lou Levov distributed the skins along with his own patterns, people from Naples who had been glovers in the old country and the best of whom wound up working at Newark Maid's first home when he could come up with the rent for the small loft on West Market Street on the top floor of the chair factory. The old Italian grandfather or the father did the cutting on the kitchen table, with the French rule, the shears, and the spud knife he'd brought from Italy. The grandmother or the mother did the sewing, and the daughters did the laying off—ironing the glove—in the old-fashioned way, with irons heated up in a box set atop the kitchen's potbellied stove. The women worked on antique Singers, nineteenth-century machines that Lou Levov, who'd learned to reassemble them, had bought for a song and then repaired himself; at least once a week, he'd have to drive all the way Down Neck at night and spend an hour getting a machine running right again. Otherwise, both day and night, he was all over Jersey peddling the gloves the Italians had made for him, selling them at first out of the trunk of the car, right on a main downtown street, and, in time, directly to apparel shops and department stores that were Newark Maid's first solid accounts. It was in a tiny kitchen not half a mile from where the Swede was now standing that the boy had seen a pair of gloves cut by the oldest of the old Neapolitan artisans. He believed that he could remember sitting in his father's lap while Lou Levov sampled a glass of the family's homemade wine and across from them a cutter said to be a hundred years old who was supposed to have made gloves for the queen of Italy smoothed the ends of a trank with half a dozen twists of his knife's dull blade. "Watch him, Seymour. See how small the skin is? The most difficult thing in the world to cut a kidskin efficiently. Because it's so small. But watch what he does. You're watching a genius and you're watching an artist. The Italian cutter, son, is always more artistic in his outlook. And this is the master of them all." Sometimes hot meatballs would be frying in a pan, and he remembered how one of the Italian cutters, who always purred "Che bellezza . . ." and called him Piccirell', sweet little thing, when he stroked the Swede's blond head, taught him how to dip the crisp Italian bread in a pot of tomato sauce. No matter how tiny the yard out back, there were tomato plants growing, and a grapevine and a pear tree, and in every household there was always a grandfather. It was he who had made the wine and to whom Lou Levov uttered, in a Neapolitan dialect and with what he took to be the appropriate gesture, his repertoire's one complete Italian sentence, "'Na mano lava 'nad"—One hand washes the other—when he laid out on the oilcloth the dollar bills for the week's piecework. Then the boy and his father got up from the table with the finished lot and left for home, where Sylvia Levov would examine each glove, with a stretcher meticulously examine each seam of each finger and each thumb of every glove. "A pair of gloves," his father told the Swede, "are supposed to match perfectly—the grain of the leather, the color, the shading, everything. The first thing she looks to see is if the gloves match." While his mother worked she taught the boy about all the mistakes that can occur in the making of a glove, mistakes she had been taught to recognize as her husband's wife. A skipped stitch can turn into an open seam, but you can't see it, she told the child, without putting the stretcher into the glove and tensioning the seam. There are stitch holes that aren't supposed to be there but are because the sewer stitched wrong and then just tried to go on. There is something called butcher cuts that occur if the animal was cut too deeply when it was flayed. Even after the leather is shaved they're there, and though they don't necessarily break when you stress the glove with the stretcher, they could break if someone put the glove on. In every batch they brought up from Down Neck his father found at least one glove where the thumb didn't match the palm. This drove him wild. "See that? See, the cutter is trying to make his quota out of a skin, and he can't get a thumb out of the same hide as the trank, so he cheats—he takes the next skin and cuts the thumb, and it doesn't match, and it's no goddamn good to me at all. See here? Twisted fingers. This is what Mario was showing you this morning. When you're cutting a fourchette or a thumb or anything, you got to pull it straight. If you don't pull it straight, you're going to have a problem. If he pulled that fourchette crookedly on the bias, then when it's sewn together the finger is going to corkscrew just like this. That's what your mother is looking for. Because remember *and don't forget*—a Levov makes a glove that is *perfect*." Whenever his mother found something wrong she gave the glove to the Swede, who stuck a pin where the defect was, through the stitch and never through leather. "Holes in leather stay," his father warned him. "It's not like fabric, where the holes disappear. Always through the stitch, always!" After the boy and his mother had inspected the gloves in a lot, his mother used special thread to tack the gloves together, thread that breaks easily, his father explained, so that when the buyer pulls them apart the knots sewn on each side won't tear through the leather. After the gloves were tacked, the Swede's mother tissued them—laid a pair down on a sheet of tissue paper, folded the paper over, then over again so that each pair was protected together. A dozen pairs, counted out loud for her by the Swede, went into a box. It wasn't a fancy box back in the early days, just a plain brown box with a size scale on the end showing the sizes. The fancy black box with the gold trim and the name Newark Maid stamped in gold came along only when his father landed the breakthrough Bamberger's account and, afterward, the account with Macy's Little Accessory Shop. A distinctive, attractive box with the company name and a gold and black woven label in every glove made all the difference not only to the shop but to the knowledgeable upscale customer.

Every Saturday when they drove Down Neck to collect that week's finished gloves, they'd bring along the gloves the Swede had marked with a pin where his mother had discovered a defect. If a glove bristled with three pins or more, his father would have to warn the family who had made it that if they wanted to work for Newark Maid, sloppiness would not be tolerated. "Lou Levov doesn't sell a table-cut glove unless it is a *perfect* table-cut glove," he told them. "I'm not here to play games. I'm here like you are—I'm here to make money. 'Na mano lava 'nad, *and don't forget it.*"

"What is calfskin, Seymour?" "The skin from young calves." "What kind of grain?" "It has a tight, even grain. Very smooth. Glossy." "What's it used for?" "Mostly for men's gloves. It's heavy." "What is Cape?" "The skin of the South African haired sheep." "Cabretta?" "Not the wool-type sheep but the hair-type sheep." "From where?" "South America. Brazil." "That's part of the answer. The animals live a little north and south of the equator. Anywhere around the world. Southern India. Northern Brazil. A band across Africa—" "We got ours from *Brazil.*" "Right. That's true. You're right. I'm only telling you they come from other countries too. So you'll know. What's the key operation in preparing the skin?" "Stretching." "And never forget it. In this business, a sixteenth of an inch makes all the difference in the world. Stretching! Stretching is a hundred percent right. How many parts in a pair of gloves?" "Ten, twelve if there's a binding." "Name 'em." "Six fourchettes, two thumbs, two tranks." "The unit of measurement in the glove trade?" "Buttons." "What's a one-button glove?" "A one-button glove is one inch long if you measure from the base of the thumb to the top." "Approximately one inch long. What is silking?" "The three rows of stitching on the back of the glove. If you don't do the end pulling, all the silking is going to come right out." "Excellent. I didn't even ask you about end pulling. Excellent. What's the most difficult seam to make on a glove?" "Full piqué." "Why? Take your time, son—it's difficult. Tell me why." The prixseam. The gauge seam. Single draw points. Spear points. Buckskin. Mocha. English does. Soaking. Dehairing. Pickling. Sorting. Taxing. The grain finish. The velvet finish. Pasted linings. Skeleton linings. Seamless knitted wool. Cut-and-sewed knitted wool. . . .

As they drove back and forth Down Neck, it never stopped. Every Saturday morning from the time he was six until he was nine and Newark Maid became a company with its own loft.

The dog and cat hospital was located on the corner in a small, decrepit brick building next door to an empty lot, a tire dump, patchy with weeds nearly as tall as he was, the twisted wreckage of a wire-mesh fence lying at the edge of the sidewalk where he waited for his daughter . . . who lived in Newark . . . and for how long . . . and where, in what kind of quarters in this city? No, he did not lack imagination any longer—the imagining of the abhorrent was now effortless, even though it was impossible still to envisage how she had got herself from Old Rimrock to here. There was no delusion that he could any longer clutch at to soften whatever surprise was next.

This place where she worked certainly didn't make it look as if she continued to believe her calling was to change the course of American history. The building's rusted fire escape would just come down, just come loose from its moorings and crash onto the street, if anyone stepped on it—a fire escape whose function was not to save lives in the event of a fire but to uselessly hang there testifying to the immense loneliness inherent to living. For him it was stripped of any other meaning—no meaning could make better use of that building. Yes, alone we are, deeply alone, and always, in store for us, a layer of loneliness even deeper. There is nothing we can do to dispose of that. No, loneliness shouldn't surprise us, as astonishing to experience as it may be. You can try turning yourself inside out, but all you are then is inside out and lonely instead of inside in and lonely. My stupid, stupid Merry dear, stupider even than your stupid father, not even blowing up buildings helps. It's lonely if there are buildings and it's lonely if there are no buildings. There is no protest to be lodged against loneliness—not all the bombing campaigns in history have made a dent in it. The most lethal of manmade explosives can't touch it. Stand in awe not of Communism, my idiot child, but of ordinary, everyday loneliness. On May Day go out and march with your friends to its greater glory, the superpower of superpowers, the force that overwhelms all. Put your money on it, bet on it, worship it—bow down in submission not to Karl Marx, my stuttering, angry, idiot child, not to Ho Chi Minh and Mao Tse-tung—bow down to the great god Loneliness!

I'm lonesome, she used to say to him when she was a tiny girl, and he could never figure out where she had picked up that word. Lonesome. As sad a word as you could hear out of a two-year-old's mouth. But she had learned to say so much so soon, had talked so easily at first, so *intelligently*—maybe *that* was what lay behind the stutter, all those words she uncannily knew before other kids could pronounce their own names, the emotional overload of a vocabulary that included even "I'm lonesome."

He was the one she could talk to. "Daddy, let's have a conversation." More often than not, the conversations were about Mother. She would tell him that Mother had too much say about her clothes, too much say about her hair. Mother wanted to dress her more adultlike than the other kids. Merry wanted long hair like Patti, and Mother wanted it cut. "Mother would really be happy if I had to wear a uniform the way she did at St. Genevieve's." "Mother's conservative, that's all. But you do like shopping with her." "The best part of shopping with Mother is that you get a nice little lunch, which is fun. And sometimes it's fun picking out clothes. But still, Mother has too much s-s-s-s-say." At lunch in school she never ate what Mother gave her. "Baloney on white bread is disgusting. Liverwurst is disgusting. Tuna in the lunch bag gets all wet. The only thing that I like is Virginia ham, but with the crusts *off*. I like hot s-s-soup." But when she took hot soup to school she was always breaking the thermos. If not the first week, the second. Dawn got her special breakproof ones, but even those she could break. That was the extent of her destructiveness.

After school, when she baked with her friend Patti, Merry would always have to crack the eggs because Patti said cracking eggs made her sick. Merry thought this was silly, and so one afternoon she cracked the egg right in front of her and Patti threw up. *And that was her destructiveness—breaking a thermos and cracking an egg.* And getting rid of whatever her mother gave her for lunch. Never complained about it, just wouldn't eat it. And when Dawn began suspecting what was up and asked her what she had for lunch, Merry might have thrown it out without checking. "You're sometimes a troublesome child," Dawn told her. "I'm not. I'm not that t-t-t-troublesome if you don't ask what I had for lunch." Exasperated, her mother said, "It isn't always easy being you, is it, Merry?" "I think it's easier being me, Mom, than maybe it is being n-n-near me." To her father she confided, "I didn't think the fruit was that ex-ex-citing, so I threw that out too." "And the milk you threw out." "The milk was a little bit warm, Dad." But there was always a dime at the bottom of the lunch bag for ice cream, and so that's what she would have. Didn't like mustard. That was another complaint in the years before she began to complain about capitalism. "What kid does?" she asked him. The answer was Patti. Patti would eat sandwiches with mustard and processed cheese; Merry, as she confided to her father in their conversations, didn't understand that "*at all.*" Melted cheese sandwiches were what Merry preferred to everything else. Melted Muenster cheese and white bread. After school she'd bring Patti home with her, and because Merry had thrown out her lunch, they made melted cheese sandwiches. Sometimes they would just melt cheese on a piece of foil. She was sure that she could survive on melted cheese alone, she told her father, if she ever had to. That was probably the most irresponsible thing the child had ever done—after school with Patti melting cheese on pieces of foil and gobbling it down—until she blew up the general store. She couldn't even bring herself to say how much Patti got on her nerves, for fear of hurting Patti's feelings. "The problem is when somebody comes over to your house, after a while you get s-s-s-sick of them." But always she acted with Dawn as though she wanted Patti to stay longer. *Mom, can Patti stay for dinner? Mom, can Patti stay overnight? Mom, can Patti wear my boots? Mom, can you drive me and Patti to the village?*

In fifth grade she gave her mother a Mother's Day gift. On a doily in school they were asked to write something they would do for their mothers, and Merry wrote that she would prepare dinner every Friday night, a fairly generous offer for a ten-year-old but one she made good on and kept up largely because that way she could be sure that one night a week they got baked ziti; also, if you made dinner you didn't have to clean up. With Dawn's help she would sometimes make lasagna or stuffed shells, but the baked ziti she made by herself. Sometimes on Friday it would be macaroni and cheese but mostly it was baked ziti. The important thing, she told her father, was to see that the cheese melted, though it was equally important to be sure that the top zitis got hard and crunchy. He was the one who cleaned up when she cooked the baked ziti, and there was always a lot to clean up. But he loved it. "Cooking is fun and cleaning up is not," she confided in him, but that was not his experience when Merry was cooking. When he heard from a Bloomingdale's buyer that a restaurant on West 49th Street had the best baked ziti in New York, he began to take the family to Vincent's once a month. They'd go to Radio City or to a Broadway musical, and then to Vincent's. Merry loved Vincent's. And a young waiter named Billy loved her, as it turned out, because of a kid brother he had at home who also stuttered. He told Merry about the TV stars and the movie stars who showed up at Vincent's to eat. "See where your dad is sitting? See his chair, signorina? Danny Thomas sat in that chair last night. You know what Danny Thomas says when people come up to his table and introduce themselves to him?"

"I d-d-don't," said the signorina. "He says, 'Nice to see you.'" And on Monday, at school, she repeated to Patti whatever Billy at Vincent's in New York had told her the day before. Had there ever been a happier child? A less destructive child? A little signorina any more loved by her mother and father?

No.

A black woman in tight yellow slacks, a woman colossal as a dray horse through the hindquarters, tottered up to him on her high-heeled shoes, extending a tiny scrap of paper in one hand. Her face was badly scarred. He knew she had come to inform him that his daughter was dead. That was what was written on the paper. It was a note from Rita Cohen. "Sir," she said, "can you tell me where the Salvation Army is?" "Is there one?" he asked. She did not look as though she thought there was. But she replied, "I believe so, yeah." She held up the piece of paper. "Says so. Do you know where it is, sir?" Anything beginning with sir or ending with sir usually means "I want money," and so he reached into his pocket, passed her some bills, and she lurched away, disappeared down into the underpass on those ill-fitting shoes, and after that he saw no one.

He waited for forty more minutes and would have waited another forty, have waited there until it grew dark, might well have remained long after that, a man in a seven-hundred-dollar custom-made suit with his back against a lamppost like a vagrant in threadbare rags, a man who from all appearances had meetings to attend and business to transact and social obligations to fulfill, self-consciously loitering on a blighted street near the railroad station, maybe a rich out-of-towner under the mistaken impression that he'd landed in the red-light district, pretending to stare aimlessly into space while his head is full of secrets and his heart is (as it was) thumping away. On the chance that, horribly enough, Rita Cohen was telling the truth and always had been, he might well have stood vigil there all night long and through to the next morning, thinking to catch Merry *coming* to work. But, mercifully, if that is the word, in only forty minutes she appeared, a figure tall and female but one he might never have taken for his daughter had he not been told to look for her there.

Again imagination had failed him. He felt as though he had no control over muscles that he'd mastered at the age of two—he wouldn't have been surprised if everything, not excluding his blood, had come gushing from him onto the pavement. This was too much to battle with. This was too much to bring home to Dawn's new face. Not even electrically operated skylights over a modern kitchen whose heart was a state-of-the-art cooking island would enable her to find her way back from this. Eighteen hundred nights at the mercy of a murderer's father's imagination still hadn't prepared him for her incognito. It had not required this to elude the FBI. How she got to this was too horrible for him to contemplate. But to run from his own child? In fear? There was her *soul* to cherish. "Life!" he instructed himself. "I cannot let her go! Our life!" And by then Merry had seen him, and had it even been possible for him, he did not fall to pieces and run, because it was now too late to run.

And to what would he have run anyway? To that Swede who did it all so effortlessly? To that Swede blessedly oblivious of himself and his thoughts? To the Swede Levov who once upon a time . . . He might as well turn for help to that hefty black woman with the scarred face, expect to find himself by asking her, "Madam, do you know where it is that I am? Have you any idea where I went?"

Merry had seen him. How could she miss him? How could she have missed him even on a street where there was life and not death, where there was a throng of the striving and the harried and the driven and the decisive and not this malignant void? There was her handsome, utterly recognizable six-foot-three father, the handsomest father a girl could have. She raced across the street, this frightful creature, and like the carefree child he used to enjoy envisioning back when he was himself a carefree child—the girl running from her swing outside the stone house—she threw herself upon his chest, her arms encircling his neck. From beneath the veil she wore across the lower half of her face—obscuring her mouth and her chin, a sheer veil that was the ragged foot off an old nylon stocking—she said to the man she had come to detest, "Daddy! Daddy!" faultlessly, just like any other child, and looking like a person whose tragedy was that she'd never been anyone's child.

They are crying intensely, the dependable father whose center is the source of all order, who could not overlook or sanction the smallest sign of chaos—for whom keeping chaos far at bay had been intuition's chosen path to certainty, the rigorous daily given of life—and the daughter who is chaos itself.

# 6

SHE HAD become a Jain. Her father didn't know what that meant until, in her unhampered, chantlike speech—the unimpeded speech with which she would have spoken at home had she ever been able to master a stutter while living within her parents' safekeeping—she patiently told him. The Jains were a relatively small Indian religious sect—that he could accept as fact. But whether Merry's practices were typical or of her own devising he could not be certain, even if she contended that every last thing she now did was an expression of religious belief. She wore the veil to do no harm to the microscopic organisms that dwell in the air we breathe. She did not bathe because she revered all life, including the vermin. She did not wash, she said, so as "to do no harm to the water." She did not walk about after dark, even in her own room, for fear of crushing some living object beneath her feet. There are souls, she explained, imprisoned in every form of matter; the lower the form of life, the greater is the pain to the soul imprisoned there. The only way ever to become free of matter and to arrive at what she described as "self-sufficient bliss for all eternity" was to become what she reverentially called "a perfected soul." One achieves this perfection only through the rigors of asceticism and self-denial and through the doctrine of *ahimsa* or nonviolence.

The five "vows" she'd taken were typewritten on index cards and taped to the wall above a narrow pallet of dirty foam rubber on the unswept floor. That was where she slept, and given that there was nothing but the pallet in one corner of the room and a rag pile—her clothing—in the other, that must be where she sat to eat whatever it was she survived on. Very, very little, from the look of her; from the look of her she could have been not fifty minutes east of Old Rimrock but in Delhi or Calcutta, near starvation not as a devout purified by her ascetic practices but as the despised of the lowest caste, miserably moving about on an untouchable's emaciated limbs.

The room was tiny, claustrophobically smaller even than the cell in the juveniles' prison where, when he could not sleep, he would imagine visiting her after she was apprehended. They had reached her room by walking from the dog and cat hospital down toward the station, then turning west through an underpass that led to McCarter Highway, an underpass no more than a hundred and fifty feet long but of the kind that causes drivers to hit the lock button on the door. There were no lights overhead, and the walkways were strewn with broken pieces of furniture, with beer cans, bottles, lumps of things that were unidentifiable. There were license plates underfoot. The place hadn't been cleaned in ten years. Maybe it had never been cleaned. Every step he took, bits of glass crunched beneath his shoes. There was a bar stool upright in the middle of the walkway. It had got there from where? Who had brought it? There was a twisted pair of men's pants. Filthy. Who was the man? What had happened to him? The Swede would not have been surprised to see an arm or a leg. A garbage sack blocked their way. Dark plastic. Knotted shut. What was in it? It was large enough for a dead body. And there were bodies, too, that were living, people shifting around in the filth, dangerous-looking people back in the dark. And above the blackened rafters, the thudding of a train—the noise of the trains rolling into the station heard from beneath their wheels. Five, six hundred trains a day rolling overhead.

To get where Merry rented a room just off McCarter Highway, you had to make it through an underpass not just as dangerous as any in Newark but as dangerous as any underpass in the world.

They were walking because she would not drive with him. "I only walk, Daddy, I do not go in motor vehicles," and so he had left his car out on Railroad Avenue for whoever came along to steal it, and walked beside her the ten minutes it took to reach her room, a walk that would have brought him to tears within the first ten steps had he not continued to recite to himself, "This is life! This is our life! I cannot let her go," had he not taken her hand in his and, as they traversed together that horrible underpass, reminded himself, "This is her hand. Merry's hand. Nothing matters but her hand." Would have brought him to tears because when she was six and seven years old she'd loved to play marines, either him yelling at her or her yelling at him, "'Ten*shun!* Stand at ease! Rest!"; she loved to march with him—"Forward *march!* To the left flank *march!* To the rear *march!* Right oblique *march!*"; loved to do marine calisthenics with him—"You People, hit the deck!"; she loved to call the ground "the deck," to call their bathroom "the head," to call her bed "the rack" and Dawn's food "the chow"; but most of all she loved to count Parris Island cadence for him as she started out across the pasture—mounted up on his shoulders—to find Momma's cows. "By yo leh, rah, leh, rah, leh, rah yo leh. Leh, rah, yo leh. . . ." And without stuttering. When they played marines, she did not stutter over a single word.

The room was on the ground floor of a house that a hundred years ago might have been a boardinghouse, not a bad one either, a respectable boardinghouse, brownstone below the parlor floor, neat brickwork above, curved railings of cast iron leading up the brick steps to the double doorway. But the old boardinghouse was now a wreck marooned on a narrow street where there were only two other houses left. Incredibly, two of the old Newark plane trees were left as well. The house was tucked between abandoned ware-houses and overgrown lots studded with chunks of rusted iron junk, mechanical debris scattered amid the weeds.

From over the door of the house, the pediment was gone, ripped out; the cornices had been ripped out too, carefully stolen and taken away to be sold in some New York antiques store. All over Newark, the oldest buildings were missing ornamental stone cornices—cornices from as high up as four stories plucked off in broad daylight with a cherry picker, with a hundred-thousand-dollar piece of equipment; but the cop is asleep or paid off and nobody stops whoever it is, from whatever agency that has a cherry picker, who is making a little cash on the side. The turkey frieze that ran around the old Essex produce market on Washington and Linden, the frieze with the terra-cotta turkeys and the huge cornucopias overflowing with fruit—stolen. Building caught fire and the frieze disappeared overnight. The big Negro churches (Bethany Baptist closed down, boarded up, looted, bulldozed; Wycliffe Presbyterian disastrously gutted by fire)—cornices stolen. Aluminum drainpipes even from occupied buildings, from standing buildings—stolen. Gutters, leaders, drainpipes—stolen. Everything was gone that anybody could get to. Just reach up and take it. Copper tubing in boarded-up factories, pull it out and sell it. Anyplace where the windows are gone and boarded up tells people immediately, "Come in and strip it. Whatever's left, strip it, steal it, sell it." Stripping stuff—that's the food chain. Drive by a place where a sign says this house is for sale, and there's nothing there, there's nothing to sell. Everything stolen by gangs in cars, stolen by the men who roam a city with shopping carts, stolen by thieves working alone. The people are desperate and they take anything. They "go junkin'" the way a shark goes fishing.

"If there's one brick still on top of the other," cried his father, "the idea gets into their heads that the *mortar* might be useful, so they'll push them apart and take *that*. Why not? The mortar! Seymour, this city isn't a city—it's a carcass! Get out!"

The street where Merry lived was paved with bricks. There couldn't be more than a dozen of these brick streets intact in the entire city. The last of the cobblestone streets, a pretty old cobblestone street, had been stolen about three weeks after the riots.

While the rubble still reeked of smoke where the devastation was the worst, a developer from the suburbs had arrived with a crew around one A.M., three trucks and some twenty men moving stealthily, and during the night, without a cop to bother them, they'd dug up the cobblestones from the narrow side street that cut diagonally back of Newark Maid and carted them all away. The street was gone when the Swede showed up for work the next morning.

"Now they're stealing streets?" his father asked. "Newark can't even hold on to its streets? Seymour, get the hell out!" His father's had become the voice of reason.

Merry's street was just a couple of hundred feet long, squeezed into the triangle between McCarter—where, as always, the heavy truck traffic barreled by night and day—and the ruins of Mulberry Street. Mulberry the Swede could recall as a Chinatown slum as long ago as the 1930s, back when the Newark Levovs, Jerry, Seymour, Momma, Poppa, used to file up the narrow stairwell to one of the family restaurants for a chow mein dinner on a Sunday afternoon and, later, driving home to Keer Avenue, his father would tell the boys unbelievable stories about the Mulberry Street "tong wars" of old.

Of old. Stories of old. There were no longer stories of old. There was nothing. There was a mattress, discolored and waterlogged, like a cartoon-strip drunk slumped against a pole. The pole still held up a sign telling you what corner you were on. And that's all there was.

Above and beyond the roofline of her house, he could see the skyline of commercial Newark half a mile away and those three familiar, comforting words, the most reassuring words in the English language, cascading down the elegantly ornate cliff that was once the focal point of a buzzing downtown—ten stories high the huge, white stark letters heralding fiscal confidence and institutional permanence, civic progress and opportunity and pride, indestructible letters that you could read from the seat of your jetliner descending from the north toward the international airport: FIRST FIDELITY BANK.

That's what was left, that lie. First. *Last.* LAST FIDELITY BANK. From down on the earth where his daughter now lived at the corner of Columbia and Green—where his daughter lived even worse than her greenhorn great-grandparents had, fresh from steerage, in their Prince Street tenement—you could see a mammoth signboard designed for concealing the truth. A sign in which only a madman could believe. A sign in a fairy tale.

Three generations. All of them growing. The working. The saving. The success. Three generations in raptures over America. Three generations of becoming one with a people. And now with the fourth it had all come to nothing. The total vandalization of their world.

Her room had no window, only a narrow transom over the door that opened onto the unlit hallway, a twenty-foot-long urinal whose decaying plaster walls he wanted to smash apart with his fists the moment he entered the house and smelled it. The hallway led out to the street through a door that had neither lock nor handle, nor glass in the double frame. Nowhere in her room could he see a faucet or a radiator. He could not imagine what the toilet was like or where it might be and wondered if the hallway was it for her as well as for the bums who wandered in off the highway or down from Mulberry Street. She would have lived better than this, far better, if she were one of Dawn's cattle, in the shed where the herd gathered in the worst weather with the proximity of one another's carcasses to warm them, and the rugged coats they grew in winter, and Merry's mother, even in the sleet, even on an icy, wintry day, up before six carrying hay bales to feed them. He thought of the cattle not at all unhappy out there in the winter and he thought of those two they called the "derelicts," Dawn's retired giant, Count, and the old mare Sally, each of them in human years comparable to seventy or seventy-five, who found each other when they were both over the hill and then became inseparable—one would go and the other would follow, doing all the things together that would keep them well and happy. It was fascinating to watch their routine and the wonderful life they had. Remembering how when it was sunny they would stretch out in the sun to warm their hides, he thought, If only she had become an animal.

It was beyond understanding, not only how Merry could be living in this hovel like a pariah, not only how Merry could be a fugitive wanted for murder, but how he and Dawn could have been the source of it all. How could their innocent foibles add up to this human being? Had none of this happened, had she stayed at home, finished high school, gone to college, there would have been problems, of course, big problems; she was precocious in her rebellion and there would have been problems even without a war in Vietnam. She might have wallowed a long while in the pleasures of resistance and the challenge of discovering how unrestrained she could be. But she would have been at home. At home you flip out a little and that's it. You do not have the pleasure of the *unadulterated* pleasure, you don't get to the point where you flip out a little so many times that finally you decide it's such a great, great kick, why not flip out a lot? At home there is no opportunity to douse yourself in this squalor. At home you can't live where the disorder is. At home you can't live where nothing is reined in. At home there is that tremendous discrepancy between the way she imagines the world to be and the way the world is for her. Well, no longer is there that dissonance to disturb her equilibrium. Here are her Rimrockian fantasies, and the culmination is horrifying.

Their disaster had been tragically shaped by time—they did not have enough time with her. When she's your ward, when she's there, you can do it. If you have contact with your child steadily over time, then the stuff that is off—the mistakes in judgment that are made on both sides—is somehow, through that steady, patient contact, made better and better, until at last, inch by inch, day by day and inch by inch, there is remediation, there are the ordinary satisfactions of parental patience rewarded, of things working out. . . . But this. Where was the remediation for *this?* Could he bring Dawn here to see her, Dawn in her bright, tight new face and Merry sitting cross-legged on the pallet in her tattered sweatshirt and ill-shapen trousers and black plastic shower clogs, meekly composed behind that nauseating veil? How broad her shoulder bones were. Like his. But hanging off those bones there was nothing. What he saw sitting before him was not a daughter, a woman, or a girl; what he saw, in a scarecrow's clothes, stick-skinny as a scarecrow, was the scantiest farmyard emblem of life, a travestied mock-up of a human being, so meager a likeness to a Levov it could have fooled only a bird. How could he bring Dawn here? Driving Dawn down McCarter Highway, turning off McCarter and into this street, the warehouses, the rubble, the garbage, the debris . . . Dawn seeing this room, smelling this room, her hands touching the walls of this room, let alone the unwashed flesh, the brutally cropped, bedraggled hair . . .

He kneeled down to read the index cards positioned just about where she once used to venerate, over her Old Rimrock bed, magazine photos of Audrey Hepburn.

> I renounce all killing of living beings, whether subtile or gross, whether movable or immovable.

> I renounce all vices of lying speech arising from anger, or greed, or fear, or mirth.

> I renounce all taking of anything not given, either in a village, or a town, or a wood, either of little or much, or small or great, or living or lifeless things.

> I renounce all sexual pleasures, either with gods, or men, or animals.

> I renounce all attachments, whether little or much, small or great, living or lifeless; neither shall I myself form such attachments, nor cause others to do so, nor consent to their doing so.

As a businessman the Swede was astute, and if need be, beneath the genial surface of the man's man—capitalizing on the genial surface—he could be as artfully calculating as the deal required. But he could not see how even the coldest calculation could help him here. Neither could all the fathering talent in the world collected and gathered up and mobilized in one man. He read through her five vows again, considered them as seriously as he could, all the while bewildering himself with the thought, For purity—in the name of purity.

Why? Because she'd killed someone, or because she would have needed purity whether she'd never killed a fly? Did it have to do with him? That foolish kiss? That was ten years behind them, and besides, it had been nothing, had come to nothing, did not appear to have meant anything much to her even at the time. Could something as meaningless, as commonplace, as ephemeral, as understandable, as forgivable, as innocent . . . No! How could he be asked again and again to take seriously things that were not serious? Yet that was the predicament that Merry had forced on him all the way back when she was blasting away at the dinner table about the immorality of their bourgeois life. How could anybody take that childish ranting seriously? He had done as well as any parent could have—he had listened and listened when it was all he could do not to get up from dinner and walk away until she'd spewed herself out; he had nodded and agreed to as much as he could even marginally agree to, and when he opposed her—say, about the moral efficacy of the profit motive—always it was with restraint, with all the patient reasonableness he could muster. And this was not easy for him, given that it was the profit motive to which a child requiring tens of thousands of dollars' worth of orthodontia, psychiatry, and speech therapy—not to mention ballet lessons and riding lessons and tennis lessons, all of which, growing up, she at one time or another was convinced she could not survive without—might be thought to owe if not a certain allegiance then at least a minuscule portion of gratitude. Perhaps the *mistake* was to have tried so hard to take seriously what was in no way serious; perhaps what he should have done, instead of listening so intently, so *respectfully,* to her ignorant raving was to reach over the table and whack her across the mouth.

But what would that have taught her about the profit motive—

what would it have taught her about him? Yet if he had, *if*, then the veiled mouth could be taken seriously. He could now berate himself, "Yes, I did it to her, I did it with my outbursts, my temper." But it seemed as though he had done whatever had been done to her because he could not *abide* a temper, had not wanted one or dared to have one. He had done it by kissing her. But that couldn't be. *None of this could possibly be.*

Yet it was. Here we are. Here *she* is, imprisoned in this rat hole with these "vows."

She was better off steeped in contempt. If he had to choose between angry, fat Merry stuttering with Communist outrage and *this* Merry, veiled, placid, dirty, infinitely compassionate, this raggedly attired scarecrow Merry . . . But why have to choose either? Why must she always be enslaving herself to the handiest empty-headed idea? From the moment she had become old enough to think for herself she had been tyrannized instead by the thinking of crackpots. What had he done to produce a daughter who, after excelling for years at school, refused to think for herself—a daughter who had to be either violently against everything in sight or pathetically *for* everything, right down to the microorganisms in the air we breathe? Why did a girl as smart as she was *strive* to let other people do her thinking for her? Why was it beyond her to strive—as he had every day of his life—to be all that one is, to be true to *that*? "But the one who doesn't think for himself is *you!*" she'd told him when he'd suggested that she might be parroting the clichés of others. "*You're* the living example of the person who *never* thinks for himself!" "Am I really?" he said, laughing. "Yes! You're the most conformist man I ever met! All you do is what's expec-expec-expected of you!" "That's terrible too?" "It's not *thinking*, D-d-dad! It isn't! It's being a s-s-stupid aut-aut-aut-aut-aut-automaton! A r-r-r-r-robot!" "Well," he replied, believing that it was all a phase, a bad-tempered phase she would outgrow, "I guess you're just stuck with a comformist father—better luck next time," and pretended that he had not been terrified by the sight of her distended, pulsating, frothing lips hammering "r-r-r-r-robot" into his face with the ferocity of a lunatic riveter. A phase, he thought, and felt comforted, and never once considered that thinking "a phase" might be a not bad example of not thinking for yourself.

Fantasy and magic. Always pretending to be somebody else. What began benignly enough when she was playing at Audrey Hepburn had evolved in only a decade into this outlandish myth of selflessness. First the selfless nonsense of the People, now the selfless nonsense of the Perfected Soul. What next, Grandma Dwyer's Cross? Back to the selfless nonsense of the Eternal Candle and the Sacred Heart? Always a grandiose unreality, the remotest abstraction around—*never* self-seeking, not in a million years. The lying, inhuman horror of all this selflessness.

Yes, he had liked his daughter better when she was as self-seeking as everyone else rather than blessed with flawless speech and monstrous altruism.

"How long have you been here?" he asked her.

"Where?"

"This room. This street. In Newark. How long have you been in Newark?"

"I came six months ago."

"You've been . . ." Because there was everything to say, to ask, to demand to know, he could say no more. Six months. In Newark six months. There was no here and now for the Swede, there were just two inflammatory words matter-of-factly spoken: six months.

He stood over her, facing her, his power pinned to the wall, rocking almost imperceptibly back on the heels of his shoes, as though in this way he might manage to take leave of her *through* the wall, then rocking forward onto his toes, as though at any moment to grab her, to whisk her up into his arms and out. He couldn't return home to sleep in perfect safety in the Old Rimrock house knowing that she was in those rags in that veil on that mat, looking like the loneliest person on earth, sleeping only inches from a hallway that sooner or later had to catch up with her.

This girl was mad by the time she was fifteen, and kindly and stupidly he had tolerated that madness, crediting her with nothing worse than a point of view he didn't like but that she would surely outgrow along with her rebellious adolescence. And now look what she looked like. The ugliest daughter ever born of two attractive parents. I renounce this! I renounce that! I renounce everything! *That* couldn't be it, could it? All of it to renounce his looks and Dawn's? All of it because the mother was once Miss New Jersey? Is life this belittling? It can't be. I won't have it!

"How long have you been a Jain?"

"One year."

"How did you find out about all this?"

"Studying religions."

"How much do you weigh, Meredith?"

"More than enough, Daddy."

Her eye sockets were huge. Half an inch above the veil, big, big dark eye sockets, and inches above the eye sockets the hair, which no longer streamed down her back but seemed just to have happened onto her head, still blond like his but long and thick no longer because of a haircut that was itself an act of violence. Who'd done it? She or someone else? And with what? She could not, in keeping with her five vows, have renounced any attachment as savagely as she had renounced her once-beautiful hair.

"But you don't look as though you eat *anything*," and despite his intention to state this to her unemotionally, he as good as moaned—unbidden a voice emerged from the Swede wretchedly laced with all his dismay. "What do you *eat*?"

"I destroy plant life. I am insufficiently compassionate as yet to refuse to do that."

"You mean you eat vegetables. Is that what you mean? What is wrong with that? How could you refuse to do that? Why *should* you?"

"It is an issue of personal sanctity. It is a matter of reverence for life. I am bound to harm no living being, neither man, nor animal, nor plant."

"But you would *die* if you did that. How can you be 'bound' to that? You would eat nothing."

"You ask a profound question. You are a very intelligent man, Daddy. You ask, 'If you respect life in all forms, how can you live?' The answer is you cannot. The traditional way by which a Jain holy man ends his life is by *salla khana*—self-starvation. Ritual death by *salla khana* is the price paid for perfection by the perfect Jain."

"I cannot believe this is you. I have to tell you what I think."

"Of course you do."

"I cannot believe, clever as you are, that you know what you are saying or what you are doing here or why. I cannot believe that you are telling me that a point will come when you will decide that you will not even destroy plant life, and that you won't eat anything, and that you will just doom yourself to death. For whom, Merry? For what?"

"It's all right. It's all right, Daddy. I can believe that you can't believe that you know what I'm saying or what I'm doing or why."

She addressed him as though *he* were the child and *she* were the parent, with nothing but sympathetic understanding, with that loving tolerance that he once had so disastrously extended to her. And it galled him. The condescension of a lunatic. Yet he neither bolted for the door nor leaped to do what had to be done. He remained the reasonable father. The reasonable father of someone mad. Do something! Anything! In the name of everything reasonable, stop being reasonable. This child needs a hospital. She could not be in any greater peril if she were adrift on a plank in the middle of the sea. She's gone over the edge of the ship—how that happened is not the question now. She must be rescued immediately!

"Tell me where you studied religions."

"In libraries. Nobody looks for you there. I was in libraries often, and so I read. I read a lot."

"You read a lot when you were a little girl."

"I did? I like to read."

"That's where you became a member of this religion. In a library."

"Yes."

"And church? Do you go to some sort of a church?"

"There is no church at the center. There is no god at the center. God is at the center of the Judeo-Christian tradition. And God may say, 'Take life.' And it is then not just permissible but obligatory. That's all over the Old Testament. There are examples even in the New Testament. In Judaism and Christianity the position is taken that life belongs to God. Life isn't sacred, God is sacred. But at the center for us is not a belief in the sovereignty of God but a belief in the sanctity of life."

The monotonous chant of the indoctrinated, ideologically armored from head to foot—the monotonous, spellbound chant of those whose turbulence can be caged only within the suffocating straitjacket of the most supercoherent of dreams. What was missing from her unstuttered words was not the sanctity of life—missing was the sound of life.

"How many of you are there?" he asked, working fiercely to adjust to clarifications with which she was only further bewildering him.

"Three million."

Three million people like her? It could not be. In rooms like this one? Locked away in three million terrible rooms? "Where are they, Merry?"

"In India."

"I'm not asking you about India. I don't care about India. We do not live in India. In America, how many of you are there?"

"I don't know. It's unimportant."

"I would think very few."

"I don't know."

"Merry, are you the only one?"

"My spiritual exploration I undertook on my own."

"I do not understand. Merry, I do not understand. How did you get from Lyndon Johnson to this? How do you get from point A to point Z, where there is no point of contact *at all*? Merry, it does not hang together."

"There is a point of contact. I assure you there is. It all hangs together. You just don't see it."

"Do *you?*"

"Yes."

"Tell it to me then. I want you to tell it to me so that I can understand what has *happened* to you."

"There is a logic, Daddy. You mustn't raise your voice. I will explain. It all links up. I have given it much thought. It goes like this. *Ahimsa,* the Jain concept of nonviolence, appealed to Mahatma Gandhi. He was not a Jain. He was Hindu. But when he was looking in India for a group that was genuinely Indian and not Western and that could point to charitable works as impressive as those the Christian missionaries had produced, he landed on the Jains. We are a small group. We are not Hindus but our beliefs are akin to Hindus'. We are a religion founded in the sixth century B.C. Mahatma Gandhi took from us this notion of *ahimsa,* nonviolence. We are the core of truth that created Mahatma Gandhi. And Mahatma Gandhi, in his nonviolence, is the core of truth that created Martin Luther King. And Martin Luther King is the core of truth that created the civil rights movement. And, at the end of his life, when he was moving beyond the civil rights movement to a larger vision, when he was opposing the war in Vietnam . . ."

Without stuttering. Speech that once would have impelled her to grimace and turn white and bang on the table—would have made of her an embattled speaker attacked by the words and obstinately attacking them back—delivered now patiently, graciously, still in that monotonous chant but edged with the gentlest tone of spiritual urgency. Everything she could not achieve with a speech therapist and a psychiatrist and a stuttering diary she had beautifully realized by going mad. Subjecting herself to isolation and squalor and terrible danger, she had attained control, mental and physical, over every sound she uttered. An intelligence no longer impeded by the blight of stuttering.

And intelligence was what he was hearing, Merry's quick, sharp, studious brain, the logical mind she'd had since earliest childhood.

And hearing it opened him up to pain such as he had never before imagined. The intelligence was intact and yet she was mad, her logic a brand of logic bereft totally of the power to reason with which it had already entwined itself by the time she was ten. It was absurd—this being reasonable with her was *his* madness. Sitting there trying to act as though he were respectful of her religion when her religion consisted of an absolute failure to understand what life is and is not. The two of them acting as if he had come there to be educated. Being *lectured*, by her!

". . . we do not understand salvation as in any way the union of the human soul with something beyond itself. The spirit of Jain piety lives in founder Mahavira's saying, 'O man, thou art thine own friend. Why seekest thou for a friend beyond thyself?'"

"Merry, did you do it? I must ask you this now. Did you do it?"

It was the question he had expected to ask her first, once they had reached her room and before everything else that was horrible began painfully to be sifted through and scrutinized. He thought he had waited because he did not want her to think that his first consideration was anything other than at long last seeing her and seeing to her, attending to her well-being; but now that he had asked, he knew that he hadn't already asked because he could not bear to hear an answer.

"Do what, Daddy?"

"Did you bomb the post office?"

"Yes."

"You intended to blow up Hamlin's too?"

"There was no other way to do it."

"Except not to do it. Merry, you must tell me now who made you do it?"

"Lyndon Johnson."

"That will not do. No! Answer me. Who talked you *into* it? Who brainwashed you? Who did you do it *for*?"

There had to be forces outside. The prayer went, "Lead me not into temptation." If people were not led by others, why was that the famous prayer that it was? A child who had been blessed with every privilege could not have done this on her own. Blessed with love. Blessed with a loving and ethical and prosperous family. Who had enlisted her and lured her into this?

"How strongly you still crave the idea," she said, "of your innocent offspring."

"Who was it? Don't protect them. Who is responsible?"

"Daddy, you can detest me alone. It's all right."

"You are telling me you did it all on your own. Knowing that Hamlin's would be destroyed too. That's what you are saying."

"Yes. I am the abomination. Abhor *me*."

He remembered then something she had written in the sixth or seventh grade, before she'd gone on to Morristown High. The students in her class at her Montessori school were asked ten questions about their "philosophy," one a week. The first week the teacher asked, "Why are we here?" Instead of writing as the other kids did—here to do good, here to make the world a better place, etc.—Merry answered with her own question: "Why are apes here?" But the teacher found this an inadequate response and told her to go home and think about the question more seriously—"Expand on this," the teacher said. So Merry went home and did as she was told and the next day handed in an additional sentence: "Why are kangaroos here?" It was at this point that Merry was first informed by a teacher that she had a "stubborn streak." The final question assigned to the class was "What is life?" Merry's answer was something her father and mother chuckled over together that night. According to Merry, while the other students labored busily away with their phony deep thoughts, she—after an hour of thinking at her desk—wrote a single, unplatitudinous declarative sentence: "Life is just a short period of time in which you are alive." "You know," said the Swede, "it's smarter than it sounds. She's a kid—how has she figured out that life is short? She is somethin', our precocious daughter. This girl is going to Harvard." But once again the teacher didn't agree, and she wrote beside Merry's answer, "Is that *all*?" Yes, the Swede thought now, that is all. Thank God, that is all; even that is unendurable.

The truth was that he had known all along: without a tempter's assistance, everything angry inside her had broken into the open. She was unintimidated, she was *unintimidatable,* this child who had written for her teacher not, like the other kids, that life was a beautiful gift and a great opportunity and a noble endeavor and a blessing from God but that it was just a short period of time in which you were alive. Yes, the intention had been all her own. That had to be. Her antagonism had been intent on murder and nothing less. Otherwise this mad repose would not be the result.

He tried to let reason rise once again to the surface. How hard he tried. What does a reasonable man say next? If, after being battered and once again brought nearly to tears by what he'd just heard uttered so matter-of-factly—everything incredible uttered so matter-of-factly—a man could hold on and be reasonable, what does he go ahead to say? What does a reasonable, responsible father say if he is able still to feel intact as a father?

"Merry, may I tell you what I think? I think you are terrified of being punished for what you've done. I think that rather than evade your punishment you have taken it into your own hands. I don't believe that's a difficult conclusion to reach, honey. I don't believe I'm the only person in the world who, seeing you here, seeing you here looking like this, would come up with that idea. You're a good girl and so you want to do penance. But this is not penance. Not even the state would punish you like this. I have to say these things, Merry. I have to tell you truthfully what this looks like to me."

"Of course you do."

"Just look at what you've done to yourself—you are going to *die* if you keep this up. Another year of this and you *will* die—from self-starvation, from malnutrition, from *filth.* You cannot go back and forth every day under those railroad tracks. That underpass is a home for derelicts—for derelicts who do not play by your rules. Their world is a ruthless world, Merry, a terrible world—a *violent* world."

"They won't harm me. They know that I love them."

The words sickened him, the flagrant childishness, the sentimental grandiosity of the self-deception. What does she see in the hopeless scurryings of these wretched people that could justify such an idea? Derelicts and love? To be a derelict living in an underpass is to have clobbered out of you a hundred times over the minutest *susceptibility* to love. This was awful. Now that her speech is finally cleared of the stuttering, all that comes through is this junk. What he had dreamed about—that his wonderful, gifted child would one day stop stuttering—had come to pass. She had mastered miraculously the agitated stuttering only to reveal, at the eye of the storm that was her erupted personality, this insane clarity and calm. What a great revenge to take: This is what you wanted, Daddy? Well, here it is.

Her being able successfully to explain and to talk was now the worst thing of all.

The harshness he felt but didn't want her to hear was in his voice nonetheless when he said, "You will meet a violent end, Meredith. Keep trying them out twice a day, keep it up and you'll find out just how much they know about your love. Their hunger, Merry, is not for love. Somebody will kill you!"

"But only to be reborn."

"I doubt that, honey. I seriously doubt that."

"Will you concede that my guess is as good as yours, Dad?"

"Won't you at least take off that mask while we're talking? So I can see you?"

"See me stutter, do you mean?"

"Well, I don't know if wearing that is what accounts for the disappearance of your stutter or not. You tell me that it has. You tell me that the stutter was only your way of doing no violence to the air and the things that live in the air . . . is that correct? Have I understood what you were saying?"

"Yes."

"Well . . . even if I were to concede that, I have to tell you I think you might eventually have a better life *with* your stutter. I don't minimize the hardship it was for you. But if it turns out you had to carry things to this extreme to be rid of that damn thing . . . then I really do wonder . . . well, if it's the best trade-off imaginable."

"You can't explain away what I've done by motives, Daddy. I certainly wouldn't explain away what *you've* done by motives."

"But I *do* have motives. *Everyone* has motives."

"You cannot reduce the journey of a soul to that kind of psychology. It is not worthy of you."

"Then *you* explain it. Explain it to me, *please*. How do you explain that when you took all this . . . what looks to me like misery and nothing more, that when you did that, took upon yourself real suffering, which is all this is, suffering that you have *chosen*, Merry, real suffering and nothing more or less than suffering"—his voice was wavering but on he went, reasonable, reasonable, responsible, responsible—"*then*, only *then*—do you see what I'm saying?—the stutter vanished?"

"I've told you. I am done with craving and selfhood."

"Sweet, sweet child and girl." He sat down amid the filth of the floor, helpless to do anything other than try to his utmost not to lose control.

In the tiny room, where they now sat no more than an arm's length from each other, there was no light other than what fell through the dirty transom. She lived without light. Why? Had she renounced the vice of electricity too? She lived without light, she lived without everything. This was how their life had worked out: she lived in Newark with nothing, he lived in Old Rimrock with everything except her. Was his good fortune to blame for that too? The revenge of the have-nots upon those who have and own. All the self-styled have-nots, the playacting Rita Cohens seeking to associate themselves with their parents' worst enemies, modeling themselves on whatever was most loathsome to those who most loved them.

There used to be a slogan she'd crayoned in two colors on a piece of cardboard, a handmade poster that she'd hung over her desk, replacing his Weequahic football pennant; the poster had hung there undisturbed all during the year before her disappearance. Till it went up, she had always coyly coveted the Weequahic pennant because the Swede's high school sweetheart had taken it to sewing class in 1943 and stitched into the felt along the bottom edge of the orange and brown triangle, in thick white thread, "To All-City Levov, XXXX, Arlene." The poster was the only thing he had dared to remove from her room and destroy, and even doing that much had taken three months; appropriating the property of another, adult or child, was simply repugnant to him. But three months after the bombing he marched up the stairs and into her room and tore the poster down. It read: "We are against everything that is good and decent in honky America. We will loot and burn and destroy. We are the incubation of your mother's nightmares." In large square letters the attribution: "WEATHERMEN MOTTO." And because he was a tolerant man he'd tolerated that too. "Honky" in his daughter's hand. Hanging there for a year in his own home, each red letter shadowed heavily in black.

And because even though he hadn't liked it one bit he did not believe it was his right blah-blah blah-blah blah, because—out of regard for her property and her personal freedom—he couldn't even pull down an awful poster, because he was not capable of even that much righteous violence, now the hideous realization of the nightmare had come along to test even further the limits of his enlightened tolerance. She thinks if she raises a hand she'll swat and kill an innocent mite that is innocently floating by her—so in touch is she with the environment that any and every move she makes will have the most stupendously dire consequences—and he thinks that if he removes a hateful and disgusting poster that she has put up, he'll do damage to her integrity, to her psyche, to her First Amendment rights. No, he wasn't a Jain, thought the Swede, but he might as well have been—he was just as pathetically and naively nonviolent. The idiocy of the uprightness of the goals he had set.

"Who is Rita Cohen?" he asked.

"I don't know. Who is she?"

"The girl who came to me in your behalf. In '68. After you disappeared. She came to my office."

"Nobody has ever come to you in my behalf, no one I have ever sent."

"Yes, a short little girl. Very pale. Her hair in an Afro. Dark hair. I gave her your ballet slippers and your Audrey Hepburn scrapbook and your diary. Is she the person who put you up to this? Is she the person who made the bomb? You used to talk to somebody on the phone when you were still at home—those secret conversations you had." The secret conversations that, like the poster, he had also "respected." If only he had torn down that poster and pulled the plug on her phone and locked her up then and there! "Was that the person?" he asked her now. "Tell me the truth, please."

"I only speak the truth."

"I gave her ten thousand dollars for you. I gave her cash. Did you or did you not get that money?"

Her laugh was kindly. "Ten thousand dollars? Not yet, Daddy."

"Then I must have an answer from you. Who is the Rita Cohen who told me where I could find you? Is this the Melissa from New York?"

"You found me," she replied, "because you have been looking. I never expected not to be found by you. You sought me out because you *must* seek me."

"Did you come to Newark to help me find you? Is that why you came here?"

But she replied, "No."

"Then *why* did you come? What were you thinking? *Were* you thinking? You know where the office is. You know how very close it is. Where's the logic, Merry? This close and . . . "

"I got a ride, and here I was, you see."

"Like that. Coincidence. No logic. No logic anywhere."

"The world is not a place on which I have influence or wish to have any. I relinquish all influence over everything. As to what constitutes a coincidence, you and I, Daddy—"

"Do you 'relinquish all influence'?" he cried. "*Do* you, '*all* influence'?" The most maddening conversation of his life. The know-it-all-ism of her absurdly innocent, profoundly insane, unstuttering solemnity, the awful candor of the room and of the street outside, the awful candor of *everything* outside him that was so powerfully controlling him. "You have an influence over *me*," he shouted, "you are influencing *me!* You who will not kill a mite are killing *me!* What you sit there calling 'coincidence' *is* influence—your powerlessness is power over *me*, goddamn it! Over your mother, over your grandfather, over your grandmother, over everyone who loves you—wearing that veil is bullshit, Merry, complete and absolute *bullshit!* You are the most powerful person in the world!"

There was no solace to be found in thinking, This is *not* my life, this is the *dream* of my life. That was not going to make him any less miserable. Nor was the rage with his daughter, nor was the rage with the little criminal whom he had allowed to be cast as their savior. A cunning and malicious crook who suckered him without half trying. Took him for all she could get in four ten-minute visits. The viciousness. The audacity. The unshatterable nerves. God alone knew where such kids came from.

Then he remembered that one of them came from his house. Rita Cohen merely came from somebody else's house. They were brought up in houses like his own. They were raised by parents like him. And so many were girls, girls whose political identity was total, who were no less aggressive and militant, no less drawn to "armed action" than the boys. There is something terrifyingly pure about their violence and the thirst for self-transformation. They renounce their roots to take as their models the revolutionaries whose conviction is enacted most ruthlessly. They manufacture like unstoppable machines the abhorrence that propels their steely idealism. Their rage is combustible. They are willing to do anything they can imagine to make history change. The draft isn't even hanging over their heads; they sign on freely and fearlessly to terrorize against the war, competent to rob at gunpoint, equipped in every way to maim and kill with explosives, undeterred by fear or doubt or inner contradiction—girls in hiding, dangerous girls, attackers, implacably extremist, completely unsociable. He read the names of girls in the papers who were wanted by the authorities for crimes allegedly stemming from antiwar activities, girls that he imagined Merry knew, girls with whose lives he imagined his daughter's to be now interlinked: Bernadine, Patricia, Judith, Cathlyn, Susan, Linda. . . . His father, after foolishly watching a TV news special about the police hunt for the underground Weathermen, among them Mark Rudd and Katherine Boudin and Jane Alpert—all in their twenties, Jewish, middle class, college-educated, violent in behalf of the antiwar cause, committed to revolutionary change and determined to overturn the United States government—went around saying, "I remember when Jewish kids were home doing their homework. What happened? What the hell happened to our smart Jewish kids? If, God forbid, their parents are no longer oppressed for a while, they run where they think they can find oppression. Can't live without it. Once Jews ran away from oppression; now they run away from no-oppression. Once they ran away from being poor; now they run away from being rich. It's crazy. They have parents they can't hate anymore because their parents are so good to them, so they hate America instead." But Rita Cohen was a case unto herself: a vicious slut and a common crook.

Then how is he to explain her letter, if that is all she is? What happened to our smart Jewish kids? They *are* crazy. Something is *driving* them crazy. Something has set them against everything. Something is leading them into disaster. These are not the smart Jewish children intent on getting ahead by doing what they are told better than anyone else does. They only feel at home doing better than anyone else as they are *not* told. Distrust is the madness to which they have been called.

And here on the floor is the result in one of its more heartbreaking forms: the religious conversion. If you fail to bring the world into subjection, then subject yourself to the world.

"I *love* you," he was telling Merry, "you *know* I would look for you. You are my *child.* But how could I find you in a million years, wearing that mask and weighing eighty-eight pounds and living the way you live? How could anyone have found you, even here? Where *were* you?" he cried, as angry as the angriest father ever betrayed by a daughter or a son, so angry he feared that his head was about to spew out his brains just as Kennedy's did when he was shot. "Where have you *been?* Answer me!"

So she told him where she'd been.

And how did he listen? Wondering: If there was some point in their lives *before* she took the wrong path, where and when was it? Thinking: There was no such point, there was never any controlling Merry however many years she managed to deceive them, to seem safely theirs and under their sway. Thinking: Futile, every last thing he had ever done. The preparations, the practice, the obedience; the uncompromising dedication to the essential, to the things that matter most; the systematic system building, the patient scrutiny of every problem, large or small; no drifting, no laxity, no laziness; faithfully meeting every obligation, addressing energetically every situation's demands . . . a list as long as the U.S. Constitution, his articles of faith—and all of it futility. The systemization of futility is all it had ever been. All he had ever restrained by his responsibility was himself.

Thinking: She is not in my power and she never was. She is in the power of something that does not give a shit. Something demented. We all are. Their elders are not responsible for this. They are them-selves not responsible for this. Something else is.

Yes, at the age of forty-six, in 1973, almost three-quarters of the way through the century that with no regard for the niceties of burial had strewn the corpses of mutilated children and their muti-lated parents everywhere, the Swede found out that we are all in the power of something demented. It's just a matter of time, honky. We all are!

He heard them laughing, the Weathermen, the Panthers, the angry ragtag army of the violent Uncorrupted who called him a criminal and hated his guts because he was one of those who own and have. *The Swede finally found out!* They were delirious with joy, delighted having destroyed his once-pampered daughter and ruined his privileged life, shepherding him at long last to their truth, to the truth as they knew it to be for every Vietnamese man, woman, child, and tot, for every colonized black in America, for everyone everywhere who had been fucked over by the capitalists and their insatiable greed. The something that's demented, honky, is American history! It's the American empire! It's Chase Manhattan and General Motors and Standard Oil and Newark Maid Leatherware! Welcome aboard, capitalist dog! Welcome to the fucked-over-by-America human race!

She told him that for the first seventy-two hours after the bombing she had been hidden in the Morristown home of Sheila Salzman, her speech therapist. Safely she made her way to Sheila's house, was taken in, and lived hidden away in an anteroom to Sheila's office during the day and in the office itself at night. Then her underground wandering began. In just two months she had fifteen aliases and moved every four or five days. But in Indianapolis, where she was befriended by a movement minister who knew only that she was an antiwar activist gone underground, she took a name from a tombstone in a cemetery, the name of a baby born within a year of herself who had died in infancy. She applied for a duplicate birth certificate in the baby's name, which was how she became Mary Stoltz. After that, she obtained a library card, a Social Security number, and when she turned seventeen, a driver's license. For nearly a year, Mary Stoltz washed dishes in the kitchen of an old people's home—a job she got through the minister—until one morning he reached her on the pay phone and said that she was to leave work immediately and meet him at the Greyhound station. There he gave her a ticket to Chicago, told her to stay two days, then to buy a ticket for Oregon—north of Portland was a commune where she could find sanctuary. He gave her the commune's address and some money to buy clothes, food, and the tickets, and she left for Chicago, where she was raped on the night she arrived. Held captive and raped and robbed. Just seventeen.

In the kitchen of a dive not as friendly as the kitchen at the old people's home, she washed dishes to earn the money to get to Oregon. There was no minister to advise her in Chicago and she was afraid that if she tried to make contact with the underground she would do something wrong and be apprehended. She was too frightened even to use a pay phone to call the Indianapolis minister. She was raped again (in the fourth rooming house where she went to live) but this time she wasn't robbed, and so after six weeks as a dishwasher she had put together enough money to head for the commune.

In Chicago the loneliness had been so all-enveloping, she felt it as a current coursing through her. There wasn't a day, on some days not an hour, when she did not set out to phone Old Rimrock. But instead, before remembering her childhood room could completely undo her, she would find a diner or a luncheonette and sit on a stool at the counter and order a BLT and a vanilla milk shake. Saying the familiar words, watching the bacon curl on the grill, watching for her toast to pop up, carefully removing the toothpicks when she was served, eating the layered sandwich between sips of the shake, concentrating on crunching the tasteless fibers from the lettuce, extracting the smoke-scented fat from the brittle bacon and the flowery juices from the soft tomato, swilling everything in with the mash of the mayonnaised toast, grinding patiently away with her jaws and her teeth, thoughtfully pulverizing every mouthful into a silage to settle her down—concentrating on her BLT as fixedly as her mother's livestock focusing on the fodder at the trough—gave her the courage to go on alone. She would eat the sandwich and drink the shake and remember how she got there and go on. By the time she left Chicago she had discovered she no longer needed a home; she would never again come close to suc-cumbing to the yearning for a family and a home.

In Oregon she was involved in two bombings.

Instead of stopping her, killing Fred Conlon had only inspired her; after Fred Conlon, instead of her being crippled by conscience, she was delivered from all residual fear and compunction. The horror of having killed, if only inadvertently, an innocent man, a man as good as any she would ever hope to know, had not taught her anything about that most fundamental prohibition, which, stupefyingly enough, she had failed to learn to observe from being raised by Dawn and him. Killing Conlon only confirmed her ardor as an idealistic revolutionary who did not shrink from adopting any means, however ruthless, to attack the evil system. She had proved that being in opposition to everything decent in honky America wasn't just so much hip graffiti emblazoned on her bedroom wall.

He said, "You planted the bombs."

"I did."

"At Hamlin's and in Oregon you planted the bombs."

"Yes."

"Was anyone killed in Oregon?"

"Yes."

"Who?"

"People."

"People," he repeated. "How many people, Merry?"

"Three," she said.

There was plenty to eat at the commune. They grew a lot of their own food and so there was no need, as there had been when she first got to Chicago, to scavenge for wilted produce outside supermarkets at night. At the commune she began to sleep with a woman she fell in love with, the wife of a weaver whose loom Merry learned to operate when she was not working with the bombs. Assembling bombs had become her specialty after she'd successfully planted her second and third. She loved the patience and the precision required to safely wire the dynamite to the blasting cap and the blasting cap to the Woolworth's alarm clock. That's when the stuttering first began to disappear. She never stuttered when she was with the dynamite.

Then something happened between the woman and her husband, a violent argument that necessitated Merry's leaving the commune to restore peace.

It was while hiding in eastern Idaho, where she worked in the potato fields, that she decided to flee to Cuba. At night in the farm camp barracks she began to study Spanish. Living in the camp with the other laborers, she felt even more passionately committed to her beliefs, though the men were frightening when they were drunk and again there were sexual incidents. She believed that in Cuba she could live among workers without having to worry about their violence. In Cuba she could be Merry Levov and not Mary Stoltz.

She had concluded by this time that there could never be a revolution in America to uproot the forces of racism and reaction and greed. Urban guerrilla warfare was futile against a thermonuclear superstate that would stop at nothing to defend the profit principle. Since she could not help to bring about a revolution in America, her only hope was to give herself to the revolution that was. That would mark the end of her exile and the true beginning of her life.

The next year was devoted to finding her way to Cuba, to Fidel, who had emancipated the proletariat and who had eradicated injustice with socialism. But in Florida she had her first close brush with the FBI. There was a park in Miami full of Dominican refugees. It was a good place to practice Spanish and soon she found herself teaching the boys there how to speak English. Affectionately they called her La Farfulla, the stutterer, which did not prevent them from mischievously stuttering when they repeated the English words she taught them. In Spanish her own speech was flawless. Another reason to flee to the arms of the world revolution.

One day, Merry told her father, she noticed a youngish black bum, new to the park, watching her tutoring her boys. She knew immediately what that meant. A thousand times before she'd thought it was the FBI and a thousand times she'd been wrong—in Oregon, in Idaho, in Kentucky, in Maryland, the FBI watching her at the stores where she clerked; watching in the diners and the cafeterias where she washed dishes; watching on the shabby streets where she lived; watching in the libraries where she hid out to read the newspapers and to study the revolutionary thinkers, to master Marx, Marcuse, Malcolm X, and Frantz Fanon, a French theorist whose sentences, litanized at bedtime like a supplication, had sustained her in much the same way as the ritual sacrament of the vanilla milk shake and the BLT. *It must be constantly borne in mind that the committed Algerian woman learns both her role as "a woman alone in the street" and her revolutionary mission instinctively. The Algerian woman is not a secret agent. It is without apprenticeship, without briefing, without fuss, that she goes out into the street with three grenades in her handbag. She does not have the sensation of playing a role. There is no character to imitate. On the contrary, there is an intense dramatization, a continuity between the woman and the revolutionary. The Algerian woman rises directly to the level of tragedy.*

Thinking: And the New Jersey girl descends to the level of idiocy. The New Jersey girl we sent to Montessori school because she was so bright, the New Jersey girl who at Morristown High got only A's and B's—the New Jersey girl rises directly to the level of disgraceful playacting. The New Jersey girl rises to the level of psychosis.

Everywhere, in every city where she went to hide, she thought she saw the FBI—but it was in Miami that she was finally discovered while stuttering away on a park bench trying to teach her boys to speak English. Yet how could she not teach them? How could she turn away from those who had been born to nothing, condemned to nothing, who appeared even to themselves to be human trash? On the second day when she came to the park and found the same young black bum pretending to be asleep on a bench beneath a blanket of newspapers, she turned back to the street and began to run and she did not stop until she saw a blind woman begging in the street, a large black woman with a dog. The woman was jiggling a cup and saying softly, "Blind, blind, blind." On the pavement at her feet lay a ragged wool coat inside which Merry realized she could hide. But she couldn't just take it from her; instead she asked the woman if she could help her beg, and the woman said sure, and

Merry asked if she could wear the woman's dark glasses and her coat, and the woman said, "Anything, honey," and so Merry stood in the sun in Miami in that heavy old coat, wearing the dark glasses, shaking the cup for her while the woman chanted "Blind, blind, blind." That night she hid out alone beneath a bridge, but the next day she went back to beg with the black woman, once again disguised by the coat and the glasses, and eventually she moved in with her and her dog and took care of her.

That was when she began to study religions. Bunice, the black woman, sang to her in the mornings when they awoke in the bed where they slept, she and Merry and the dog. But when Bunice got cancer and died, that was the worst: the clinics, the ward, the funeral at which she was the only mourner, losing the person she'd loved most in the world . . . that was the hardest it ever was.

During the months while Bunice was dying she found in the library the books that led her to leave behind forever the Judeo-Christian tradition and find her way to the supreme ethical imperative of *ahimsa*, the systematic reverence for life and the commitment to harm no living being.

Her father was no longer wondering at what point he had lost control over her life, no longer thinking that everything he had ever done had been futile and that she was in the power of something demented. He was thinking instead that Mary Stoltz was not his daughter, for the simple reason that his daughter could not have absorbed so much pain. She was a kid from Old Rimrock, a privileged kid from paradise. She could not have worked potato fields and slept under bridges and for five years gone about in terror of arrest. She could never have slept with the blind woman and her dog. Indianapolis, Chicago, Portland, Idaho, Kentucky, Maryland, Florida—never could Merry have lived alone in all those places, an isolated vagabond washing dishes and hiding out from the police and befriending the destitute on park benches. And never would she have wound up in Newark. No. Living for six months ten minutes away, walking to the Ironbound through that underpass, wearing that veil and walking all alone, every morning and

every night, past all those derelicts and through all that filth—no!
The story was a lie, its purpose to destroy their villain, who was
him. The story was a caricature, a sensational caricature, and she
was an actress, this girl was a professional, hired and charged with
tormenting him because he was everything they were not. They
wanted to kill him off with the story of a pariah exiled in the very
country where her family had triumphantly rooted itself in every
possible way, and so he refused to be convinced by anything she
had said. He thought, The rape? The bombs? A sitting duck for
every madman? That was more than hardship. That was hell. Merry
couldn't survive *any* of it. She could not have survived killing four
people. She could not have murdered in cold blood and survived.

And then he realized that she hadn't survived. Whatever the
truth might be, whatever had truly befallen her, her determination
to leave behind her, in ruin, her parents' contemptible life had
driven her to the disaster of destroying herself.

Of course this all could have happened to her. Things happen
like this every day all over the face of the earth. He had no idea how
people behaved.

"You're not my daughter. You are not Merry."

"If you wish to believe that I am not, that may be just as well.
That may be for the best."

"Why don't you ask me about your mother, Meredith? Should I
ask you? Where was your mother born? What is her maiden name?
What is her father's name?"

"I don't want to talk about my mother."

"Because you know nothing about her. Or about me. Or about
the person you pretend to be. Tell me about the house at the shore.
Tell me the name of your first-grade teacher. Who was your second-
grade teacher? Tell me why you are pretending to be my daughter!"

"If I answer the questions, you will suffer even more. I don't
know how much suffering you want."

"Oh, don't worry about my suffering, young lady—just answer
the questions. Why are you pretending to be my daughter? Who are
you? Who is 'Rita Cohen'? What are you two up to? Where is my

daughter? I will turn this matter over to the police unless you tell me now what is going on here and where my daughter is."

"Nothing I'm doing is actionable, Daddy."

The awful legalism. Not only the awful Jainism, but this shit too. "No," he said, "*now* it isn't—now it's just horrible! What about what you *did* do!"

"I killed four people," she replied, as innocently as she might once have told him, "I baked tollhouse cookies this afternoon."

"No!" he shouted. The Jainism, the legalism, the egregious innocence, all of it desperation, all of it to distance herself from the four who are dead. "This will not do! You are not an Algerian woman! You are not from Algeria and you are not from India! You are an American girl from Old Rimrock, New Jersey! A very, very screwed-up American girl! Four people? No!" And now *he* refused to believe it, now it was he for whom the guilt made no sense and could not be. She had been much too blessed for this to be true. So had he. He could never father a child who killed four people. Everything life had provided her, everything life offered her, everything life demanded of her, everything that had happened to her from the day she was born made that *impossible*. Killing people? It was not one of their problems. Mercifully life had omitted that from their lives. Killing people was as far as you could get from all that had been given to the Levovs to do. No, she was not, she could not, be his. "If you are so big on not lying or taking anything, small or great—all that crap, Merry, completely meaningless crap—I beg you to tell me the truth!"

"The truth is simple. Here is the truth. You must be done with craving and selfhood."

"Merry," he cried, "Merry, Merry," and, the unbridled unchecked in him, powerless *not* to attack, with all his manly brawn he fell upon her huddled there on the grimy pallet. "It isn't you! You could not have done it!" She put up no resistance as he tore from her face the veil cut from the end of a stocking. Where the heel should be was her chin. Nothing is more fetid than something where your foot has been, and she puts her mouth up against it. We loved her, she loved us—and as a result she wears her face in a stocking. "*Now* speak!" he commanded her.

But she wouldn't. He pried her mouth open, disregarding a guideline he had never before overstepped—the injunction against violence. It was the end of all understanding. There was no way for understanding to be there anymore, even though he knew violence to be inhuman and futile, and understanding—talking sense to each other for however long it took to bring about accord—all there was that could achieve a lasting result. The father who could never use force on his child, for whom force was the embodiment of moral bankruptcy, pried open her mouth and with his fingers took hold of her tongue. One of her front teeth was missing, one of her beautiful teeth. That *proved* it wasn't Merry. The years of braces, the retainer, the night brace, all those contraptions to perfect her bite, to save her gums, to beautify her smile—*this could not be the same girl.*

"Speak!" he demanded, and at last the true smell of her reached him, the lowest human smell there is, excluding only the stench of the rotting living and the rotting dead. Strangely, though she had told him she did not wash so as to do no harm to the water, he had smelled nothing before—neither when they'd embraced on the street nor sitting in the dimness across from her pallet—nothing other than a sourish, nauseatingly unfamiliar something that he ascribed to the piss-soaked building. But what he smelled now, while pulling open her mouth, was a human being and not a building, a mad human being who grubs about for pleasure in its own shit. Her foulness had reached him. She is disgusting. His daughter is a human mess stinking of human waste. Her smell is the smell of everything organic breaking down. It is the smell of no coherence. It is the smell of all she's become. She could do it, and she did do it, and this reverence for life is the final obscenity.

He tried to locate a muscle in his head somewhere to plug the opening at the top of his throat, something to stop him up and prevent their sliding still further into the filth, but there was no such muscle. A spasm of gastric secretions and undigested food started up the intestinal piping and, in a bitter, acidic stream, surged sickeningly onto his tongue, and when he cried out, "*Who are you!*" it was spewed with his words onto her face.

Even in the dimness of that room, once he was over her he knew very well who she was. It was not necessary for her to speak with her face unprotected to inform him that the inexplicable had forever displaced whatever he once thought he knew. If she was no longer branded as Merry Levov by her stutter, she was marked unmistakably by the eyes. Within the chiseled-out, oversized eye sockets, the eyes were his. The tallness was his and the eyes were his. She was all his. The tooth she was missing had been pulled or knocked out.

She looked not at him when he retreated to the door but anxiously all around her narrow room, as though in his frenzy he had battered most brutally the harmless microorganisms that dwelled with her in her solitude.

Four people. Little wonder that she had vanished. Little wonder that he had. This was his daughter, and she was unknowable. This murderer is mine. His vomit was on her face, a face that, but for the eyes, was now most unlike her mother's or her father's. The veil was off, but behind the veil there was another veil. Isn't there always?

"Come with me," he begged.

"You go, Daddy. Go."

"Merry, you are asking me to do something that is excruciatingly painful. You are asking me to leave you. I just found you. Please," he begged her, "come with me. Come home."

"Daddy, let me be."

"But I must see you. I cannot leave you here. I must see you!"

"You've seen me. Please go now. If you love me, Daddy, you'll let me be."

The most perfect girl of all, one's daughter, had been raped.

All he could think of was the two times she had been raped. Four people blown up by her—so grotesque, so out of scale, it was unimaginable. It had to be. To see the faces, to hear the names, to learn that one was a mother of three, the second just married, the third about to retire. . . . Did *she* know what or who they were . . . care who they were . . . ? He could not imagine any of it. Wouldn't. Only the rape was imaginable. Imagine the rape and the rest is blocked out: their faces remain out of sight, their spectacles, their hairdos, their families, their jobs, their birth dates, their addresses, their blameless innocence.

Not one Fred Conlon—four Fred Conlons.

The rape. The rape obscured everything else. Concentrate on the rape.

What *were* the details? Who were these men? Was it somebody who was part of that life, somebody who was against the war and on the run like her, was it somebody she knew or was it a stranger, a bum, an addict, a madman who'd followed her home and into the hallway with a knife? What went on? Had they held her down and threatened her with a knife? Had they beaten her? What did they make her do? Were there no people to help her? Just what did they make her do? He would kill them. She had to tell him who they were. I want to find out who those people are. I want to know where it happened. I want to know when it happened. We're going to go back and find those people and I'm going to kill them!

Now that he could not stop imagining the rapes, there was no relief, not for one second, from the desire to go out and kill somebody. With all the walls he'd built up, she gets raped. All of that protection and he could not prevent her from getting raped. Tell me everything about it! I'm going to kill them!

But it was too late. It had happened. He could do nothing to make it not happen. For it to not happen, he would have had to kill them before it happened—and how could he manage that? Swede Levov? Off the playing field, when had Swede Levov laid a hand on anyone? Nothing so repelled this muscular man as the use of force.

The places she was in. The people. How did she survive without people? That place she was in now. Were all her places like that or even worse? All right, she should not have done what she did, should never have done it, yet to think of how she'd had to live. . . .

He was sitting at his desk. He had to get some relief from seeing what he did not want to see. The factory was empty. There was only the night watchman who'd come on duty with his dogs. He was down in the parking lot, patrolling the perimeter of the double-thick chain-link fence, a fence topped off, after the riots, with supplemental scrolls of razor ribbon that were to admonish the boss each and every morning he pulled in and parked his car, "Leave! Leave! Leave!" He was sitting alone in the last factory left in the worst city in the world. And it was worse even than sitting there during the riots, Springfield Avenue in flames, South Orange Avenue in flames, Bergen Street under attack, sirens going off, weapons firing, snipers from rooftops blasting the street lights, looting crowds crazed in the street, kids carrying off radios and lamps and television sets, men toting armfuls of clothing, women pushing baby carriages heavily loaded with cartons of liquor and cases of beer, people pushing pieces of new furniture right down the center of the street, stealing sofas, cribs, kitchen tables, stealing washers and dryers and ovens—stealing not in the shadows but out in the open. Their strength is tremendous, their teamwork is flawless. The shattering of the glass windows is thrilling. The not paying for things is intoxicating. The American appetite for ownership is dazzling to behold. *This* is shoplifting. Everything free that everyone craves, a wanton free-for-all free of charge, everyone uncontrollable with thinking, Here it is! Let it come! In Newark's burning Mardi Gras streets, a force is released that feels redemptive, something purifying is happening, something spiritual and revolutionary perceptible to all. The surreal vision of household appliances out under the stars and agleam in the glow of the flames incinerating the Central Ward promises the liberation of all mankind. Yes, here it is, let it come, yes, the magnificent opportunity, one of human history's rare transmogrifying moments: the old ways of suffering are burning blessedly away in the flames, never again to be resurrected, instead to be superseded, within only hours, by suffering that will be so gruesome, so monstrous, so unrelenting and abundant, that its abatement will take the next five hundred years. The fire this time—and next? After the fire? Nothing. Nothing in New-ark ever again.

And all the while the Swede is there in the factory with Vicky, waiting with just Vicky beside him for his place to go up, waiting for police with pistols, for soldiers with submachine guns, waiting for protection from the Newark police, the state police, the Na-tional Guard—from *someone*—before they burn to the ground the business built by his father, entrusted to him by his father . . . and that wasn't as bad as this. A police car opens fire into the bar across the street, out his window he sees a woman go down, buckle and go down, shot dead right on the street, a woman killed in front of his eyes . . . and not even that was as bad as this. People screaming, shouting, firemen pinned to the ground by gunfire so they cannot fight the flames; explosions, the sound suddenly of bongo drums, in the middle of the night a volley of pistol shots blowing out every one of the street-level windows displaying Vicky's signs . . . and this is worse by far. And then they left, everyone, fled the smoldering rubble—manufacturers, retailers, the banks, the shop owners, the corporations, the department stores; in the South Ward, on the residential blocks, there are two moving vans per day on every street throughout the next year, homeowners fleeing, deserting the modest houses they treasure for whatever they can get . . . but he stays on, refuses to leave, Newark Maid remains behind, and that did not prevent her from getting raped. Not even during the worst of it does he abandon his factory to the vandals; he does not abandon his workers afterward, does not turn his back on these people, and *still* his daughter is raped.

Hanging on the wall directly back of his desk, framed and under glass, there is a letter from the Governor's Select Commission on Civil Disorder thanking Mr. Seymour I. Levov for his testimony as an eyewitness to the riots, praising him for his courage, for his devotion to Newark, an official letter signed by ten distinguished citizens, two of them Catholic bishops, two of them ex-governors of the state; and on the wall alongside that, also framed and under glass, an article that six months earlier appeared in the *Star-Ledger,* with his photograph and the headline, "Glove Firm Lauded for Staying in Newark"—and still she is raped.

The rape was in his bloodstream and he would never get it out. The odor of it was in his bloodstream, the look of it, the legs and the arms and the hair and the clothing. There were the sounds— the thud, her cries, the careening in a tiny enclosure. The horrible bark of a man coming. His grunting. Her whimpering. The stupendousness of the rape blotted out everything. All unsuspectingly, she had stepped out of her doorway and they had grabbed her from behind and thrown her down and there was her body for them to do with as they wished. Only some cloth covered her body and they tore it off. There was nothing between her body and their hands. Inside her body. Filling the inside of her body. The tremendous force with which they did it. The tearing force. They knocked out her tooth. One of them was insane. He sat over her and let loose a stream of shit. They were all over her. These men. They were speaking a foreign language. Laughing. Whatever they felt the urge to do, they did. One waited behind the other. She saw him waiting. There was nothing she could do.

And nothing he could do. The man grows crazier and crazier to do something just when there is nothing left for him to do.

Her body in the crib. Her body in the bassinet. Her body when she starts to stand on his stomach. The belly showing between her dungarees and her shirt while she hangs upside down from him when he comes home from work. Her body when she leaves the earth and leaps into his arms. The abandon of her body flying into his arms, granting him a father's permission to touch. The unquestioning adoration of him that is in that leaping body, a body seemingly all finished, a perfected creation in miniature, with all of the miniature's charm. A body that looks quickly put on after having just been freshly ironed—no folds anywhere. The naive freedom with which she discloses it. The tenderness this evokes. Her bare feet padded like a little animal's feet. New and unworn, her uncorrupted paws. Her grasping toes. The stalky legs. Utilitarian legs. Firm. The most muscular part of her. Her sorbet-colored underpants. At the great divide, her baby tuchas, the gravity-defying behind, improbably belonging to the upper Merry and not as yet to the lower. No fat. Not an ounce anywhere. The cleft, as though an awl had made it—that beautifully beveled joining that will petal outward, evolving in the cycle of time into a woman's origami-folded cunt. The implausible belly button. The geometric torso. The anatomical precision of the rib cage. The pliancy of her spine. The bony ridges of her back like keys on a small xylophone. The lovely dormancy of the invisible bosom before the swell begins. All the turbulent wanting-to-become blessedly, blessedly dormant. Yet in the neck somehow is the woman to be, there in that building block of a neck ornamented with down. The face. That's the glory. The face that she will not carry with her and that is yet the fingerprint of the future. The marker that will disappear and yet be there fifty years later. How little of her story is revealed in his child's face. Its youngness is all he can see. So very new in the cycle. With nothing as yet totally defined, time is so powerfully present in her face. The skull is soft. The flare of the unstructured nose is the whole nose. The color of her eyes. The white, white whiteness. The limpid blue. Eyes unclouded. It's *all* unclouded, but the eyes particularly, windows, washed windows with nothing yet of the revelation of what's within. The history in her brow of the embryo. The dried apricots that are her ears. Delicious. If once you started eating them you'd never stop. The little ears always older than she is. The ears that were never just four years old and yet hadn't really changed since she was fourteen months. The preternatural fineness of her hair. The *health* of it. More reddish, more like his mother's than his then, still touched with fire then. The smell of the whole day in her hair. The carefreeness, the abandon of that body in his arms. The catlike abandon to the all-powerful father, the reassuring giant. It is so, it is true—in the abandon of her body to him, she excites an instinct for reassurance that is so abundant that it must be close to what Dawn says she felt when she was lactating. What he feels when his daughter leaves the earth to leap into his arms is the absoluteness of their intimacy. And built into it always is the knowledge that he is not going too far, that he cannot, that it is an enormous freedom and an enormous pleasure, the equivalent of her breast-feeding bond with Dawn. It's true. It's undeniable. He was wonderful at it and so was she. So wonderful. How did all this happen to this wonderful kid? She stuttered. So what? What was the big deal? How did all this happen to this perfectly normal child? Unless this is the sort of thing that *does* happen to the wonderful, perfectly normal kids. The nuts don't do these things—the normal kids do. You protect her and protect her—and she is unprotectable. If you don't protect her it's unendurable, if you *do* protect her it's unendurable. It's all unendurable. The awfulness of her terrible autonomy. The worst of the world had taken his child. If only that beautifully chiseled body had never been born.

He calls his brother. It is the wrong brother from whom to seek consolation, but what can he do? When it comes to consolation, it is always the wrong brother, the wrong father, the wrong mother, the wrong wife, which is why one must be content to console oneself and be strong and go on in life consoling others. But he needs some relief from this rape, needs the rape taken out of his heart, where it is stabbing him to death, *he cannot put up with it,* and so he calls the only brother he has. If he had another brother he would call him. But for a brother he has only Jerry and Jerry has only him. For a daughter he has only Merry. For a father she has only him. There is no way around any of this. Nothing else can be made to come true.

It is half past five on a Friday afternoon. Jerry is in the office seeing postoperative patients. But he can talk, he says. The patients can wait. "What is it? What's wrong with you?"

He has only to hear Jerry's voice, the impatience in it, the acerbic cocksuredness in it, to think, He's no good to me. "I found her. I just came from Merry. I found her in Newark. She's here. In a room. I saw her. What this girl has been through, what she looks like, where she lives—you can't imagine it. You cannot begin to imagine it." He proceeds to recount her story, not breaking down, trying to repeat what she said to him about where she had been, how she had lived, and what had become of her, trying to get it into his head, his own head, trying to find in his head the room for it all when he could not even find enough room for that room in which she lived. He comes closest to crying when he tells his brother that she had twice been raped.

"Are you done?" asks Jerry.

"What?"

"If you're done, if that's it, tell me what you are going to do now. What are you going to do, Seymour?"

"I don't know what there is to do. She did it. She blew up Hamlin's. She killed Conlon." He cannot tell him about Oregon and the other three. "She did it on her own."

"Well, sure she did it. Jesus. Who did we think did it? Where is she now, in that room?"

"Yes. It's awful."

"Then go back to the room and get her."

"I can't. She won't let me. She wants me to leave her alone."

"*Fuck* what she wants. Get back in your fucking car and get over there and drag her out of that fucking room by her hair. Sedate her. Tie her up. But get her. Listen to me. You're paralyzed. I'm not the one who thinks holding his family together is the most important thing in existence—you are. Get back in that car and get her!"

"That won't work. I can't drag her. There's more to this than you understand. Once you get beyond the point of forcing somebody back into their house—then what? There's bravado about it—but then what? It's complicated, too complicated. It won't work your way."

"That's *just* the way it works."

"She killed three other people. She has killed four people."

"*Fuck* the four people. What's the matter with you? You're acceding to her the way you acceded to your father, the way you have acceded to everything in your life."

"She was raped. She's crazy, she's gone crazy. You just look at her and you know it. *Twice* she was raped."

"What did you think was going to happen? You sound surprised.

Of course she got raped. Either get off your ass and do something or she's going to get raped for a third time. Do you love her or don't you love her?"

"How can you ask that?"

"You force me to."

"Please, not now, don't tear me down, don't undermine me. I love my daughter. I never loved anything more in the world."

"As a thing."

"What? What is that?"

"As a thing—you loved her as a fucking thing. The way you love your wife. Oh, if someday you could become conscious of why you are doing what you are doing. Do you know why? Do you have any idea? Because you're afraid of creating a bad scene! You're afraid of letting the beast out of the bag!"

"What are you talking about? What beast? What beast?" No, he is not expecting perfect consolation, but this attack—why is he launching this attack without even the pretext of consoling? Why, when he has just explained to Jerry how everything has turned out thousands and thousands of times worse than the worst they'd expected?

"What are you? Do you know? What you are is you're always trying to smooth everything over. What you are is always trying to be moderate. What you are is never telling the truth if you think it's going to hurt somebody's feelings. What you are is you're always compromising. What you are is always complacent. What you are is always trying to find the bright side of things. The one with the manners. The one who abides everything patiently. The one with the ultimate decorum. The boy who never breaks the code. Whatever society dictates, you do. Decorum. Decorum is what you spit in the *face* of. Well, your daughter spit in it for you, didn't she? Four people? Quite a critique she has made of decorum."

If he hangs up, he will be alone in that hallway behind the man who is waiting behind the man who is down on the stairs tearing at Merry, he will be seeing everything he does not want to see, knowing everything he cannot stand to know. He cannot sit there imagining the rest of that story. If he hangs up, he will never know what Jerry has to say after he says all this stuff that he for some reason wants to say about the beast. What beast? All his relations with people are like this—it isn't an attack on me, it is Jerry. Nobody can control him. He was born like this. I knew that before I called him. I've known it all my life. We do not live the same way. A brother who isn't a brother. I panicked. I am in a panic. This is panic. I called the worst person to call in the world. This is a guy who wields a knife for a living. Remedies what is ailing with a knife. Cuts out what is rotting with a knife. I am on the ropes, I am dealing with something that nobody can deal with, and for him it's business as usual—he just keeps coming at me with his knife.

"I'm not the renegade," the Swede says. "I'm not the renegade—you are."

"No, you're not the renegade. You're the one who does everything right."

"I don't follow this. You say that like an insult." Angrily he says, "What the hell is wrong with doing things right?"

"Nothing. Nothing. Except that's what your daughter has been blasting away at all her life. You don't reveal yourself to people, Seymour. You keep yourself a secret. Nobody knows what you are. You certainly never let *her* know who you are. That's what she's been blasting away at—that façade. All your fucking *norms*. Take a good look at what she did to your *norms*."

"I don't know what you want from me. You've always been too smart for me. Is this your response? Is this it?"

"You win the trophy. You always make the right move. You're loved by everybody. You marry Miss New Jersey, for God's sake. There's thinking for you. Why did you marry her? For the appearance. Why do you do everything? For the appearance!"

"I loved her! I opposed my own father I loved her so much!"

Jerry is laughing. "Is that what you believe? You really think you stood up to him? You married her because you couldn't get out of it. Dad raked her over the coals in his office and you sat there and didn't say shit. Well, isn't that true?"

"My daughter is in that room, Jerry. What is this all about?"

But Jerry does not hear him. He hears only himself. Why is this Jerry's grand occasion to tell his brother the truth? Why does someone, in the midst of your worst suffering, decide the time has come to drive home, disguised in the form of character analysis, all the contempt they have been harboring for you for all these years? What in your suffering makes their superiority so fulsome, so capacious, makes the expression of it so enjoyable? Why this occasion for launching his protest at living in the shadow of me? Why, if he had to tell me all this, couldn't he have told it to me when I was feeling my oats? Why does he even believe he's in my shadow? Miami's biggest cardiac surgeon! The heart victim's savior, Dr. Levov!

"Dad? He fucking let you slide through—don't you know that? If Dad had said, 'Look, you'll never get my approval for this, never, I am not having grandchildren half this and half that,' then you would have had to make a choice. But you *never* had to make a choice. *Never.* Because he let you slide through. Everybody has always let you slide through. And that is why, to this day, nobody knows who you are. You are unrevealed—that is the story, Seymour, *unrevealed.* That is why your own daughter decided to blow you away. You are never straight about anything and she hated you for it. You keep yourself a secret. You don't choose *ever.*"

"Why are you saying this? What do you want me to choose? What are we talking about?"

"You think you know what a man is? You have no *idea* what a man is. You think you know what a daughter is? You have no *idea* what a daughter is. You think you know what this country is? You have no *idea* what this country is. You have a false image of *everything.* All you know is what a fucking glove is. This country is *frightening.* Of course she was raped. What kind of company do you think she was keeping? Of course out there she was going to get raped. This isn't Old Rimrock, old buddy—she's out there, old buddy, in the USA. She enters that world, that loopy world out there, with what's going on out there—what do you *expect?* A kid from Rimrock, New Jersey, *of course* she doesn't know how to behave out there, *of course* the shit hits the fan. What could she know? She's like a wild child out there in the world. She can't get enough of it—she's *still* acting up. A room off McCarter Highway. And why not? Who wouldn't? You prepare her for life milking the cows? For what kind of life? Unnatural, all artificial, all of it. Those *assumptions* you live with. You're still in your old man's dream-world, Seymour, still up there with Lou Levov in glove heaven. A household tyrannized by gloves, bludgeoned by gloves, the only thing in life—ladies' gloves! Does he still tell the great one about the woman who sells the gloves washing her hands in a sink between each color? Oh where oh where is that outmoded America, that decorous America where a woman had twenty-five pairs of gloves? Your kid blows your norms to kingdom come, Seymour, and you still think you know what life is!"

Life is just a short period of time in which we are alive. Meredith Levov, 1964.

"You wanted Miss America? Well, you've got her, with a vengeance—she's your daughter! You wanted to be a real American jock, a real American marine, a real American hotshot with a beautiful Gentile babe on your arm? You longed to belong like everybody else to the United States of America? Well, you do now, big boy, thanks to your daughter. The reality of this place is right up in your kisser now. With the help of your daughter you're as deep in the shit as a man can get, the real American crazy shit. America amok! America amuck! Goddamn it, Seymour, goddamn you, if you were a father who loved his daughter," thunders Jerry into the phone—and the hell with the convalescent patients waiting in the corridor for him to check out their new valves and new arteries, to tell how grateful they are to him for their new lease on life, Jerry shouts away, shouts all he wants if it's shouting he wants to do, and the hell with the rules of the hospital. He is one of the surgeons who shouts: if you disagree with him he shouts, if you cross him he shouts, if you just stand there and do nothing he shouts. He does not do what hospitals tell him to do or fathers expect him to do or wives want him to do, he does what *he* wants to do, does as he pleases, tells people just who and what he is every minute of the day so that *nothing* about him is a secret, not his opinions, his frustrations, his urges, neither his appetite nor his hatred. In the sphere of the will, he is unequivocating, uncompromising; he is king. He does not spend time regretting what he has or has not done or justifying to others how loathsome he can be. The message is simple: You will take me as I come—there is no choice. He cannot endure swallowing anything. He just lets loose.

And these two are brothers, the same parents' sons, one for whom the aggression's been bred out, the other for whom the aggression's been bred in.

"If you were a father who loved his daughter," Jerry shouts at the Swede, "you would never have left her in that room! You would never have let her out of your sight!"

The Swede is in tears at his desk. It is as though Jerry has been waiting all his life for this phone call. That something's grotesquely out of whack has made him furious with his older brother, and now there is nothing he will not say. All his life, thinks the Swede, waiting to lay into me with these terrible things. People are infallible: they pick up on what you want and then they don't give it to you.

"I didn't *want* to leave her," says the Swede. "You don't understand. You don't want to understand. That isn't why I left her. It *killed* me to leave her! You don't understand me, you won't. Why do you say I don't love her? This is terrible. Horrible." He suddenly sees his vomit on her face and he cries out, "Everything is horrible!"

"*Now* you're getting it. Right! My brother is developing the beginning of a point of view. A point of view of his own instead of everybody else's point of view. Taking something other than the party line. Good. Now we're getting somewhere. Thinking becoming just a little untranquilized. Everything is horrible. And so what are you going to do about it? Nothing. Look, do you want me to come up there and get her? Do you want me to get her, yes or no?"

"No."

"Then why did you call me?"

"I don't know. To help me."

"Nobody can help you."

"You're a hard man. You are a hard man with me."

"Yeah, I don't come off looking very good. I never do. Ask our father if I do. You're the one who always comes off looking good. And look where it's got you. Refusing to give offense. Blaming yourself. Tolerant respect for every position. Sure, it's 'liberal'—I know, a liberal father. But what does that mean? What is at the *center* of it? Always holding things together. And look where the fuck it's got you!"

"I didn't make the war in Vietnam. I didn't make the television war. I didn't make Lyndon Johnson Lyndon Johnson. You forget where this begins. Why she threw the bomb. That fucking *war.*"

"No, you didn't make the war. You made the angriest kid in America. Ever since she was a kid, every word she *spoke* was a bomb."

"I gave her all I could, everything, everything, I gave everything. I swear to you I gave everything." And now he is crying easily, there is no line between him and his crying, and an amazing new experience it is—he is crying as though crying like this has been the great aim of his life, as though all along crying like this was his most deeply held ambition, and now he has achieved it, now that he remembers everything he gave and everything she took, all the spontaneous giving and taking that had filled their lives and that one day, inexplicably (despite whatever Jerry might say, despite all the blame that it is his pleasure now to heap upon the Swede), quite inexplicably, became repugnant to her. "You talk about what I'm dealing with as though *anybody* could deal with it. But *nobody* could deal with it. Nobody! Nobody has the weapons for this. You think I'm inept? You think I'm inadequate? If I'm inadequate, where are you going to get people who *are* adequate . . . if I'm . . . do you understand what I'm saying? What am I supposed to be? What are other people if I am inadequate?"

"Oh, I understand you."

Crying easily was always about as difficult for the Swede as losing his balance when he walked or deliberately being a bad influence on somebody; crying easily was something he sometimes almost envied in other people. But whatever chunks and fragments remain of the big manly barrier against crying, his brother's response to his pain demolishes. "If what you are telling me is what I was . . ." he begins, ". . . wasn't, wasn't enough, then, then . . . I'm telling *you*—I'm telling you that what *anybody* is *is not enough.*"

"You got it! Exactly! We are *not* enough. We are *none* of us enough! Including even the man who does everything right! Doing things right," Jerry says with disgust, "going around in this world doing things right. Look, are you going to break with appearances and pit your will against your daughter's or aren't you? Out on the *field* you did it. That's how you scored, remember? You pitted your will against the other guy's and you *scored.* Pretend it's a game if that helps. It doesn't help. For the typical male activity you're there, the man of action, but this isn't the typical male activity. Okay. Can't see yourself doing that. Can only see yourself playing ball and making gloves and marrying Miss America. Out there with Miss America, dumbing down and dulling out. Out there playing at being Wasps, a little Mick girl from the Elizabeth docks and a Jewboy from Weequahic High. The cows. Cow society. Colonial old America. And you thought all that façade was going to come without cost. Genteel and innocent. *But that costs, too, Seymour. I* would have thrown a bomb. *I* would become a Jain and live in Newark. That Wasp bullshit! I didn't know just how entirely muffled you were internally. But this is how muffled you are. Our old man really swaddled you but good. What do you want, Seymour? You want to bail out? That's all right too. Anybody else would have bailed out a long time ago. Go ahead, bail out. Admit her contempt for your life and bail out. Admit that there is something very personal about you that she hates and bail the fuck out and never see the bitch again. Admit that she's a monster, Seymour. Even a monster has to be from somewhere—even a monster needs parents. But parents don't need monsters. Bail out! But if you are *not* going to bail out, if that is what you are calling to tell me, then for Christ's sake go in there and get her. *I'll* go in and get her. How about that? Last chance. Last offer. You want me to come, I'll clear out the office and get on a plane and I'll come. And I'll go in there, and, I assure you, I'll get her off the McCarter Highway, the little shit, the selfish little fucking shit, playing her fucking games with you! She won't play them with me, I assure you. Do you want that or not?"

"I don't want that." These things Jerry thinks he knows that he doesn't know. His idea that things are connected. But there *is* no connection. How we lived and what she did? Where she was raised and what she did? It's as disconnected as everything else—it's all a part of the same mess! *He* is the one who knows nothing. Jerry rants. Jerry thinks he can escape the bewilderment by ranting, shouting, but everything he shouts is wrong. None of this is true. Causes, clear answers, who there is to blame. Reasons. But there are no reasons. She is obliged to be as she is. We all are. Reasons are in books. Could how we lived as a family ever have come back as this bizarre horror? It couldn't. It hasn't. Jerry tries to rationalize it but you can't. This is all something else, something he knows absolutely nothing about. No one does. It is not rational. It is chaos. It is chaos from start to finish. "I don't want that," the Swede tells him. "I can't have that."

"Too brutal for you. In this world, too brutal. The daughter's a murderer but this is too brutal. A drill instructor in the Marine Corps but this is too brutal. Okay, Big Swede, gentle giant. I got a waiting room full of patients. You're on your own."

# III

# Paradise Lost

# 7

IT WAS the summer of the Watergate hearings. The Levovs had
spent nearly every night on the back porch watching the replay of
the day's session on Channel 13. Before the farm equipment and the
cattle had been sold off, it was from there, on warm evenings, that
they looked out onto Dawn's herd grazing along the rim of the hill.
Up a ways from the house was a field of eighteen acres, and some
years they'd have the cows up there all summer and forget them.
But if they were merely out of sight nearby, and Merry, in her
pajamas, wanted to see them before she went to bed, Dawn would
call out, "*Here*boy, *Here*boy," the kind of thing people had been
calling to them for thousands of years, and they'd sound off in
return and start up the hill and out from the swamp, come out of
wherever they were, bellowing their response as they trudged toward the sound of Dawn's voice. "Aren't they beautiful, our girls?"
Dawn would ask her daughter, and the next day Merry and Dawn
would be out at sunrise getting them all together again, and he'd
hear Dawn say, "Okay, we're going to cross the road," and Merry
would open the gate and just with a stick and the dog, Apu the
Australian sheepdog, mother and tiny daughter would move some
twelve or fifteen or eighteen beasts, each weighing about two thousand pounds. Merry, Apu, and Dawn, sometimes the vet, and the
boy down the road to help with the fencing and the haying when an

extra hand was needed. *I've got Merry to help me hay. If there's a stray calf, Merry gets after it. Seymour goes in there and those two cows will be very unpleasant, they'll paw the grass, they'll shake their heads at him—but Merry goes in, well, they know her, and they just tell her what they want. They know her and they know exactly what she's going to do with them.*

How could she ever say to him, "I don't want to talk about my mother"? What in God's name had her mother done? What crime had her mother committed? The crime of being gentle master to these compliant cows?

During this last week, while his parents had been with them, up from Florida for the annual late-summer visit, Dawn hadn't even worried about keeping the two of them entertained. Whenever she returned from the new building site or drove back from the architect's office, they were seated before the set with the father-in-law in the role of assistant counsel to the committee. Her in-laws watched the proceedings all day and then saw the whole thing over again at night. In what time he had left to himself during the day, the Swede's father composed letters to the committee members which he read to everyone at dinner. "Dear Senator Weicker: You're surprised at what was going on in Tricky Dicky's White House? Don't be a shnook. Harry Truman had him figured out in 1948 when he called him Tricky Dicky." "Dear Senator Gurney: Nixon equals Typhoid Mary. Everything he touches he poisons, you included." "Dear Senator Baker: You want to know WHY? Because they're a bunch of common criminals, that's WHY!" "Dear Mr. Dash:" he wrote to the committee's New York counsel, "I applaud you. God bless you. You make me proud to be an American and a Jew."

His greatest contempt he reserved for a relatively insignificant figure, a lawyer named Kalmbach, who'd arranged for large illegal contributions to sift into the Watergate operation, and whose disgrace could not be profound enough to suit the old man. "Dear Mr. Kalmbach: If you were a Jew and did what you did the whole world would say, 'See those Jews, real money-grubbers.' But who is the money-grubber, my dear Mr. Country Club? Who is the thief and the cheat? Who is the American and who is the gangster? Your smooth talk never fooled me, Mr. Country Club Kalmbach. Your golf never fooled me. Your manners never fooled me. Your clean hands I always knew were dirty. And now the whole world knows. You should be ashamed."

"You think I'll get an answer from the son of a bitch? I ought to publish these in a book. I ought to find somebody to print 'em up and just distribute them free so people could know what an ordinary American feels when these sons of bitches . . . look, look at that one, *look* at him." Ehrlichman, Nixon's former chief of staff, had appeared on the screen.

"He makes me nauseous," the Swede's mother said. "Him and that Tricia."

"Please, she's unimportant," her husband said. "This is a real fascist—the whole bunch of 'em, Von Ehrlichman, Von Haldeman, Von Kalmbach—"

"She still makes me nauseous," his wife said. "You'd think she was a princess, the way they carry on about her."

"These so-called patriots," Lou Levov said to Dawn, "would take this country and make Nazi Germany out of it. You know the book *It Can't Happen Here?* There's a wonderful book, I forget the author, but the idea couldn't be more up-to-the-moment. These people have taken us to the edge of something terrible. *Look* at that son of a bitch."

"I don't know which one I hate more," his wife said, "him or the other one."

"They're the same thing," the old man told her, "they're interchangeable, the whole bunch of them."

Merry's legacy. That his father might have been no less incensed if she were there, sitting with them all in front of the set, the Swede recognized, but now that she was gone who better was there to hate for what had become of her than these Watergate bastards?

It was during the Vietnam War that Lou Levov had begun mailing Merry copies of the letters he sent to President Johnson, letters that he had written to influence Merry's behavior more than the president's. Seeing his teenage granddaughter as enraged with the war as he could get when things started to go too wrong with the business, the old man became so distressed that he would take his son aside and say, "Why does she care? Where does she even get this stuff? Who feeds it to her? What's the difference to her anyway? Does she carry on like this at school? She can't do this at school, she could harm her chances at school. She can harm her chances for college. In public people won't put up with it, they'll chop her head off, she's only a child. . . ." To control, if he could, not so much Merry's opinions as the ferocity with which she sputtered them out, he would ostentatiously ally himself with her by sending articles clipped from the Florida papers and inscribed in the margins with his own antiwar slogans. When he was visiting he would read aloud to her from the portfolio of his Johnson letters that he carried around the house under his arm—in his effort to save her from herself, tagging after the child as though *he* were the child. "We've got to nip this in the bud," he confided to his son. "This won't do, not at all."

"Well," he'd say—after reading to Merry yet another plea to the president reminding him what a great country America was, what a great president FDR had been, how much his own family owed to this country and what a personal disappointment it was to him and his loved ones that American boys were halfway around the world fighting somebody else's battle when they ought to be at home with their loved ones—"well, what do you think of your grandfather?"

"J-j-johnson's a war criminal," she'd say. "He's not going to s-s-s-stop the w-w-war, Grandpa, because you tell him to."

"He's also a man trying to do his job, you know."

"He's an imperialist dog."

"Well, that is one opinion."

"There's no d-d-d-difference between him and Hitler."

"You're exaggerating, sweetheart. I don't say Johnson didn't let us down. But you forget what Hitler did to the Jews, Merry dear. You weren't born then, so you don't remember."

"He did nothing that Johnson isn't doing to the Vietnamese."

"The Vietnamese aren't being put into concentration camps."

"Vietnam is one *b-b-big* camp! The 'American boys' aren't the issue. That's like saying, 'Get the storm troopers out of Auschwitz in time for Chris-chris-chris-*christ*mas.'"

"I *gotta* be political with the guy, sweetheart. I can't write the guy and call him a murderer and expect that he's going to listen. Right, Seymour?"

"I don't think that would help," the Swede said.

"Merry, we all feel the way you do," her grandfather told her. "Do you understand that? Believe me, I know what it is to read the newspaper and start to go nuts. Father Coughlin, that son of a bitch. The hero Charles Lindbergh—pro-Nazi, pro-Hitler, and a so-called national hero in this country. Mr. Gerald L. K. Smith. The great Senator Bilbo. Sure we have bastards in this country—home-grown and plenty of 'em. Nobody denies that. Mr. Rankin. Mr. Dies. Mr. Dies and his committee. Mr. J. Parnell Thomas from New Jersey. Isolationist, bigoted, know-nothing fascists right there in the U.S. Congress, crooks like J. Parnell Thomas, crooks who wound up in jail and their salaries were paid for by the U.S. taxpayer. Awful people. The worst. Mr. McCarran. Mr. Jenner. Mr. Mundt. The Goebbels from Wisconsin, the Honorable Mr. McCarthy, may he burn in hell. His sidekick Mr. Cohn. A disgrace. A *Jew* and a disgrace! There have always been sons of bitches here just like there are in every country, and they have been voted into office by all those geniuses out there who have the right to vote. And what about the newspapers? Mr. Hearst. Mr. McCormick. Mr. Westbrook Pegler. Real fascist, reactionary dogs. And I have hated their guts. Ask your father. Haven't I, Seymour—hated them?"

"You have."

"Honey, we live in a democracy. Thank God for that. You don't have to go around getting angry with your family. You can write letters. You can vote. You can get up on a soapbox and make a speech. Christ, you can do what your father did—you can join the marines."

"Oh, Grandpa—the marines are the *prob-prob-prob*—"

"Then damn it, Merry, join the *other* side," he said, momentarily losing his grip. "How's that? You can join *their* marines if you want to. It's been done. That's true. Look at history. When you're old enough you can go over and fight for the other army if you want it. I don't recommend it. People don't like it, and I think you're smart enough to understand why they don't. 'Traitor' isn't a pleasant thing to be called. But it's been done. It's an option. Look at Benedict Arnold. Look at him. He did it. He went over to the other side, as far as I remember. From school. And I suppose I respect him. He had guts. He stood up for what he believed in. He risked his own life for what he believed in. But he happened to be wrong, Merry, in my estimation. He went over to the other side in the Revolutionary War and, as far as I'm concerned, the man was dead wrong. Now you don't happen to be wrong. You happen to be *right*. This family is one hundred percent against this goddamn Vietnam thing. You don't have to rebel against your family *because your family is not in disagreement with you*. You are not the only person around here against this war. We are against it. Bobby Kennedy is against it—"

"*Now*," said Merry, with disgust.

"Okay, now. Now is better than not now, isn't it? Be realistic, Merry—it doesn't help anything not to be. Bobby Kennedy is against it. Senator Eugene McCarthy is against it. Senator Javits is against it, and he's a Republican. Senator Frank Church is against it. Senator Wayne Morse is against it. And how he is. I admire that man. I've written him to tell him and I have gotten the courtesy of a hand-signed reply. Senator Fulbright, of course, is against it. It's Fulbright who, admittedly, introduced the Tonkin Gulf resolu—"

"F-f-f-ful—"

"Nobody is saying—"

"Dad," said the Swede, "let Merry finish."

"I'm sorry, honey," said Lou Levov. "Finish."

"Ful-ful-fulbright is a racist."

"Is he? What are you talking about? Senator William Fulbright from Arkansas? Come on with that stuff. I think there's where you've got your facts wrong, my friend." She had slandered one of his heroes who'd stood up to Joe McCarthy, and to prevent himself from lashing out at her about Fulbright took a supreme effort of will. "But now just let *me* finish what I was saying. What *was* I saying? Where was I? Where the hell was I, Seymour?"

"Your point," the Swede said, acting evenhandedly as the moderator for these two dynamos, a role he preferred to being the adversary of either, "is that both of you are against the war and want it to stop. There's no reason for you to argue on that issue—I believe *that's* your point. Merry feels it's all gone beyond writing letters to the president. She feels that's futile. You feel that, futile or not, it's something within your power to do and you're going to do it, at least to continue to put yourself on record."

"Exactly!" the old man cried. "Here, listen to what I tell him here. 'I am a lifetime Democrat.' Merry, listen—'I am a lifetime Democrat—'"

But nothing he told the president ended the war, nor did anything he told Merry nip the catastrophe in the bud. Yet alone in the family he had seen it coming. "I saw it coming. I saw it clear as day. I saw it. I knew it. I sensed it. I fought it. She was out of control. Something was wrong. I could smell it. I told you. 'Something has to be done about that child. Something is going wrong with that child.' And it went in one ear and out the other. I got, 'Dad, take it easy.' I got, 'Dad, don't exaggerate. Dad, it's a phase. Lou, leave her alone, don't argue with her.' 'No, I will *not* leave her alone. This is my granddaughter. I *refuse* to leave her alone. I refuse to lose a granddaughter by leaving her alone. Something is *haywire* with that child.' And you looked at me like I was nuts. All of you. Only I wasn't nuts. I was *right*. With a *vengeance* I was right!"

There were no messages for him when he got home. He had been praying for a message from Mary Stoltz.

"Nothing?" he said to Dawn, who was in the kitchen preparing a salad out of greens she'd pulled from the garden.

"Nope."

He poured a drink for himself and his father and carried the glasses out to the back porch, where the set was still on.

"You going to make a steak, darling?" his mother asked him.

"Steak, corn, salad, and Merry's big beefsteak tomatoes." He'd meant Dawn's tomatoes but did not correct himself once it was out.

"No one makes a steak like you," she said, after the first shock of his words had worn off.

"Good, Ma."

"My big boy. Who could want a better son?" she said, and when he embraced her she went to pieces for the first time that week. "I'm sorry. I was remembering the phone calls."

"I understand," he said.

"She was a little girl. You'd call, you'd put her on, and she'd say, 'Hi, Grandma! Guess what?' 'I don't know, honey—what?' And she'd tell me."

"Come on, you've been terrific so far. You can keep it up. Come on. Buck up."

"I was looking at the snapshots, when she was a baby . . ."

"Don't look at them," he said. "Try not to look at them. You can do it, Ma. You have to."

"Oh, darling, you're so brave, you're such an inspiration, it's such a tonic when we come to see you. I love you so."

"Good, Ma. I love you. But you mustn't lose control in front of Dawn."

"Yes, yes, whatever you say."

"That's my girl."

His father, continuing to watch the television set—and after having miraculously contained himself for ten full days—said to him, "No news."

"No news," the Swede replied.

"Nothing."

"Nothing."

"O-kay," his father said, feigning fatalism, "o-kay—if that's the way it is, that's the way it is," and went back to watching TV.

"Do you still think she's in Canada, Seymour?" his mother asked.

"I never thought she was in Canada."

"But that's where the boys went . . ."

"Look, why don't we save this discussion? There's nothing wrong with asking questions but Dawn will be in and out—"

"I'm sorry, you're right," his mother replied. "I'm terribly sorry."

"Not that the situation has changed, Mother. Everything is exactly the same."

"Seymour . . ." She hesitated. "Darling, one question. If she gave herself up now, what would happen? Your father says—"

"Why are you bothering him with that?" his father said. "He told you about Dawn. Learn to control yourself."

"*Me* control myself?"

"Mother, you must stop thinking these thoughts. She is gone. She may never want to see us again."

"*Why?*" his father erupted. "Of course she wants to see us again. This I refuse to believe!"

"Now who's controlling himself?" his mother asked.

"Of course she wants to see us again. The problem is *she can't.*"

"Lou dear," his mother said, "there are children, even in ordinary families, who grow up and go away and that's the end of it."

"But not at *sixteen.* For Christ's sake, not under these circumstances. What are you talking about 'ordinary' families? *We* are an ordinary family. This is a child who needs help. This is a child who is in trouble and we are not a family who walks out on a child in trouble!"

"She's twenty years old, Dad. Twenty-one."

"Twenty-one," his mother said, "last January."

"Well, she's not a child," the Swede told them. "All I'm saying is that you must not set yourself up for disappointment, neither of you."

"Well, I don't," his father said. "I have more sense than that. I assure you I don't."

"Well, you mustn't. I seriously doubt that we will ever see her again."

The only thing worse than their never seeing her again would be their seeing her as he had left her on the floor of that room. Over these last few years, he had been moving them in the direction, if not of total resignation, of adaptation, of a realistic appraisal of the future. How could he now tell them what had happened to Merry, find words to describe it to them that would not destroy them? They haven't the faintest picture in their mind of what they'd see if they were to see her. Why does anyone have to know? What is so indispensable about any of them knowing?

"You got reason to say that, son, that we'll never see her?"

"The five years. The time that's gone by. That's reason enough."

"Seymour, sometimes I'm walking on the street, and I'm behind someone, a girl who's walking in front of me, and if she's tall—"

He took his mother's hands in his. "You think it's Merry."

"Yes."

"That happens to all of us."

"I can't stop it."

"I understand."

"And every time the phone rings," she said.

"I know."

"I tell her," his father said, "that she wouldn't do it with a phone call anyway."

"And why not?" she said to her husband. "Why not phone us? That's the safest thing she could possibly do, to phone us."

"Ma, none of this speculation means anything. Why not try to keep it to a minimum tonight? I know you can't help having these thoughts. You can't be free of it, none of us can be. But you have to try. You can't make happen what you want to happen just by thinking about it. Try to free yourself from a little of it."

"Whatever you say, darling," his mother replied. "I feel better now, just talking about it. I can't keep it inside me all the time."

"I know. But we can't start whispering around Dawn."

It was never difficult, as it was with his restless father—who spent so much of life in a transitional state between compassion and antagonism, between comprehension and blindness, between gentle intimacy and violent irritation—to know what to make of his mother. He had never feared battling with her, never uncertainly wondered what side she was on or worried what she might be inflamed by next. Unlike her husband, she was a big industry of nothing other than family love. Hers was a simple personality for whom the well-being of the boys was everything. Talking to her he'd felt, since earliest boyhood, as though he were stepping directly into her heart. With his father, to whose heart he had easy enough access, he had first to collide with that skull, the skull of a brawler, to split it open as bloodlessly as he could to get at whatever was inside.

It was astonishing how small a woman she had become. But what hadn't been consumed by osteoporosis had, in the last five years, been destroyed by Merry. Now the vivacious mother of his youth, who well into middle age was being complimented on her youthful vigor, was an old lady, her spine twisted and bent, a hurt and puzzled expression embedded in the creases of her face. Now, when she did not realize people were watching her, tears would rise in her eyes, eyes bearing that look both long accustomed to living with pain and startled to have been in so much pain so long. Yet all his boyhood recollections (which, however hard to credit, he knew to be genuine; even the ruthlessly unillusioned Jerry would, if asked, have to corroborate them) were of his mother towering over the rest of them, a healthy, tall reddish blonde with a wonderful laugh, who adored being the woman in that masculine household. As a small child he had not found it nearly so odd and amazing as he did looking at her now to think that you could recognize people as easily by their laugh as by their face. Hers, back when she had something to laugh about, was light and like a bird in flight, rising, rising, and then, delightfully, if you were her child, rising yet again. He didn't even have to be in the same room to know where his mother was—he'd hear her laughing and could pinpoint her on the map of the house that was not so much *in* his brain as it *was* his brain (his cerebral cortex divided not into frontal lobes, parietal lobes, temporal lobes, and occipital lobes but into the downstairs, the upstairs, and the basement—the living room, the dining room, the kitchen, etc.).

What had been oppressing her when she arrived from Florida the week before was the letter she was carrying secreted in her purse, a letter addressed by Lou Levov to the second wife Jerry had left, from whom he had only recently separated. Sylvia Levov had been given a stack of letters to mail by her husband, but that one she simply could not send. Instead she had dared to go off alone and open it, and now she had brought the contents north with her to show Seymour. "You know what would happen with Jerry if Susan ever got this? You know the rampage Jerry would go on? He is not a boy without a temper. He never was. He's not you, dear, he is not a diplomat. But your father has to stick his nose in everywhere, and what the results will be means nothing to him, so long as he's got his nose in the wrong place. All he has to do is send her this, and put Jerry in the wrong like this, and there will be hell to pay with your brother—unmitigated hell."

The letter, two pages long, began, "Dear Susie, The check enclosed is for you and for nobody else's information. It is found money. Put it somewhere where nobody knows about it. I'll say nothing and you say nothing. I want you to know that I have not forgotten you in my will. This money is yours to do whatever you want with. The children I'll take care of separately. But if you decide to invest it, *and I strongly hope you do,* my suggestion is gold stocks. The dollar isn't going to be worth a thing. I myself have just put ten thousand into three gold stocks. I will give you the names. Bennington Mines. Castworp Development. Schley-Waiggen Mineral Corp. Solid investments. I got the names from the Barrington Newsletter that has never steered me wrong yet."

Stapled to the letter—stapled so that when she opened the letter the enclosure didn't just flutter away to get lost under the sofa— there was a check made out to Susan R. Levov for seventy-five hundred dollars. A check for twice that amount had gone off to her the day after she had called, sobbing and screaming for help, to say that Jerry had left her that morning for the new nurse in his office. The position of new nurse in the office was one that she had herself occupied before Jerry began the affair with her that ended in his divorcing his first wife. According to the Swede's mother, after Jerry found out about the check for fifteen thousand he proceeded over the phone to call his father "every name in the book," and that night, for the first time in his life, Lou Levov had chest pain that necessitated her calling their doctor at two A.M.

And now, four months later, he was at it again. "Seymour, what should I do? He goes around screaming, 'A second divorce, a second broken family, *more* grandchildren in a broken home, three more wonderful children without parental guidance.' *You* know how he goes on. It's on and on, it's over and over, till I think I'm going out of my mind. 'Where did my son get so good at getting divorced? Who in the history of this entire family has ever been divorced? No one!' I cannot take it anymore, dear. He screams at me, 'Why doesn't your son just go to a whorehouse? Marry a whore out of a whorehouse and get it over with!' He'll get in another fight with Jerry, and Jerry doesn't pull his punches. Jerry doesn't have your considerateness. He never did. When they had that fight about the coat, when Jerry made that coat out of the hamsters—do you remember? Maybe you were in the service by then. Hamster skins Jerry got somewhere, I think at school, and made them into a coat for some girl. He thought he was doing her a favor. But she received this thing, I think by mail, in a box, all wrapped up and it smelled to high heaven, and the girl burst into tears, and her mother telephoned, and your father was fit to be tied. He was mortified. And they had an argument, he and Jerry, and it scared me to death. A fifteen-year-old boy and he screamed so at his own father, his 'rights,' his 'rights,' you could have heard him on Broad and Market about his 'rights.' Jerry does not back down. He doesn't know the meaning of 'back down.' But now he won't be shouting at a man who is forty-five, he will be shouting at a man who is *seventy*-five, and with angina, and this time it won't be indigestion afterwards. There won't be a headache. This time there will be a full-scale heart attack." "There won't be a heart attack. Mother, calm down." "Did I do the wrong thing? I never touched another person's mail in my life. But how could I let him send this to Susan? Because she won't keep it to herself. She'll do what she did the last time. She'll use it against Jerry—she'll tell him. And this time Jerry *will* kill him." "Jerry won't kill him. He doesn't want to kill him and he won't. Mail it, Momma. You still have the envelope?" "Yes." "It isn't torn? You didn't tear it?" "I'm ashamed to tell you—it's not torn, I used steam. But I don't want him to drop *dead*." "He won't. He hasn't yet. You stay out of it, Ma. Mail Susan the envelope with the check, with the letter. And when Jerry calls, you just go out and take a walk." "And when he gets chest pains again?" "If he gets chest pains again, you'll call the doctor again. You just stay out of it. You cannot intervene to protect him from himself. It's too late in the day for that." "Oh, thank goodness I have you. You're the only one I can turn to. All your own troubles, all you've gone through, and you're the only one in this family who says things to me that are not completely insane."

"Dawn's holding up?" his father asked.

"She's doing fine."

"She looks like a million bucks," his father said. "That girl looks like herself again. Getting rid of those cows was the smartest thing you ever did. I never liked 'em. I never saw why she needed them. Thank God for that face-lift. I was against it but I was wrong. Dead wrong. I got to admit it. That guy did a wonderful job. Thank God our Dawn doesn't look anymore like all that she went through."

"He did do a great job," the Swede said. "Erased all that suffering. He gave her back her face." No longer does she have to look in the mirror at the record of her misery. It had been a brilliant stroke: she had got the thing out from directly in front of her.

"But she's waiting. I see it, Seymour. A mother sees such things. Maybe you erase the suffering from the face, but you can't remove the memory inside. Under that face, the poor thing is waiting."

"Dawn's not a poor thing, Ma. She's a fighter. She's fine. She's made tremendous strides." True—all the while he has been stoically enduring it she has made tremendous strides by finding it *unendurable*, by being devastated by it, destroyed by it, and then by denuding herself of it. She doesn't resist the blows the way he does; she *receives* the blows, falls apart, and when she gets herself up again, decides to make herself over. Nothing that isn't admirable in that— abandon first the face assaulted by the child, abandon next the house assaulted by the child. This is her life, after all, and she will get the original Dawn up and going again if it's the last thing she does. "Ma, let's stop this. Come on outside with me while I start the coals."

"No," his mother said, looking ready to cry again. "Thank you, darling. I'll stay here with Daddy and watch the television."

"You watched it all day. Come outside and help me."

"No, thank you, dear."

"She's waiting for them to get Nixon on," his father said. "When they get Nixon on and drive a stake through his heart, your mother will be in seventh heaven."

"And you won't?" she said. "He can't sleep," she told the Swede, "because of that *mamzer*. He's up in the middle of the night writing him letters. Some I have to censor myself, I have to physically stop him, the language is so filthy."

"That skunk!" the Swede's father said bitterly. "That miserable fascist dog!" and out of him, with terrifying force, poured a tirade of abuse, vitriol about the president of the United States that, absent the stuttering that never failed to impart to her abhorrence the exterminating adamance of a machine gun, Merry herself couldn't have topped in her heyday. Nixon liberates him to say anything—as Johnson liberated Merry. It is as though in his uncensored hatred of Nixon, Lou Levov is merely mimicking his granddaughter's vituperous loathing of LBJ. Get Nixon. Get the bastard in some way. Get Nixon and all will be well. If we can just tar and feather Nixon, America will be America again, without everything loathsome and lawless that's crept in, without all this violence and malice and madness and hate. Put him in a cage, cage the crook, and we'll have our great country back the way it was!

Dawn ran in from the kitchen to see what was wrong, and soon they were all in tears, holding one another, huddled together and weeping on that big old back porch as though the bomb had been planted right under the house and the porch was all that was left of the place. And there was nothing the Swede could do to stop them or to stop himself.

The family had never seemed so wrecked as this. Despite all that he had summoned up to lessen the aftershock of the day's horror and to prevent *himself* from cracking—despite the resolve with which he had rearmed himself after hurrying through the underpass and finding his car still there, undamaged, where he had left it on that grim Down Neck street; despite the resolve with which he had for a *second* time rearmed himself after Jerry pummeled him on the phone; despite the resolve he'd had to summon up a *third* time, beneath the razor ribbon of his parking lot fence, with the key to his car in his hand; despite the self-watchfulness, despite the painstaking impersonation of impregnability, despite the elaborate false front of self-certainty with which he was determined to protect those he loved from the four she had killed—he had merely to misspeak, to say "Merry's big beefsteak tomatoes" instead of "Dawn's," for them to sense that something unsurpassingly awful had happened.

In addition to the Levovs there were six guests for dinner that evening. The first to arrive were Bill and Jessie Orcutt, Dawn's architect and his wife, who'd been friendly enough neighbors a few miles down the road all these years, in Orcutt's old family house, and became acquaintances and then dinner guests when Bill Orcutt began designing the new Levov home. Orcutt's family had long been the prominent legal family in Morris County, lawyers, judges, state senators. As president of the local landmarks society, already established as the historical conscience of a new conservationist generation, Orcutt had been a leader in the losing battle to keep

Interstate 287 from cutting through the historical center of Morristown and a victorious opponent of the jetport that would have destroyed the Great Swamp, just west of Chatham, and with it much of the county's wildlife. He was trying now to keep Lake Hopatcong from devastation by pollutants. Orcutt's bumper sticker read, "Morris Green, Quiet, and Clean," and he'd good-naturedly slapped one on the Swede's car the first time they met. "Need all the help we can get," he said, "to keep the modern ills at bay." Once he learned that his new neighbors were originally city kids to whom the rural Morris Highlands was an unknown landscape, he volunteered to take them on a county tour, one that, as it turned out, went on all one day and would have extended into the next had not the Swede lied and said he and Dawn and the baby had to be in Elizabeth, at his in-laws', Sunday morning.

Dawn had said no to the tour right off. Something in Orcutt's proprietary manner had irritated her at that first meeting, something she found gratingly egotistical in his expansive courtesy, causing her to believe that to this young country squire with the charming manners she was nothing but laughable lace-curtain Irish, a girl who'd somehow got down the knack of aping her betters so as now to come ludicrously barging into his privileged backyard. The confidence, that's what unstrung her, that great confidence. Sure she'd been Miss New Jersey, but the Swede had seen her on a few occasions with these rich Ivy League guys in their shetland sweaters. Her affronted defensiveness always came as a surprise. She didn't seem ever to feel deficient in confidence until she met them and felt the class sting. "I'm sorry," she'd say, "I know it's just my Irish resentment, but I don't like being looked down on." And as much as this resentment of hers had always secretly attracted him—in the face of hostility, he thought proudly, my wife is no pushover—it perturbed and disappointed him as well; he preferred to think of Dawn as a young woman of great beauty and accomplishment who was too *renowned* to have to feel resentful. "The only difference between them and us"—by "them" she meant Protestants—"is, on our side, a little more liquor. And not much at that. 'My new Celtic neighbor. *And* her Hebrew husband.' I can hear him already with the other nobs. I'm sorry—if you can do it that's fine with me, but I for one cannot revere his contempt for our embarrassing origins."

The mainspring of Orcutt's character—and this she was sure of without having even to speak to him—was knowing all too well just how far back he and his manners reached into the genteel past, and so she stayed at home the day of the tour, perfectly content to be alone with the baby.

Her husband and Orcutt, promptly at eight, headed diagonally to the northwest corner of the county and then, backtracking, followed the southward meandering spine of the old iron mines, Orcutt all the while recounting the glory days of the nineteenth century, when iron was king, millions of tons pulled from this very ground; starting from Hibernia and Boonton down to Morristown, the towns and villages had been thick with rolling mills, nail and spike factories, foundries and forging shops. Orcutt showed him the site of the old mill in Boonton where axles, wheels, and rails were manufactured for the original Morris and Essex Railroad. He showed him the powder company plant in Kenvil that made dynamite for the mines and then, for the First World War, made TNT and more or less paved the way for the government to build the arsenal up at Picatinny, where they'd manufactured the big shells for the Second World War. It was at the Kenvil plant that there'd been the munitions explosion in 1940—fifty-two killed, carelessness the culprit, though at first foreign agents, spies, were suspected. He drove him partway along the western course of the old Morris Canal, where barges had carried the anthracite in from Phillipsburg to fuel the Morris foundries. With a little smile, Orcutt added—to the Swede's surprise—that directly across the Delaware from Phillipsburg was Easton, and "Easton," he said, "was where the whorehouse was for young men from Old Rimrock."

The eastern terminus of the Morris Canal had been Jersey City and Newark. The Swede knew of the Newark end of the canal from when he was a boy and his father would remind him, if they were downtown and anywhere near Raymond Boulevard, that until as recently as the year the Swede was born a real canal ran up by High Street, near where the Jewish Y was, and down through to where there was now this wide city thoroughfare, Raymond Boulevard, leading traffic from Broad Street under Penn Station and out old Passaic Avenue onto the Skyway.

In the Swede's young mind, the "Morris" in Morris Canal never connected with Morris County—a place that seemed as remote as Nebraska then—but with his father's enterprising oldest brother, Morris. In 1918, at the age of twenty-four, already the owner of a shoe store he ran with his young wife—a cubbyhole Down Neck on Ferry Street, amid all the poor Poles and Italians and Irish, and the family's greatest achievement until the wartime contract with the WACs put Newark Maid on the map—Morris had perished virtually overnight in the influenza epidemic. Even on his tour of the county that day, every time Orcutt mentioned the Morris Canal, the Swede thought first of the dead uncle he had never known, a beloved brother who was much missed by his father and for whom the child had come to believe the canal beneath Raymond Boulevard was named. Even when his father bought the Central Avenue factory (no more than a hundred yards from the very spot where the canal had turned north toward Belleville, a factory that virtually backed on the city subway built beneath the old canal route), he persisted in associating the name of the canal with the story of the struggles of their family rather than with the grander history of the state.

After going around Washington's Morristown headquarters—where he politely pretended he hadn't already seen the muskets and the cannonballs and the old eyeglasses as a Newark fourth grader—he and Orcutt drove southwest a ways, out of Morristown to a church cemetery dating back to the American Revolution. Soldiers killed in the war were buried there, as well as twenty-seven soldiers, buried in a common grave, who were victims of the smallpox epidemic that swept the encampments in the countryside in the spring of 1777. Out among those old, old tombstones, Orcutt was no less historically edifying than he'd been all morning on the road, so that at the dinner table that evening, when Dawn asked where Mr. Orcutt had taken him, the Swede laughed. "I got my money's worth all right. The guy's a walking encyclopedia. I never felt so ignorant in my life." "How boring was it?" Dawn asked. "Why, not at all," the Swede told her. "We had a good time. He's a good guy. Very nice. More there than you think when you first meet him. Much more to Orcutt than the old school tie." He was thinking particularly of the Easton whorehouse but said instead, "Family goes back to the Revolution." "Doesn't that come as a surprise," Dawn replied. "The guy knows everything," he said, feigning indifference to her sarcasm. "For instance, that old graveyard where we were, it's at the top of the tallest hill around, so the rain that falls on the northern roof of the old church there finds its way north to the Passaic River and eventually to Newark Bay, and the rain that falls on the southern side finds its way south to a branch of the Raritan, which eventually goes to New Brunswick." "I don't believe that," said Dawn. "Well, it's true." "I refuse to believe it. *Not* to New Brunswick." "Oh, don't be a kid, Dawn. It's interesting *geologically.*" Deliberately he added, "Very interesting," to let her know he was having no part of the Irish resentment. It was beneath him and happened also to be beneath her.

In bed that night, he thought that when Merry got to be a schoolgirl he'd inveigle Orcutt into taking her along on this very same trip so she could learn firsthand the history of the county where she was growing up. He wanted her to see where, at the turn of the century, a railroad line used to run up into Morristown from Whitehouse to carry the peaches from the orchards in Hunterdon County. Thirty miles of railroad line just to transport peaches. Among the well-to-do there was a peach craze then in the big cities and they'd ship them from Morristown into New York. The Peach Special. Wasn't that something? On a good day seventy cars of peaches hauled from the Hunterdon orchards. Two million peach trees down there before a blight carried them all away. But he could himself tell her about that train and the trees and the blight when the time came, take her on his own to show her where the tracks used to be. It wouldn't require Orcutt to do it for him.

"The first Morris County Orcutt," Orcutt told him at the cemetery, pointing to a brown weathered gravestone decorated at the top with the carving of a winged angel, a gravestone set close up to the back wall of the church. "Thomas. Protestant immigrant from northern Ireland. Arrived 1774. Age of twenty. Enlisted in a local militia outfit. A private. January 2, 1777, fought at Second Trenton. Battle that set the stage for Washington's victory at Princeton the next day."

"Didn't know that," the Swede said.

"Wound up at the logistical base at Morristown. Commissary support for the Continental artillery train. After the war bought a Morristown ironworks. Destroyed by a flash flood, 1795. Two flash floods, '94 *and* '95. Big supporter of Jefferson. Political appointment from Governor Bloomfield saved his life. Surrogate of Morris County. Máster in chancery. Eventually county clerk. There he is. The sturdy, fecund patriarch."

"Interesting," said the Swede—interesting at just the moment he found it all about as deadly as it could get. How it *was* interesting was that he'd never met anybody like this before.

"Over here," said Orcutt, leading him some twenty feet on to another old brownish stone with an angel carved at the top, this one with an indecipherable rhyme of four lines inscribed near the bottom. "His son William. Ten sons. One died in his thirties but the rest lived long lives. Spread out all over Morris County. None of them farmers. Justices of the peace. Sheriffs. Freeholders. Postmasters. Orcutts everywhere, even into Warren and up into Sussex. William was the prosperous one. Turnpike development. Banking. New Jersey presidential elector in 1828. Pledged to Andrew Jackson. Rode the Jackson victory to a big judicial appointment. State's highest judicial body. Never a member of the bar. That didn't matter then. Died a much-respected judge. See, on the stone? 'A virtuous and useful citizen.' It's *his* son—over here, this one here—his son George who clerked for August Findley and became a partner. Findley was a state legislator. Slavery issue drove him into the Republican Party. . . ."

As the Swede told Dawn, whether she wanted to hear it or not—no, because she did *not* want to hear it—"It was a lesson in American history. John Quincy Adams. Andrew Jackson. Abraham Lincoln. Woodrow Wilson. His grandfather was a classmate of Woodrow Wilson's. At Princeton. He told me the class. I forget it now. Eighteen seventy-nine? I'm full of dates, Dawnie. He told me *everything*. And all we were doing was walking around a cemetery out back of a church at the top of a hill. It was something. It was *school*."

But once was enough. He'd paid all the attention he could, never stopped trying to keep straight in his mind the progress of the Orcutts through almost two centuries—though each time Orcutt had said "Morris" as in Morris County, the Swede had thought "Morris" as in Morris Levov. He couldn't remember ever in his life feeling more like his father—not like his father's son but like his *father*—than he did marching around the graves of those Orcutts. His family couldn't compete with Orcutt's when it came to ancestors—they would have run out of ancestors in about two minutes. As soon as you got back earlier than Newark, back to the old country, no one knew anything. Earlier than Newark, they didn't know their names or anything about them, how anyone made a living, let alone whom they'd voted for. But Orcutt could spin out ancestors forever. Every rung into America for the Levovs there was another rung to attain; this guy was *there*.

Is that why Orcutt had laid it on a little thick? Was it to make clear what Dawn accused him of making clear simply by the way he smiled at you—just who he was and just who you weren't? No, that was thinking not too much like Dawn but *way* too much like his father. Jewish resentment could be just as bad as the Irish resentment. It could be worse. They hadn't moved out here to get caught up in that stuff. He was no Ivy Leaguer himself. He'd been educated, like Dawn, at lowly Upsala in East Orange, and thought "Ivy League" was a name for a kind of clothes before he knew it had anything to do with a university. Little by little the picture came into focus, of course—a world of Gentile wealth where the buildings were covered with ivy and the people had money and dressed in a certain style. Didn't admit Jews, didn't know Jews, probably didn't like Jews all that much. Maybe they didn't like Irish Catholics—he'd take Dawn's word for it. Maybe they looked down on them, too. But Orcutt was Orcutt. He had to be judged according to his own values and not the values of "the Ivy League." As long as he's fair and respectful to me, I'll be fair and respectful to him.

All it came down to, in his mind, was that the guy could get boring on the subject of the past. The Swede wasn't going to take it to mean more until somebody proved otherwise. They weren't out there to get all worked up about neighbors across the hill whose house they couldn't even see—they were out there because, as he liked to joke to his mother, "I want to own the things that money can't buy." Everybody else who was picking up and leaving Newark was headed for one of the cozy suburban streets in Maplewood or South Orange, while they, by comparison, were out on the frontier. During the two years when he was down in South Carolina with the marines, it used to thrill him to think, "This is the Old South. I am below the Mason-Dixon line. I am Down South!" Well, he couldn't commute from Down South but he could skip Maplewood and South Orange, leapfrog the South Mountain Reservation, and just keep going, get as far out west in New Jersey as he could while still being able to make it every day to Central Avenue in an hour. Why not? A hundred acres of America. Land first cleared not for agriculture but to furnish timber for those old iron forges that consumed a thousand acres of timber a year. (The real-estate lady turned out to know almost as much local history as Bill Orcutt and was no less generous in ladling it out to a potential buyer from the streets of Newark.) A barn, a millpond, a mill-stream, the foundation remains of a gristmill that had supplied grain for Washington's troops. Back on the property somewhere, an abandoned iron mine. Just after the Revolution, the original house, a wood structure, and the sawmill had burned down and the house was replaced by this one—according to a date engraved on a stone over the cellar door and carved into a corner beam in the front room, built in 1786, its exterior walls constructed of stones collected from the fireplaces of the Revolutionary army's former campsites in the local hills. A house of stone such as he had always dreamed of, with a gambrel roof no less, and, in what used to be the kitchen and was now the dining room, a fireplace unlike any he'd ever seen, large enough for roasting an ox, fitted out with an oven door and a crane to swing an iron kettle around over the fire; a nineteen-inch-high lintel beam extending seventeen feet across the whole width of the room. Four smaller fireplaces in other rooms, all working, with the original chimneypieces, the wooden carving and moulding barely visible beneath coats and coats of a hundred and sixty-odd years of paint but waiting there to be restored and revealed. A central hallway ten feet wide. A staircase with newel posts and railings carved of pale-striped tiger maple—according to the real-estate lady, tiger maple a rarity in these parts at that time. Two rooms to either side of the staircase both upstairs and downstairs, making in all eight rooms, plus the kitchen, plus the big back porch. . . . Why the hell shouldn't it be his? Why shouldn't he own it? "I don't want to live next door to anybody. I've done that. I grew up doing that. I don't want to see the stoop out the window—I want to see the *land.* I want to see the streams running everywhere. I want to see the cows and the horses. You drive down the road, there's a *falls* there. We don't *have* to live like everybody else—we can live any way we want to now. We did it. Nobody stopped us. They couldn't. We're married. We can go anywhere, we can do anything. Dawnie, we're free!"

Moreover, getting to be free had not been painless, what with the pressure from his father to buy in the Newstead development in suburban South Orange, to buy a modern house with everything in it brand new instead of a decrepit "mausoleum." "You'll never heat it," predicted Lou Levov the Saturday he first laid eyes on the huge, vacant old stone house with the For Sale sign, a house on a hilly country road out in the middle of nowhere, eleven miles west of the nearest train stop, the Lackawanna station in Morristown, where the screen-door-green cars with the yellowish cane seats took people all the way into New York. Because it came with the hundred acres and with a collapsing barn and a fallen-down gristmill, because it had been vacant and up for sale for almost a year, it was going for about half the price of things that sat on just a two-acre lot in Newstead. "Heat this place, cost you a fortune, and you'll still freeze to death. When it snows out here, Seymour, how are you going to get to the train? On these roads, you're not. What the hell does he need all that ground for anyway?" Lou Levov demanded of the Swede's mother, who was standing between the two men in her coat and trying her best to stay out of the discussion by studying the tops of the roadside trees. (Or so the Swede thought; later he learned that, in vain, she had been looking down the road for street lights.) "What are you going to do with all the ground," his father asked him, "feed the starving Armenians? You know what? You're dreaming. I wonder if you even know where this is. Let's be candid with each other about this—this is a narrow, bigoted area. The Klan thrived out here in the twenties. Did you know that? The Ku Klux Klan. People had crosses burned on their property out here." "Dad, the Ku Klux Klan doesn't exist anymore." "Oh, doesn't it? This is rock-ribbed Republican New Jersey, Seymour. It is Republican out here from top to bottom." "Dad, Eisenhower is president— the whole *country* is Republican. Eisenhower's the president and Roosevelt is dead." "Yeah, and this place was Republican when Roosevelt was *living.* Republican during the New Deal. Think about that. Why did they hate Roosevelt out here, Seymour?" "I don't know why. Because he was a Democrat." "No, they didn't like Roosevelt because they didn't like the Jews and the Italians and the Irish—that's why they moved out here to begin with. They didn't like Roosevelt because he accommodated himself to these new Americans. He understood what they needed and he tried to help them. But not these bastards. They wouldn't give a Jew the time of day. I'm talking to you, son, about bigots. Not about the goose step even—just about hate. And this is where the haters live, out here."

The answer was Newstead. In Newstead he would not have the headache of a hundred acres. In Newstead it would be rock-ribbed Democrat. In Newstead he could live with his family among young Jewish couples, the baby could grow up with Jewish friends, and the commute door-to-door to Newark Maid, taking South Orange Avenue straight in, was half an hour tops. . . . "Dad, I drive to Morristown in fifteen minutes." "Not if it snows you don't. Not if you obey the traffic laws you don't." "The 8:28 express gets me to Broad Street 8:56. I walk to Central Avenue and I'm at work six minutes after nine." "And if it snows? You still haven't answered me. If the train breaks down?" "Stockbrokers take this train to work. Lawyers, businessmen who go into Manhattan. Wealthy people. It's not the milk train—it doesn't break down. On the early-morning trains they've got their own parlor car, for God's sake. It's not the sticks." "You could have fooled me," his father replied.

But the Swede, rather like some frontiersman of old, would not be turned back. What was impractical and ill-advised to his father was an act of bravery to him. Next to marrying Dawn Dwyer, buying that house and the hundred acres and moving out to Old Rimrock was the most daring thing he had ever done. What was Mars to his father was *America* to him—he was settling Revolutionary New Jersey as if for the first time. Out in Old Rimrock, all of America lay at their door. That was an idea he loved. Jewish resentment, Irish resentment—the hell with it. A husband and wife each just twenty-five years of age, a baby of less than a year—it had been *courageous* of them to head out to Old Rimrock. He'd already heard tell of more than a few strong, intelligent, talented guys in the leatherware business beaten down by their fathers, and he wasn't going to let it happen to him. He'd fallen in love with the same business as his old man had, he'd taken his birthright, and now he was moving beyond it to damn well live where he wanted.

No, we are not going to have *anybody's* resentment. We are thirty-five miles out *beyond* that resentment. He wasn't saying it was always easy to blend across religious borders. He wasn't saying there wasn't prejudice—he'd faced it as a recruit in the Marine

Corps, in boot camp on a couple of occasions faced it head-on and faced it down. She'd had her own brush with blatant anti-Semitism at the pageant in Atlantic City when her chaperone referred distastefully to 1945, when Bess Myerson became Miss America, as "the year the Jewish girl won." She'd heard plenty of casual cracks about Jews as a kid, but Atlantic City was the real world and it shocked her. She wouldn't repeat it at the time because she was fearful that he would turn against her for remaining politely silent and failing to tell the stupid woman where to get off, especially when her chaperone added, "I grant she was good-looking, but it was a great embarrassment to the pageant nonetheless." Not that it mattered one way or the other anymore. Dawn was a mere contestant, twenty-two years old—what could she have said or done? His point was that they both were aware, from firsthand experience, that these prejudices existed. In a community as civilized as Old Rimrock, however, differences of religion did not have to be as hard to deal with as Dawn was making them. If she could marry a Jew, she could surely be a friendly neighbor to a Protestant—sure as hell could if her husband could. The Protestants are just another denomination. Maybe they were rare where she grew up—they were rare where he grew up too—but they happen not to be rare in America. Let's face it, they *are* America. But if you do not assert the superiority of the Catholic way the way your mother does, and I do not assert the superiority of the Jewish way the way my father does, I'm sure we'll find plenty of people out here who won't assert the superiority of the Protestant way the way their fathers and mothers did. Nobody dominates anybody anymore. That's what the war was about. Our parents are not attuned to the possibilities, to the realities of the postwar world, where people can live in harmony, all sorts of people side by side no matter what their origins. This is a new generation and there is no need for that resentment stuff from anybody, them *or* us. And the upper class is nothing to be frightened of either. You know what you're going to find once you know them? That they are just other people who want to get along. Let's be intelligent about all this.

As it worked out, he never had to make a case as thorough as this to get Dawn to lay off about Orcutt, since Orcutt was never much in their lives after the sightseeing trip that Dawn kept referring to as "The Orcutt Family Cemetery Tour." Nothing like a social life developed back then between the Orcutts and the Levovs, not even a casual friendship, though the Swede did show up Saturday mornings at the pasture back of Orcutt's house for the weekly touch-football game with Orcutt's local friends and some other fellows like the Swede, ex-GIs from around Essex County trickling out with new families to the wide-open spaces.

Among them was an optician named Bucky Robinson, a short, muscular, pigeon-toed guy with a round angelic face, who'd been second-string quarterback for Hillside High, Weequahic's traditional Thanksgiving Day rival, when Swede was finishing high school. The first week Bucky showed up, the Swede overheard him telling Orcutt about Swede Levov's senior year, enumerating on his fingers, "all-city end in football; all-city, all-county center in basketball; all-city, all-county, all-state first baseman in baseball. . . ." Though ordinarily the Swede would have found this awe of him, so nakedly demonstrated, not at all to his liking in an environment where he only wished to inspire neighborly goodwill, where being just another of the guys who showed up to play ball was fine with him, he seemed not to mind that Orcutt was the one standing there enduring the excess of Bucky's enthusiasm. He had no quarrel with Orcutt and no reason to have any, yet seeing everything he would ordinarily prefer to hide behind a modest demeanor being revealed so passionately to Orcutt by Bucky was more pleasurable than he might have imagined, almost like the satisfaction of a desire he personally knew nothing about—a desire for revenge.

When, for several weeks running, Bucky and the Swede wound up together on the same team, the newcomer couldn't believe his good fortune: while to everybody else the new neighbor was Seymour, Bucky at every opportunity called him Swede. It did not matter who else might be in the clear, wildly waving his arms in the air—the Swede was the receiver Bucky saw. "Big Swede, way to go!" he'd shout whenever the Swede came back to the huddle having gathered in yet another Robinson pass—Big Swede, which nobody but Jerry had called him since high school. And with Jerry it was always sardonic.

One day Bucky hitched a ride with the Swede to a local garage where his car was being repaired and, as they were driving along, announced surprisingly that he was Jewish too and that he and his wife had recently become members of a Morristown temple. Out here, he said, they were more and more involving themselves with the Morristown Jewish community. "It can be very sustaining in a Gentile town," Bucky told the Swede, "to know you have Jewish friends nearby." Though not enormous, Morristown's was an established Jewish community, went back to before the Civil War, and included quite a few of the town's influential people, among them a trustee at Morristown Memorial Hospital—through whose insistence the first Jewish doctors had, two years back, finally been invited to join the hospital staff—and the owner of the town's best department store. Successful Jewish families had been living in the big stucco houses on Western Avenue for fifty years now, though on the whole this wasn't an area known to be terribly friendly toward Jews. As a child Bucky had been taken by his family up to Mt. Freedom, the resort town in the nearby hills, where they would stay for a week each summer at Lieberman's Hotel and where Bucky first fell in love with the beauty and serenity of the Morris countryside. Up at Mt. Freedom, needless to say, it was great for Jews: ten, eleven large hotels that were all Jewish, a summer turnover in the tens of thousands that was entirely Jewish—the vacationers themselves jokingly referred to the place as "Mt. Friedman." If you lived in an apartment in Newark or Passaic or Jersey City, a week in Mt. Freedom was heaven. And as for Morristown, although solidly Gentile, it was nonetheless a cosmopolitan community of lawyers, doctors, and stockbrokers where Bucky and his wife loved going to the movies at the Community, loved the shops, which were excellent, loved the beautiful old buildings and where there were the

Jewish shopkeepers with their neon signs up and down Speedwell Avenue. But did the Swede know that before the war there'd been a swastika scrawled on the golf-course sign at the edge of Mt. Freedom? Did he know that the Klan held meetings in Boonton and Dover, rural people, working-class people, members of the Klan? Did he know that crosses were burned on people's lawns not five miles from the Morristown green?

From that day on, Bucky kept trying to land the Swede, who would have been a considerable catch, and to haul him in for the Morristown Jewish community, to get him, if not to join the temple outright, at least to play evening basketball in the Interchurch League for the team the temple fielded. Robinson's mission irritated the Swede in just the way his mother had when, some months after Dawn became pregnant, she'd astonished him by asking if Dawn was going to convert before the baby was born. "A man to whom practicing Judaism means nothing, Mother, doesn't ask his wife to convert." He had never been so stern with her in his life, and, to his dismay, she had walked away near tears, and it had taken numerous hugs throughout the day to get her to understand that he wasn't "angry" with her—he had only been making clear that he was a grown man with the prerogatives of a grown man. Now with Dawn he talked about Robinson—talked a lot about him as they lay in bed at night. "I didn't come out here for that stuff. I never got that stuff anyway. I used to go on the High Holidays with my father, and I just never understood what they were getting at. Even seeing my father there never made sense. It wasn't him, it wasn't like him—he was bending to something that he didn't have to, something he didn't even understand. He was just bending to this because of my grandfather. I never understood what any of that stuff had to do with his being a man. What the glove factory had to do with his being a man anybody could understand—just about everything. My father knew what he was talking about when he was talking about gloves. But when he started about that stuff? You should have heard him. If he'd known as little about leather as he knew about God, the family would have wound up in the poorhouse." "Oh, but Bucky Robinson isn't talking about God, Sey-mour. He wants to be your friend," she said, "that's all." "I guess. But I never was interested in that stuff, Dawnie, back for as long as I can remember. I never understood it. Does anybody? I don't know what they're talking about. I go into those synagogues and it's all foreign to me. It always has been. When I had to go to Hebrew school as a kid, all the time I was in that room I couldn't wait to get out on the ball field. I used to think, 'If I sit in this room any longer, I'm going to get sick.' There was something unhealthy about those places. Anywhere near any of those places and I knew it wasn't where I wanted to be. The factory was a place I wanted to be from the time I was a boy. The ball field was a place I wanted to be from the time I started kindergarten. That this is a place where I want to be I knew the moment I laid eyes on it. Why shouldn't I be where I want to be? Why shouldn't I be with *who* I want to be? Isn't that what this country's all about? I want to be where I want to be and I don't want to be where I don't want to be. That's what being an American is—isn't it? I'm with you, I'm with the baby, I'm at the factory during the day, the rest of the time I'm out here, and that's everywhere in this world I *ever* want to be. We own a piece of America, Dawn. I couldn't be happier if I tried. I did it, darling, I did it—I did what I set out to do!"

For a while, the Swede stopped showing up at the touch-football games just to avoid having to deflect Bucky Robinson on the sub-ject of his temple. With Robinson he did not feel like his father—he felt like Orcutt. . . .

No, no. You know whom he really felt like? Not during the hour or two a week he happened to be on the receiving end of a Bucky Robinson pass, but whom he felt like all the rest of the time? He couldn't tell anybody, of course: he was twenty-six and a new father and people would have laughed at the childishness of it. He laughed at it himself. It was one of those kid things you keep in your mind no matter how old you get, but whom he felt like out in Old Rimrock was Johnny Appleseed. Who cares about Bill Orcutt? Woodrow Wilson knew Orcutt's grandfather? Thomas Jefferson knew his grandfather's uncle? Good for Bill Orcutt. Johnny Apple-seed, that's the man for me. Wasn't a Jew, wasn't an Irish Catholic, wasn't a Protestant Christian—nope, Johnny Appleseed was just a happy American. Big. Ruddy. Happy. No brains probably, but didn't need 'em—a great walker was all Johnny Appleseed needed to be. All physical joy. Had a big stride and a bag of seeds and a huge, spontaneous affection for the landscape, and everywhere he went he scattered the seeds. What a story that was. Going everywhere, walking everywhere. The Swede had loved that story all his life. Who wrote it? Nobody, as far as he could remember. They'd just studied it in grade school. Johnny Appleseed, out there everywhere planting apple trees. That bag of seeds. I loved that bag. Though maybe it was his hat—did he keep the seeds in his hat? Didn't matter. "Who told him to do it?" Merry asked him when she got old enough for bedtime stories—though still baby enough, should he try to tell any other story, like the one about the train that used to carry only peaches, to cry, "Johnny! I want Johnny!" "Who told him? Nobody told him, sweetheart. You don't have to tell Johnny Appleseed to plant trees. He just takes it on himself." "Who is his wife?" "Dawn. Dawn Appleseed. That's who his wife is." "Does he have a child?" "Sure he has a child. And you know what her name is?" "What?" "Merry Appleseed!" "Does she plant apple seeds in a hat?" "Sure she does. She doesn't plant them in the hat, honey, she stores them in the hat—and then she throws them. Far as she can, she casts them out. And everywhere she throws the seed, wherever it lands on the ground, do you know what happens?" "What?" "An apple tree grows up, right there." And every time he walked into Old Rimrock village he could not restrain himself—first thing on the weekend he pulled on his boots and walked the five hilly miles into the village and the five hilly miles back, early in the morning walked all that way just to get the Saturday paper, and he could not help himself—he thought, "Johnny Appleseed!" The pleasure of it. The pure, buoyant unrestrained pleasure of striding. He didn't care if he played ball ever again—he just wanted to step out and stride. It seemed somehow that the ballplaying had cleared the way to *allow* him to do this, to stride in an hour down to the village, pick up the Lackawanna edition of the *Newark News* at the general store with the single Sunoco pump out front and the produce out on the steps in boxes and burlap bags. It was the only store down there in the fifties and hadn't changed since the Hamlin son, Russ, took it over from his father after World War I—they sold washboards and tubs, there was a sign up outside for Frostie, a soft drink, another nailed to the clapboards for Fleischmann's Yeast, another for Pittsburgh Paint Products, even one out front that said "Syracuse Plows," hanging there from when the store sold farm equipment too. Russ Hamlin could remember from earliest boyhood a wheelwright shop perched across the way, could still recall watching wagon wheels rolled down a ramp to be cooled in the stream; remembered, too, when there was a distillery out back, one of many in the region that had made the famous local applejack and had shut down only with the passage of the Volstead Act. Clear at the back of the store there was one window that was the U.S. post office—one window was it, and thirty or so of those boxes with the combination locks. Hamlin's general store, with the post office inside, and outside the bulletin board and the flagpole and the gas pump—that's what had served the old farming community as its meeting place since the days of Warren Gamaliel Harding, when Russ became proprietor. Diagonally across the street, alongside where there'd been the wheelwright shop, was the six-room schoolhouse that would be the Levovs' daughter's first school. Kids sat on the steps of the store. Your girl would meet you there. A meeting place, a greeting place. The Swede loved it. The familiar old *Newark News* he picked up had a special section out here, the second section, called "Along the Lackawanna." Even that pleased him, and not just reading through it at home for the local Morris news but merely carrying it home in his hand. The word "Lackawanna" was pleasing to him in and of itself. From the front counter he'd pick up the paper with "Levov" scrawled at the top in Mary Hamlin's hand, charge a quart of milk if they needed it, a loaf of bread, a dozen fresh-laid eggs from Paul Hamlin's farm up the road, say "See ya,

Russell" to the owner, and then he'd turn and stride all the way back, past the white pasture fences he loved, the rolling hay fields he loved, the corn fields, the turnip fields, the barns, the horses, the cows, the ponds, the streams, the springs, the falls, the watercress, the scouring rushes, the meadows, the acres and acres of woods he loved with all of a new country dweller's puppy love for nature, until he reached the century-old maple trees he loved and the substantial old stone house he loved—pretending, as he went along, to throw the apple seed everywhere.

Once, from an upstairs window, Dawn saw him approaching the house from the foot of their hill while he was doing just that, flinging out one arm, flinging it out not as though he were throwing a ball or swinging a bat but as though he were pulling handfuls of seed from the grocery bag and throwing them with all his strength across the face of the historic land that was now no less his than it was William Orcutt's. "What are you practicing out there?" she said, laughing at him when he burst into the bedroom looking, from all that exercise, handsome as hell, big, carnal, ruddy as Johnny Appleseed himself, someone to whom something marvelous was happening. When people raise their glasses and toast a youngster, when they say to him, "May you have health and good fortune!" the picture that they have in mind—or that they should have in mind—is of the earthy human specimen, the very image of unrestricted virility, who burst so happily into that bedroom and found there, all alone, a little magnificent beast, his young wife, stripped of all maidenly constraints and purely, blissfully his. "Seymour, what *are* you doing down at Hamlin's—taking ballet lessons?" Easily, so easily, with those large protecting hands of his he raised the hundred and three pounds of her up from the floor where she stood barefoot in her nightgown, and using all his considerable strength, he held her to him as though he were holding together, binding together, into one unshatterable entity, the wonderful new irreproachable existence of husband and father Seymour Levov, Arcady Hill Road, Old Rimrock, New Jersey, USA. What he had been doing out on the road—which, as though it were a shameful or superficial endeavor, he could not bring himself openly to confess even to Dawn—was making love to his life.

About the intensity of his physical intimacy with his young wife he was actually more discreet. Together they were rather prudish around people, and no one would have guessed at the secret that was their sexual life. Before Dawn he had never slept with anybody he'd dated—he'd slept with two whores while he was in the Marine Corps, but that didn't count really, and so only after they were married did they discover how passionate he could be. He had tremendous stamina and tremendous strength, and her smallness next to his largeness, the way he could lift her up, the bigness of his body in bed with her seemed to excite them both. She said that when he would fall asleep after making love she felt as though she were sleeping with a mountain. It thrilled her sometimes to think she was sleeping beside an enormous rock. When she was lying under him, he would plunge in and out of her very hard but at the same time holding himself at a distance so she would not be crushed, and because of his stamina and strength he could keep this up for a long time without getting tired. With one arm he could pick her up and turn her around on her knees or he could sit her on his lap and move easily under the weight of her hundred and three pounds. For months and months following their marriage, she would begin to cry after she had reached her orgasm. She would come and she would cry and he didn't know what to make of it. "What's the matter?" he asked her. "I don't know." "Do I hurt you?" "No. I don't know where it comes from. It's almost as if the sperm, when you shoot it into my body, sets off the tears." "But I don't hurt you." "No." "Does it please you, Dawnie? Do you like it?" "I love it. There's something about it . . . it just gets to a place that nothing else gets to. And that's the place where the tears are. You reach a part of me that nothing else ever reaches." "Okay. As long as I don't hurt you." "No, no. It's just strange . . . it's just strange . . . it's just strange not being alone," she said. She stopped crying only when he went down on her for the first time. "You don't cry this way," he said. "It was so different," she said. "How? Why?" "I guess

. . . I don't know. I guess I'm alone again." "Do you want me not to do it again?" "Oh, no," she laughed, "absolutely not." "Okay." "Seymour . . . how did you know how to do that? Did you ever do that before?" "Never." "Why did you then? Tell me." But he couldn't explain things as well as she could and so he didn't try. He was just overtaken by the desire to do something more, and so he lifted her buttocks in one hand and raised her body into his mouth. To stick his face there and just go. Go to where he had never been before. Ecstatically complicitous, he and Dawn. He had no reason to believe she would ever do it for him, of course, and then one Sunday morning she just did it. He didn't know what to think. His little Dawn put her beautiful little mouth around his cock. He was stunned. They both were. It was taboo for both of them. From then on, it just went on for years and years. It never stopped. "There's something so touching about you," she whispered to him, "when you get to the point where you're out of control." So touching to her, she told him, this very restrained, good, polite, well-brought-up man, a man always so in charge of his strength, who had *mastered* his tremendous strength and had no violence in him, when he got past the point of no return, beyond the point of anyone's being embarrassed about anything, when he was beyond the point of being able to judge her or to think that somehow she was a bad girl for wanting it as much as she wanted it from him then, when *he* just wanted it, those last three or four minutes that would culminate in the screaming orgasm. . . . "It makes me feel so extremely feminine," she told him, "it makes me feel extremely powerful . . . it makes me feel *both*." When she got out of bed after they made love and she looked wildly disheveled, flushed and with her hair all over the place and her eye makeup smudged and her lips swollen, and she went off into the bathroom to pee, he would follow her there and lift her off the seat after she had wiped herself and look at the two of them together in the bathroom mirror, and she would be taken aback as much as he was, not simply by how beautiful she looked, how beautiful the fucking *allowed* her to look, but how *other* she looked. The social face was gone—there was

Dawn! But all this was a secret from others and had to be. Particularly from the child. Sometimes after Dawn had been all day on her feet with the cows, he would pull his chair up to hers after dinner and he would rub her feet, and Merry would make a face and say, "Oh, Daddy, that's disgusting." But that was the only truly demonstrative thing they ever did in front of her. Otherwise there was just the usual affectionate stuff around the house that kids expect to see from parents and would miss if it didn't go on. The life they led together behind their bedroom door was a secret about which their daughter knew no more than anyone else. And on it went, on and on for years; it never stopped until the bomb went off and Dawn wound up in the hospital. After she came out was when it began stopping.

Orcutt had married the granddaughter of one of his grandfather's law partners at Orcutt, Findley, the Morristown firm that he had been expected to join. After graduating from Princeton, he had declined, however, to accept a place at Harvard Law School—Princeton and Harvard Law had for over a hundred years constituted the education of an Orcutt boy—and breaking with the traditions of the world he'd been born to, he moved to a lower Manhattan studio to become an abstract painter and a new man. Only after three depressive years feverishly painting behind the dirty windows over the truck traffic on Hudson Street did he marry Jessie and come back to Jersey to begin architecture studies at Princeton. He never relinquished entirely his dream of an artistic calling, and though his architectural work—mostly on the restoration of the eighteenth- and nineteenth-century houses out in their moneyed quarter of Morris County and, from Somerset and Hunterdon counties all the way down through Bucks County in Pennsylvania, the converting of old barns into elegant rustic homes—kept him happily occupied, every three or four years there was an exhibition of his at a Morristown frame shop that the Levovs, always flattered to be invited to the opening, faithfully attended.

The Swede was never so uncomfortable in any social situation as he was standing in front of Orcutt's paintings, which were said by the flier you got at the door to be influenced by Chinese calligraphy but looked like nothing much to him, not even Chinese. Right from the beginning Dawn had found them "thought-provoking"—to her they showed a most unlikely side to Bill Orcutt, a sensitivity she'd never seen a single indicator of before—but the thought the exhibition most provoked in the Swede was how long he should continue pretending to look at one of the canvases before moving on to pretend to be looking at another one. All he really had any inclination to do was to lean forward and read the titles pasted up on the wall beside each painting, thinking they might help, but when he did—despite Dawn's telling him not to, pulling his jacket and whispering, "Forget those, look at the *brushwork*"—he was only more disheartened than when he did look at the brushwork. *Composition #16, Picture #6, Meditation #11, Untitled #12* . . . and what was there on the canvas but a band of long gray smears so pale across a white background that it looked as though Orcutt had tried not to paint the painting but to rub it out? Consulting the description of the exhibition in the flier, written and signed by the young couple who owned the frame shop, didn't do any good either. "Orcutt's calligraphy is so intense the shapes dissolve. Then, in the glow of its own energy, the brush stroke dissolves itself. . . ." Why on earth would a guy like Orcutt, no stranger to the natural world and the great historical drama of this country—and a helluva tennis player—why on earth did he want to paint pictures of nothing? Since the Swede had to figure the guy wasn't a phony—why would someone as well educated and as self-confident as Orcutt devote all this effort to being a phony?—he could for a while put the confusion down to his own ignorance about art. Intermittently the Swede might continue to think, "There's something wrong with this guy. There is some big dissatisfaction there. This Orcutt does not have what he wants," but then the Swede would read something like that flier and realize that he didn't know what he was talking about. "Two decades after the Greenwich Village years, Orcutt's ambition remains lofty: to create," the flier concluded, "a personal expression of universal themes that include the enduring moral dilemmas which define the human condition."

It never occurred to the Swede, reading the flier, that enough could not be claimed for the paintings just because they *were* so hollow, that you had to say they were pictures of everything *because* they were pictures of nothing—that all those words were merely another way of saying Orcutt was talentless and, however earnestly he might try, could never hammer out for himself an artistic prerogative or, for that matter, any but the prerogative whose rigid definitions had swaddled him at birth. It did not occur to the Swede that he was right, that this guy who seemed so at one with himself, so perfectly attuned to the place where he lived and the people around him, might be inadvertently divulging that to be *out* of tune was, in fact, a secret and long-standing desire he hadn't the remotest idea of how to achieve except by oddly striving to paint paintings that looked like they didn't look like anything. Apparently the best he could do with his craving to be otherwise was this stuff. Sad. Anyway, it didn't matter how sad it was or what the Swede did or did not ask or understand or know about the painter once one of those calligraphic paintings expressing the universal themes that define the human condition made its way onto the Levov living room wall a month after Dawn returned from Geneva with her new face. And that's when things got a little sad for the Swede.

It was a band of brown streaks and not gray ones that Orcutt had been trying to rub out of *Meditation #27*, and the background was purplish rather than white. The dark colors, according to Dawn, signaled a revolution of the painter's formal means. That's what she told him, and the Swede, not knowing quite how to respond and with no interest in what "formal means" meant, settled lamely on "Interesting." They didn't have any art hanging on the walls when he was a kid, let alone "modern" art—art hadn't existed in his house any more than it did in Dawn's. The Dwyers had religious pictures, which might even be what accounted for Dawn's having all of a sudden become a connoisseur of "formal means": a secret embarrassment about growing up where, aside from the framed photos of Dawn and her kid brother, the only pictures were pictures of the Virgin Mary and of Jesus' heart. These tasteful people have modern art on the wall, *we're* going to have modern art on the wall. Formal means on the wall. However much Dawn might deny it, wasn't there something of that going on here? Irish *envy?*

She'd bought the painting right out of Orcutt's studio for exactly half as much as it had cost them to buy Count when he was a baby bull. The Swede told himself, "Forget the dough, write it off—you can't compare a bull to a painting," and in this way managed to control his disappointment when he saw *Meditation #27* go up on the very spot where once there had been the portrait of Merry that he'd loved, a painstakingly perfect if somewhat overly pinkish likeness of the glowing child in blond bangs she had been at six. It had been painted in oils for them by a jovial old gent down in New Hope who wore a smock and a beret in his studio there—he'd taken the time to serve them mulled wine and tell them about his apprenticeship copying paintings in the Louvre—and who'd come to the house six times for Merry to sit for him at the piano, and wanted only two thousand smackers for the painting *and* the gilt frame. But as the Swede was told, since Orcutt hadn't asked for the additional thirty percent it would have cost had they purchased *#27* from the frame shop, the five grand was a bargain.

His father's comment, when he saw the new painting, was "How much the guy charge you for that?" With reluctance Dawn replied, "Five thousand dollars." "Awful lot of money for a first coat. What's it going to be?" "*Going* to be?" Dawn had replied sourly. "Well, it ain't finished . . . I hope it ain't. . . . Is it?" "That it isn't 'finished,'" said Dawn, "is the idea, Lou." "Yeah?" He looked again. "Well, if the guy ever wants to finish it, I can tell him how." "Dad," said the Swede, to forestall further criticism, "Dawn bought it because she likes it," and though he also could have told the guy how to finish it (probably in words close to those his father had in mind), he was more than willing to hang anything Dawn bought from Orcutt *just because she had bought it.* Irish envy or no Irish envy, the painting was another sign that the desire to live had become stronger in her than the wish to die that had put her into the psychiatric clinic twice. "So the picture is shit," he told his father later. "The thing is, *she wanted it.* The thing is she *wants* again. Please," he warned him, feeling himself—strangely, given the slightness of the provocation—at the edge of anger, "no more about that picture." And Lou Levov being Lou Levov, the next time he visited Old Rimrock the first thing he did was to walk up to the picture and say loudly, "You know something? I like that thing. I'm gettin' used to it and I actually like it. Look," he said to his wife, "look at how the guy didn't finish it. See that? Where it's blurry? He did that on purpose. That's art."

In the back of Orcutt's van was his large cardboard model of the new Levov house, ready to unveil to the guests after dinner. Sketches and blueprints had been piling up in Dawn's study for weeks now, among them a diagram prepared by Orcutt charting how sunlight would angle into the windows on the first day of each month of the year. "A flood of sunlight," said Dawn. "Light!" she exclaimed. "Light!" And if not with the brutal directness that could truly test to the limit his understanding of her suffering and of the panacea she'd devised, by implication she was damning yet again the stone house he loved and, too, the old maple trees he loved, the giant trees that shaded the house against the summer heat and every autumn ceremoniously cloaked the lawn in a golden wreath at whose heart he'd hung Merry's swing once upon a time.

The Swede couldn't get over those trees in the first years out in Old Rimrock. *I own those trees.* It was more astonishing to him that he owned trees than that he owned factories, more astonishing that he owned trees than that a child of the Chancellor Avenue playing field and the unbucolic Weequahic streets should own this stately old stone house in the hills where Washington had twice made his winter camp during the Revolutionary War. It was *puzzling* to own trees—they were not owned the way a business is owned or even a house is owned. If anything, they were held in trust. In trust. Yes, for all of posterity, beginning with Merry and *her* kids.

To protect against ice storms and high winds, he had cables installed in each of the big maples, four cables forming a rough parallelogram against the sky where the heavy branches opened dramatically out some fifty feet up. The lightning rods that snaked from the trunk to the topmost point of each tree he arranged to have inspected annually, just to be on the safe side. Twice a year, the trees were sprayed against insects, every third year they were fertilized, and regularly an arborist came around to prune out the deadwood and check the overall health of the private park beyond their door. Merry's trees. Merry's family's trees.

In the fall—just as he had always planned it—he'd be sure to get home from work before the sun went down, and there she would be—just as he had planned it—swinging high up over the fallen leaves encircling the maple by the front door, their largest tree, from which he'd first suspended that swing for her when she was only two. Up she would swing, nearly into the leaves of the branches that spread just beyond the panes of their bedroom windows . . . and, though to him those precious moments at the end of each day had symbolized the realization of his every hope, to her they had meant not a goddamn thing. She turned out to love the trees no more than Dawn had loved the house. What *she* worried about was Algeria. *She* loved Algeria. The kid in that swing, the kid in that tree. The kid in that tree who was now on the floor of that room.

The Orcutts had come early so that Bill and Dawn would have time together to go over the problem of the link that was to join the one-story house to the two-story garage. Orcutt had been away in New York for a couple of days, and Dawn was impatient to get this, their last problem, resolved after weeks of thinking and rethinking how to create a harmonious relationship between the very different buildings. Even if the garage was more or less disguised as a barn, Dawn didn't want it too close, overwhelming the distinctiveness of the house, but she was afraid that a link twenty-four feet long, which was Orcutt's proposal, might impart the look of a motel.

They ruminated together almost daily, not only over the dimensions but now over whether the effect should perhaps be that of a greenhouse rather than of the simple passageway first planned. Whenever Dawn felt that Orcutt was trying to impose on her, however graciously, a solution that had more to do with some old-fashioned architectural aesthetic of his own than with the rigorous modernity she had in mind for their new home, she could be quite peeved, and she even wondered, on those few occasions when she was outright furious with him, if it hadn't been a mistake to turn to someone who, though he had considerable authority with the local contractors—guaranteeing a first-class construction job— and an excellent professional reputation, was "essentially a restorer of antiques." Years had passed since she'd been intimidated by the snobbery that, fresh from Elizabeth and the family home (and the pictures on the wall and the statue in the hallway), she'd taken to be more or less Orcutt's whole story. Now his credentials as county gentry were what she was most cutting about when the two of them were at odds. The angry disdain disappeared, however, when Orcutt came back to her, usually within twenty-four hours, having alighted on—in Dawn's words—"a perfectly elegant plan," whether it was for the location of the washer-dryer or a bathroom skylight or the stairway to the guest room above the garage.

Orcutt had brought with him, along with the large one-six-teenth-inch scale model out in the van, samples of a new transparent plastic material he wanted her to consider for the walls and the roof of the link. He'd gone into the kitchen to show it to her. And there the two of them remained, the resourceful architect and the exacting client, debating all over again—while Dawn cleaned the lettuce, sliced the tomatoes, shucked the two dozen ears of corn the Orcutts had brought over in a bag from their garden—the pros and cons of a transparent link rather than the board-and-batten enclosure Orcutt had first proposed to unify it with the exterior of the garage. And meanwhile on the back terrace that looked out toward the hill where, in another time, on an evening like this one, Dawn's herd would be silhouetted against the flamboyance of the late-summer sunset, the Swede prepared the barbecue coals. Keeping him company were his father and Jessie Orcutt, who rarely these days was seen out socializing with Bill but who, according to Dawn, was going through what had wearily been described—by Orcutt, phoning to ask if they wouldn't mind his wife's coming along with him for dinner—as "the calm that heralds the manic upswing."

The Orcutts had three boys and two girls, all grown now, living and working at jobs in New York, five kids to whom Jessie, from all reports, had been a conscientious mother. It was after they'd gone that the heavy drinking began, at first only to lift her spirits, then to suppress her misery, and in the end for its own sake. Yet back when the two couples had first met, it was Jessie's *soundness* that had impressed the Swede: so fresh, so outdoorsy, so cheerily at one with life, not the least bit false or insipid . . . or that's how she'd struck the Swede, if not his wife.

Jessie was a Philadelphia heiress, a finishing-school girl, who always during the day, and sometimes in the evening, wore her mud-spattered jodhpurs and who generally had her hair arranged in flossy flaxen braids. What with those braids and her pure, round, unblemished face—behind which, said Dawn, if you bit into it, you'd find not a brain but a McIntosh apple—she could have passed for a Minnesota farm girl well into her forties, except on those days when her hair was worn up and she could look as much like a young boy as like a young girl. The Swede would never have imagined that there was anything missing from Jessie's endowment to prevent her from sailing right on through into old age as the laudable mother and lively wife who could make a party for everyone's children out of raking the leaves and whose Fourth of July picnics, held on the lawn of the old Orcutt estate, were a treasured tradition among her friends and neighbors. Her character struck the Swede back then as a compound in which you'd find just about everything *toxic* to desperation and dread. At the core of her he could imagine a nucleus of confidence plaited just as neatly and tightly as her braided hair.

Yet hers was another life broken cleanly in two. Now the hair was a ganglion of iron-gray hemp always in need of brushing, and Jessie was a haggard old woman at fifty-four, an undernourished drunk hiding the bulge of a drunk's belly beneath her shapeless sack dresses. All she could ever find to talk about—on the occasions when she managed to leave the house and go out among people—was the "fun" she'd had back before she'd ever had a drink, a husband, a child, or a single thought in her head, before she'd been enlivened (as she certainly had looked to him to be) by the stupendous satisfactions of being a dependable person.

That people were manifold creatures didn't come as a surprise to the Swede, even if it was a bit of a shock to realize it anew when someone let you down. What was astonishing to him was how people seemed to run out of their own being, run out of whatever the stuff was that made them who they were and, drained of themselves, turn into the sort of people they would once have felt sorry for. It was as though while their lives were rich and full they were secretly sick of themselves and couldn't wait to dispose of their sanity and their health and all sense of proportion so as to get down to that other self, the *true* self, who was a wholly deluded fuckup. It was as though being in tune with life was an accident that might sometimes befall the fortunate young but was otherwise something for which human beings lacked any real affinity. How odd. And how odd it made him seem to himself to think that he who had always felt blessed to be numbered among the countless unembattled normal ones might, in fact, be the abnormality, a stranger from real life *because* of his being so sturdily rooted.

"We had a place outside Paoli," Jessie was telling his father. "We always raised animals. When I was seven I got the most wonderful thing. Somebody gave me a pony and a cart. And after that there was nothing to stop me. I just loved horses. I've ridden all my life. Showed and hunted. Was involved in a drag down there in school in Virginia. When I went to school in Virginia I was the whip."

"Wait a minute," said Mr. Levov. "Whoa. I don't know what a drag and a whip is. Slow down, Mrs. Orcutt. You got a guy from Newark here."

She pursed her lips—when he called her "Mrs. Orcutt"—seemingly for his having addressed her as though he were her social inferior, which, the Swede knew, was in part why his father *had* called her "Mrs. Orcutt." But she was "Mrs. Orcutt" to Lou Levov also because of the distancing disdain he had for the drink in her glass, her third Scotch and water in under an hour, and the cigarette—her fourth—burning down between the fingers of her trembling hand. He was amazed by her lack of control—by *anyone's* lack of control but particularly by the lack of control of the goy who drank. Drink was the devil that lurked in the goy—"Big-shot goyim," his father said, "the presidents of companies, and they're like Indians with firewater."

"'Jessie,'" she said, "'Jessie,' please," her grin painfully artificial, disguising, by the Swede's estimate, about ten percent of the agony she now felt at having decided against staying alone at home with her dogs and her TV tray and her own J&B and, in a ridiculous eruption of hope, opting instead for going out like a wife with her husband. At home there was a phone next to the J&B; she could reach over her glass and pick it up and dial, and even if only half dressed, she could tell the people she knew, without having to face the terror of facing them, how much she liked them. Months might go by without one of Jessie's phone calls, and then she'd phone three times after they were already in bed for the night. "Seymour, I'm calling to tell you how much I like you." "Well, Jessie, thank you. I like you too." "Do you?" "Of course I do. You know that." "Yes, I like you, Seymour. I always liked you. Did you know I liked you?" "Yes, I did." "I always admired you. So does Bill. We've always admired you and liked you. We like Dawn." "Well, we like you, Jessie." The night after the bombing, around midnight, after Merry's photograph had been on television and everybody in America knew that the day before she had said to somebody at school that Old Rimrock was in for a big surprise, Jessie tried to walk the three miles to their house to see the Levovs but on the unpaved country road, alone in the dark, had twisted her ankle and, two hours later, still lying there, was nearly run over by a pickup truck.

"Okay, my friend Jessie, fill me in. What is a drag and a whip?" You couldn't say his father didn't try to get along with people for all that he really couldn't. If she was a guest of his children, then she was his friend, regardless of how repelled he might be by the cigarettes, by the whiskey, by the unkempt hair and the rundown shoes and the burlap tent concealing the ill-used body—by all the privilege she had squandered and the disgrace she had made of her life.

"A drag is a hunt and it's not with a fox. It's over a line that's laid by a man on a horse ahead of you . . . that has a scent in a bag. It's to make the *effect* of a hunt. The hounds go after it. There are huge, huge fences, and it's done in a sort of a course. It's a lot of fun. You go very fast. Huge, huge, thick brush fences. Eight, ten feet wide with bars on top. Quite exciting. Down there there's a lot of stee-plechasing and a lot of good riders and everybody gets out there and bombs through those places and it's fun."

It appeared to the Swede to be as much her confoundment with her predicament—a tipsy woman, out at a party, blabbing uncontrollably—as his father's genial I'm-just-a-dope inquiry that drew her disastrously on, each slurred word unsuccessfully stimulating her mouth to try to produce one that rang clear as a bell. Clear as the "Daddy!" that had pealed out perfectly from behind the veil of his daughter the Jain.

He knew what his father was thinking without bothering to look up from where he was using the tongs to make a pyramid of the reddest coals. Fun, his father was thinking, what *is* it with them and fun? What is this fun? What is so much *fun?* His father was wondering, as he had ever since his son had bought the house and the hundred acres forty miles west of Keer Avenue, Why does he want to live with these people? Forget the drinking. Sober's just as bad. They would bore me to death in two minutes.

Dawn had one brief against them, his father had another.

"Anyway," Jessie was saying, trying, with the cigarette-holding hand, to stir into being some sort of conclusion, "that was why I went to school with my horse."

"You went to school with a horse?"

Again she impatiently pursed her lips, probably because this father, who thought he was helping her out with his questions, was driving her even more rapidly than usual to whatever collapse was in store. "Yes. We both got on the train at the same time," she told him. "Wasn't I *lucky?*" she asked, and to the surprise of both Levov men, as though she weren't at all in serious straits—as though that was just a laughable illusion that disgustingly self-satisfied sober people persisted in having about drunks—laid a flirtatious hand on the side of Lou Levov's head.

"I'm sorry, I don't understand how you got on the train with a horse. How big was this horse?"

"In those days horses were on horsecars."

"Ah-hah," said Mr. Levov, as though his lifelong bewilderment at the pleasures of Gentiles had at last been put to rest. He took her hand from where it lay on his hair and, as though to squeeze into her everything he knew about life's purpose that she would seem to have forgotten, held it firmly between his own hands. Meanwhile, under the impetus of that force which, by failing to size up the situation, would lead her into humiliation before the night was through, Jessie went waveringly on.

"They were all leaving with the polo circuit and they were all going down south in the winter train. The train stopped in Philadelphia. So I put my horse in with them. I put my horse in the car two cars up from where I was bunked in, waved good-bye to the family, and it was great."

"How old were you?"

"I was thirteen. I didn't feel homesick at all, and it was just great, great, great"—here she began to cry—"fun."

Thirteen, his father was thinking, a *pisherke*, and you waved good-bye to the family? What was the matter? Was something the matter with them? What the hell were you waving good-bye to your family for at thirteen? No wonder you're *shicker* now.

But what he said was "That's all right, let it all out. Why not? You're among friends." Unsavory as the job must have seemed to him, it had to be done, and so he removed the glass from her one hand, discarded for her the freshly lit cigarette in the other, and took her into his arms, which was perhaps all she had been asking for all along.

"I see where I have to be a father again," he said to her softly, and she could say nothing, she could only weep and let herself be rocked by the Swede's father, whom, on the one other occasion she had met him in her life—when, some fifteen years back, they had gone to picnic on the Orcutts' lawn for Fourth of July—she had tried to interest in skeet shooting, yet another of those diversions that had long defied Lou Levov's Jewish comprehension. For "fun" pulling a trigger and shooting with a gun. They're meshugeh.

That was the day when, on the way back home, they'd passed a handmade sign on the road by the Congregational church that said "Tent Sale" and Merry had begged the Swede, in her fervent way, to stop and buy one for her.

If Jessie could cry on his father's shoulder over waving good-bye to her family at the age of thirteen, about being shipped off alone at thirteen with nothing but a horse, why shouldn't that memory of his—"Daddy, *stop*, they're selling t-t-t-*tents!*"—bring the Swede to the edge of tears about his daughter the Jain when she was six?

Figuring that Orcutt ought to know what was happening to Jessie and needing time to collect himself, feeling suddenly the full weight of the situation he was so strenuously working to obliterate from his thinking at least until the guests went home—the situation he was in as the father of a daughter who had killed not just one person more or less accidentally but, in the name of truth and justice, three more people quite indifferently, a daughter who, having repudiated everything she had ever learned from him and her mother, had now gone on to disown virtually the whole of civilized existence, beginning with cleanliness and ending with reason—the Swede left his father temporarily to tend alone to Jessie and went around, by way of the back of the house, to the rear kitchen door to get Orcutt. Through the door's glass panes he could see a stack of papers on the table, a new batch of Orcutt's drawings, probably of the troublesome link, and then, by the sink, he saw Orcutt himself.

Orcutt had on his raspberry-colored linen pants and, hanging clear of the pants, a loose-fitting Hawaiian shirt decorated with a colorful array of tropical flora best described in a word favored by Sylvia Levov for everything distasteful to her in wearing apparel: "loud." Dawn maintained that the outfit was just part of that superconfident Orcutt façade by which, as a young newcomer to Old Rimrock, she had once been so ridiculously intimidated. According to Dawn's interpretation—which, when she told it to him, struck the Swede as not without a tinge still of the old resentment—the message of the Hawaiian summer shirts was simply this: I am William Orcutt III and I can wear what other people around here wouldn't dare to wear. "The grander you believe you are in the great world of Morris County," said Dawn, "the more flamboyant you think you can be. The Hawaiian shirt," she said, smiling her mocking smile, "is Wasp extremism—Wasp motley. That's what I've learned living out here—even the William Orcutt the Thirds have their little pale moments of exuberance."

Just the year before, the Swede's father had made a similar observation. "I've noticed this about the rich goyim in the summertime. Comes the summer, and these reserved, correct people wear the most incredible costumes." The Swede had laughed. "It's a form of privilege," he said, repeating Dawn's line. "Is it?" asked Lou Levov, laughing along with him. "Maybe it is," Lou concluded. "Still, I got to hand it to this goy: you have to have guts to wear those pants and those shirts."

Certainly, seeing Orcutt dressed like that down in the village, a burly guy, big and substantial-looking, you would not have imagined—if you were the Swede—his paintings having that rubbed-out look as their distinctive feature. A person as unsophisticated about abstract art as the Swede was said to be by Dawn might easily have imagined the guy who went everywhere in those shirts as painting pictures like the famous one of Firpo knocking Dempsey out of the ring in the second round at the old Polo Grounds. But then artistic creation obviously was not achieved in any way or for any of the reasons Swede Levov could understand. According to the Swede's interpretation, all of the guy's effervescence seemed rather to go into wearing those shirts—all his flamboyance, his boldness, his defiance, and perhaps, too, his disappointment and his despair.

Well, perhaps not *all*, the Swede discovered as he stood peering in through the kitchen door from the big granite step outside. Why he hadn't just opened the door and gone straight ahead into his own kitchen to say that Jessie was in serious need of her husband was because of the way that Orcutt was leaning over Dawn while Dawn was leaning over the sink, shucking the corn. In the first instant it looked to the Swede—despite the fact that Dawn needed no such instruction—as though Orcutt were showing Dawn *how* to shuck corn, bending over her from behind and, with his hands on hers, helping her get the knack of cleanly removing the husk and the silk. But if he was only helping her learn to shuck corn, why, beneath the florid expanse of Hawaiian shirt, were his hips and his buttocks moving like that? Why was his cheek pressed against hers like that? And why was Dawn saying—if the Swede was correctly reading her lips—"Not here, not here . . ."? Why *not* shuck the corn here? The kitchen was as good a place as any. No, it took a moment to figure out that, one, they were not merely shucking corn together and, two, not all of the effervescence, flamboyance, boldness, defiance, disappointment, and despair nibbling at the edges of the old-line durability was necessarily sated by wearing those shirts.

So *this* was why she was always losing her patience with Orcutt—to put me off the track! Making cracks about his bloodlessness, his breeding, his empty warmth, putting him down like that *whenever we are about to get into bed.* Sure she talks that way—she has to, she's in love with him. The unfaithfulness to the house was never unfaithfulness to the house—it was unfaithfulness. "The poor wife doesn't drink for no reason. Always holding everything back. So busy being so polite," Dawn said, "so Princeton," Dawn said, "so *unerring*. He works so hard to be one-dimensional. That Wasp blandness. Living completely off what they once were. The man is simply not *there* half the time."

Well, Orcutt was there now, right there. What the Swede believed he'd seen, before quickly turning back to the terrace and the steak on the fire, was Orcutt putting himself exactly where he intended to be, while telling Dawn exactly where he was. "There! There! There! There!" And he did not appear to be holding anything back.

# 8

A T DINNER—outdoors, on the back terrace, with darkness
coming on so gradually that the evening seemed to the Swede
stalled, stopped, suspended, provoking in him a distressing sense of
nothing more to follow, of nothing ever to happen again, of having
entered a coffin carved out of time from which he would never be
extricated—there were also the Umanoffs, Marcia and Barry, and
the Salzmans, Sheila and Shelly. Only a few hours had passed since
the Swede learned that it was Sheila Salzman, the speech therapist, who had hidden Merry after the bombing. The Salzmans had
not told him. And if only they had—called when she showed up
there, done their duty to him then . . . He could not complete the
thought. If he were to contemplate head-on all that would not have
happened had Merry never been permitted to become a fugitive
from justice . . . Couldn't complete that thought either. He sat at
dinner, eternally inert—immobilized, ineffectual, inert, estranged
from those expansive blessings of openness and vigor conferred on
him by his hyperoptimism. A lifetime's agility as a businessman,
as an athlete, as a U.S. Marine, had in no way conditioned him
for being a captive confined to a futureless box where he was not
to think about what had become of his daughter, was not to
think about how the Salzmans had assisted her, was not to think
about . . . about what had become of his wife. He was supposed

to get through dinner not thinking about the only things he could think about. He was supposed to do this forever. However much he might crave to get out, he was to remain stopped dead in the moment in that box. Otherwise the world would explode.

Barry Umanoff, once the Swede's teammate and closest high school friend, was a law professor at Columbia, and whenever the folks flew up from Florida Barry and his wife were invited for dinner. Seeing Barry always made his father happy, in part because Barry, the son of an immigrant tailor, had evolved into a university professor but also because Lou Levov—wrongly, though the Swede pretended not to care—credited Barry Umanoff with getting Seymour to lay down his baseball glove and enter the business. Every summer Lou reminded Barry—"Counselor" as he'd been calling him since high school—of the good deed Barry had done for the Levov family by the example of his professional seriousness, and Barry would say that, if he'd been one-hundredth the ballplayer the Swede was, nobody would have gotten him near a law school.

It was Barry and Marcia Umanoff with whom Merry had stayed overnight a couple of times in New York before the Swede finally forbade her going into New York at all, and it was Barry from whom the Swede had sought legal advice after Merry's disappearance from Old Rimrock. Barry took him to meet Schevitz, the Manhattan litigator. When the Swede asked Schevitz to level with him—what was the worst that could be laid on his daughter if she was apprehended and found guilty?—he was told, "Seven to ten years." "But," said Schevitz, "if it's done in the passion of the antiwar movement, if it's done accidentally, if everything was done to try to prevent anyone from getting hurt . . . And do we know she did it alone? We don't. Do we even know she did it? We don't. No significant political history, a lot of rhetoric, a lot of violent rhetoric, but is this a kid who, on her own, would kill someone deliberately? How do we know she made the bomb or set the bomb? To make a bomb you have to be fairly sophisticated—could this kid light a match?" "She was excellent in science," the Swede said. "For her chemistry project she got an A." "Did she make a bomb for her chemistry project?" "No, of course not—no." "Then we don't know, do we, whether she could light a match or not. It might have been all rhetoric to her. We don't know what she did and we don't know what she meant to do. We don't know anything and neither does anyone else. She could have won the Westinghouse Science Prize and we wouldn't know. What can be proved? Probably very little. The worst, since you ask me, is seven to ten. But let's assume she's treated as a juvenile. Under juvenile law she gets two to three, and even if she pleads guilty to something, the record is sealed and nobody can get at it. Look, it all depends on her role in the homicide. It doesn't have to be too bad. If the kid will come in, even if she did have something to do with it, we might get her off with practically nothing." And until a few hours ago—when he'd learned that on the Oregon commune making bombs was her specialty, when from her own unstuttering mouth he heard that it was not a single possibly accidental death for which she was responsible but the coldhearted murder of four people—Schevitz's words were sometimes all he had to keep him from giving up hope. This man did not deal in fairy tales. You could see that as soon as you walked into his office. Schevitz was somebody who liked to be proved right, somebody whose wish to prevail was his *vocation*. Barry had made it clear beforehand that Schevitz was not a guy interested in making people feel good. He was not addressing the Swede's yearnings when he said, *If the kid will come in we might get her off.* But this was back when they thought they could find a jury that would believe she didn't know how to light a match. This was before five o'clock that afternoon.

Barry's wife, Marcia, a literature professor in New York, was, by even the Swede's generous estimate, "a difficult person," a militant nonconformist of staggering self-certainty much given to sarcasm and calculatedly apocalyptic pronouncements designed to bring discomfort to the lords of the earth. There was nothing she did or said that didn't make clear where she stood. She had barely to move a muscle—swallow while you were speaking, tap with a fingernail on the arm of her chair, even nod her head as if she were in total agreement—to inform you that nothing you were saying was correct. To encompass all her convictions she dressed in large block-printed caftans—an extensive woman, for whom a disheveled appearance was less a protest against convention than a sign that she was a thinker who got right to the point. No nonsense, no commonplace stood between her and the harshest truths.

Yet Barry enjoyed her. Since they couldn't have been more dissimilar, perhaps theirs was one of those so-called attractions of opposites. In Barry, there was such thoughtfulness and kindly concern—ever since he was a kid, and the poorest kid the Swede had known, he'd been a diligent, upright gentleman, a solid catcher in baseball, eventually the class valedictorian, who, after his stint in the service, went to NYU on the GI Bill. That's where he met and married Marcia Schwartz. It was hard for the Swede to understand how a strongly built, not unhandsome guy like Barry could free himself at the age of twenty-two from the desire to be with anybody else in this world but Marcia Schwartz, already so opinionated as a college girl that the Swede had to battle in her presence to stay awake. Yet Barry liked her. Sat there and listened to her. Didn't at all seem to care that she was a slob, dressed even in college like somebody's grandmother, and with those buoyant eyes, unnervingly enlarged by the heavy spectacles. Dawn's opposite in every way. For Marcia to have spawned a self-styled revolutionary —yes, had Merry been raised within earshot of Marcia's mouth . . . but Dawn? Pretty, petite, unpolitical Dawn—why *Dawn?* Where do you look for the cause? Where is the explanation for this mismatch? Was it nothing more than a trick played by their genes? During the March on the Pentagon, the march to stop the war in Vietnam, Marcia Umanoff had been thrown into a paddy wagon with some twenty other women and, very much to her liking, locked up overnight in a D.C. jail, where she didn't stop talking protest talk till they were all let out in the morning. If Merry had been *her* daughter, things *would* make sense. If only Merry had fought a war of words, fought the world with words alone, like this strident yenta. Then Merry's would be not a story that begins and ends with a bomb but another story entirely. But a bomb. A bomb. A bomb tells the whole fucking story.

Hard to grasp Barry's marrying that woman. Maybe it had to do with his family's being so poor. Who knows? Her animus, her superior airs, the sense she gave of being unclean, everything intolerable to the Swede in a friend, let alone in a mate—well, those were the very characteristics that seemed to enliven Barry's appreciation of his wife. It was a puzzle, it truly was, how one perfectly reasonable man could adore what a second perfectly reasonable man couldn't abide for half an hour. But just because it was a puzzle, the Swede tried his best to restrain his aversion and neutralize his judgment and see Marcia Umanoff as simply an oddball from another world, the academic world, the intellectual world, where always to be antagonizing people and challenging whatever they said was apparently looked on with admiration. What it was they got out of being so negative was beyond him; it seemed to him far more productive when everybody grew up and got over that. Still, that didn't mean that Marcia was really out to needle people and work them over just because she was so often needling people and working them over. He couldn't call her vicious once he'd recognized that this was the way she was accustomed to socializing in Manhattan; moreover, he couldn't believe that Barry Umanoff— who at one time was closer to him than his own kid brother— could marry someone vicious. As usual, the Swede's default reaction to not being able to fathom cause and effect (as opposed to his father's reflexive suspiciousness) was to fall back on a lifelong strategy and become tolerant and charitable. And so he was content to chalk up Marcia as "difficult," allowing at worst, "Well, let's just say she's no bargain."

But Dawn loathed her. Loathed her because she knew herself to be loathed by Marcia for having been Miss New Jersey. Dawn couldn't stand people who made that story the whole of her story, and Marcia was especially exasperating because the pleasure of explaining Dawn by a story that had never explained her—and hardly explained her now—was so smugly exhibited. When they'd all first met, Dawn told the Umanoffs about her father's heart attack and how no money was coming into the house and how she realized that the door to college was about to be slammed shut on her brother . . . the whole scholarship story, but none of it made Miss New Jersey seem like anything but a joke to Marcia Umanoff. Marcia barely bothered to hide the fact that when she looked at Dawn Levov she saw no one there, that she thought Dawn pretentious for raising cows, thought she was doing it for the image—it wasn't a serious operation Dawn ran twelve, fourteen hours a day, seven days a week; as far as Marcia was concerned it was a pretty *House and Garden* fantasy contrived by a rich, silly woman who lived, not in stinky-smelling New Jersey, no, no, who lived *in the country.* Dawn loathed Marcia because of her undisguised superiority to the Levovs' wealth, to their taste, to the rural way of life they loved, and loathed her beyond loathing because she was convinced that privately Marcia was altogether pleased about what Merry was alleged to have done.

The privileged place in Marcia's feelings went to the Vietnamese—the North Vietnamese. She never for a moment compromised her political convictions or her compassionate comprehension of international affairs, not even when she saw from six inches away the misery that had befallen her husband's oldest friend. And this was what led Dawn to make the accusations that the Swede knew to be false, not because he could swear to Marcia's honorableness but because for him the probity of Barry Umanoff was beyond question. "I will not have her in this house! A *pig* has more humanity in her than that woman does! I don't care how many degrees she has—she is callous and she is *blind!* She is the most blind, self-involved, narrow-minded, obnoxious so-called intelligent person I have ever met in my life and I will not have her in my house!" "Well, I can't very well ask Barry to come by himself." "Then Barry can't come." "Barry has to come. I want Barry to come. My father gets a terrific boot out of seeing Barry here. He *expects* to see Barry here. It's Barry, Dawn, who got me to Schevitz." "But that woman took

Merry *in*. Don't you see? That's where Merry went! To New York—
to them! That's who gave her a hiding place! Somebody did, somebody *had* to. A real bomb thrower in her house—that *excited* her.
She hid her from us, hid Merry from her parents when she needed
her parents most. Marcia Umanoff is the one who sent her underground!" "Merry didn't want to stay there even before. She
stayed exactly twice at Barry's. That was it. The third time she never
showed up. You don't remember. She went somewhere else to stay
and never showed up at the Umanoffs' again." "Marcia is the *one*,
Seymour. Who else has her connections? Wonderful Father This
One, wonderful Father That One, pouring blood on the draft records. So cozy she is with her war-resister priests, so buddy-buddy—
but they're not priests, Seymour! Priests are *not* great forward-
thinking liberals. Otherwise they don't *become* priests. It's just that
that's not what priests are supposed to *do*—no more than they're
supposed to stop praying for the boys who go over there. What *she*
likes about these priests is that these *aren't* priests. She doesn't love
them because they are in the Church, she loves them because they
are doing something that, in her estimation, *taints* the Church.
Because they are doing something *outside* the Church, outside the
regular *role* of the priest. That these priests are an affront to what
people like me grew up with, *that's* what she likes. That's what this
fat bitch likes about *everything*. I hate her. I hate her guts!" "Fine.
Fine with me. Hate her all you want," he said, "but not for something she hasn't done. She didn't do it, Dawn. You are driving
yourself crazy with something that cannot be true."

And it wasn't true. It wasn't Marcia who had taken Merry in.
Marcia *was* all talk—always had been: senseless, ostentatious talk,
words with the sole purpose of scandalously exhibiting themselves,
uncompromising, quarrelsome words expressing little more than
Marcia's intellectual vanity and her odd belief that all her posturing
added up to an independent mind. It was Sheila Salzman who'd
taken Merry in, the Morristown speech therapist, the pretty, kindly,
soft-spoken young woman who for a while had given Merry so
much hope and confidence, the teacher who provided Merry all

those "strategies" to outwit her impediment and replaced Audrey Hepburn as her heroine. In the months when Dawn was on sedatives and was in and out of the hospital; in the months before Sheila and the Swede would back off from ignoring the whole responsible orientation of their lives; in the months before these two well-ordered, well-behaved people could bring themselves to stop endangering their precious stability, Sheila Salzman had been Swede Levov's mistress, the first and last.

Mistress. A most un-Swede-like acquisition, incongruous, implausible, even ridiculous. "Mistress" does not quite make sense in the untarnished context of that life—and yet, for the four months after Merry disappeared, that is what Sheila was to him.

At dinner the conversation was about Watergate and about *Deep Throat.* Except for the Swede's parents and the Orcutts, everybody at the table had been to see the X-rated movie starring a young porno actress named Linda Lovelace. The picture was no longer playing only in the adult houses but had become a sensation in neighborhood theaters all over Jersey. What surprised him, Shelly Salzman was saying, was that the electorate who overwhelmingly chose as president and vice president Republican politicians hypocritically pretending to deep moral piety should make a hit out of a movie that so graphically caricatured acts of oral sex.

"Maybe it's not the same people," said Dawn, "who are going to the movie."

"It's McGovernites?" Marcia Umanoff asked her.

"At this table it is," answered Dawn, already inflamed at the outset of dinner by this woman she could not bear.

"Please," said the Swede's father, "what these two things have got to do with each other is a mystery to me. I don't know why you people pay good money to go to that trash in the first place. It's pure trash—am I right, Counselor?" He looked to Barry for support.

"It's a kind of trash," Barry said.

"Then why do you let it into your lives?"

"It leaks in, Mr. Levov," Bill Orcutt said to him pleasantly, "whether we like it or not. Whatever is out there leaks in. It pours in. It's not the same out there anymore, in case you haven't heard."

"Oh, I heard, sir. I come from the late city of Newark. I heard more than I want to hear. Look, the Irish ran the city, the Italians ran the city, now let the colored run the city. That's not my point. I got nothing against that. It's the colored people's turn to reach into the till? I wasn't born yesterday. In Newark corruption is the name of the game. What is new, number one, is race; number two, taxes. Add *that* to the corruption, *there's* your problem. Seven dollars and seventy-six cents. That is the tax rate in the city of Newark. I don't care how big you are or how small you are, I'm here to tell you that you cannot run a business with those kind of taxes. General Electric already moved out in 1953. GE, Westinghouse, Breyer's down on Raymond Boulevard, Celluloid, all left the city. Everyone of them big employers, and *before* the riots, *before* the racial hatred, they got out. Race is just the icing on the cake. Streets aren't cleaned. Burned-out cars nobody takes away. People in abandoned buildings. *Fires* in abandoned buildings. Unemployment. Filth. Poverty. More filth. More poverty. Schooling nonexistent. Schools a disaster. On every street corner dropouts. Dropouts doing nothing. Dropouts dealing drugs. Dropouts looking for trouble. The projects— don't get me started on the projects. Police on the take. Every kind of disease known to man. As far back as the summer of '64 I told my son, 'Seymour, get out.' 'Get out,' I said, but he won't listen. Paterson goes up, Elizabeth goes up, Jersey City goes up. You got to be blind in both eyes not to see what is next. And I told this to Seymour. 'Newark is the next Watts,' I told him. 'You heard it here first. The summer of '67.' I predicted it in those very words. Didn't I, Seymour? Called it practically to the *day.*"

"That is true," the Swede acknowledged.

"Manufacturing is finished in Newark. *Newark* is finished. The riots were just as bad if not worse in Washington, in Los Angeles, in Detroit. But, mark my words, Newark will be the city that never comes back. It can't. And gloves? In America? Kaput. Also finished.

Only my son hangs on. Five more years and outside of the government contracts there won't be a pair of gloves made in America. Not in Puerto Rico either. They're already in the Philippines, the big boys. It will be India, it'll be Indonesia, Pakistan, Bangladesh—you'll see, every place around the world making gloves except here. The union alone didn't break us, however. Sure, the union didn't understand, but some of the manufacturers didn't understand either—'I wouldn't pay the sons of bitches another five cents,' and here the guy is driving a Cadillac and sitting in Florida in the winter. No, a lot of the manufacturers didn't think straight. But the unions never understood the competition from overseas, and there is no doubt in my mind that the union speeded up the demise of the glove industry by being tough and making it so that people couldn't make money. The union rate on piecework ran a lot of people out of business or offshore. In the thirties our competition was heavy from Czechoslovakia, from Austria, from Italy. The war came along and saved us. Government contracts. Seventy-seven million pairs of gloves purchased by the quartermaster. The glove man got rich. But then the war ended, and I tell you, as far back as that, even in the good days, it was already the beginning of the end. Our downfall was that we could never compete with overseas. We hastened it because there wasn't some good judgment on either side. But it could not be saved regardless. The only thing that could have stopped it—and I was not for this, I don't think you can stop world trade and I don't think you should try—but the only thing that could have stopped it is if we put up trade barriers, making it not just five percent duties but thirty percent, forty percent—"

"Lou," said his wife, "what does any of this have to do with this movie?"

"This movie? These goddamn movies? Well, of course, they're not new either, you know. We had a pinochle club, this is years ago . . . you remember, the Friday Night Club? And we had a guy in the electrical business. You remember him, Seymour, Abe Sacks?"

"Sure," the Swede said.

"Well, I hate to tell you but he had all these kind of movies right in his house. Sure they existed. On Mulberry Street, where we used to go with the kids to eat Chinks, was a saloon where you could go in and buy whatever filth you wanted. And you know something? I watched five minutes and I went back in the kitchen and, to his credit, so did my dear friend, he's dead now, a wonderful fella, my mind is going, the glove cutter, what the hell was his name—"

"Al Haberman," said his wife.

"Right. The two of us just played gin for an hour, until there was this hullabaloo in the living room where they were showing the movie, and what happened was the whole damn movie, the camera, the whole what-do-you-call-it caught fire. I couldn't have been happier. That is thirty, forty years ago, and to this day I remember sitting with Al Haberman playing cards while the rest of them were drooling like idiots in the living room."

He was by now telling this to Orcutt, directing his remarks solely at him. As though, despite the evidence of the drunken woman Lou Levov was sitting next to, despite the incontrovertible evidence of so much of Jewish lore, the anarchy of a highborn Gentile remained essentially unimaginable to him, and Orcutt, therefore, of everyone at the table, could best appreciate the platitude he was getting at. They're supposed to be the dependable ones in control of themselves. Aren't they? They marked the territory. Didn't they? They made the rules, the very rules that the rest of us who came here have agreed to follow. Could Orcutt fail to admire him for sitting in that kitchen, sitting there patiently playing gin until at last the forces of good overcame the forces of evil and that dirty movie went up in smoke back in 1935?

"Well, I'm sorry to say, Mr. Levov, that you can't keep it out any longer just by playing cards," Orcutt told him. "That was a way to keep it out that doesn't exist any longer."

"Keep what out?" Lou Levov asked.

"What you're talking about," said Orcutt. "The permissiveness. Abnormality cloaked as ideology. The perpetual protest. Time was you could step away from it, you could make a stand against it. As you point out, you could even just play cards against it. But these days it's getting harder and harder to find relief. The grotesque is supplanting everything commonplace that people love about this country. Today, to be what they call 'repressed' is a source of shame to people—as not to be repressed used to be."

"That is true, that is true. Let me tell you about Al Haberman. You want to talk about the old-style world and what used to be, let's talk about Al. A wonderful fella, Al, a handsome fella. Got rich cutting gloves. You could in those days. A husband and a wife who had any ambition could get a few skins and make some gloves. Ended up in a small room, two men cutting, a couple of women sewing, they could make the gloves, they could press them and ship them. They made money, they were their own bosses, they could work sixty hours a week. Way, way back when Henry Ford was paying the unheard-of sum of a dollar a day, a fine table cutter would make five dollars a day. But look, in those days it was nothing for an ordinary woman to own twenty, twenty-five pair of gloves. Quite common. A woman used to have a glove wardrobe, different gloves for every outfit—different colors, different styles, different lengths. A woman wouldn't go outside without a pair in any weather. In those days it wasn't unusual for a woman to spend two, three hours at the glove counter and try on thirty pair of gloves, and the lady behind the desk had a sink and she would wash her hands between each color. In a fine ladies' glove, we had quarter sizes into the fours and up to eight and a half. Glove cutting is a wonderful trade—was, anyway. Everything now is 'was.' A cutter like Al always had a shirt and a tie on. In those days a cutter never worked without a shirt and a tie. You could work at seventy-five and eighty years old too. They could start in the way Al did, at fifteen, or even younger, and they could go to eighty. Seventy was a spring chicken. And they could work at their leisure, Saturday and Sunday. These people could work constantly. Money to send their kids to school. Money to fix up their homes nicely. Al could take a piece of leather, say to me, for a gag, 'What do you want, Lou, eight and nine-sixteenths?' And just snip it off without a ruler, measuring it perfectly with just his eye. The cutter was the prima donna. But all that pride of craftsmanship is gone, of course. Of the actual table cutters who could cut a sixteen-button white glove, I think Al Haberman may have been the last guy in America who could do it. The long glove, of course, vanished. Another 'was.' There was the eight-button glove which became very popular, silk-lined, but that was gone by '65. We were already taking gloves that were longer, chopping off the tops, making shorties, and using the top to make another glove. From this point where the thumb seam is, every inch on out they used to put a button, so we still talk, in terms of length, of buttons. Thank God in 1960 Jackie Kennedy walked out there with a little glove to the wrist, and a glove to the elbow, and a glove above the elbow, and a pillbox hat, and all of a sudden gloves were in style again. First Lady of the glove industry. Wore a size six and a half. People in the glove industry were praying to that lady. She herself stocked up in Paris, but so what? That woman put the ladies' fine leather glove back on the map. But when they assassinated Kennedy and Jacqueline Kennedy left the White House, that and the miniskirt was the end of the ladies' fashion glove. The assassination of John F. Kennedy and the arrival of the miniskirt, and together that was the death knell for the ladies' dress glove. Till then it was a twelve-month, year-round business. There was a time when a woman would not go out unless she wore a pair of gloves, even in the spring and the summer. Now the glove is for cold weather or for driving or for sports—"

"Lou," his wife said, "nobody is talking about—"

"Let me finish, please. Don't interrupt me, please. Al Haberman was a great reader. No schooling but he loved to read. His favorite author was Sir Walter Scott. And Sir Walter Scott, in one of his classic books, gets an argument going between the glovemaker and the shoemaker about who is the better craftsman, and the glovemaker wins the argument. You know what he says? 'All you do,' he tells the shoemaker, 'is make a mitten for the foot. You don't have to articulate around each toe.' But Sir Walter Scott was the son of a glover, so it makes sense he would win the argument. You didn't know Sir Walter Scott was the son of a glover? You know who else, aside from Sir Walter and my two sons? William Shakespeare. Father was a glover who couldn't read and write his own name. You know what Romeo says to Juliet when she's up on the balcony? Everybody knows 'Romeo, Romeo, where are you, Romeo'—that *she* says. But what does Romeo say? I started in a tannery when I was thirteen, but I can answer for you because of my friend Al Haberman, who since has passed away, unfortunately. Seventy-three years old, he came out of his house, slipped on the ice, and broke his neck. Terrible. He told me this. Romeo says, 'See the way she leans her cheek on her hand? I only wish I was the glove on that hand so that I could touch that cheek.' Shakespeare. Most famous author in history."

"Lou dear," Sylvia Levov said again softly, "what does this have to do with what everybody is talking about?"

"*Please*," he said, and impatiently, with one hand, without even looking at her, waved away her objection. "And McGovern," he went on, "this is an idea I don't follow at all. What does McGovern have to do with that lousy movie? I voted for McGovern. I campaigned in the whole condominium for McGovern. You should hear what I put up with from Jewish people, how Nixon was this for Israel and that for Israel, and I reminded them, in case they forgot, that Harry Truman had him pegged for Tricky Dicky back in 1948, and now look, the reward they're reaping, my good friends who voted for Mr. Von Nixon and his storm troopers. Let me tell you who goes to those movies: riffraff, bums, and kids without adult supervision. Why my son takes his lovely wife to such a movie is something I'll go to my grave not understanding."

"To see," said Marcia, "how the other half lives."

"My daughter-in-law is a lady. She has no interest in those things."

"Lou," his wife said to him, "maybe not everybody sees it your way."

"I cannot believe that. These are intelligent, educated people."

"You put too much stock in intelligence," Marcia teased him. "It doesn't annihilate human nature."

"That's human nature, those movies? Tell me, what do you tell to children about that movie when they ask? That it's good, wholesome fun?"

"You don't have to tell them a thing," Marcia said. "They don't ask. These days they just go."

And what puzzled him, of course, was that what was happening these days did not seem to displease her, a professor, a *Jewish* professor—with *children.*

"I wouldn't say children are going," Shelly Salzman put in, as much, seemingly, to disrupt the unpromising dialogue as to give comfort to the Swede's father. "I would say adolescents."

"And, Dr. Salzman, *you* approve of this?"

Shelly smiled at the title Lou Levov insisted on using with him after all these years. Shelly was a pale, plump, round-shouldered man in a bow tie and a seersucker jacket, a hardworking family doctor who could not keep the kindness out of his voice. The pallor and the posture, the old-fashioned steel-rimmed glasses, the hairless crown of his head, the wiry white curls above his ears—this unstudied lack of luster had made the Swede feel particularly sorry for him during the months of the love affair with Sheila Salzman. . . . Yet he, nice Dr. Salzman, had harbored Merry in his house, hidden her not only from the FBI but from him, her father, the person she'd needed most in the world.

And I was the one, the Swede was thinking, guilty over *my* secret—even as Shelly was gently saying to the Swede's father, "My approval or disapproval is beside the point of whether they go to those movies or not."

When Dawn had first proposed going for a face-lift to the clinic of a Geneva doctor she had read about in *Vogue*—a doctor they didn't know, a procedure they knew nothing about—the Swede had quietly contacted Shelly Salzman and went off to see him alone in his office. Their own family doctor was a man the Swede respected, a cautious and thorough elderly man who would have counseled the Swede and answered his questions and tried, on the Swede's behalf, to dissuade Dawn from the idea, but instead the Swede had called Shelly and asked if he might come over to talk about a family problem. Only when he got to Shelly's office did he understand that he had gone there to confess, four years after the fact, to having had the affair with Sheila in the aftermath of Merry's disappearance. When Shelly smiled and asked, "How can I help you?" the Swede found himself on the brink of saying, "By forgiving me." Throughout the conversation, every time the Swede spoke he had to quash the impulse to tell Shelly everything, to say, "I'm not here because of the face-lift. I'm here because I did what I should never have done. I betrayed my wife, I betrayed you, I betrayed myself." But saying this would be a betrayal of Sheila, would it not? He could no more justify his taking it solely upon himself to confess to her husband than he could had she taken it upon herself to confess to his wife. However much he might yearn to be rid of a secret that stained and oppressed him, and imagine that a confession might unburden him, did he have the right to free himself at Sheila's expense? At Shelly's expense? At Dawn's expense? No, there was such a thing as ethical stability. No, he could not be so ruthlessly self-regarding. A cheap stunt, a treacherous stunt, and one that probably wouldn't pay off in long-term relief—yet each time the Swede opened his mouth to speak, he needed desperately to say to this kindly man, "I was the lover of your wife," to seek from Shelly Salzman the magical restitution of equilibrium that Dawn must be hoping she'd find in Geneva. But instead he only told Shelly how against the face-lift he was, only enumerated his reasons against it, and then, to his surprise, listened to Shelly telling him that Dawn had perhaps begun to entertain a potentially promising idea. "If she thinks this will help her start over again," Shelly said, "why not give her the opportunity? Why not give this woman *every* opportunity? There's nothing wrong with it, Seymour. This is life—not a life sentence but life. Nothing immoral about having a face-lift. Nothing frivolous about a woman wanting one. She found the idea in *Vogue* magazine? That shouldn't throw you off. She only found what she was looking for. You don't know how many women come to me who've been through a terrible trauma and they want to talk about something or other, and what turns out to be on their mind is just this, plastic surgery. And without *Vogue* magazine. The emotional and psychological implications can turn out to be something. The relief they get, those that get relief, is not to be minimized. I can't say I know how it happens, I'm not saying it always happens, but I've seen it happen again and again, women who've lost their husbands, who've been seriously ill . . . You don't look like you believe me." But the Swede knew what he looked like: like a man with "Sheila" written all over his face. "I know," said Shelly, "it seems like a purely physical way of dealing with something profoundly emotional, but for many people it's a wonderful survival strategy. And Dawn may be one of them. I don't think you want to be puritanical about this. If Dawn feels strongly about a face-lift, and if you were to go along with her, if you were to support her . . ." Later that same day Shelly phoned the Swede at the factory—he'd made some inquiries about Dr. LaPlante. "We've got people as good as him here, I'm sure, but if you want to go to Switzerland and get away and let her recuperate there, why not? This LaPlante is tops." "Shelly, thanks, it's awfully kind of you," said the Swede, disliking himself more than ever in the light of Shelly's generosity . . . and yet this was the same guy who, with his co-conspirator wife, had provided Merry a hiding place not only from the FBI but from her father and mother. A fact about as fantastic as a fact could be. What kind of mask is everyone wearing? I thought these people were on my side. But the mask is all that's on my side—that's it! For four months I wore the mask myself, with him, with my wife, and I could not stand it. I went there to tell him that. I went to tell him that I had betrayed him, and only didn't so as not to compound the betrayal, and never once did he let on how cruelly he'd betrayed me.

"My approval or disapproval," Shelly had been saying to Lou Levov, "is beside the point of whether they go to those movies or not."

"But you are a physician," the Swede's father insisted, "a respected person, an ethical person, a responsible person—"

"Lou," said his wife, "maybe, dear, you're monopolizing the conversation."

"Let me finish, *please.*" To the table at large, he asked, "Am I? Am
I monopolizing the conversation?"

"Absolutely not," said Marcia, throwing an arm good-naturedly
across his back. "It's delightful to hear your delusions."

"I don't know what that means," he told her.

"It means social conditions may have altered in America since
you were taking the kids to eat at the Chinks and Al Haberman was
cutting gloves in a shirt and a tie."

"Really?" Dawn said to her. "They've altered? Nobody told us,"
and, to contain herself, got up and left for the kitchen. Waiting
there for Dawn's instructions were a couple of local high school
girls who helped to do the serving and the cleaning up whenever
the Levovs had dinner guests.

Marcia was to one side of Lou Levov, Jessie Orcutt to the other.
Jessie's new glass of Scotch, which she must have managed to pour
for herself in the kitchen, he had picked up from her place and
moved out of her reach only minutes into the cold cucumber soup.
When she then made a move to leave the table, he would not allow
her to get up. "Just sit," he told her. "Sit and eat. You don't need
that. You need food. Eat your dinner." Each time she so much as
shifted in her chair, he laid a hand firmly on hers to remind her she
was going nowhere.

A dozen candles burned in two tall ceramic candelabra, and to
the Swede, who sat flanked by his mother and by Sheila Salzman, everyone's eyes—deceptively enough, even Marcia's eyes—
appeared blessed in that light with spiritual understanding, with
kindly lucidity, alive with all the meaning one so craves to find in
one's friends. Sheila, like Barry, was on hand every year at Labor
Day because of what she had come to mean to his folks. On the
phone to Florida the Swede almost never got through a conversation without his father's asking, "And how is that lovely Sheila, that
lovely woman, how is she doing?" "She is such a dignified woman,"

his mother said, "such a refined person. Isn't she Jewish, darling? Your father says no. He insists she isn't."

Why this disagreement should persist for years he could not understand exactly, but the subject of fair-haired Sheila Salzman's religious origins had proved indispensable to his parents' lives. To Dawn, who'd been trying for decades to be as tolerant of the Swede's imperfect parents as he was of her imperfect mother, this was their most inexplicable preoccupation—their most enraging as well (particularly as Dawn knew that, for her adolescent daughter, Sheila had something Dawn didn't have, that somehow Merry had come to trust the speech therapist in a way she no longer trusted her mother). "Are there no Jewish blonds in the world other than you?" Dawn asked him. "It hasn't anything to do with her appearance," the Swede explained, "it has to do with Merry." "What does her being Jewish have to do with Merry?" "I don't know. She was the speech therapist. They're in awe of her," the Swede said, "because of all she did for Merry." "She wasn't the child's mother by any chance—or was she?" "They know that, darling," calmly answered the Swede, "but because of the speech therapy, they've made her into some kind of magician."

And so had he, not so much while she was Merry's therapist—when he had merely found her composure a curious stimulus to sexual imaginings—but after Merry disappeared and grief absconded with his wife.

Thrown violently off his own narrow perch, he felt an intangible need open hugely within him, a need with no bottom to it, and he yielded to a solution so foreign to him that he did not even recognize how improbable it was. In the quiet, thoughtful woman, who had once made Merry less strange to herself by teaching her how to overcome her word phobias and to control the elaborate circumlocutionary devices that, paradoxically, only increased her child's sense of being out of control, was someone he found himself wanting to incorporate into himself. The man who had lived correctly within marriage for almost twenty years was determined to be senselessly, worshipfully in love. It was three months before he could begin to understand that this was no way around anything, and it was Sheila who had to tell him. He hadn't gotten a romantic mistress—he'd gotten a candid mistress. She sensibly told him what all his adoration of her meant, told him that he was no more himself with her than Dawn was Dawn at the psychiatric clinic, explained to him that he was out to sabotage everything—but he was in such a state that he went on anyway telling her how, when they ran away together to Ponce, she could learn Spanish and teach techniques of speech therapy at the university there, and he could operate the business from his Ponce plant and they could live in a modern hacienda up in the hills, among the palms, above the Caribbean. . . .

What she did not tell him about was Merry in her house—after the bombing, Merry hiding in her house. She told him everything except that. The candor stopped just where it should have begun.

Was everyone's brain as unreliable as his? Was he the only one unable to see what people were up to? Did everyone slip around the way he did, in and out, in and out, a hundred different times a day go from being smart to being smart enough, to being as dumb as the next guy, to being the dumbest bastard who ever lived? Was it stupidity deforming him, the simpleton son of a simpleton father, or was life just one big deception that everyone was on to except him?

This sense of inadequacy he might once have described to *her;* he could talk to Sheila, talk about his doubts, his bewilderment— all the serenity in her allowed for that, this magician of a woman who had given Merry the great opportunity that Merry had thrown away, who had supplanted with "a wonderful floating feeling," according to Merry, half at least of her stutterer's frustration, the lucid woman whose profession was to give sufferers a second chance, the mistress who knew everything, including how to harbor a murderer.

Sheila had been with Merry and she had told him nothing.

All the trust between them, like all the happiness he'd ever known (like the killing of Fred Conlon—like *everything*), had been an accident.

She'd been with Merry and said nothing.

And said nothing now. The eagerness with which others spoke seemed, under the peculiar intensity of her gaze, to strike her as a branch of pathology. Why would anyone say *that?* She herself was to say nothing all evening, nothing about Linda Lovelace or Richard Nixon or H. R. Haldeman and John Ehrlichman, her advantage over other people being that her head was not filled by what filled everybody else's head. This way of hers, of lying in wait behind herself, the Swede had once taken to be a mark of her superiority. Now he thought, "Icy bitch. *Why?*" Once she had said to him, "The influence you allow others to have on you, it's absolute. Nothing so captivates you as another person's needs." And he had said, "I think you are describing Sheila Salzman," and, as always, he was wrong.

He thought she was omniscient and all she was was cold.

Whirling about inside him now was a frenzied distrust of everyone. The excision of certain assurances, the *last* assurances, made him feel as though he had gone in one day from being five to being one hundred. It would give him comfort, he thought, it would help him right then if, of all things, he knew that resting out in the pasture beyond their dinner table was Dawn's herd, with Count, the big bull, protecting them. If Dawn still had Count, if only Count. . . . A relief-filled, realityless moment passed before he realized that of course it would be a comfort to have Count roaming the dark pasture among the cows, because then Merry would be roaming among the guests, here, Merry, in her circus pajamas, leaning up against the back of her father's chair, whispering into her father's ear. *Mrs. Orcutt drinks whiskey. Mrs. Umanoff has BO. Dr. Salzman is bald.* A mischievous intelligence that was utterly harmless—back then unanarchic and childish and well within bounds.

Meanwhile he heard himself saying, "Dad, take some more steak," in what he knew was a hopeless effort—a good son's effort—to get his self-abandoned father to be, if not tranquil, less insistently chagrined over the inadequacies of the non-Jewish human race.

"I'll tell you who I'll take some steak for—for this young lady." Spearing a slice from the platter that one of the serving girls was holding beside him, he dumped it onto Jessie's plate; he had taken Jessie on as a full-scale project. "Now pick up your knife and fork and eat," he told her, "you could use some red meat. Sit up straight," and, as though she believed he could well resort to violence if she did otherwise, Jessie Orcutt drunkenly mumbled, "I was going to," but began to fiddle with the meat in such a clumsy way that the Swede feared his father was going to start cutting her food for her. All that crude energy that, try as it might, could not remake the troubled world.

"But this is serious business, this children business." Having gotten Jessie taking nourishment, he was in a state again about *Deep Throat*. "If that isn't serious, what is anymore?"

"Dad," said the Swede, "what Shelly is saying is not that it's not serious. He agrees it's serious. He's saying that once you've made your case to an adolescent child, you've made your case and you can't then take these kids and lock them up in their rooms and throw away the key."

His daughter was an insane murderer hiding on the floor of a room in Newark, his wife had a lover who dry-humped her over the sink in their family kitchen, his ex-mistress had knowingly brought disaster upon his house, and he was trying to propitiate his father with on-the-one-hand-this and on-the-other-hand-that.

"You'd be surprised," Shelly told the old man, "how much the kids today have learned to take in their stride."

"But degrading things should *not* be taken in their stride! I say *lock* them in their rooms if they take this in their stride! I remember when kids used to be at home doing their homework and not out seeing movies like this. This is the morality of a country that we're talking about. Well, isn't it? Am I nuts? It is an affront to decency and to decent people."

"And what," Marcia asked him, "is so inexhaustibly interesting about decency?"

The question so surprised him that it left him looking a little frantically around the table for somebody with an opinion learned enough to subdue this woman.

It turned out to be Orcutt, that great friend of the family. Bill Orcutt was coming to Lou Levov's aid. "And what is wrong with decency?" Orcutt asked, smiling broadly at Marcia.

The Swede could not look at him. On top of all the things he could not think about there were two people—Sheila and Orcutt—he could not look at. Did Dawn consider Bill Orcutt handsome? He never thought so. Round face, snout nose, puckering lower lip . . . piggy-looking bastard. Must be something else that drove her to that frenzy over the kitchen sink. What? The easy assurance? Was that what got her going? The comfort taken by Bill Orcutt in being Bill Orcutt, his contentment in being Bill Orcutt? Was it because he wouldn't dream of slighting you even if both you and he knew that you weren't up to snuff? Was it his appropriateness that got her going like that, the flawless appropriateness, how very appropriately he played his role as steward of the Morris County past? Was it the sense he exuded of never having had to grub for anything or take shit from anyone or be at a loss as to how to behave even when the wife on his arm was a hopeless drunk? Was it because he'd entered the world expecting things not even a Weequahic three-letterman begins to expect, that none of us begin to expect, that the rest of us, if we even get those things by working our asses off for them, still never feel entitled to? Was that why she was in heat over the sink—because of his inbred sense of entitlement? Or was it the laudable environmentalism? Or was it the great art? Or was it simply his cock? Is that it, Dawn dear? I want an answer! I want it tonight! *Is it just his cock?*

The Swede could not stop imagining the particulars of Orcutt fucking his wife any more than he could stop imagining the particulars of the rapists fucking his daughter. Tonight the imagining would not let him be.

"Decency?" Marcia said to Orcutt, foxily smiling back at him. "Much overvalued, wouldn't you say, the seductions of decency and civility and convention? Not the richest response to life I can think of."

"So what *do* you recommend for 'richness'?" Orcutt asked her. "The high road of transgression?"

The patrician architect was amused by the literature professor and the menacing figure she tried to cut in order to appall the squares. Amused he was. Amused! But the Swede could not turn the dinner party into a battle for his wife. Things were bad enough without colliding with Orcutt in front of his parents. All he had to do was to not listen to him. Yet each time that Orcutt spoke, every word antagonized him, convulsed him with spite and hatred and sinister thoughts; and when Orcutt wasn't speaking, the Swede was constantly looking down the table to see what in God's name there was in that face that could so excite his wife.

"Well," Marcia was saying, "without transgression there isn't very much knowledge, is there?"

"My God," cried Lou Levov, "*that's* one I never heard before. Excuse me, Professor, but where the hell do you get that idea?"

"The Bible," said Marcia, deliciously, "for a start."

"The *Bible? Which* Bible?"

"The one that begins with Adam and Eve. Isn't that what they tell us in Genesis? Isn't that what the Garden of Eden story is telling us?"

"What? Telling us *what?*"

"Without transgression there is no knowledge."

"Well, that ain't what they taught me," he replied, "about the Garden of Eden. But then I never got past eighth grade."

"What *did* they teach you, Lou?"

"That when God above tells you not to do something, you damn well don't do it—that's what. Do it and you pay the piper. Do it and you will suffer from it for the rest of your days."

"Obey the good Lord above," said Marcia, "and all the terrible things will vanish."

"Well . . . yes," he replied, though without conviction, realizing that he was being mocked. "Look, we are way off the subject—we are not talking about the Bible. Forget the Bible. This is no place to talk about the Bible. We are talking about a movie where a grown woman, from all reports, goes in front of a movie camera, and for money, openly, for millions and millions of people to see, children, everyone, does everything she can think of that is degrading. *That's* what we're talking about."

"Degrading to whom?" Marcia asked him.

"To *her*, for God's sake. Number one, *her*. She has made herself into the scum of the earth. You can't tell me you are in favor of *that*."

"Oh, she hasn't made herself into the scum of anything, Lou."

"To the contrary," said Orcutt, laughing. "She has eaten of the Tree of Knowledge."

"*And*," announced Marcia, "made herself into a superstar. The highest of the high. I think Miss Lovelace is having the time of her life."

"Adolf Hitler had the time of his life, Professor, shoveling Jews into the furnace. That does not make it *right*. This is a woman who is poisoning young minds, poisoning the country, and in the bargain she *is* making herself the scum of the earth—period!"

There was nothing inactive in Lou Levov when he argued, and it looked as though just observing the phenomenon of an opinionated old man, fettered still to his fantasy of the world, was all that was prompting Marcia to persist. To bait and bite and draw blood. Her sport. The Swede wanted to kill her. Leave him alone! Leave him alone and he'll shut up! It's no big deal getting him to say more and more and more—so stop it!

But this problem that he had long ago learned to circumnavigate, in part by subduing his own personality, seemingly subjugating it to his father's while maneuvering around Lou where he could—this problem of the father, of maintaining filial love against the onslaught of an unrelenting father—was not a problem that she'd had decades of experience integrating into her life. Jerry just told their father to fuck off; Dawn was driven almost crazy by him; and Sylvia Levov stoically and impatiently endured him, her only successful form of resistance being to freeze him out and live with the isolation—and see more of herself evaporating year by year. But Marcia took him on as the fool that he was for still believing in the power of his indignation to convert the corruptions of the present into the corruptions of the past.

"So what would you want her to be instead, Lou? A cocktail waitress?" Marcia asked.

"Why not? That's a job."

"Not much of one," Marcia replied. "Not one that would interest anyone here."

"Oh?" said Lou Levov. "They'd prefer what she does instead?"

"I don't know," said Marcia. "We'll have to poll the girls. Which would you prefer," she said to Sheila, "cocktail waitress or porn star?"

But Sheila was not about to be engulfed in Marcia's mockery, and with eyes that seemed to stare past it and right on through to the egotism, she gave her unequivocal reply. The Swede remembered that after Sheila had first met Marcia and Barry Umanoff here, at the Old Rimrock house, he had asked her, "How can he love this person?" and instead of answering him as Dawn did, "Because he's a ball-less wonder," Sheila had replied, "By the end of a dinner party, everybody is probably thinking that about somebody. Sometimes everybody is thinking that about everybody." "Do you?" he'd asked her. "I think that about couples all the time," she'd said.

The wise woman. And yet this wise woman had harbored a murderer.

"What about Dawn?" Marcia asked. "Cocktail waitress or porno actress?"

Smiling sweetly, exhibiting her best Catholic schoolgirl posture—the girl who makes the nuns happy by sitting at her desk without slouching—Dawn said, "Up yours, Marcia."

"What kind of conversation is this?" Lou Levov asked.

"A dinner conversation," Sylvia Levov replied.

"And what makes *you* so blasé?" he asked her.

"I'm not blasé. I'm listening."

Now Bill Orcutt said, "Nobody's polled you, Marcia. Which would you prefer, assuming you had the choice?"

She laughed merrily at the slighting innuendo. "Oh, they've got big fat mamas in dirty movies. They, too, appear in the dreams of men. And not only for comic relief. Listen, you folks are too hard on Linda. Why is it that if a girl takes off her clothes in Atlantic City it's for a scholarship and makes her an American goddess, but if she takes off her clothes in a sex flick it's for filthy money and makes her a whore? Why is that? Why? All right—nobody knows. But seriously, folks, I love this word 'scholarship.' A hooker comes to a hotel room. The guy asks her how much she gets. She says, 'Well, if you want blank I get a three-hundred-dollar scholarship. And if you want blank-blank I get a five-hundred-dollar scholarship. And if you want blank-blank-blank—'"

"Marcia," said Dawn, "try as you will, you can't get under my skin tonight."

"Can't I?"

"Not tonight."

There was a beautiful floral arrangement at the center of the table. "From Dawn's garden," Lou Levov had told them all proudly as they were sitting down to eat. There were also large platters of the beefsteak tomatoes, sliced thickly, dressed in oil and vinegar, and encircled by slices of red onion fresh from the garden. And there were two wooden buckets—old feed buckets that they'd picked up at a junk shop in Clinton for a dollar apiece—each lined gaily with a red bandanna and brimming with the ears of corn that Orcutt had helped her shuck. Cradled in wicker baskets near either end of the table were freshly baked loaves of French bread, those new baguettes from McPherson's, reheated in the oven and pleasant to tear apart with your hands. And there was good strong Burgundy wine, half a dozen bottles of the Swede's best Pommard, four of them open on the table, bottles that five years back he had laid down for drinking in 1973—according to his wine register, Pommards laid down in his cellar just one month to the day before Merry killed Dr. Conlon. Yes, earlier in the evening he had found 1/3/68 inscribed, in his handwriting, in the spiral notebook he used for recording the details of each new purchase . . . "1/3/68" he had written, with no idea that on 2/3/68 his daughter would go ahead and outrage all of America, except perhaps for Professor Marcia Umanoff.

The two high school kids who were doing the serving emerged from the kitchen every few minutes, silently offering around the steaks he'd cooked, arranged on pewter platters, all carved up and running with blood. The Swede's set of carving knives were from Hoffritz, the best German stainless steel. He'd gone over to New York to buy the set and the big carving block for their first Thanksgiving in the Old Rimrock house. He once had cared about all that stuff. Loved to hone the blade on the long conical file before he went after the bird. Loved the sound of it. The sad inventory of his domestic bounty. Wanted his family to have the best. Wanted his family to have everything.

"Please," said Lou Levov, "can I get an answer about the effect of this on the children? You are all way, way off the topic. Haven't we seen enough tragedy with the young children? Pornography. Drugs. The violence."

"Divorce," Marcia threw in to help him out.

"Professor, don't get me started on divorce. You understand French?" he asked her.

"I do if I have to," she said, laughing.

"Well, I got a son down in Florida, Seymour's brother, whose *spécialité* is divorce. *I* thought his *spécialité* was cardiac surgery. But no, it's divorce. I thought I sent him to medical school—I thought that's where all the bills were coming from. But no, it was divorce school. That's what he's got the diploma in—divorce. Has there ever been a more terrible thing for a child than the specter of divorce? I don't think so. And where will it end? What is the limit? *You* didn't all grow up in this kind of world. Neither did I. We grew up in an era when it was a different place, when the feeling for community, home, family, parents, work . . . well, it was different. The changes are beyond conception. I sometimes think that more has changed since 1945 than in all the years of history there have ever been. I don't know what to make of the end of so many things. The lack of feeling for individuals that a person sees in that movie, the lack of feeling for places like what is going on in Newark—how did this happen? You don't have to revere your family, you don't have to revere your country, you don't have to revere where you live, but you have to know you *have* them, you have to know that you are *part* of them. Because if you don't, you are just out there on your own and I feel for you. I honestly do. Am I right, Mr. Orcutt, or am I wrong?"

"To wonder where the limit is?" Orcutt replied.

"Well, yes," said Lou Levov, who, the Swede observed—and not for the first time—had spoken of children and violence without any sense that the subject intersected with the life of his immediate family. Merry had been used for somebody else's evil purposes— that was the story to which it was crucial for them all to remain anchored. He kept such a sharp watch over each and every one of them to be certain that nobody wavered for a moment in their belief in that story. No one in this family was going to fall into doubt about Merry's absolute innocence, not so long as he was alive.

Among the many things the Swede could not think about from within the confines of his box was what would happen to his father when he learned that the death toll was four.

"You're right," Bill Orcutt was saying to Lou Levov, "to wonder where the limit is. I think everybody here is wondering where the limit is and worrying where the limit is every time they look at the papers. Except the professor of transgression. But then we're all stifled by convention—we're not great outlaws like William Burroughs and the Marquis de Sade and the holy saint Jean Genet. The Let Every Man Do Whatever He Wishes School of Literature. The brilliant school of Civilization Is Oppression and Morality Is Worse."

And he did not blush. "Morality" without batting an eye. "Transgression" as though he were a stranger to it, as though it were not he of all the men here—William III, latest in that long line of Orcutts advertised in their graveyard as virtuous men—who had transgressed to the utmost by violating the unity of a family already half destroyed.

His wife had a lover. And it was for the lover that she'd undergone the rigors of a face-lift, to woo and win *him*. Yes, now he understood the gushing letter profusely thanking the plastic surgeon for spending "the five hours of your time for my beauty," thanking him as if the Swede had not paid twelve thousand dollars for those five hours, plus five thousand more for the clinic suite where they had spent the two nights. *It is quite wonderful, dear doctor. It is as though I have been given a new life. Both from within and from the outside.* In Geneva he had sat up with her all night, held her hand through the nausea and the pain, and all of it for the sake of somebody else. It was for the sake of somebody else that she was building the house. The two of them were designing the house for each other.

To run away to Ponce to live with Sheila after Merry disappeared—no, Sheila had made him come to his senses and recover his rectitude and go back to his wife and as much of their life as remained intact, to the wife even a mistress knew he could not wound, let alone desert, in such a crisis. Yet these other two were going to pull it off. He knew it the moment he saw them in the kitchen. Their pact. Orcutt dumps Jessie and she dumps me and the house is for them. She thinks our catastrophe is over and so she is going to bury the past and start anew—face, house, husband, all new. *Try as you will, you can't get under my skin tonight. Not tonight.*

*They* are the outlaws. Orcutt, said Dawn to her husband, lived completely off what his family once was—well, she was living off what she'd just become. Dawn and Orcutt: two predators.

The outlaws are everywhere. They're inside the gates.

# 9

H E H A D a phone call. One of the girls came out of the kitchen to tell him. She whispered, "It's from I *think* Czechoslovakia."

He took the call in Dawn's downstairs study, where Orcutt had already moved the large cardboard model of the new house. After leaving Jessie on the terrace with the Swede and his parents and the drinks, Orcutt must have gone back to the van to get the model and carried it into Dawn's study and set it up on her desk before proceeding into the kitchen to help her shuck the corn.

Rita Cohen was on the line. She knew about Czechoslovakia because "they" were following him: they'd followed him earlier in the summer to the Czech consulate; they'd followed him that afternoon to the animal hospital; they'd followed him to Merry's room, where Merry had told him there was no such person as Rita Cohen.

"How can you do this to your own daughter?" she asked.

"I've done nothing to my daughter. I went to see my daughter. You wrote and told me where she was."

"You told her about the hotel. You told her we didn't fuck."

"I did not mention any hotel. I don't know what this is all about."

"You are lying to me. You told your daughter you did not fuck me. I warned you about that. I warned you in the letter."

Directly in front of the Swede sat the model of the house. He could see now what he had not been able to envision from Dawn's explanations—exactly how the long shed roof let the light into the main hallway through the high row of windows running the length of the front wall. Yes, now he saw how the sun would arc through the southern sky and the light would wash—and how happy it seemed to make her just to say "wash" after "light"—wash over the white walls, thus changing everything for everyone.

The cardboard roof was detachable, and when he lifted it up he could look right into the rooms. All the interior walls were in place, there were doors and closets, in the kitchen there were cabinets, a refrigerator, a dishwasher, a range. Orcutt had gone so far as to install in the living room tiny pieces of furniture also fashioned out of cardboard, a library table by the western wall of windows, a sofa, end tables, an ottoman, two club chairs, a coffee table in front of a raised fireplace hearth that extended the width of the room. In the bedroom, across from the bay window, where there were the built-in drawers—Shaker drawers, Dawn called them—was the large bed, awaiting its two occupants. On the wall to either side of the headboard were built-in shelves for books. Orcutt had made some books and put them on the shelves, miniaturized books fashioned out of cardboard. They even had titles on them. He was good at all this. Better at this, thought the Swede, than at the painting. Yes, wouldn't life be so much less futile if we could do it at the scale of one-sixteenth inch to a foot? The only thing missing from the bedroom was a cardboard cock with Orcutt's name on it. Orcutt should have made a sixteenth-inch scale model of Dawn on her stomach, with her ass in the air and, from behind, his cock going in. It would have been nice for the Swede to have found that, too, while he stood over her desk, looking down at Dawn's cardboard dreaming and absorbing the fury of Rita Cohen.

What does Rita Cohen have to do with Jainism? What does one thing have to do with the other? No, Merry, it does *not* hang together. What does any of this ranting have to do with you, who will not even do harm to *water*? *Nothing* hangs together—*none* of it is linked up. It is only in your head that it is linked up. Nowhere else is there any logic.

She's been tracking Merry, trailing her, tracing her, but they're not connected and they never were! There's the logic!

"You've gone too far. You *go* too far. You think you are running the show, D-d-daddy? You are not running *anything!*"

But whether he was or wasn't running the show no longer mattered, because if Merry and Rita Cohen *were* connected, in any way, if Merry had lied to him about not knowing Rita Cohen, then she might as easily have been lying about being taken in by Sheila after the bombing. If that was so, when Dawn and Orcutt ran off to live in this cardboard house, he and Sheila could run off to Puerto Rico after all. And if, as a result, his father dropped dead, well, they'd just have to bury him. That's what they'd do: bury him deep in the ground.

(He was all at once remembering the death of his grandfather—what it did to his father. The Swede was a little kid, seven years old. His grandfather had been rushed to the hospital the evening before, and his father and his uncles sat at the old man's bedside all night long. When his father arrived home it was seven-thirty in the morning. The Swede's grandfather had died. His father got out of the car, went as far as the front steps of the house, and then just sat himself down. The Swede watched him from behind the living room curtains. His father did not move, even when the Swede's mother came out to comfort him. He sat without moving for over an hour, all the time leaning forward, his elbows on his knees and his face invisible in his hands. There was such a load of tears inside his head that he had to hold it like that in his two strong hands to prevent it from tumbling off of him. When he was able to raise the head up again, he got back in the car and drove to work.)

*Is* Merry lying? Is Merry brainwashed? Is Merry a lesbian? Is Rita the girlfriend? Is Merry running the whole insane thing? Are they out to do nothing but torture me? Is that the game, the entire game, to torture and torment me?

No, Merry's not lying—Merry is *right*. Rita Cohen does not exist. If Merry believes it, I believe it. He did not have to listen to somebody who did not exist. The drama she'd constructed did not exist. Her hateful accusations did not exist. Her authority did not exist, her power. If she did not exist, she could not *have* any power. Could Merry have these religious beliefs *and* Rita Cohen? You had only to listen to Rita Cohen howling into the phone to know that she was someone to whom there was no sacred form of life on earth *or* in heaven. What does she have to do with self-starvation and Mahatma Gandhi and Martin Luther King? She does not exist because she does not fit in. These are not even her words. These are not a young girl's words. There are no *grounds* for these words. This is an imitation of someone. Someone has been telling her what to do and what to say. From the beginning this has all been an act. She's an act; she did not arrive at this by herself. Someone is behind her, someone corrupt and cynical and distorted who sets these kids to do these things, who strips a Rita Cohen and a Merry Levov of everything good that was their inheritance and lures them into this *act*.

"*You* are going to take her back to all your dopey pleasures? Take her from her holiness into that shallow, soulless excuse for a life? Yours is the lowest species on this earth—don't you know that *yet*? Are you really able to believe that *you*, with your conception of life, you basking unpunished in the crime of your wealth, have anything whatsoever to offer *this woman*? Just exactly what? A life of bad faith lived to the hilt, that's what, the ultimate in bloodsucking propriety! Don't you know who this woman *is*? Don't you realize what this woman has *become*? Don't you have any inkling of what she is in *communion* with?" The perennial indictment of the middle class, from somebody who did not exist; the celebration of his daughter's degradation and the excoriation of his class: Guilty!— according to somebody who did not exist. "*You* are going to take her away from *me*? You, who felt *sick* when you saw her? Sick because she refuses to be captured in your shitty little moral universe? Tell me, Swede—how did you get so smart?"

He hung up. Dawn has Orcutt, I have Sheila, Merry has Rita or she doesn't have Rita—*Can Rita stay for dinner? Can Rita stay overnight? Can Rita wear my boots? Mom, can you drive me and Rita to the village?*—and my father drops dead. If it has to be, it has to be. He got over *his* father's dying, I'll get over *my* father's dying. I'll get over everything. I do not care what meaning it has or what meaning it doesn't have, whether it fits or whether it doesn't fit— they are not dealing with me anymore. *I* don't exist. They are dealing now with an irresponsible person; they are dealing with someone who does not care. *Can Rita and I blow up the post office?* Yes. Whatever you want, dear. And whoever dies, dies.

Madness and provocation. Nothing recognizable. Nothing plausible. No context in which it hangs together. *He* no longer hangs together. Even his capacity for suffering no longer exists.

A great idea takes hold of him: his capacity for suffering no longer exists.

But that idea, however great, did not make it out of the room with him. Never should have hung up—never. She'd make him pay a huge price for that. Six foot three, forty-six years old, a multimillion-dollar business, and broken for a second time by a ruthless, pint-sized slut. This is his enemy and she *does* exist. But where did she come from? Why does she write me, phone, strike out at me—what does she have to do with my poor broken girl? Nothing!

Once again she leaves him soaked with sweat, his head a ringing globe of pain; the entire length of his body is suffused with a fatigue so extreme that it feels like the onset of death, and yet his enemy evinces little more substance than a mythical monster. Not a shadow enemy exactly, *not* nothing—but what then? A courier. Yes. Does her number on him, indicts him, exploits him, eludes him, resists him, brings him to a total bewildered standstill by saying whatever mad words come into her head, encircles him in her lunatic clichés and is in and out like a courier. But a courier from whom? From where?

He knows nothing about her. Except that she expresses perfectly the stupidity of her kind. Except that he is still her villain, that her hatred of him is resolute. Except that she's now twenty-seven. Not a kid anymore. A woman. But grotesquely fixed in her position. Behaves like a mechanism of human parts, like a loudspeaker, human parts assembled as a loudspeaker designed to produce shattering sound, a sound that is disruptive and maddening. After five years the change is only in the direction of more of the same sound. The deterioration of Merry comes as Jainism; the deterioration of Rita Cohen comes as *more*. He knows nothing about her except that she needs more than ever to be in charge—to be more and more and more *unexpected*. He knows he is dealing with an unbending destroyer, with something big in someone very small. Five years have passed. Rita is back. Something is up. Something unimaginable is about to happen again.

He would never get across the line that was tonight. Ever since leaving Merry in that cell, behind that veil, he has known that he's no longer a man who can endlessly forestall being crushed.

I am done with craving and selfhood. Thanks to you.

Someone opened the study door. "Are you all right?" It was Sheila Salzman.

"What do you want?"

She pulled the door shut behind her and came into the room. "You looked ill at dinner. Now you look even worse."

Over Dawn's desk was a framed photograph of Count. All the blue ribbons Count won were pinned to the wall on either side of the picture. It was the same picture of Count that used to appear in Dawn's annual ad in the Simmental breeder's magazine. Merry had been the one to choose the slogan for the ad from the three Dawn had proposed to them in the kitchen after dinner one night. COUNT CAN DO WONDERFUL THINGS FOR YOUR HERD. IF EVER THERE WAS A BULL TO USE, IT'S COUNT. A BULL UPON WHICH A HERD CAN BE BUILT. Merry at first argued for a suggestion of her own— YOU CAN COUNT ON COUNT—but after Dawn and the Swede each made the case against it, Merry chose A BULL UPON WHICH A HERD CAN BE BUILT, and that became the slogan for Arcady Breeders for as long as Count was Dawn's stylish superstar.

On the desk there used to be a snapshot of Merry, age thirteen, standing at the head of their long-bodied prize bull, the Golden Certified Meat Sire, holding him by a leather lead shank clipped into his nose ring. As a 4-H kid she'd been taught how to lead and walk and wash and handle a bull, first a yearling, but then the big boys, and Dawn had taught her how to show Count—to hold her hand up on the strap so that his head was up and to keep a bit of tension on the lead and move it a little with her hand, first so as to show Count off to advantage but also to be in communication with him so that he'd listen a little more than he might if her hand was slack and down at her side. Even though Count wasn't difficult or arrogant, Dawn taught Merry never to trust him. He could sometimes have a strong attitude, even with Merry and Dawn, the two people he was most used to in the world. In just that photograph—a picture he'd loved in the same way he'd loved the picture that had appeared on page one of the *Denville-Randolph Courier* of Dawn in her blazer at the fireplace mantel—he could see all that Dawn had patiently taught Merry and all that Merry had eagerly learned from her. But it was gone, as was the sentimental memento of Dawn's childhood, a photograph of the charming wooden bridge down at Spring Lake that led across the lake to St. Catherine's, a picture taken in the spring sunshine, with the azaleas in bloom at either end of the bridge and, resplendent in the background, the weathered copper dome of the grand church itself, where, as a kid, she had liked to imagine herself a bride in a white bridal gown. All there was on Dawn's desk now was Orcutt's cardboard model.

"Is this the new house?" Sheila asked him.

"You bitch."

She did not move; she looked directly back at him but did not speak or move. He could take Count's picture off the wall and bludgeon her over the head with it and she would *still* be unruffled, still somehow deprive him of a heartfelt response. Five years earlier, for four months, they had been lovers. Why tell him the truth now if she was able to withhold it from him even then?

"Leave me alone," he said.

But when she turned to do as he gruffly requested, he grabbed her arm and swung her flat against the closed door. "You took her in." The force of the rage was in no way concealed by the whisper that rasped up from his throat. Her skull was locked between his hands. Her head had been held in his powerful grip before but never, never like this. "You took her in!"

"Yes."

"You never told me!"

She did not answer.

"I could kill you!" he said, and, immediately upon saying it, let her go.

"You've seen her," Sheila said. Her hands neatly folded before her. That nonsensical calm, only moments after he had threatened to kill her. All that ridiculous self-control. Always that ridiculous, careful, self-controlled thinking.

"You know everything," he snarled.

"I know what you've been through. What can be done for her?"

"By *you*? Why did you let her go? She went to your house. She'd blown up a building. You knew all about it—why didn't you call me, get in touch with me?"

"I didn't know about it. I found out later that night. But when she came to me she was just beside herself. She was upset and I didn't know why. I thought something had happened at home."

"But you knew within the next few hours. How long was she with you? Two days, three days?"

"Three. She left on the third day."

"So you knew what happened."

"I found out later. I couldn't believe it, but—"

"It was on television."

"But she was in my house by then. I had already promised her that I would help her. And that there was no problem she could tell me that I couldn't keep to myself. She asked me to trust her. That was before I watched the news. How could I betray her then? I'd been her therapist, she'd been my client. I'd always wanted to do what was in her best interest. What was the alternative? For her to get arrested?"

"Call me. That was the alternative. Call her father. If you had gotten to me right there and then, and said, 'She's safe, don't worry about her,' and then not let her out of your sight—"

"She was a big girl. How can you not let her out of your sight?"

"You lock her in the house and keep her there."

"She's not an animal. She's not like a cat or a bird that you can keep in a cage. She was going to do whatever she was going to do. We had a trust, Seymour, and violating her trust at that point . . . I wanted her to know that there was someone in this world she could trust."

"*At that moment, trust was not what she needed! She needed me!*"

"But I was sure that your house was where they'd be looking. What good was calling you? I couldn't drive her out here. I even started thinking they would know she would be at my house. All of a sudden it seemed like it was the most obvious place for her to be. I started thinking *my* phone was bugged. How could I call you?"

"You could have somehow made contact."

"When she first came she was agitated, something had gone wrong, she was just yelling about the war and her family. I thought something terrible had happened at home. Something terrible had happened to *her*. She wasn't the same, Seymour. Something very wrong had happened to that girl. She was talking as if she hated you so. I couldn't imagine . . . but sometimes you start to believe the worst about people. I think maybe that's what I was trying to figure out when we were together."

"What? What are you talking about?"

"Could there really be something wrong? Could there really be something that she was subjected to that could lead her to something like that? I was confused too. I want you to know that I never really believed it and I didn't want to believe it. But of course I had to wonder. Anyone would have."

"And? And? Having had an affair with me—what the hell did you find out, having had your little affair with me?"

"That you're kind and compassionate. That you do just about everything you can to be an intelligent, decent person. Just as I would have imagined before she'd blown up that building. Seymour, believe me, please, I just wanted her to be safe. So I took her in. And got her showered and clean. And gave her a place to sleep. I really had no idea—"

"She blew up a building, Sheila! Somebody was killed! It was all over the goddamn television!"

"But I didn't know until I turned on the TV."

"So at six o'clock at night you knew. She was there for three days. And you do not contact me."

"What good would it have done to contact you?"

"I'm her father."

"You're her father and she blew up a building. What good was it going to do bringing her back to you?"

"Don't you grasp what I'm saying? She's my daughter!"

"She's a very strong girl."

"Strong enough to look after herself in the world? No!"

"Turning her over to you wasn't going to help any. She wasn't going to sit and eat her peas and mind her business. You don't go from blowing up a building to—"

"It was your duty to tell me that she came to your house."

"I just thought that would make it easier for them to find her. She'd come so far, she'd gotten so much stronger, I thought that she could make it on her own. She *is* a strong girl, Seymour."

"She's a crazy girl."

"She's troubled."

"Oh, Christ! The father plays no role with the troubled daughter?"

"I'm sure he played plenty of a role. That was why I couldn't . . . I just thought something terrible had happened at home."

"Something terrible happened at the general store."

"But you should have seen her—she'd gotten so fat."

"I should have *seen* her? Where do you think she'd been? It was your responsibility to get in touch with her parents! Not to let the child run off into nowhere! She never needed me more. She never needed her father more. And you're telling me she never needed him less. You made a terrible error. I hope you know it. A terrible, terrible error."

"What could you have done for her then? What could anyone have done for her then?"

"I deserved to know. I had a right to know. She's a minor. She's my daughter. You had an obligation to get to me."

"My first obligation was to her. She was my client."

"She was no longer your client."

"She had been my client. A very special client. She'd come so far. My first obligation was to her. How could I violate her confidence? The damage had already been done."

"I don't believe you are saying any of this."

"It's the law."

"What's the law?"

"That you don't betray your client's confidence."

"There's another law, idiot—a law against committing murder! She was a fugitive from justice!"

"Don't talk about her like that. Of course she ran. What else could she do? I thought that maybe she would turn herself in. But that she would do it in her own time. In her own way."

"And me? And her mother?"

"Well, it killed me to see you."

"You saw me for four months. It killed you every day?"

"Each time I thought that maybe it would make a difference if I let you know. But I didn't see what difference it would really make. It wouldn't change anything. You were already so broken."

"You are an inhuman bitch."

"There was nothing else I could do. She asked me not to tell. She asked me to trust her."

"I don't understand how you could be so shortsighted. I don't understand how you could be so taken in by a girl who was so obviously crazy."

"I know it's difficult to face. The whole thing is impossible to understand. But to try to pin it on me, to try to act like anything I could have done would have made a difference—it wouldn't have made a difference in her life, it wouldn't have made a difference in your life. She was running. There was no bringing her back there. She wasn't the same girl that she'd been. Something had gone wrong. I saw no point in bringing her back. She'd gotten so fat."

"Stop that! What difference did *that* make!"

"I just thought she was so fat and so angry that something very bad must have gone on at home."

"That it was my fault."

"I didn't think that. We all have homes. That's where everything always goes wrong."

"So you took it on yourself to let this sixteen-year-old who had killed somebody run off into the night. Alone. Unprotected. Knowing God knows what could happen to her."

"You're talking about her as if she were a defenseless girl."

"She *is* a defenseless girl. She was *always* a defenseless girl."

"Once she'd blown up the building there's nothing that could have been done, Seymour. I would have betrayed her confidence and what difference would it have made?"

"I would have been with my daughter! I could have protected her from what has happened to her! You don't know what has happened to her. You didn't see her the way I saw her today. She's completely crazy. I saw her today, Sheila. She's not fat anymore—she's a stick, a stick wearing a rag. She's in a room in Newark in the most awful situation imaginable. I cannot describe to you how she lives. If you had only told me, it would all be different!"

"We wouldn't have had an affair—that's all that would have been different. Of course I knew that you might be hurt."

"By what?"

"By my having seen her. But to bring it all up again? I didn't know where she was. I didn't have any more information on her. That's the whole thing. She wasn't crazy. She was upset. She was angry. But she wasn't crazy."

"It's not crazy to blow up the general store? It's not crazy to make a bomb, to plant a bomb in the post office of the general store?"

"I'm saying that at my house she wasn't crazy."

"She'd already *been* crazy. You *knew* she'd been crazy. What if she went on to kill somebody else? Isn't that a bit of a responsibility? She did, you know. She did, Sheila. She killed three more people. What do you think of that?"

"Don't say things just to torture me."

"I'm telling you something! She killed three more people! You could have prevented that!"

"You're torturing me. You're trying to torture me."

"She killed three more people!" And that was when he pulled Count's picture off the wall and hurled it at her feet. But that did not faze her—that seemed only to bring her under her own control again. Acting the role of herself, without rage, without even a reaction, dignified, silent, she turned and left the room.

"What can be *done* for her?" he was growling, and all the while, down on his knees, carefully gathering together the shattered fragments of the glass and dumping them into Dawn's wastebasket. "What can be done for her? What can be done for *anyone? Nothing* can be done. She was sixteen. Sixteen years old and completely crazy. She was a minor. She was my daughter. She blew up a building. She was a lunatic. You had no *right* to let her go!"

Without its glass, the picture of the immovable Count he hung again over the desk, and then, as though listening to people unabatedly chattering on about something or other were the task assigned him by the forces of destiny, he returned from the savagery of where he'd been to the solid and orderly ludicrousness of a dinner party. That's what was left to hold him together—a dinner party. All there was for him to cling to as the entire enterprise of his life continued careering toward destruction—a dinner party.

To the candlelit terrace he duteously returned, while bearing within him everything that he could not understand.

*

Dishes had been cleared, the salad eaten, and dessert served, fresh strawberry-rhubarb pie from McPherson's. The Swede saw that the guests had rearranged themselves for the last course. Orcutt, hiding still the vicious shit that he was behind the Hawaiian shirt and the raspberry trousers, had moved across the table and sat talking with the Umanoffs, all of them amiable and laughing together now that *Deep Throat* was off the agenda. *Deep Throat* had never been the real subject anyway. Boiling away beneath *Deep Throat* was the far more disgusting and transgressive subject of Merry, of Sheila, of Shelly, of Orcutt and Dawn, of wantonness and betrayal and deception, of treachery and disunity among neighbors and friends, the subject of cruelty. The mockery of human integrity, every ethical obligation destroyed—that was the subject here tonight!

The Swede's mother had come around to sit beside Dawn, who was talking with the Salzmans, and his father and Jessie were nowhere to be seen.

Dawn asked, "Important?"

"The Czech guy. The consul. The information I wanted. Where's my dad?"

He waited for her to say "Dead," but after she looked around she mouthed only "Don't know" and turned back to Shelly and Sheila.

"Daddy left with Mrs. Orcutt," his mother whispered. "They went somewhere together. I think in the house."

Orcutt came up to him. They were the same size, both big men, but the Swede had always been the stronger, going back to their twenties, to when Merry was born and the Levovs moved out to Old Rimrock from their apartment on Elizabeth Avenue in Newark and the newcomer had showed up for the Saturday morning touch-football games back of Orcutt's house. Out there just for the fun of it, to enjoy the fresh air and the feel of the ball and the camaraderie, to make some new friends, the Swede had not the slightest inclination to appear showy or superior, except when he simply had no choice: when Orcutt, who off the field had never been other than kind and considerate, began to use his hands more recklessly than the Swede considered sportsmanlike—in a way that the Swede considered cheap and irritating, for a pickup game the worst sort of behavior even if Orcutt's team did happen to have fallen behind. After it had occurred for two weeks in a row, he decided the third week to do what he of course could have done at any time—to dump him. And so, near the end of the game, with a single, swift maneuver—employing the other person's weight to do the damage—he managed at once to catch a long pass from Bucky Robinson and to make sure Orcutt was sprawled in the grass at his feet, before he pranced away to pile on the score. Pranced away and thought, of all things, "I don't like being looked down on," the words that Dawn had used to decline joining The Orcutt Family Cemetery Tour. He had not realized, not till he was speeding alone toward the goal line, how much Dawn's assailability had gotten to him nor how unsettled he was by the remotest likelihood (a likelihood that, to her face, he had dismissed) of his wife's being ridiculed out here for growing up in Elizabeth the daughter of an Irish plumber. When, after scoring, he turned around and saw Orcutt still on the ground, he thought, "Two hundred years of Morris County history, flat on its ass—that'll teach you to look down on Dawn Levov. Next time you'll play the whole *game* on your ass," before trotting back up the field to see if Orcutt was all right.

The Swede knew that once he got him on the floor of the terrace he would have no difficulty in slamming Orcutt's head against the flagstones as many times as might be required to get him into that cemetery with his distinguished clan. Yes, something is wrong with this guy, there always was, and the Swede had known it all along— knew it from those terrible paintings, knew it from the reckless use of his hands in a backyard pickup game, knew it even at the cemetery, when for one solid hour Orcutt got to goyishly regale a Jewish sightseer. . . . Yes, big dissatisfaction there right from the start. Dawn said it was art, modern art, when all the time, baldly displayed on their living room wall, was William Orcutt's dissatisfaction. But now he has my wife. Instead of that misfortune Jessie, he's got revamped and revitalized Miss New Jersey of 1949. Got it made, got it *all* now, the greedy, thieving son of a bitch.

"Your father's a good man," Orcutt said. "Jessie doesn't usually get all this attention when she goes out. It's why she doesn't go out. He's a very generous man. He doesn't hold anything back, does he? Nothing left undisclosed. You get the whole person. Unguarded. Unashamed. Works himself up. It's wonderful. An amazing person, really. A huge presence. Always himself. Coming from where I do, you have to envy all that."

Oh, I'll bet you do, you son of a bitch. Laugh at us, you fucker. Just keep laughing.

"Where are they?" the Swede asked.

"He told her there's only one way to eat a fresh piece of pie. That's sitting at a kitchen table with a nice cold glass of milk. I guess they're in the kitchen with the milk. Jessie's learning a lot more about making a glove than she may ever need to know, but that's all right too. No harm in that. I hope you didn't mind that I couldn't leave her home."

"We wouldn't want you to leave her home."

"You're all very understanding."

"I was looking at the model of your house," the Swede told him, "in Dawn's study." But what he was looking at was a mole on the left side of Orcutt's face, a dark mole buried in the crease that ran from his nose to the corner of his mouth. Along with the snout nose Orcutt had an ugly mole. Does she find the mole appealing? Does she kiss the mole? Doesn't she ever find this guy just a wee bit fat in the face? Or, when it comes to an upper-class Old Rimrock boy, is she as unmindful of his looks, as unperturbed, as professionally detached as the whorehouse ladies over in Easton?

"Uh-oh," said Orcutt, amiably feigning how uncertain he was. Uses his hands when he plays football, wears those shirts, paints those paintings, fucks his neighbor's wife, and manages through it all to maintain himself as the ever-reasonable unknowable man. All façade and subterfuge. *He works so hard*, Dawn said, *at being one-dimensional.* Up top the gentleman, underneath the rat. Drink the devil that lurks in his wife; lust and rivalry the devils lurking in him. Sealed and civilized and predatory. To reinforce the genealogical aggression—the overpowering by origins—the aggression of scrupulous manners. The humane environmentalist and the calculating predator, protecting what he has by birthright and taking surreptitiously what he doesn't have. The civilized savagery of William Orcutt. His civilized form of animal behavior. I prefer the cows. "It's supposed to be seen *after* dinner—with the spiel," Orcutt said. "Did it make any sense without the spiel?" he asked. "I wouldn't think so."

But of course—being unknowable is the *goal.* Then you move instrumentally through life, appropriating the beautiful wives. In the kitchen he should have hit those two over the head with a skillet.

"It did. A lot," the Swede said. And then, as he could never stop himself from doing with Orcutt, he added, "It's interesting. I get the idea now about the light. I get the idea of the light washing over those walls. That's going to be something to see. I think you're going to be very happy in it."

Orcutt laughed. "You, you mean."

But the Swede had not heard his own error. He hadn't heard it because of the huge thought that had just come at him: what he should have done and failed to do.

He should have overpowered her. He should not have left her there. Jerry was right. Drive to Newark. Leave immediately. Take Barry. The two of them could subdue her and bring her back in the car to Old Rimrock. And if Rita Cohen is there? I'll kill her. If she is anywhere near my daughter, I'll pour gasoline all over that hair and set the little cunt on fire. Destroying my daughter. Showing me her pussy. Destroying my child. *There's* the meaning—they are destroying her for the pleasure of *destroying* her. Take Sheila. Take Sheila. Calm down. Take Sheila to Newark. Merry listens to Sheila. Sheila will talk to her and get her out of that room.

"—leave it to our visiting intellectual to get everything wrong. The complacent rudeness with which she plays the old French game of beating up on the bourgeoisie. . . ." Orcutt was confiding to the Swede his amusement with Marcia's posturing. "It's to her credit, I suppose, that she doesn't defer to the regulation dinner-party discipline of not saying anything about anything. But still it's amazing, constantly amazes me, how emptiness always goes with cleverness. She hasn't the faintest idea, really, of what she's talking about. Know what my father used to say? 'All brains and no intelligence. The smarter the stupider.' Applies."

Not Dawn? No. Dawn wanted nothing further to do with their catastrophe. She was just biding her time with him until the house was built. Go and do it yourself. *Get back in the fucking car and get her. Do you love her or don't you love her? You're acceding to her the way you acceded to your father, the way you have acceded to everything in your life. You're afraid of letting the beast out of the bag. Quite a critique she has made of decorum. You keep yourself a secret. You don't choose ever!* But how could he bring Merry home, now, tonight, in that veil, with his father here? If his father were to see her, he'd expire on the spot. To where else then? Where would he take her? Could the two of *them* go live in Puerto Rico? Dawn wouldn't care where he went. As long as she had her Orcutt. He had to get her before she again set foot in that underpass. Forget Rita Cohen. Forget that inhuman idiot Sheila Salzman. Forget Orcutt. He does not matter. Find a place for Merry to live where there is not that underpass. That's *all* that matters. Start with the underpass. Save her from getting herself killed in the underpass. Before the morning, before she has even left her room—*start there.*

He had been cracking up in the only way he knew how, which is not really cracking up at all but sinking, all evening long being unmade by steadily sinking under the weight. A man who never goes full out and explodes, who only sinks . . . but now it was clear what to do. Go get her out of there before dawn.

After Dawn. After Dawn life was inconceivable. There was nothing he could do without Dawn. But she wanted Orcutt. "That Wasp blandness," she'd said, all but yawning to make her point. But that blandness had terrific glamour for a little Irish Catholic girl. The mother of Merry Levov needs nothing less than William Orcutt III. The cuckolded husband understands. Of course. Understands everything now. Who will get her back to the dream of where she has always wanted to go? Mr. America. Teamed up with Orcutt she'll be back on the track. Spring Lake, Atlantic City, now Mr. America. Rid of the stain of our child, the stain on her credentials, rid of the stain of the destruction of the store, she can begin to resume the uncontaminated life. But I was stopped at the general store. And she knows it. Knows that I am allowed in no farther. I'm of no use anymore. This is as far as she goes with me.

He brought a chair around, sat himself down between his wife and his mother, and, even as Dawn spoke, took her hand in his. There are a hundred different ways to hold someone's hand. There are the ways you hold a child's hand, the ways you hold a friend's hand, the ways you hold an elderly parent's hand, the ways you hold the hands of the departing and of the dying and of the dead. He held Dawn's hand the way a man holds the hand of a woman he adores, with all that excitement passing into his grip, as though pressure on the palm of the hand effects a transference of souls, as though the interlinking of fingers symbolizes every intimacy. He held Dawn's hand as though he possessed no information about the condition of his life.

But then he thought: She wants to be back with me, too. But she can't because it's all too awful. What else can she do? She must think she's poison. She gave birth to a murderer. She *has* to put on a new crown.

He should have listened to his father and never married her. He had defied him, just that one time, but that was all it had taken— that did it. His father had said, "There are hundreds and thousands of lovely Jewish girls, but you have to find *her*. You found one down in South Carolina, Dunleavy, and finally you saw the light and got rid of her. So now you come home and find Dwyer up here. *Why,* Seymour?" The Swede could not say to him, "The girl in South Carolina was beautiful, but not half as beautiful as Dawn." He could not say to him, "The authority of beauty is a very irrational thing." He was twenty-three years old and could only say, "I'm in love with her."

"'In love,' what does that mean? What is 'in love' going to do for you when you have a child? How are you going to raise a child? As a Catholic? As a Jew? No, you are going to raise a child who won't be one thing or the other—all because you are 'in love'."

His father was right. That was what happened. They raised a child who was neither Catholic nor Jew, who instead was first a stutterer, then a killer, then a Jain. He had tried all his life never to do the wrong thing, and that was what he had done. All the wrongness that he had locked away in himself, that he had buried as deep as a man could bury it, had come out anyway, because a girl was beautiful. The most serious thing in his life, seemingly from the time he was *born,* was to prevent the suffering of those he loved, to be kind to people, a kind person through and through. That was why he had brought Dawn to meet secretly with his father at the factory office—to try to resolve the religious impasse and avoid making either of them unhappy. The meeting had been suggested by his father: face to face, between "the girl," as Lou Levov charitably referred to her around the Swede, and "the ogre," as the girl called him. Dawn hadn't been afraid; to the Swede's astonishment she agreed. "I walked out on that runway in a bathing suit, didn't I? It wasn't easy, in case you didn't know. Twenty-five thousand people. It's not a very dignified feeling, in a bright white bathing suit and bright white high heels, being looked at by twenty-five thousand people. I appeared in a *parade* in a bathing suit. In Camden. Fourth of July. I had to. I hated that day. My father almost died. But I did it. I taped the back of that damn bathing suit to my skin, Seymour, so it wouldn't ride up on me—masking tape on my own behind. I felt like a *freak.* But I took the job of Miss New Jersey and so I did the work. A very tiring job. Every town in the state. Fifty dollars an appearance. But if you work hard, the money adds up, so I did it. Working hard at something totally different that scared me to death—but I did it. The Christmas I broke the news to my parents about Miss Union County—you think that was fun? *But I did it.* And if I could do all that, I can do this, because this isn't being a silly girl on a float, this is my *life,* my entire *future.* This is for *keeps!* But you'll be there, won't you? I cannot go there by myself. You *have* to be there!"

She was so incredibly gutsy there was no choice but to say, "Where else would I be?" On the way down to the factory, he warned her not to mention rosary beads or the cross or heaven and to stay away from Jesus as much as possible. "If he asks if there are any crosses hanging in the house, say no." "But that's a lie. I can't say no." "Then say one." "That's a lie." "Dawnie, it won't help anything if you say three. One is just the same as three. It gets your point over. Say it. For me. Say one." "We'll see." "And you don't have to mention the other stuff." "What other stuff?" "The Virgin Mary." "That is not *stuff.*" "The statues. Okay? Just forget it. If he asks, 'Do you have any statues?' just tell him no, just tell him, 'We don't have statues, we don't have pictures, the one cross and that's it.'" Religious ornaments, he explained, statues like those in her dining room and her mother's bedroom, pictures like those her mother had on the walls were sore subjects with his father. He wasn't defending his father's position. He was just explaining that the man had been brought up a certain way, and that's the way he was, and there was nothing anybody could do about it, so why stir him up?

Opposing the father is no picnic and not opposing the father is no picnic—that's what he was discovering.

Anti-Semitism was another sore subject. Watch out what you say about Jews. Best to say nothing about Jews. And stay away from priests, don't talk about priests. "Don't tell him that story about your father and the priests when he was a caddie at the country club as a kid." "Why would I ever tell him that?" "I don't know, but don't go near it." "*Why?*" "I don't *know*—just *don't.*"

But he knew why. Because if she told him that the first time her father realized priests had genitals was in the locker room when he used to caddie on weekends, that up until then he didn't even think they were *anatomically* sexual, his own father might very well be tempted to ask her, "You know what they do with the foreskins of the little Jewish boys after the circumcision?" And she would have to say, "I don't know, Mr. Levov. What *do* they do with the fore-skins?" and Mr. Levov would reply—the joke was one of his favor-ites—"They send them to Ireland. They wait till they got enough of them, they collect them all together, then they send them to Ireland and they make priests out of them."

It was a conversation the Swede would never forget, and not so much because of what his father said—all that he'd expected. It was Dawn who made it an unforgettable exchange. Her truthful-ness, how she had not seriously fudged about her parents or about anything that he knew was important to her—her courage was what was unforgettable.

She was more than a full foot shorter than her fiancé and, according to one of the judges who'd confided in Danny Dwyer after the pageant, had failed to be in the top ten in Atlantic City only because without her high heels she measured five foot two and a half, in a year when half a dozen other girls equally talented and pretty were positively statuesque. This petiteness (which may or may not have disqualified her from a serious shot at runner-up—it hardly explained to the Swede's satisfaction why Miss Arizona should walk off winner of the whole shebang at only five *three*) had simply deepened the Swede's devotion to Dawn. In a youngster as innately dutiful as the Swede—and a handsome boy always making the extra effort not to be mistaken for the owner of his startling good looks—Dawn's being only five foot two quickened in him a manly urge to shield and to shelter. Up until that drawn-out, drain-ing negotiation between Dawn and his father, he'd had no idea he was in love with a girl as strong as this. He even wondered if he *wanted* to be in love with a girl as strong as this.

Aside from the number of crosses in her house, the only other thing she lied about outright was the baptism, an issue on which she finally appeared to capitulate, but only after three solid hours of negotiations during which it seemed to the Swede that, amazingly enough, his *father* had yielded on that issue almost right off the bat. Not until later did he realize that his father had deliberately let the negotiation string out until the twenty-two-year-old girl was at the end of her strength and *then*, shifting by a hundred and eighty degrees his position on baptism, wrapped up the deal giving her only Christmas Eve, Christmas Day, and the Easter bonnet.

But after Merry was born, Dawn got the child baptized anyway. She could have performed the baptism herself or got her mother to do it but she wanted the real thing, and so she got a priest and some godparents and took the baby to the church, and until Lou Levov happened to come upon the baptismal certificate in a dresser in the unused back bedroom of the Old Rimrock house, no one ever knew—only the Swede, whom Dawn told in the evening, after the freshly baptized baby had been put to bed cleansed of original sin and bound for heaven. By the time the baptismal certificate was unearthed, Merry was a family treasure six years old, and the up-roar was short-lived. Though that didn't mean that the Swede's father could shake the conviction that what lay behind Merry's dif-ficulties all along was the secret baptism: that, and the Christmas tree, and the Easter bonnet, enough for that poor kid *never* to know who she was. That and her grandma Dwyer—she didn't help either. Seven years after Merry was born, Dawn's father had the second heart attack, dropped dead while installing a furnace, and from then on there was no dragging Grandma Dwyer out of St. Genevieve's. Every time she could get her hands on Merry, she spirited the child off to church, and God alone knew what they pumped into her there. The Swede, far more confident with his father—about this, about everything, really, than he'd been before becoming a father himself—would tell him, "Dad, Merry takes it all with a grain of salt. It's just Grandma to her, and what Grandma does. Going to church with Dawn's mother doesn't mean a thing to Merry either way." But his father wasn't buying it. "She kneels, doesn't she? They're up there doing all that stuff, and Merry is kneeling—right?" "Well, sure, I guess so, sure, she kneels. But it doesn't *mean* any-thing to her." "Yeah? Well it does to me—it means plenty!"

Lou Levov backed off—that is, with his son—from attributing Merry's screaming to the baptism. But alone with his wife he wasn't so cautious, and when he was riled up about "some Catholic crap" the Dwyer woman had inflicted on his granddaughter, he wondered aloud if it wasn't the secret baptism that all along lay behind the screaming that scared the hell out of the whole family during Merry's first year. Perhaps everything bad that *ever* happened to Merry, not excluding the *worst* thing that happened to her, had originated then and there.

She entered the world screaming and the screaming did not stop. The child opened her mouth so wide to scream that she broke the tiny blood vessels in her cheeks. At first the doctor figured it was colic, but when it went on for three months, another explanation was needed and Dawn took her for all kinds of tests, to all kinds of doctors—and Merry never disappointed you, she screamed there too. At one point Dawn even had to wring some urine out of the diaper to take it to the doctor for a test. They had happy-go-lucky Myra as their housekeeper then, a large, cheery bartender's daughter from Morristown's Little Dublin, and though she would pick up Merry and nestle her into that pillowy, plentiful bosom of hers and coo and coo at her as sweetly as though she were her own, if Merry was already off and screaming, Myra got results no better than Dawn's. There was nothing Dawn didn't try to outwit whatever mechanism triggered the screaming. When she took Merry with her to the supermarket, she made elaborate preparations beforehand, as though to *hypnotize* the child into a state of calm. Just to go out shopping, she would give her a bath and a nap, put her in nice clean clothes, get her all set in the car, wheel her around the store in the shopping cart—and everything might be going fine, until somebody came along and leaned over the cart and said, "Oh, what a cute baby," and that would be it: inconsolable for the next twenty-four hours. At dinnertime, Dawn would tell the Swede, "All that hard work for nothing. I'm going crazier and crazier. I'd stand on my *head* if it helped—but *nothing* helps." The home movie of Merry's first birthday showed everybody singing "Happy Birthday" and Merry, in her high chair, screaming. But only weeks later, for no apparent reason, the fury of the screaming began to ebb, then the frequency, and by the time she was one and a half, everything was wonderful and remained wonderful and went on being wonderful until the stuttering.

What had gone wrong for Merry was what her Jewish grandfather had known would go wrong from the morning of the meeting on Central Avenue. The Swede had sat in a chair in the corner of the office, well out of the line of fire; whenever Dawn said the name Jesus, he looked miserably through the glass at the hundred and twenty women working at the sewing machines on the floor—the rest of the time he looked at his feet. Lou Levov sat iron-faced at his desk, not his favorite desk, out amid the clamorous activity of the making department, but at the desk he rarely ever used, tucked away for the sake of quiet within the glass enclosure. And Dawn didn't cry, didn't go to pieces, and lied, really, hardly at all—just held her ground throughout, all sixty-two and a half inches of her. Dawn—whose only preparation for such a grilling was the Miss New Jersey prepageant interview, heavily weighted in the scoring, when she stood before five seated judges and answered questions about her biography—was sensational.

Here's the opening of the inquisition that the Swede never forgot:

WHAT IS YOUR FULL NAME, MISS DWYER?

Mary Dawn Dwyer.

DO YOU WEAR A CROSS AROUND YOUR NECK, MARY DAWN?

I have. In high school I did for a while.

SO YOU THINK OF YOURSELF AS A RELIGIOUS PERSON.

No. That isn't why I wore it. I wore it because I'd been to a retreat and when I got home I just started wearing a cross. It wasn't a huge religious symbol. It was just a sign really of having been to this weekend retreat, where I made a lot of friends. It was much more that than a sign of being a devout Catholic.

ANY CROSSES IN YOUR HOUSE? HANGING UP?

Only one.

IS YOUR MOTHER DEVOUT?

Well, she goes to church.

HOW OFTEN?

Often. Every Sunday. Without fail. And then there'll be times during Lent when they'll go every day.

AND WHAT DOES SHE GET OUT OF IT?

Get out of it? I don't know if I understand. She gets comfort. There's a comfort about being in a church. When my grandmother died she went to church a lot. When someone dies or someone is sick, it helps give you some kind of comfort. Something to do. You start saying your rosary for special intentions—

ROSARIES ARE THE BEADS?

Yes, sir.

AND YOUR MOTHER DOES THAT?

Well, sure.

I SEE. AND YOUR FATHER'S LIKE THAT TOO?

Like what?

DEVOUT.

Yes. Yes, he is. Going to church makes him feel like a good man. That he's doing his duty. My father is very conventional in terms of morality. He grew up with a much more extremely Catholic upbringing than I did. He's a workingman. He's a plumber. Oil heating. In his view the Church is a big powerful thing that makes you do what's right. He's someone who is very caught up in issues of right and wrong and being punished for doing wrong and the prohibitions against sex.

I WOULDN'T DISAGREE WITH THAT.

I don't think you would. You and my father aren't that different, when you come down to it.

EXCEPT THAT HE IS CATHOLIC. HE IS A DEVOUT CATHOLIC AND I AM A JEW. THAT'S NO SMALL DIFFERENCE.

Well, maybe it's not such a big difference either.

IT IS.

Yes, sir.

WHAT ABOUT JESUS AND MARY?

What about them?

WHAT DO YOU THINK ABOUT THEM?

As individuals? I don't think in terms of them as individuals. I do remember being little and telling my mother that I loved her more than anybody else, and she told me that wasn't right, I had to love God more.

GOD OR JESUS?

I think it was God. Maybe it was Jesus. But I didn't like it. I wanted to love her the most. Other than that, I can't remember any specific examples of Jesus as a person or an individual. The only time for me the people are real is when you do the Stations of the Cross on Good Friday and you follow Jesus up the hill to his crucifixion. That's a time when he becomes a real figure. And, of course, Jesus in the manger.

JESUS IN THE MANGER. WHAT DO YOU THINK ABOUT JESUS IN THE MANGER?

What do I think about it? I like little baby Jesus in the manger.

WHY?

Well, there's always something so pleasant and comforting about the scene. And important. This moment of humility. There's all that straw and little animals around, all cuddled up. It's just a nice, warming scene. You never imagine it as cold and windy out there. There's always some candles. Everyone's just adoring this little baby.

THAT'S ALL. EVERYBODY IS JUST ADORING THIS LITTLE BABY.

Yes. I don't see anything wrong with that.

AND WHAT ABOUT JEWS? LET'S GET DOWN TO BRASS TACKS, MARY DAWN. WHAT DO YOUR PARENTS SAY ABOUT JEWS?

(*Pause.*) Well, I don't hear much about Jews at home.

WHAT DO YOUR PARENTS SAY ABOUT JEWS? I WOULD LIKE AN ANSWER.

I think what's more remarkable than what I think you're getting at is that my mother might be aware that she doesn't like people for being Jewish but she doesn't realize that there are people who might not like her for being Catholic. One thing I didn't like, I remember, was that on Hillside Road one of my friends was Jewish, and I remember that I didn't like that I was going to go to heaven and she wasn't.

WHY WASN'T SHE GOING TO HEAVEN?

If you weren't Christian, you weren't going to heaven. It seemed very sad to me that Charlotte Waxman wasn't going to be up in heaven with me.

WHAT DOES YOUR MOTHER HAVE AGAINST JEWS, MARY DAWN?

Could you just call me Dawn, please?

WHAT DOES YOUR MOTHER HAVE AGAINST JEWS, DAWN?

Well, it isn't that Jews are Jews. It's that you're non-Catholics. To my parents you're just lumped with the Protestants.

WHAT DOES YOUR MOTHER HAVE AGAINST JEWS? ANSWER ME.

Well, the usual things you hear.

I DON'T HEAR THEM, DAWN. YOU'RE GOING TO HAVE TO TELL ME.

Well, mostly about being pushy. (*Pause.*) And materialistic. (*Pause.*) The term "Jewish lightning" would be used.

JEWISH LIGHT?

Jewish lightning.

WHAT DOES THAT MEAN?

You don't know what Jewish lightning is?

NOT YET.

When a fire is set for insurance purposes. There's lightning. You never heard that?

NO, THAT'S A NEW ONE ON ME.

You're shocked. I didn't mean to.

YES, I AM SHOCKED ALL RIGHT. BUT WE MIGHT AS WELL GET THIS OUT IN THE OPEN, DAWN. THAT IS WHAT WE ARE HERE FOR.

It wouldn't be all Jews. It would be New York Jews.

WHAT ABOUT NEW JERSEY JEWS?

(*Pause.*) Well, yes, I think they're probably a variant of New York Jews.

I SEE. TO JEWS IN UTAH IT DOESN'T APPLY, JEWISH LIGHT-NING. JEWS IN MONTANA. IS THAT RIGHT? IT DOESN'T APPLY TO JEWS IN MONTANA.

I don't know.

AND WHAT ABOUT YOUR FATHER AND JEWS? LET'S GET IT OUT IN THE OPEN AND SPARE EVERYBODY A LOT OF SUFFERING LATER ON.

Mr. Levov, even though those things are said, most of the time nothing is said. My family doesn't say very much about anything. Two or three times a year we go out to a restaurant, my father and my mother, my younger brother and me, and I'm always surprised when I look around and see all the other families talking away amongst themselves. We just sit there and eat.

YOU ARE CHANGING THE SUBJECT.

I'm sorry. I don't mean this as a way to excuse it, because I don't like it, but I'm only trying to say that it isn't even something they strongly feel. There's no real anger or hatred behind it. What I'm pointing out is that on rare occasions he uses the word "Jew" in a derogatory fashion. It isn't really an issue one way or another, but every once in a while something will come up. That is true.

AND HOW WOULD THEY FEEL ABOUT YOU MARRYING A JEW?

They feel about the same way you feel about your son marrying a Catholic. One of my cousins married a Jew. They might tease about it but it wasn't a big scandal. She was a little older, so everybody was glad, in a way, she found somebody.

SHE WAS SO OLD EVEN A JEW WOULD DO. HOW OLD WAS SHE, A HUNDRED?

She was thirty. But nobody was brought to tears. It's not a big deal until somebody wants to insult somebody.

AND THEN?

Well, then you might want to get in a snide remark if you were angry at the person. I don't think the issue of marrying a Jew is a huge deal necessarily.

UNTIL THE ISSUE OF WHAT TO RAISE THE KIDS AS.

Well, yes.

SO HOW WOULD YOU RESOLVE THIS ISSUE WITH YOUR PARENTS?

I'd have to resolve the issue with myself.

WHAT DOES THAT MEAN?

I would like my child baptized.

YOU WOULD LIKE THAT.

You can be as liberal as you want, Mr. Levov, but not when it comes to baptism.

WHAT IS BAPTISM? WHAT IS SO IMPORTANT ABOUT THAT?

Well, it's technically washing away original sin. But what it does, it gets the child into heaven if they die. Otherwise, if they die before they're baptized, they just go into limbo.

WELL, WE WOULDN'T WANT THAT. LET ME ASK YOU SOMETHING ELSE. SUPPOSE I SAY OKAY, YOU CAN BAPTIZE THE CHILD. WHAT ELSE WOULD YOU WANT?

I guess when the time came, I'd want my children to make their first communion. There are the sacraments, you see—

SO ALL YOU WANT IS THE BAPTISM, SO IF THE KID DIES IT GETS INTO HEAVEN AS FAR AS YOU'RE CONCERNED, AND THE FIRST COMMUNION. EXPLAIN TO ME WHAT THAT IS.

It's the first time we take the Eucharist.

AND WHAT IS THAT?

This is my body, this is my blood—

THIS IS ABOUT JESUS?

Yes. You don't know that? You know, when everybody kneels. "This is my body, eat of it. This is my blood, drink of it." And then you say "My Lord and my God" and eat the body of Christ.

I CAN'T GO THAT FAR. I'M SORRY, I CANNOT GO THAT FAR.

Well, as long as there's baptism, we'll worry about the rest later. Why don't we leave it up to the child when the time comes?

I'D RATHER NOT LEAVE IT UP TO A CHILD, DAWN. I'D RATHER MAKE THE DECISION MYSELF. I DON'T WANT TO LEAVE IT UP TO A CHILD TO DECIDE TO EAT JESUS. I HAVE THE HIGHEST RESPECT FOR WHATEVER YOU DO, BUT MY GRANDCHILD IS NOT GOING TO EAT JESUS. I'M SORRY. THAT IS OUT OF THE QUESTION. HERE'S WHAT I'LL DO FOR YOU. I'LL GIVE YOU THE BAPTISM. THAT'S ALL I CAN DO FOR YOU.

That's *all?*

AND I'LL GIVE YOU CHRISTMAS.

Easter?

EASTER. SHE WANTS EASTER, SEYMOUR. TO ME YOU KNOW
WHAT EASTER IS, DAWN DEAR? EASTER IS A HUGE TARGET
FOR DELIVERIES. HUGE, HUGE PRESSURES TO GET GLOVES IN
STOCK FOR PEOPLE TO BUY THEIR EASTER OUTFITS. I'LL TELL
YOU A STORY. EVERY NEW YEAR'S EVE, IN THE AFTERNOON,
WE'D CLEAN UP ALL THE ORDERS FOR THE YEAR, SEND EVERY-
BODY HOME, AND WITH MY FORELADY AND MY FOREMAN I'D
POP A BOTTLE OF CHAMPAGNE, AND BEFORE WE'D FINISHED
TAKING THE FIRST SIP WE WOULD GET A CALL FROM A STORE
DOWN IN WILMINGTON, IN DELAWARE, A CALL FROM THE
BUYER THERE FOR A HUNDRED DOZEN LITTLE WHITE SHORT
LEATHER GLOVES. FOR TWENTY YEARS OR MORE WE KNEW
THAT CALL WAS GOING TO COME FOR THE HUNDRED DOZEN AS
WE WERE TOASTING IN THE NEW YEAR, AND THOSE WERE
GLOVES THAT WERE FOR EASTER.

That was your tradition.

IT WAS, YOUNG LADY. NOW TELL ME, WHAT IS EASTER ANY-
WAY?

He rises.

WHO?

Jesus. Jesus rises.

MISS, YOU MAKE IT AWFULLY HARD FOR ME. I THOUGHT
THAT'S WHEN YOU HAVE THE PARADE.

We do have the parade.

WELL, ALL RIGHT, I'LL GIVE YOU THE PARADE. HOW'S THAT?

We have ham on Easter.

YOU WANT A HAM ON EASTER, YOU CAN HAVE A HAM ON
EASTER. WHAT ELSE?

We go to church in an Easter bonnet.

AND IN A PAIR OF GOOD WHITE GLOVES, I HOPE.

Yes.

YOU WANT TO GO TO CHURCH ON EASTER AND TAKE MY
GRANDCHILD WITH YOU?

Yes. We'll be what my mother calls once-a-year Catholics.

IS THAT IT? ONCE A YEAR? *(Claps his hands together.)* LET'S SHAKE ON THAT. ONCE A YEAR. YOU'VE GOT A DEAL!

Well, it would be twice a year. Easter and Christmas.

WHAT ARE YOU GOING TO DO CHRISTMAS?

When the child's small we can just go to the Mass where they sing all the Christmas carols. You have to be there when they sing all the Christmas carols. Otherwise it's not worth it. You hear the Christmas carols on the radio, but in church they won't give you the Christmas carols until Jesus is born.

I DON'T CARE ABOUT THAT. THOSE CAROLS DON'T INTEREST ME ONE WAY OR THE OTHER. HOW MANY DAYS IS THIS GOING TO GO ON AT CHRISTMAS?

Well, there's Christmas Eve. There's Midnight Mass. Midnight Mass is a High Mass—

I DON'T KNOW WHAT THAT MEANS. I DON'T WANT TO. I'LL GIVE YOU CHRISTMAS EVE AND I'LL GIVE YOU CHRISTMAS DAY AND I'LL GIVE YOU EASTER. BUT I'M NOT GIVING YOU THE STUFF WHERE THEY EAT HIM.

Catechism. What about catechism?

I CAN'T GIVE YOU THAT.

Do you know what it is?

I DON'T HAVE TO KNOW WHAT IT IS. THAT'S AS FAR AS I GO. I THINK THIS IS A GENEROUS OFFER. MY SON WILL TELL YOU, HE KNOWS ME—I AM MEETING YOU MORE THAN HALFWAY. WHAT IS CATECHISM?

Where you go to school and learn about Jesus.

ABSOLUTELY NOT. ALL RIGHT? IS IT CLEAR? SHOULD WE SHAKE? SHOULD WE WRITE THIS DOWN? CAN I TRUST YOU OR SHOULD WE WRITE THIS DOWN?

This is scaring me, Mr. Levov.

YOU'RE SCARED?

Yes. *(Near tears.)* I don't think I can fight this fight.

I ADMIRE YOU FIGHTING THIS FIGHT.

Mr. Levov, we'll work it out later.

LATER NEVER WORKS. WE WORK IT OUT NOW OR NEVER. WE
STILL WANT TO TALK ABOUT BAR MITZVAH LESSONS.

If it's a boy and he's going to be bar mitzvahed, then he has to be
baptized. And then he can decide.

DECIDE WHAT?

After he grows up, he can decide which he likes better.

NO, HE'S NOT GOING TO DECIDE ANYTHING. YOU AND I ARE
GOING TO DECIDE RIGHT HERE.

But why don't we just wait and we'll see?

WE WILL NOT SEE.

(*To the Swede.*) I can't have this conversation anymore with your
father. He's too tough. I can only lose. We can't negotiate like this,
Seymour. I don't want a bar mitzvah.

YOU DON'T WANT A BAR MITZVAH?

With the Torah and all that?

THAT'S RIGHT.

No.

NO? THEN I DON'T THINK WE CAN REACH AN AGREEMENT.

Then we won't have any children. I love your son. We just won't
have children.

AND I'LL NEVER BE A GRANDFATHER. IS THAT THE DEAL?

You have another son.

NO, NO, THAT WON'T DO. NO HARD FEELINGS BUT I THINK
MAYBE EVERYBODY SHOULD JUST GO THEIR OWN WAY.

Can't we wait and see what happens? Mr. Levov, it's all a lot of
years away. Why can't we just let him or her decide what they want?

ABSOLUTELY NOT. I'M NOT LETTING SOME CHILD MAKE
THESE KIND OF DECISIONS. HOW THE HELL CAN HE DECIDE?
WHAT DOES HE KNOW? WE'RE ADULTS. THE CHILD IS NOT AN
ADULT. (*Stands at his desk.*) MISS DWYER, YOU ARE PRETTY AS A
PICTURE. I CONGRATULATE YOU ON HOW FAR YOU'VE COME.
NOT EVERY GIRL REACHES YOUR HEIGHTS. YOUR PARENTS
MUST BE VERY PROUD. I THANK YOU FOR COMING TO MY
OFFICE. THANK YOU AND GOOD-BYE.

No. I'm not leaving. I'm not going to go. I'm not a picture, Mr. Levov. I'm myself. I'm Mary Dawn Dwyer of Elizabeth, New Jersey. I'm twenty-two years old. I love your son. That is why I'm here. I love Seymour. I love him. Let's go on, please.

So the deal was cut, the youngsters were married, Merry was born and secretly baptized, and until Dawn's father died of the second heart attack in 1959, both families got together every year for Thanksgiving dinner up in Old Rimrock, and to everyone's surprise—except maybe Dawn's—Lou Levov and Jim Dwyer would wind up spending the whole time swapping stories about what life had been like when they were boys. Two great memories meet, and it is futile to try to contain them. They are on to something even more serious than Judaism and Catholicism—they are on to Newark and Elizabeth—and all day long nobody can tear them apart. "All immigrants down at the port." Jim Dwyer always began with the port. "Worked at Singer's. That was the big one down there. There was the shipbuilding industry down there too, of course. But everyone in Elizabeth worked at Singer's at one time or another. Some maybe out on Newark Avenue, at the Burry Biscuit Cookie Company. People either making sewing machines or making cookies. But mostly it was at Singer's, see, right at the port, down at the end, right by the river. Biggest hirer in the community," Dwyer said. "Sure, all the immigrants, when they come over, could get a job at Singer's. That was the biggest thing around. That and Standard Oil. Standard Oil out in Linden. The Bayway section. Right at the edge of what they called then Greater Elizabeth. . . . The mayor? Joe Brophy. Sure. He owned the coal company and he was also the mayor of the city. Then Jim Kirk took over. . . . Oh, sure, Mayor Hague. Quite a character. Ned, my brother-in-law, can tell you all about Frank Hague. He's the Jersey City expert. If you voted the right way in that town, you had a job. All I know is the ballpark. Jersey City had a great ballpark. Roosevelt Stadium. Beautiful. And they never got Hague, as you know, never put him away. Winds up with a place at the shore, right next to Asbury Park. A beautiful place he has. . . . The thing is, see, Elizabeth is a great sports town, but without having the great sports facilities. A baseball park where you could charge fifty cents or something to get in, never had that. We had open fields, we had Brophy Field, Mattano Park, Warananco Park, all public facilities, and still we had great teams and great players. Mickey McDermott pitched for St. Patrick's Elizabeth. Newcombe, the colored fella, an Elizabeth boy. Lives in Colonia now but an Elizabeth boy, pitched for Jefferson. . . . Swimming in the Arthur Kill, that was it. Sure. Close as I ever got to a vacation. Went twice a year to Asbury Park on the excursion. That was the vacation. Did my swimming in the Arthur Kill, underneath the Goethals Bridge. Bareback, you know. I'd come home with grease in my hair and my mother would say, 'You are swimming in the Arthur Kill again.' And I'd say, 'Elizabeth River? You think I'm crazy?' And all the while my hair is sticking up greasy, you know. . . ."

It was not quite so easy as this for the two mothers-in-law to find common ground and hit it off, for though Dorothy Dwyer could be a bit loquacious herself at Thanksgiving—just about as loquacious as she was nervous—her subject always was church. "St. Patrick's, that was the original one down there, at the port, and that was Jim's parish. The Germans started St. Michael's parish and the Polish had St. Adalbert's, at Third Street and East Jersey Street, and St. Patrick's is right behind Jackson Park, around the corner. St. Mary's is up in south Elizabeth, in the West End section, and that's where my parents started. They had the milk business there on Murray Street. St. Patrick's, Sacred Heart in north Elizabeth, Blessed Sacrament, Immaculate Conception Church, all Irish. And St. Catherine's. That's up in Westminster. Well, it's on the city line. Actually it's in Hillside, but the school across the street is in Elizabeth. And then our church, St. Genevieve's. St. Genevieve's, when it started, was a missionary church, you see, just a part of St. Catherine's. Just a wooden church. It's a big, beautiful church now. But the building that stands now—and I remember when I first went in it—"

That was as trying as it ever got: Dorothy Dwyer prattling on about Elizabeth as though this were the Middle Ages and beyond the fields tilled by the peasants the only points of demarcation were the spires of the parish churches on the horizon. Dorothy Dwyer prattling on about St. Gen's and St. Patrick's and St. Catherine's while Sylvia Levov sat across from her too polite to do anything other than nod and smile but her face as white as a sheet. Just sat there and endured it, and good manners got her through. So all in all, it was never anywhere near as bad as everybody had been expecting. And it was never but once a year that they were brought together anyway, and that was on the neutral, dereligion-ized ground of Thanksgiving, when everybody gets to eat the same thing, nobody sneaking off to eat funny stuff—no kugel, no gefilte fish, no bitter herbs, just one colossal turkey for two hundred and fifty million people—one colossal turkey feeds all. A moratorium on funny foods and funny ways and religious exclusivity, a morato-rium on the three-thousand-year-old nostalgia of the Jews, a mora-torium on Christ and the cross and the crucifixion for the Chris-tians, when everyone in New Jersey and elsewhere can be more passive about their irrationalities than they are the rest of the year. A moratorium on all the grievances and resentments, and not only for the Dwyers and the Levovs but for everyone in America who is suspicious of everyone else. It is the American pastoral par excel-lence and it lasts twenty-four hours.

"It was wonderful. The Presidential Suite. Three bedrooms and a living room. That's what you got in those days for having been a Miss New Jersey. The U.S. Line. I guess it wasn't booked, so we got on board and they just gave it to us."

Dawn was telling the Salzmans about their trip abroad to look at the Simmentals in Switzerland.

"I'd never been to Europe before, and all the way over everybody was telling me, 'There's nothing like France, just wait until we come into Le Havre in the morning and you smell France. You'll love it.' So I waited, and early in the morning Seymour was still in bed and

I knew we had docked and so I raced on deck and I sniffed," Dawn said, laughing, "and it was just garlic and onions all over the place."

She had raced out of the cabin with Merry while he was still in bed, but in the story she was on deck alone, astonished to find that France didn't smell like one big flower.

"The train to Paris. It was sublime. You see miles and miles of woods, but every tree is in line. They plant their forests in a line. We had a wonderful time, didn't we, darling?"

"We did," said the Swede.

"We walked around with great big bread sticks sticking out of our pockets. They practically said, 'Hey, look at us, a couple of rubes from New Jersey.' We were probably just the kind of Americans they laugh at. But who cared? We walked around, nibbling at the tops of them, looking at everything, the Louvre, the garden of the Tuileries—it was just wonderful. We stayed at the Crillon. The greatest treat of the whole trip. I loved it. Then we got on the night train, the Orient Express to Zurich, and the porter didn't get us up on time. Remember, Seymour?"

Yes, he remembered. Merry wound up on the platform in her pajamas.

"It was absolutely horrendous. The train had already started up. I had to get all our things and throw them all out the window—you know, that's the way people get out of the train there—and we ran out half dressed. They never woke us up. It was ghastly," Dawn said, again laughing happily at the recollection of the scene. "There we were, Seymour and me and our suitcases, wearing our underwear. So, anyway"—for a moment she was laughing too hard to go on—"we got to Zurich, and we went to wonderful restaurants—smelled of delicious croissants and good pâtés—and *pâtisseries* everywhere. Things like that. Oh, it was so good. All of the papers were on canes, they were hung up on racks, so you take your paper down and sit and have your breakfast and it was wonderful. So from there we took a car and we went down to Zug, the center of the Simmentals, and then we went to Lucerne, which was beautiful, absolutely beautiful, and then we went to the Beau Rivage in Lausanne. Remember the Beau Rivage?" she asked her husband, her hand still firmly held in his.

And he did remember it. Never had forgotten it. Coincidentally enough, had himself been thinking of the Beau Rivage just that afternoon, on the drive back to Old Rimrock from Central Avenue. Merry at afternoon tea, with the band playing, before she'd been raped. She had danced with the headwaiter, his six-year-old child, before she'd killed four people. Mademoiselle Merry. On his own, on their last afternoon at the Beau Rivage, the Swede had gone down to the jewelry shop off the lobby, and while Merry and Dawn were out walking on the promenade to take a last look together at the boats on Lake Geneva and the Alps out across the way, he had bought Dawn a diamond necklace. He had a vision of her wearing the diamond necklace along with the crown she kept in a hatbox at the top of her closet, the silver crown with the double row of rhinestones that she had worn as Miss New Jersey. Since he couldn't even get her to wear the crown to show to Merry—"No, no, it's just too silly a thing," Dawn told him; "to her I'm 'Mom,' which is perfectly fine"—he'd never get her to put it on with the new necklace. Knowing Dawn and her sense of herself as well as he did, he realized that even to cajole her into trying them on, the necklace and the crown together, in the bedroom, just modeling them there for him alone, would be impossible. She was never more stubborn about anything than about not being an ex–beauty queen. "It's not a beauty pageant," she was already telling people back then who persisted in asking about her year as Miss New Jersey. "Most people involved with the pageant will fight with anyone who says they were in a beauty pageant, and I'm one of them. Your only prize for winning at any level is a *scholarship.*" And yet it was with the crown in her hair, the crown not of a scholarship winner but of a beauty queen, that he had imagined her wearing that necklace when he caught sight of it in the window of the shop at the Beau Rivage.

In one of their photograph albums there was a series of pictures he used to like to look at back when they were first married and even on occasion to show to people. They always made him so proud of her, these glossy photos taken in 1949–50, when she'd held down the fifty-two-week-a-year job that the head man over at the Miss New Jersey Scholarship Pageant liked to describe as serving as the state's official "hostess"—the job of accommodating as many cities and towns and groups as possible for every kind of event, working like a dog, really, and receiving in compensation the $500 cash scholarship, a pageant trophy, and the fifty bucks for each personal appearance. There was, of course, a picture of her at the Miss New Jersey coronation on the night of Saturday, May 21, 1949, Dawn in a strapless evening gown of silk, stiff and scalloped at the top, very tight to the waist, and below, to the floor, a full, voluptuous skirt, thickly embroidered with flowers and sparkling with beads. And on her head her crown. "You don't feel ridiculous in your evening gown wearing a crown," she told him, "but you definitely feel ridiculous in your clothes and your crown. Little girls always asking if you're a princess. People coming up and asking if the crown is diamonds. In just a suit and wearing that thing, Seymour, you feel absolutely *silly*." But she hardly looked silly—wearing her very simple, tailored clothes and that crown, she looked stunning. There was a picture of her in a suit and her crown—and her Miss New Jersey sash, pinned at the waist with a brooch—at an agricultural fair with some farmers, another of her in her crown and the sash at a manufacturer's convention with some businessmen, and one of her in that strapless silk evening gown and her crown at the governor's Princeton mansion, Drumthwacket, dancing with the governor of New Jersey, Alfred E. Driscoll. Then there were the pictures of her at parades and ribbon cuttings and charity fund-raisers around the state, pictures of her assisting at the crowning in local pageants, pictures of her opening the department stores and the auto showrooms—"That's Dawnie. The beefy guy owns the place." There were a couple of her visiting schools where, seated at the piano in the auditorium, she generally played the popularized Chopin polonaise that she'd performed to become Miss New Jersey, leaving out clots and clots of black notes to get it in at two and a half minutes so she wouldn't be disqualified by the stopwatch at the state level. And in all of those pictures, whatever clothes she might be wearing that were appropriate to the event, she would always have the crown set in her hair, making her look, as much to her husband as to the little girls who came up to ask, like a princess—more like a princess was supposed to look than any of a whole string of European princesses whose photographs he'd seen in *Life*.

Then there were the pictures taken at Atlantic City, at the Miss America Pageant in September, pictures of her in her swimsuit and in evening wear, which made him wonder how she ever could have lost. She told him, "When you're out on that runway you can't imagine how ridiculous you feel in that swimsuit and your high heels, and you know that when you walk a ways the back end is going to ride up, and you can't reach behind you and pull it down. . . ." But she hadn't been ridiculous at all: he never looked at the swimsuit pictures that he didn't say aloud, "Oh, she was beautiful." And the crowd had been with her; at Atlantic City most of the audience was naturally rooting for Miss New Jersey, but during the parade of states Dawn had received a spontaneous ovation that bespoke more than local pride. The pageant wasn't on TV back then, it was still for the folks jammed into Convention Hall, so afterward, when the Swede, who'd sat in the hall beside Dawn's brother, called to tell his parents that Dawn hadn't won, he could still say of her reception, without exaggerating, "She brought the house down."

Certainly, of the five other former Miss New Jerseys at their wedding, none could compare to Dawn in any way. Together they constituted a kind of sorority, these former Miss New Jerseys, and for a while there in the fifties they all attended one another's weddings, so that he must have met up with at least ten girls who had won the state crown and probably twice as many who'd become friends of this or that bride during the days of rehearsal for the state competition, girls who'd gotten as far as being Miss Shore Resort and Miss Central Coast and Miss Columbus Day and Miss

Northern Lights, and there wasn't a one who could rival his wife in any category—talent, intelligence, personality, poise. If he should ever happen to remark to someone that why Dawn hadn't become Miss America was something he would never understand, Dawn always begged him not to go around saying that, because it gave the impression that her having not become Miss America was something she was embittered about when, in many ways, losing had been a relief. Just getting through without humiliating herself and her family had been a relief. Sure, after all the buildup the New Jersey people had given her she was surprised and a little let down not to have made the Court of Honor or even the top ten, but that, too, might have been a blessing in disguise. And though losing would not be a relief for a competitor like him, not a blessing of any kind, he nonetheless admired Dawn's graciousness—gracious was how the folks over at the pageant liked to describe all the girls who lost—even if he couldn't understand it.

Losing allowed her, for one thing, to begin to restore the relations with her father that had nearly been ruined because of her persisting at something he so strongly disapproved of. "I don't care what they're giving away," Mr. Dwyer said when she tried to explain about the pageant scholarship money. "The whole damn thing," he told her, "is about being ogled. Those girls are there to be ogled. The more money they give for it, the worse it is. The answer is *no*."

That Mr. Dwyer agreed finally to come down to Atlantic City had been due to the persuasive skills of Dawn's favorite aunt, Peg, her mother's sister, the schoolteacher who'd married rich Uncle Ned and taken Dawn as a kid to the hotel in Spring Lake. "It would make any father uncomfortable seeing his baby up there," Peg had told her brother-in-law in that gentle, diplomatic way Dawn always admired and wanted to emulate. "It brings certain images to mind that a father would just as soon not have associated with his daughter. I'd feel that way if it were my daughter," she told him, "and I don't have what it is that fathers naturally feel for their daughters. It would bother me, of course it would. I would think that what you feel is the case with a lot of dads. They're really proud, their buttons are popping and all that, but at the same time, 'Oh, my God, that's my baby up there.' But Jim, this is so clean and beyond reproach there is just nothing to worry about. The trashy ones get sifted out early—they go on to work the truckers' convention. These are just ordinary kids from small towns, decent, sweet girls whose fathers own the grocery store and don't belong to the country club. They get them up to look like debutantes but there is nothing big in their backgrounds. They're just good kids who go home and settle down and marry the boy next door. And the judges are serious people. Jim, this is for Miss *America*. If it were compromising to the girls, they wouldn't allow it. It is an *honor*. Dawn wants you there to share in that honor. She will not be very happy if you are not there, Jimmy. She will be crushed, especially if you are the *only* father who isn't there." "Peggy, it's beneath her. It's beneath all of us. I'm not going." So that's when she laid into him about his responsibility not merely to Dawn but to the nation. "You wouldn't come when she won at the local level. You wouldn't come when she won at the state level. Are you now telling me that you are not going to come if she wins at the national level? If she is awarded Miss America and you're not there to walk up on the stage and hug your daughter with pride, what will they think? They'll think, 'A great tradition, a part of the American heritage, and her father isn't there. Photographs of Miss America with her family, and her father isn't in a one of them.' Tell me, how's that going to go down the next day?"

And so he humbled himself and he did it—against his better judgment, consented to come for the big night to Atlantic City with the rest of Dawn's relatives, and it was a disaster. When Dawn saw him waiting there in his Sunday suit in the lobby with her mother and her aunts and her uncles and her cousins, every last Dwyer in Union *and* Essex *and* Hudson counties, all she was allowed to do by her chaperone was to shake his hand, and he was fit to be tied. But that was a pageant rule, in case anybody who was watching might not know it was her father and see some kind of embrace and think something untoward was going on. It was all so that absolutely *nothing* smacked of impropriety, but Jim Dwyer, who had only recently recovered from the first heart attack and so was on edge anyway, had misunderstood, thinking that now she was such a big shot she had dared to rebuff her own dad, actually given her father the cold shoulder, and in public, before the entire public.

Of course, for the week that she was in Atlantic City under the watchful eye of the pageant, she had not been allowed to see the Swede *at all,* not in the company of her chaperone, not even in a public place, and so, until the very last night, he'd just stayed up in Newark and had to be content, like her family, to talk to her on the phone. But Dawn's sincerity in recounting to her father this hardship—of her being deprived, for a whole week, of the company of her Jewish beau—did not much impress him when, back in Elizabeth, she attempted to assuage his grudge at what he remembered for many years afterward as "the snub."

"That was just an Old World hotel that was the most wonderful place," Dawn was telling the Salzmans. "Huge place. Glorious. Right on the water. Something you see in a movie. Big rooms overlooking Lake Geneva. We loved that. I'm boring you," she suddenly said.

"No, no," they replied in unison.

Sheila pretended to be listening intently to every word Dawn spoke. She had to be pretending. Not even she could have recovered so completely from the eruption in Dawn's study. If she had—well, it would be hard then to say what sort of woman she was. She was nothing like the one he had imagined. And that was not because she had been passing herself off with him as something else or somebody else but because he had understood her no better than he was able to understand anyone. How to penetrate to the interior of people was some skill or capacity he did not possess. He just did not have the combination to that lock. Everybody who flashed the signs of goodness he took to be good. Everybody who flashed the signs of loyalty he took to be loyal. Everybody who flashed the signs of intelligence he took to be intelligent. And so he had failed to see into his daughter, failed to see into his wife, failed to see into his one and only mistress—probably had never even begun to see into himself. What was *he*, stripped of all the signs he flashed? People were standing up everywhere, shouting "This is me! This is me!" Every time you looked at them they stood up and told you who they were, and the truth of it was that they had no more idea of who or what they were than he had. *They* believed their flashing signs too. They ought to be standing up and shouting, "This *isn't* me! This *isn't* me!" They would if they had any decency. "This *isn't* me!" Then you might know how to proceed through the flashing bullshit of this world.

Sheila Salzman may or may not have been listening to Dawn's every word, but Shelly Salzman surely was. The kindly doctor wasn't merely acting like the kindly doctor but appeared to have fallen somewhat under Dawn's spell—the spell of that alluring surface whose underside, as she presented it to people, was as charmingly straightforward as it could be. Yes, after all she'd been through, she looked and she behaved as though nothing had happened. For him there was this two-sidedness to everything: side by side, the way it had been and the way it was now. But Dawn made it sound as though the way it had been was *still* the way it was. After the tragic detour their lives had taken, she'd managed in the last year to arrive back at being herself, apparently just by not thinking about certain things. And arrived back not merely at Dawn with her face-lift and her petite gallantry and her breakdowns and her cattle and her decisions to change her life but back at the Dawn of Hillside Road, Elizabeth, New Jersey. A gate, some sort of psychological gate, had been installed in her brain, a mighty gate past which nothing harmful could travel. She locked the gate, and that was that. Miraculous, or so he'd thought, until he'd learned that the gate had a name. The William Orcutt III Gate.

Yes, if you'd missed her back in the forties, here once again was Mary Dawn Dwyer of Elizabeth's Elmora section, an up-and-coming Irish looker from a working-class family that was starting to do okay, respectable parishioners at St. Genevieve's, the classiest Catholic church in town—miles uptown from the church by the docks where her father and his brothers had been altar boys. Once again she was in possession of that power she'd had even as a twenty-year-old to stir up interest in whatever she said, somehow to touch you *inwardly,* which was not often true of the contestants who *won* at Atlantic City. But she could do that, lay bare something juvenile even in adults, by nothing more than venting ordinary lively enthusiasms through that flagrantly perfect, strikingly executed heart-shaped face. Maybe, until she spoke and revealed her attitudes as not so different from any decent person's, people were frightened of her for looking like that. Discovering that she was not at all a goddess, had no interest in pretending to be one—discovering in her almost an excess of *no* pretense—made even more riveting the brilliant darkness of her hair, the angular mask not much bigger than a cat's, and the eyes, the big pale eyes almost alarmingly keen and vulnerable. From the message in those eyes one would never have believed that this girl was going to grow up to be a shrewd businesswoman resolutely determined about turning a profit as a cattle breeder. What excited the Swede's tenderness always was that she who wasn't at all frail nonetheless looked so delicate and frail. This always impressed him: how strong she was (once was) and how vulnerable her kind of beauty caused her to appear, even to him, her husband, long after one might imagine that married life had dulled the infatuation.

And how plain Sheila looked sitting alongside her, purportedly listening to her, plain and proper, sensible, dignified, and dreary. So dreary. Everything in her severely withheld. Hidden. There was nothing hearty in Sheila. There was lots in Dawn. There once was in him. That once described everything there was in him. It was not easy to understand how he could ever have found in this prim, severe, hidden whatever-she-was a woman more magnetic than Dawn. How pathetic he must have been, how depleted, a broken, helpless creature escaping from everything that had collapsed, running in the headlong way that someone in trouble will take flight in order to make a bad thing worse. Almost all there was to attract him was that Sheila was someone else. Her clarity, her candor, her equilibrium, her perfect self-control were at first almost beside the point. Shrinking from such a blinding catastrophe—disconnected as he'd never been before from his ready-made life; notorious and disgraced as he'd never been before—he turned in a daze to the one woman other than his wife whom he knew even remotely in a personal way. That was how he got there, seeking asylum, hounded—the forlorn reason for a straight arrow so assertively uxorious, so intensely and spotlessly monogamous, hurling himself at such an extraordinary moment into a situation he would have thought he hated, the shameful fiasco of being untrue. But amorousness had little to do with his clutching. He could not offer the passionate love that Dawn drew from him. Lust was far too natural a task for someone suddenly so misshapen—the father of someone gruesomely misbegotten. He was there for the illusion. He lay atop Sheila like a person taking cover, digging in, a big male body in hiding, a man disappearing: because she was somebody else, maybe he could be somebody else too.

But that she *was* someone else was what made it all wrong. Alongside Dawn, Sheila was a well-groomed impersonal thinking-machine, a human needle threaded with a brain, nobody he could want to touch, let alone sleep with. Dawn was the woman who had inspired the feat for which even his record-breaking athletic career had barely fortified him: vaulting his father. The feat of standing up to his father. And how she had inspired it was by looking as spectacular as she looked and yet talking like everyone else.

Was it bigger, more important, worthier things that inclined others to a lifelong mate? Or at the heart of everyone's marriage was there something irrational and unworthy and odd?

Sheila would know. She knew it all. Yes, she'd have an answer to that one too. . . . She'd come so far, Sheila had said, she'd gotten so much stronger I thought that she could make it on her own. She's a strong girl, Seymour. *She's a crazy girl. She's crazy!* She's troubled. *And the father plays no role with the troubled daughter?* I'm sure he played plenty of a role. I just thought something terrible had happened at home. . . .

Oh, he wanted his wife back—it was impossible to exaggerate the extent to which he wanted her back, the wife so serious about being a serious mother, the woman so fiercely disinclined to be thought spoiled or vain or frivolously nostalgic for her once-glamorous eminence that she would not wear even as a joke for her family the crown in the hatbox at the top of her closet. His endurance had run out—he wanted that Dawn back *right now*.

"What were the farms like?" Sheila asked her. "In Zug. You were going to tell us about the farms." This interest of Sheila's in figuring it all out—how could he have wanted *anything* to do with her? These deep thinkers were the only people he could not stand to be around for long, these people who'd never manufactured anything or seen anything manufactured, who did not know what things were made of or how a company worked, who, aside from a house or a car, had never sold anything and didn't know how to sell anything, who'd never hired a worker, fired a worker, trained a worker, been fleeced by a worker—people who knew nothing of the intricacies or the risks of building a business or running a factory but who nonetheless imagined that they knew everything worth knowing. All that *awareness*, all that introspective Sheila-like gazing into every nook and cranny of one's soul went repellently against the grain of life as he had known it. To his way of thinking it was simple: you had only to carry out your duties strenuously and unflaggingly like a Levov and orderliness became a natural condition, daily living a simple story tangibly unfolding, a deeply unagitating story, the fluctuations predictable, the combat containable, the surprises satisfying, the continuous motion an undulation carrying you along with the utmost faith that tidal waves occur only off the coast of countries thousands and thousands of miles away—or so it all had seemed to him *once upon a time*, back when the union of beautiful mother and strong father and bright, bubbly child rivaled the trinity of the three bears.

"I got lost, yes. Oh, lots and lots of farms," said Dawn, gratified just by the thought of all those farms. "They showed us their best cows. Wonderful warm barns. We were there in the early spring when they haven't been out to pasture yet. They're living under the house and the chalet is on top. Porcelain stoves, very ornate . . ." *I don't understand how you could be so shortsighted. So taken in by a girl who was obviously crazy.* She was running. There was no bringing her back there. She wasn't the same girl that she'd been. Something had gone wrong. She'd gotten so fat. I just thought she was so fat and so angry that something very bad must have gone on at home. *That it was my fault.* I didn't think that. We all have homes. That's where everything always goes wrong. ". . . and they gave us wine that they made, little things to eat, and so friendly," Dawn said. "When we went back the second time it was fall. The cows live up in the mountains all summer and they milk them and the cow that made the most milk all summer would be the first one to come down with a great bell on her neck. That was the number-one cow. They put flowers on her horns and had great celebrations. When they come down from the high mountain pastures they come down in a line, the leading cow the first one." *What if she went on to kill somebody else? Isn't that a bit of a responsibility? She did, you know. She killed three more people. What do you think of that?* Don't say these things just to torture me. *I'm telling you something! She killed three more people! You could have prevented that!* You're torturing me. You're trying to torture me. *She killed three more people!* "And all the people, all the children, the girls and the women who had been milking all summer would come in beautiful clothes, all dressed in Swiss outfits, and a band, music, a big fiesta down in the square. And then the cows would all go in for the winter in the barns under the houses. Very clean and very nice. Oh, that was an occasion, seeing that. Seymour took lots of pictures of all their cows so we could put them on the projector."

"Seymour took pictures?" his mother asked. "I thought you couldn't take a picture if it killed you," and she leaned over and kissed him. "My wonderful son," whispered Sylvia Levov, in her eyes adoring admiration shining for her firstborn boy.

"Well, he did back then, the wonderful son. He was a Leica man back then," Dawn was saying. "You took good pictures, didn't you, dear?"

Yes, he had. That was him all right. That was the wonderful son himself who had taken the pictures, who had bought Merry the Swiss girl's outfit, who had bought Dawn the jewelry in Lausanne, and who had told his brother and Sheila that Merry killed four people. Who had bought for the family, as a memento of Zug, of the gloriously Switzerlandish state of their lives, the ceramic candelabra, now half encased with candle drippings, and who had told his brother and Sheila that Merry killed four people. Who had been a Leica man and told those two—the two he could least trust in the world and over whom he had no control—what Merry had done.

"Where else did you go?" Sheila asked Dawn, careful to give no indication that in the car she would tell Shelly, and Shelly would say, "My God, my God"; because he was such a mild and decent person, he might even cry. But when they got home, the instant they were home, the first thing he would do would be to call the police. Once before he had harbored this murderer. For three days. That had been frightening, awful, brutally nerve-racking. But only one was dead, and bad as it was, you could wrap your mind around that number—and as his wife had insisted, as idiotically, he had agreed, they had no alternative; the girl was her client, a promise had been made, professional conscience wouldn't allow . . . But four people. This was too much. This was unacceptable. Four innocent people, to kill them off—no, this was barbarism, gruesome, depraved, this was evil, and they certainly did have an alternative: the law. Obligation to the law. They knew where she was. They could be prosecuted for keeping a secret like this. No, it was not going to spin any farther out of Shelly's control. The Swede saw it all. Shelly would phone the police—he had to. "Four people. She's in Newark. Seymour Levov knows the address. He was there. He was with her there today." Shelly was exactly as Lou Levov had described him—"a physician, a respected person, an ethical person, a responsible person"—and he would not allow his wife to become accessory to the murder of four people by this wretched, loathsome girl, another homicidal savior of the world's oppressed. Insane terroristic behavior coupled with that bogus ideology—she had done the worst thing that anyone can do. That would be Shelly's interpretation and what could the Swede do to change it? How could he get Shelly to see it otherwise when *he* could no longer see it otherwise? Take him aside immediately, the Swede thought, tell him, explain to Shelly now, say whatever has to be said to stop him from taking action, to stop him from thinking that turning her in is his duty as a law-abiding citizen, that it's a way of protecting innocent lives—tell him, "She was used. She was malleable. She was a compassionate child. She was a wonderful child. She was *only* a child, and she got herself in with the wrong people. She could never have masterminded anything like that on her own. She just hated the war. We all did. We all felt angry and impotent. But she was a kid, a confused adolescent, a high-strung girl. She was too young to have had any real experience, and she got herself caught up in something that she did not understand. She was attempting to save lives. I'm not trying to give a political excuse for her, because there is no political excuse—there is no justification, none. But you can't just look at the appalling effect of what she did. She had her reasons, which were very strong for her, and the reasons don't matter now—she has changed her philosophy and the war is over. None of us really know all that happened and none of us can really know why. There is more behind it, much, much more than we can understand. She was wrong, of course—she made a tragic, terrible, ghastly mistake. There's no defense of her to be made. But she's not a risk to anyone anymore. She is now a skinny, pathetic wreck of a girl who wouldn't hurt a fly. She's quiet, she's harmless. She's not a hardened criminal, Shelly. She is a broken creature who did something terrible and who regrets it to the bottom of her soul. What good will it do to call the police? Of course justice must be served, but she is no longer a danger. There is no need for you to get involved. We don't have to call the police to protect anyone. And there's no need for vengeance. Vengeance has been taken on her, believe me. I know she's guilty. The question is not if she's guilty. The question is what is to be done now. Leave her to me. I will look after her. She won't do anything—I'll see to that. I'll see that she is taken care of, that she is given help. Shelly, give me a chance to bring her back to human life—*don't call the police!*"

But he knew what Shelly would think: Sheila had done enough for that family. They both had. That family was in real trouble now, but there was no more help from Dr. Salzman. This wasn't a face-lift. Four people were dead. That girl should get the electric chair. Yes, the number four would transform even Shelly into an outraged citizen ready to pull the switch. He would go ahead and turn her in because she was a little bitch who deserved it.

"That second time? Oh, we went everywhere," Dawn was saying. "It doesn't really matter in Europe where you go, everywhere you go there are things that are beautiful, and we sort of followed that path."

But the police knew. From Jerry. It's inevitable. Jerry has already called the FBI. Jerry. To give Jerry her address. To tell Jerry. To tell anyone. To sit here so battered as to overlook the implications of disclosing what Merry had done! Battered, doing nothing—holding Dawn's hand, thinking back again to Atlantic City, to the Beau Rivage, to Merry dancing with the headwaiter—mindless of the consequences of his reckless disclosure, bereft of his lifelong talent for being Swede Levov, instead floating free of the battering ram that is this world, dreaming, dreaming, helplessly dreaming, while down in Florida the hotheaded brother who thought the worst of him and wasn't a brother to him at all, who'd been antagonized from the beginning by all the Swede had been blessed with, by that impossible perfection they'd both had to contend with, the in-flamed and willful and ruthless brother who never did anything halfway, who would like nothing better than a reckoning—yes, a final reckoning for all the world to see. . . .

He'd turned her in. Not his brother, not Shelly Salzman, but *he*, he was the one who'd done it. What would it have taken to keep my mouth shut? What did I expect to get by opening it? Relief? Childish relief? Their reaction? I was after something so ridiculous as their *reaction?* By opening his mouth he had made things as bad as they could be—by retelling to them what Merry had told him, the Swede had done it: turned her in for killing four people. Now he had planted his own bomb. Without wanting to, without knowing what he was doing, without even being importuned, he had yielded—he had done what he should do and he had done what he shouldn't do: he had turned her in.

It would have taken another day entirely to keep his mouth shut—a different day, the abolition of this day. Lead me not into this day! Seeing so much so fast. And how stoical he had always been in his ability not to see, how prodigious had been his powers to regularize. But in the three extra killings he had been confronted by something impossible to regularize, even for him. Being told it was horrible enough, but only by retelling it had he understood how horrible. One plus three. Four. And the instrument of this unblinding is Merry. The daughter has made her father see. And perhaps this was all she had ever wanted to do. She has given him sight, the sight to see clear through to that which will never be regularized, to see what you can't see and don't see and won't see until three is added to one to get four.

He had seen how improbable it is that we should come from one another and how improbable it is that we do come from one another. Birth, succession, the generations, history—utterly improbable.

He had seen that we *don't* come from one another, that it only appears that we come from one another.

He had seen the way that it is, seen out beyond the number four to all there is that cannot be bounded. The order is minute. He had thought most of it was order and only a little of it was disorder. He'd had it backwards. He had made his fantasy and Merry had unmade it for him. It was not the specific war that she'd had in mind, but it was a war, nonetheless, that she brought home to America—home into her very own house.

And just then they heard his father scream: "No!" They heard

Lou Levov screaming, "Oh my God! *No!*" The girls in the kitchen were screaming. The Swede understood instantaneously what was happening. Merry had appeared in her veil! And told her grandfather that the death toll was four! She'd taken the train up from Newark and walked the five miles from the village. She'd come on her own! Now everyone knew!

The thought of her walking the length of that underpass one more time had terrified him all through dinner—in her rags and sandals walking alone through that filth and darkness among the underpass derelicts who understood that she loved them. However, while he had been at the table formulating no solution, she had been nowhere near the underpass but—he all at once envisioned it—already back in the countryside, here in the lovely Morris County countryside that had been tamed over the centuries by ten American generations, back walking the hilly roads that were edged now, in September, with the red and burnt orange of devil's paintbrush, with a matted profusion of asters and goldenrod and Queen Anne's lace, an entangled bumper crop of white and blue and pink and wine-colored flowers artistically topping their workaday stems, all the flowers she had learned to identify and classify as a 4-H Club project and then on their walks together had taught him, a city boy, to recognize—"See, Dad, how there's a n-notch at the tip of the petal?"—chicory, cinquefoil, pasture thistle, wild pinks, joe-pye weed, the last vestiges of yellow-flowered wild mustard sturdily spilling over from the fields, clover, yarrow, wild sunflowers, stringy alfalfa escaped from an adjacent farm and sporting its simple lavender blossom, the bladder campion with its clusters of white-petaled flowers and the distended little sac back of the petals that she loved to pop loudly in the palm of her hand, the erect mullein whose tonguelike velvety leaves she plucked and wore inside her sneakers—so as to be like the first settlers, who, according to her history teacher, used mullein leaves for insoles—the milkweed whose exquisitely made pods she would carefully tear open as a kid so she could blow into the air the silky seed-bearing down, thus feeling herself at one with nature, imagining that she was the everlasting wind. Indian Brook flowing rapidly on her left, crossed by little bridges, dammed up for swimming holes along the way and opening into the strong trout stream where she'd fished with her father—Indian Brook crossing under the road, flowing eastward from the mountain where it arises. On her left the pussy willows, the swamp maples, the marsh plants; on her right the walnut trees nearing fruition, only weeks from dropping the nuts whose husks when she pulled them apart would darkly stain her fingers and pleasantly stink them up with an acid pungency. On her right the black cherry, the field plants, the mowed fields. Up on the hills the dogwood trees; beyond them the woodlands—the maples, the oaks, and the locusts, abundant and tall and straight. She used to collect their beanpods in the fall. She used to collect everything, catalog everything, explain to him everything, examine with the pocket magnifying glass he'd given her every chameleonlike crab spider that she brought home to hold briefly captive in a moistened mason jar, feeding it on dead houseflies until she released it back onto the goldenrod or the Queen Anne's lace ("Watch what happens now, Dad") where it resumed adjusting its color to ambush its prey. Walking northwest into a horizon still thinly alive with light, walking up through the twilight call of the thrushes: up past the white pasture fences she hated, up past the hay fields, the corn fields, the turnip fields she hated, up past the barns, the horses, the cows, the ponds, the streams, the springs, the falls, the watercress, the scouring rushes ("The pioneers used them, Mom, to scrub their pots and pans"), the meadows, the acres and acres of woods she hated, up from the village, tracing her father's high-spirited, happy Johnny Appleseed walk until, just as the first few stars appeared, she reached the century-old maple trees that she hated and the substantial old stone house, imprinted with her being, that she hated, the house in which there lived the substantial family, also imprinted with her being, that she also hated.

At an hour, in a season, through a landscape that for so long now has been bound up with the idea of solace, of beauty and sweetness and pleasure and peace, the ex-terrorist had come, quite on her own, back from Newark to all that she hated and did not want, to a coherent, harmonious world that she despised and that she, with her embattled youthful mischief, the strangest and most unlikely attacker, had turned upside down. Come back from Newark and immediately, *immediately* confessed to her father's father what her great idealism had caused her to do.

"Four people, Grandpa," she'd told him, and his heart could not bear it. Divorce was bad enough in a family, but *murder,* and the murder not merely of one but of one plus three? The murder of *four?*

"No!" exclaimed Grandpa to this veiled intruder reeking of feces who claimed to be their beloved Merry, "*No!*" and his heart gave up, gave out, and he died.

There was blood on Lou Levov's face. He was standing beside the kitchen table clutching his temple and unable to speak, the once-imposing father, the giant of the family of six-footers at five foot seven, speckled now with blood and, but for his potbelly, looking barely like himself. His face was vacant of everything except the struggle not to weep. He appeared helpless to prevent even that. He could not prevent anything. He never could, though only now did he look prepared to believe that manufacturing a superb ladies' dress glove in quarter sizes did not guarantee the making of a life that would fit to perfection everyone he loved. Far from it. You think you can protect a family and you cannot protect even yourself. There seemed to be nothing left of the man who could not be diverted from his task, who neglected no one in his crusade against disorder, against the abiding problem of human error and insufficiency—nothing to be seen, in the place where he stood, of that eager, unbending stalk of a man who, just thirty minutes earlier, would jut his head forward to engage even his allies. The combatant had borne all the disappointment he could. Nothing blunt remained within him for bludgeoning deviancy to death. What should be did not exist. Deviancy prevailed. You can't stop it. Improbably, what was not supposed to happen had happened and what was supposed to happen had not happened.

The old system that made order doesn't work anymore. All that was left was his fear and astonishment, but now concealed by nothing.

At the table was Jessie Orcutt, seated before a half-empty dessert plate and an untouched glass of milk and holding in her hand a fork whose tines were tipped red with blood. She had stabbed at him with it. The girl at the sink was telling them this. The other girl had run screaming out of the house, so there was just the one still in the kitchen to recount the story as best she could through her tears. Because Mrs. Orcutt would not eat, the girl said, Mr. Levov had started to feed Mrs. Orcutt the pie himself, a bite at a time. He was explaining to her how much better it was for her to drink milk instead of Scotch whiskey, how much better for herself, how much better for her husband, how much better for her children. Soon she would be having grandchildren and it would be better for them. With each bite she swallowed he said, "Yes, Jessie good girl, Jessie very good girl," and told her how much better it would be for everybody in the world, even for Mr. Levov and his wife, if Jessie gave up drinking. After he had fed her almost all of one whole slice of the strawberry-rhubarb pie, she had said, "*I* feed Jessie," and he was so happy, so pleased with her, he laughed and handed over the fork, and she had gone right for his eye.

It turned out she'd missed it by no more than an inch. "Not bad," Marcia said to everyone in the kitchen, "for somebody as drunk as this babe is." Meanwhile Orcutt, appalled by a scene exceeding any previously contrived by his wife to humiliate her civic-minded, adulterous mate, who looked not at all invincible, not at all important to himself or anyone else, who looked just as silly as he had the morning the Swede had dumped him in the midst of their friendly football game—Orcutt tenderly lifted Jessie up from the chair and to her feet. She showed no remorse, none, seemed to have been stripped of all receptors and all transmitters, without a single cell to notify her that she had overstepped a boundary fundamental to civilized life.

"One drink less," Marcia was saying to the Swede's father, whose wife was already dabbing at the tiny wounds in his face with a damp napkin, "and you'd be blind, Lou." And then this large, unimpeded social critic in a caftan could not help herself. Marcia sank into Jessie's empty chair, in front of the brimming glass of milk, and with her face in her hands, she began to laugh at their obtuseness to the flimsiness of the whole contraption, to laugh and laugh and laugh at them all, pillars of a society that, much to her delight, was going rapidly under—to laugh and to relish, as some people, historically, always seem to do, how far the rampant disorder had spread, enjoying enormously the assailability, the frailty, the enfeeblement of supposedly robust things.

Yes, the breach had been pounded in their fortification, even out here in secure Old Rimrock, and now that it was opened it would not be closed again. They'll never recover. Everything is against them, everyone and everything that does not like their life. All the voices from without, condemning and rejecting their life!

And what is wrong with their life? What on earth is less reprehensible than the life of the Levovs?